THE
SHAPESHIFTER'S
LAIR

PETER TREMAYNE

THE SHAPESHIFTER'S LAIR

HEADLINE

First published in Great Britain in 2020 by
HEADLINE PUBLISHING GROUP

1

Cataloguing in Publication Data is available from the British Library

ISBN 978 1 4722 6537 1

Typeset in Times New Roman PS by Palimpsest Book Production Limited,
Falkirk, Stirlingshire

Printed and bound in Great Britain by Clays Ltd, Elcograf S.p.A.

MIX
Paper from
responsible sources
FSC® C104740

Headline's policy is to use papers that are natural, renewable and recyclable
products and made from wood grown in well-managed forests and other
controlled sources. The logging and manufacturing processes are expected
to conform to the environmental regulations of the country of origin.

HEADLINE PUBLISHING GROUP
An Hachette UK Company
Carmelite House
50 Victoria Embankment
London EC4Y 0DZ

www.headline.co.uk
www.hachette.co.uk

For Maria V. Soteriades
The years have passed and times have changed since 1969.
But our friendship has remained constant.
Thanks for being there.

Tiagaid thra in lucht sin isidaib. Ocus tiagaid fo muirib agis tiagaid i conrechtaibh ocus tiaigaid eo hamaide, ocu tiagait eo tuath clingtha. Is as sin is bunadas doibh uile, i muintir deamain.

Lebor Gabála Érenn

So they go in the currents of the wind. They go under the seas, they go in wolf-shapes and they go to fools and to the powerful. Thence is it that this is the nature of all of them, to be followers of the devil.

A Christian scribe's notation in *Lebor Gabála Érenn*

PRINCIPAL CHARACTERS

Sister Fidelma of Cashel, *a dálaigh* or advocate of the law courts of 7th-century Ireland
Brother Eadulf of Seaxmund's Ham, in the land of the South Folk of the East Angles, her companion

At Cashel
Colgú, King of Muman, Fidelma's brother
Enda, warrior of the Nasc Niadh, warriors of the Golden Collar, the élite bodyguard to King Colgú

Missing in the mountains
Princess Gelgéis of Osraige
Spealáin, her steward

At the Abbey of the Blessed Cáemgen
Cétach, a pedlar arriving at the abbey
Abbot Daircell Ciotóg
Brother Aithrigid, his *rechtaire* or steward
Brother Dorchú, the *dorseóracht* or gatekeeper
Brother Lachtna, the physician
Brother Eochaí, the *echaire* or stable master

Brother Gobbán, the smith
Brother Cuilínn, a stable boy

At Láithreach
Iuchra, a soothsayer
Brehon Rónchú, a local judge, who is missing
Beccnat, a *baran* or steward judge, assistant to Brehon Rónchú
Serc, a prostitute
Síabair, the town's physician
Teimel, a hunter and tracker
Muirgel, widow of Murchad, a boatman

At Sliabh Céim an Doire
Corbmac, commander of Dicuil Dóna's warriors

At Ghleann Uí Máil
Dicuil Dóna, lord of The Cuala
Scáth, steward and son of Dicuil Dóna
Aróc, daughter of Dicuil Dóna

At Dún Árd
Garrchú, steward of the mines of The Cuala

Others mentioned
Brehon Brocc, the murdered Brehon
Alchú, son of Fidelma and Eadulf
Tuaim Snámha, petty King of Osraige from AD 660–678
Fianamail of the Uí Máil, King of Laigin from AD 666–680

THE CUALA

KINGDOM OF LAIGIN
7TH CENTURY A.D.

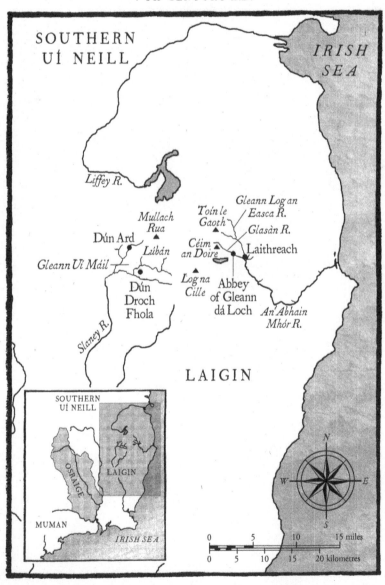

SOUTHERN
UÍ NEILL

IRISH
SEA

Liffey R.

*Toín le
Gaoth*

*Gleann Log an
Easca R.*

Glasàn R.

*Mullach
Rua*

Dún Ard

Liibán

*Céim
an Doire*

Laithreach

Gleann Uí Máil

*Log na
Cille*

Abbey
of Gleann
dá Loch

Dún
Droch
Fhola

Slaney R.

*An Abhain
Mhór R.*

LAIGIN

SOUTHERN
UÍ NEILL

OSRAIGE

LAIGIN

MUMAN

IRISH SEA

0   5   10   15 miles

0   5   10   15   20 kilometres

N
W   E
S

AUThOR'S NOTE

This story is set in AD 672, during the period known as *Laethanta na Bó Riabhai* (the days of the brindled cow), which corresponds to the last three days of March and the first three days of April in the modern calendar. The setting is the remote and forbidding peaks of The Cuala – today called the Wicklow Mountains – containing some of Ireland's highest peaks and the island's largest continuous upland.

It was here that the *Annales Ríoghachta Éireann* (Annals of the Kingdom of Ireland) stated that in The Age of the World 3656, during the reign of the High King, Tigernmas, gold was first found and smelted in a wooded glen east of the River Liffey by Uchadan, the smith, of the *Fear Cualann*, the men of The Cuala. Tigernmas, son of Fothal mac Ethriel, was said to rule in 1621–1544 BC, and is recorded as being killed during a wildly abandoned orgy to Crom Cruach, a gold pagan idol, whose cult demanded human sacrifice during the feast of Samhain. Could this have been a symbolic warning about the effect of greed for gold and power on men and women?

Gold has certainly long been used by the smiths of Ireland. One gold collar, known as the Blessington Lunala, shaped like a crescent moon, is generally dated 2400–2000 BC. Blessington stands at the edge of The Cuala. The Broighter gold hoard is dated to the 1st century BC. Gold was even discovered in the 18th century AD in the foothills of these same Wicklow Mountains at Croghan, Kinshela, where a stream was afterwards named Gold River.

To help people with locations a sketch map is included. The Abbey of the Blessed Cáemgen at Gleann Dá Loch (today Anglicised as Glendalough) is 'the valley of the two lakes'. The abbey was founded by Cáemgen (Saint Kevin) a century before these events. The forbidding mountain of Log na Coille (Anglicised as Lugnaquilla), 'the mountain of the wood', is the fourth highest peak standing at 905 metres. Nearby is Mullach Cliabháin (Anglicised as Mullagh Cleevaun) or 'the summit of the cradle', which stands at 849 metres and is the eighth highest mountain in Ireland.

Readers may wish to know that the background details of the clash in Durlus Éile and Osraige, mentioned in this story, are recounted in *The Seventh Trumpet* (2012). How Fidelma resolved the relationship she had as a student is told in *Act of Mercy* (1999). The rescue of Eadulf from execution in Laigin occurs in *Our Lady of Darkness* (2000). The incident of how Fidelma defended her friend Liadin, charged with murdering her husband, occurs in the short story 'At the Tent of Holofernes', collected in *Hemlock at Vespers: A Collection of Sister Fidelma Mysteries* (2000).

CHAPTER ONE

A bbot Daircell raised his head from the manuscript that he was copying. Had he not been a religious man, he might have uttered a profanity. That he thought it brought a moment of guilt to his conscience. As a result, he pressed his thin lips in a tight grimace before shouting sternly to his steward. The fact that he even raised his voice to a pitch that echoed from the small scriptorium, in which he was working in isolation, to reach the ears of his steward in the adjacent chamber, demonstrated the irritated mood of the abbot.

'Brother Aithrigid, for the love of God, find out who is making that unholy clamour and tell them to desist!'

The clamour was the constant pealing of the bell at the gates of the abbey to announce the arrival of wayfarers and guests of importance. Generally such visitors were few and far between because the lonely abbey in the Valley of the Two Lakes was not on any major route between settlements among the tall mountains that surrounded it. It was not just the pealing of the bell that aggravated the abbot, however, but its frenetic, almost panic-inducing sound, and the fact that Brother Dorchú, the abbey's *dorseóracht,* or gatekeeper, had apparently not responded to its summons. The abbot decided that unless Brother Dorchú had a pressing reason for his lack of diligence, his penance would not be a light one. He had been accepted into the abbey only a year before, having abandoned service as a bodyguard to the lord of The Cuala, the noble who ruled the mountainous territory in which the abbey was sited. The abbot had made Brother Dorchú the gatekeeper because he felt a former warrior would be best suited as a protector of the entrance to the abbey. Abbot Daircell sat back and scowled, making his hawk-like features more forbidding as he heard the hurried slapping of leather-soled sandals across the stone-flagged floor as the steward went off on his errand. Indeed, it was only a short while before the gate bell sounded a few hesitant, isolated notes and fell silent.

Abbot Daircell gave a sigh of relief and turned back to the manuscript page he had been contemplating. He tried to regain his concentration but his mood had changed. It was hard enough to decipher the Latin characters of the letter he had received from Abbot Failbe mac Pipáin of Iona, let alone the arguments in favour of the methods of Rome in their new computing of the Paschal celebrations. However, the complex arguments, which Abbot Failbe favoured, were beyond him. He had long ago admitted that he was neither astronomer nor mathematical scholar, nor had knowledge enough to approve or disapprove of such radical changes to the calendar. Had not the Blessed Augustine of Hippo once dismissed such matters in a letter, stating the Holy Spirit had wanted to create Christians, not mathematicians? He sighed once more and pushed the paper away.

At that moment he heard his steward hurrying back, the slap of his sandals now sounding as frantically as had the ringing of the bell. To the abbot's surprise, the scriptorium door burst open. Framed in the doorway was not his steward but a tall youth whose robes did not disguise his tough muscular form. Abbot Daircell stared in surprise. Above all rules, the brethren were taught respect and decorum; to pause outside the abbot's chambers and knock thrice, before entering once permission was given. Abbot Daircell's face darkened in annoyance, trying to remember the name of the boy.

It was one of the stable lads, recently joined. Before he could utter the admonishment, the youth seemed to recover his breath.

'The steward sent me,' he gasped. 'A man . . . a man . . .' he began to stutter. 'A man at the gate . . .'

Abbot Daircell paused, suppressing his inclination to reprove the youth. He remembered his name now.

'Calm yourself, Brother Cuilínn. So, there is a man at the gate? I hardly thought it was a straying sheep that would ring the gate bell in such agitation.' Abbot Daircell admitted to favouring irony in his speech. 'Tell me, who is this man and what does he seek here?'

Brother Cuilínn swallowed, still breathless from running with his message.

'It is a pedlar. Brother Aithrigid told me to tell you that it is Cétach the pedlar.'

Abbot Daircell's frown deepened. He knew Cétach and his reputation. He was a trader from the local township with a reputation for cunning. He was deemed both disingenuous and untrustworthy but the Abbey occasionally did business with him.

'And so? Why does Cétach the pedlar come and announce himself in such an unusual and conceited manner by ringing our gate bell as if to wake the dead for the Day of Judgment? Does he bring some news of importance? And do you know why our gatekeeper was unable to answer the summons of the bell?'

The young boy was still standing, hesitating, and the abbot grew impatient.

'Speak,' he instructed sternly. 'Do I have to repeat myself? Does the pedlar bring some news? He is not a person that I would welcome here at the best of times – a man of little worth and even less religion – but if he brings news . . .?'

The stable boy's expression and voice remained agitated. 'He brings a body, Father Abbot. The steward, Brother Aithrigid . . . he . . . er . . . requests that you examine it.'

'A body? He requests that I . . .?' Abbot Daircell hesitated, holding his temper as he realised that the boy was only the conveyor of a message.

He rose abruptly from his chair without another word and preceded the youth from the scriptorium, making his way through the abbey buildings, across the expanse of ground towards the inner gate. This gate stood before a wooden bridge, which crossed a stream to a second gate, which was the main gate of the abbey complex.

Outside this gate, the short and portly figure of Cétach stood by a mule cart, twisting the reins of the animal in his nervous hands. Cétach was a man of unprepossessing appearance. The hair on his forehead was receding, but grew dirty red, soiled and matted at the back. His beard was ample but also thick and dirty, and what little that could be seen of his cheeks was coarse and ruddy. He lowered his head in deference as the abbot approached.

'What is all this nonsense I hear, Brother Aithrigid?' Abbot Daircell demanded, ignoring the pedlar and speaking directly to his steward. 'I am told that you request that I look at a body.'

Brother Aithrigid was a tall, elderly, silver-haired man. He was softly spoken and exuded calmness in the face of all excitement. Before joining the abbey, Abbot Daircell knew Brother Aithrigid had once trained in law. Although he had not reached the highest qualification, he was at the level of an *Aire Árd*, one skilled in the preparations of judgments. In this capacity he handled the abbey's legal affairs.

His voice was almost pacifying as he replied: 'I think the pedlar should explain. It is he who brought the body here.'

As Abbot Daircell turned to Cétach, the pedlar began speaking in a soft whining manner.

'If it pleases you, Lord Abbot, I brought it here as quickly as I could and—'

Abbot Daircell held up his hand as the man seemed about to plunge on.

'You brought a body here? Where did you find this body?'

'Not far away. I was coming through the mountains, following the river through the valley of Glasán. It was there, at the pass of the oak wood, near the track where you begin to ascend the mountain to the summit to the Lake of the Water Monster . . . That's where I found it . . .'

'But why bring it here? Why not stop and bury the body? To come here is surely a deviation of your route, as I assume you would be heading to your home in Láithreach . . . or did you think this body stood in need of a special ecclesiastical ceremony and burial?'

Once more Abbot Daircell could not prevent his irony rising.

'I did, Lord Abbot,' replied the pedlar.

The abbot stood staring at him in surprise; he had expected some denial.

'Why so?' he demanded when he had recovered.

'I thought you might also feel some recompense was due for my trouble.'

The abbot knew that Cétach was a man of few morals, earning what he could by guile and cunning, but even so, it was astounding that he would expect some sort of reward for bringing a body to the abbey.

'Why should I give you a reward for bringing a body to me?' the abbot demanded.

Cétach, in spite of his tough, rugged appearance, almost simpered.

'I recognised the body as one of a party that had left Durlus Éile several days ago. I knew then that they were on their way here.'

There was a silence. A shadow crossed the abbot's features.

'On their way here from Durlus Éile?' the abbot repeated quietly. Durlus Éile was a few days' ride away on the western side of the high peaks, a small trading township in the petty kingdom of Osraige, outside the borders of the kingdom of Laigin, in which the abbey lay.

'Are you saying that you have come from Durlus Éile?' the abbot intoned slowly. 'You were following a party of travellers, of which this body was one of them? Where are the others? I don't understand.'

'I was doing business in Durlus Éile,' the pedlar hastened to explain. 'While I was waiting in the town, I saw the party leaving. There were two men and a woman. That was a full nine days ago. They took the road eastwards through the mountains. I left several days later but along the same trail. It was on that trail that I found this body. I knew the travellers to be of noble rank for I have often traded in that town.'

'Of noble rank?' The abbot's voice was icy as if a threatening thought was weighing on him. 'Show me this body.'

'It is here, Lord Abbot.' The pedlar jerked his thumb over his shoulder to indicate something covered in brown sacking in the back of his cart.

Abbot Daircell moved forward and was helped by his steward to pull back a piece of the sacking. He stood for moment staring down at the white, decomposing face of the cadaver. There was dried blood across the throat. The abbot could not suppress a gasp of recognition.

'Do you know him, my lord?' asked the pedlar nervously, watching the expression on the abbot's face.

Abbot Daircell ignored him but turned to his steward. 'I suppose you have already recognised the body?'

'I have,' agreed Brother Aithrigid solemnly. 'Am I not of Osraige and your cousin? It is the body of Brehon Brocc.'

'Brocc; Brehon to our cousin, the Princess Gelgéis of Durlus Éile,' echoed Abbot Daircell grimly. He turned to the pedlar, questions tumbling in his mind, but he was unable to speak.

'Indeed, my lord,' the pedlar said, pre-empting the unasked questions. 'I recognised the Brehon while I was in Durlus Éile. He and the princess and her steward, Spealáin, were leaving the township.'

'Where are the others? Where is Princess Gelgéis?' snapped Abbot Daircell.

'There was only this body lying on the mountain track. There was no sign of anyone else.'

Abbot Daircell's mouth was a thin grim line as he stared at the pedlar. He seemed to be struggling with emotion.

'When did you say that you saw the princess and her party set out from Durlus Éile? When were you there?'

'Nine days ago,' the pedlar repeated. 'They were all on horseback. I set out with my wagon along the same route only a few days ago.'

Abbot Daircell was shaking his head as if he had difficulty comprehending events. He seemed incapable of forming the next obvious question.

'There was no sign of their horses or other traces; no sign of who had done this deed?' Brother Aithrigid intervened.

The pedlar shook his head. 'Nothing. No sign. It was just the man's body that lay on the ground.'

'And you said that you found the body in the pass just below Sliabh Céim an Doire?'

'The mountain of the pass of the oak trees,' confirmed the pedlar, repeating the name. 'The mountains are high there and the valleys are dark with impenetrable forests, where it is rumoured beings called the *Cumachtae* – the shapeshifters – are active. Although I have never been troubled by them,' he added with a sniff.

It was true that Céim an Doire was one of the highest peaks in the whole of The Cuala, the great mountain range that covered the north of the kingdom of Laigin. The area was replete with deserted mines in forest valleys.

The abbot, seeming to recover himself, turned to beckon to a small, bald man in the group of brothers now gathering with growing curiosity.

'Brother Lachtna, come and tell us how long you think this man has been dead.'

Brother Lachtna was the abbey's physician. He came forward reluctantly and barely glanced at the body but sniffed in distaste.

'There is already putrefaction to the extent that comes after several days of exposure to the elements,' he offered.

'I want a more careful observation,' Abbot Daircell pressed harshly.

Wrinkling up his nose in distaste, the physician reached forward and took off the sackcloth covering completely, the better to examine the corpse.

'The man still wears his clothes and his leather purse. That's rather strange if he were attacked by brigands. I see the throat's been cut . . . Ah, what's that arrow there?'

'I took it from out of the man's back,' the pedlar explained. 'It was after that I saw that the man's throat had been cut.'

'It has been mild during the last few days, mild for this time of year,' Brother Lachtna muttered thoughtfully. 'But, as I said, perhaps the corpse has lain in the open for several days.' He seemed about to say something further but stopped.

'There is something else?' queried the abbot, who had a sharp eye.

Brother Lachtna hesitated. 'He has obviously been dead a week or so but . . . but I am curious . . .' His voice trailed off as he stood regarding the body.

'Curious? What is curious about a body?' It was Brother Aithrigid, the steward, who asked.

'The putrefaction indicating the time from when the body was killed to this date does not accord to the conditions of where the body has lain all this time.'

'What do you mean?' demanded Abbot Daircell.

'I think we all know the valley of Glasán and are aware of the mountains surrounding it. The area is replete in wolves, foxes and other scavenging animals. Carrion birds constantly fly the skies. I find it curious that this body has not been molested by any of them.'

'What are you implying?' pressed the abbot.

The little physician shrugged. 'I cannot say that I am prepared to draw a conclusion. I say only what I observe. There are no apparent marks of any animal, or any scavenger species – mammal or bird. None of these scavengers has paid any attention to this cadaver – that is, if it has lain abandoned on a mountainside for a week or more. Contrary to that, the decomposition of the corpse indicates that it has been protected from such an exposure to the weather. That is beyond my comprehension at this time.'

There was silence for a moment before the abbot addressed the pedlar again.

'You say that you saw nothing, no sign of anyone except the corpse lying on the mountainside? No sign of a struggle, no sign of horses, or of a conflict of any sort? You saw nothing to indicate what might have befallen Princess Gelgéis and her companion?'

'Nothing at all,' said Cétach with a nervous glance around. 'The man's body lay there and there were no items scattered nearby: no torn cloth, no rusty dagger, no part of any item that might be abandoned during an attack.'

'The body lay on its own?' demanded the abbot once again. 'You saw nothing else?'

'Nothing else,' confirmed the pedlar. 'It was as if the Aos Sí, the Otherworld folk, the shapeshifters, had swept down from the mountains and carried everything off in their Otherworld mist.'

CHAPTER TWO

Several of the religious who had gathered started to mutter, and several performed an exaggerated sign of the Cross, calling on the sanctified Cáemgen, the founder of the abbey, to appear and protect them.

'Nonsense!' the physician, Brother Lachtna, snapped at the pedlar. 'Stick to the facts.'

The pedlar turned to him defiantly. 'Is it not said that Dallahan of the Aos Sí rides these mountain passes? That Dallahan, the headless horseman, goes riding in search of unwary souls to accompany him to the dark world below the hills?'

'There is nothing supernatural in the way this corpse met its death,' sniffed the physician. 'There is nothing of the Otherworld about this arrow that you say you pulled out of his back. The cut in the man's throat, which severed him from life, is not the work of the supernatural.'

'But there were no signs of tracks or anything like that,' the pedlar insisted, defensively. 'It was as if the corpse had just appeared there. If the Brehon and his companions were attacked, there would have been signs. It was as if they were then swallowed by a great mist, leaving the corpse alone.'

'A corpse with an arrow in its back and its throat cut.' Brother Lachtna seemed amused. 'Since when do the Aos Sí resort to such tactics?'

'Are you sure the tracks had not been obliterated by the weather?' Abbot Daircell demanded.

'I am a pedlar, not a tracker,' the pedlar replied defensively. 'But I could see no tracks though the area was muddy, being not far from the river.'

Abbot Daircell was clearly troubled. 'Brother Lachtna, take the corpse to the apothecary and examine it carefully to see if you can find further information. Then you may have the body washed and prepared for burial, which will have to be done at midnight tonight, according to custom. As a Brehon, he is due that respect. You will report when you are ready so that the steward may order the ringing of the *clog-estachtlae*.'

This was the traditional tolling of the 'death bell' prior to the burial.

Brother Aithrigid frowned. 'Should there not be a night of the watching, the *aire*, before the corpse is buried?' he pointed out, his legal mind leading him to mention the protocol.

'We can forgo that,' Abbot Daircell dismissed sharply. 'The corpse has already been left on the mountainside long enough. We shall simply say a few words of the *écnaire* calling for the intercession of God for the repose of Brocc's soul.'

The physician was about to cover the body for removal when something caught his eye.

'The corpse is still wearing a belt,' he reminded them. 'There is a small leather pouch sewn to it.'

The abbot glanced at the face of the pedlar.

'I suppose you have already examined it?' he asked cynically.

'Me? I have not.' The pedlar made a poor show of indignant protest. However, the physician intervened.

'It seems to have something still in it.'

'Well?' Abbot Daircell barked.

The physician bent over the body without disguising his repugnance at the putrid odours. The pouch flap was not fastened and he reached one hand inside and pulled a small item out. It looked like a tiny piece of rock.

'It's nothing.' The physician was about to throw it aside. 'It's just a pebble.'

The abbot held out his open hand for it. 'A pebble? I suppose he could have picked it up as a weapon to throw,' he muttered, examining it.

'Not much of a weapon,' remarked Brother Aithrigid. 'And why would he have put it in the pouch?'

'It's heavy enough to cause an injury to someone if thrown with force,' Abbot Daircell said, feeling the weight in the lump of rock. He waved a dismissal to the physician before turning and spotting the gaunt features of Brother Dorchú, who had joined them. He stood awkwardly, waiting for the abbot's censure for not attending to the gate bell. He was a tall, sinewy man, who looked nothing like a member of the religieux. But the abbot had not forgotten about the former warrior's inattention in not answering the bell.

'Take charge of the pedlar,' he instructed. 'Give him a meal but be sparing of alcohol.' Cétach looked indignantly at the implication. 'I suspect you have already rewarded yourself, judging by the empty purse.' The pedlar protested again that he had touched nothing, but the abbot simply held up his hand to silence him. He continued to address the gatekeeper. 'Have a look at the man's wares and see what items he has to trade. If there is anything worthy you may make a purchase.'

Brother Dorchú led the protesting pedlar away.

Abbot Daircell turned to Brother Aithrigid, who was still waiting for instruction. 'We had best quench all that talk of the Aos Sí among the brethren. We hear too many folk tales of the demons who haunt these mountains.'

'There are a few who still firmly believe in the old tales,' Brother Aithrigid replied.

Abbot Daircell glanced thoughtfully at his steward, knowing well there might be a hidden rebuke in the words. Brother Aithrigid was aware that the abbot's hobby was collecting such tales with the purpose of adding to a text that he was expanding in the abbey's library.

He paused for a moment and then exhaled in annoyance. 'Send Brother Eochaí to me.'

'Brother Eochaí?' The steward hesitated. 'Why do you need to see the master of the stables? Are you about to make a journey?'

Abbot Daircell turned now with an expression of annoyance. 'You know I am not accustomed to repeating myself, Brother Aithrigid.' He articulated the words slowly and coldly. 'I am going to sit in my herb garden for a while. Send Brother Eochaí to me there.'

Brother Aithrigid paused then grimaced, as if he had been considering a difficult problem, and left. Watching him go, the abbot knew that the steward realised that the herb garden was a place where no one could eavesdrop without being observed. It was obvious that the abbot had something to say that he did not wish overheard.

Abbot Daircell seated himself on a small wooden bench, vacantly tossing with one hand the heavy little stone, no more than a pebble, that the physician had handed him. He tried not to seem impatient and was pleased that he did not have to wait long.

Brother Eochaí was a short individual whose small frame did not disguise his well-trained muscles, nor did his features veil the hidden strength and determination of purpose. Usually he affected a lopsided grin of amusement at the world. His demeanour before the abbot was that of an equal, not of a person awaiting orders, nor of one who was curious about being summoned by the abbot.

Abbot Daircell stopped tossing the stone. He was about to throw it away but then decided to thrust it into his leather *bossán,* the purse hanging from his belt. He glanced round to ensure that they were alone in the garden.

'Do I find you well, *echaire*?' he asked, addressing the man by his title of 'master of the stables'.

'I am, thanks be,' Brother Eochaí replied solemnly.

'And the horses in your charge . . . are they all fit and strong?'

'All save a cob who cast a shoe this morning. Brother Gobbán, the smith, is preparing to shoe the beast even as we speak. And, of course, we have a mare that is going to foal in a few days' time.'

'But you have some strong horses immediately available in the stable? Horses that can travel distances without tiring?'

Only by a slight lifting of his eyebrows did the master of the stables indicate that the abbot had asked an unusual question.

'My stable can compete with the best in the land, Father Abbot. Indeed, I have a two-year-old colt that is a match for any in the Five Kingdoms for stamina and speed.' There was no boast in his voice; just a statement of fact.

Abbot Daircell was silent for a minute or two as if contemplating something. Then he turned to stare up directly at the man.

'Like me, I know you to be a man of Osraige. That is why I have sent for you.'

Brother Eochaí regarded his superior with disapproval.

'I am a man of God first and foremost, Father Abbot. Where ever He sends me, my first duty is to serve Him. I am a simple man, not related to noble families such as yourself or Brother Aithrigid. But I am sure that we are all of the same mind – we serve the Faith and the Abbey, and not individual princes or kingdoms.'

The abbot forced an uneasy smile. 'That is certainly as it should be,' he agreed in a pious tone. It sounded false. 'But, my son, we have to accept that service to the Faith is also service to truth and justice. So I presume that you have heard of the news that has been brought to the abbey by Cétach?'

'I have heard that the pedlar found the body of Brehon Brocc.'

'Brehon Brocc was one of a party that was accompanying Princess Gelgéis to this very abbey.'

Brother Eochaí shrugged. 'I am afraid news of misfortune spreads like a fire lit among dry bracken at the height of summer, especially when some fools want to embellish it with stories about the wraiths of the Aos Sí haunting the mountain passes.'

The abbot's expression was one of anger. 'So that story is being spread already? Fools! Fools!'

'Frightened fools,' the stable master observed grimly.

'Frightened? Indeed, frightened. That is why I have need of you, especially as you are of Osraige.'

'If you enquire as to my birthplace, Father Abbot, I admit that I am of the Uí Dróna, born on the west bank of the great River Fheoir. But I say once again that I serve the Faith, not Osraige, nor the kingdom of Laigin.'

'I believe there is no conflict,' the abbot said emphatically. 'But you will remember that scarcely more than a year has passed since the King of Laigin, Fianamail of the Uí Máil, was preparing to raise his warriors to march on the Kingdom of Muman and use Osraige as an excuse for his invasion.'

The story was well known. The territory of Osraige lay sandwiched between the bigger kingdoms of Muman and Laigin. Both kingdoms traditionally claimed sovereignty over the territory and had long been in conflict over it. The rulers of the petty kingdom found themselves playing one ruler off against the other to maintain their independence. Laigin, and its rulers of the Uí Máil dynasty, had devised many plans to invade, finding the smaller border territory an easy means to exert pressure on Muman and its ruler.

The most recent conflict had been when a noble of Osraige had entered into a conspiracy with rebellious members of the King of Muman's family to overthrow him. The plan had been that, as soon as Muman could be destabilised by in-fighting, Fianamail of Laigin would strike. Princess Gelgéis had played a crucial role with King Colgú of Muman in overcoming the threat and Fianamail had reluctantly withdrawn his army. Tuaim Snámha, the petty King of Osraige, had managed to avoid culpability but there had been fines and tributes claimed by the High King and Chief Brehon of the Five

Kingdoms. Muman had increased Osraige's tribute to King Colgú in retribution.

'That conflict is common knowledge,' Brother Eochaí admitted, uncertain where the abbot was leading.

'Is it also common knowledge that Princess Gelgéis is now the betrothed to Colgú, King of Muman. That the forthcoming union of the families is one desired by Colgú and Gelgéis.'

The man's eyelids raised a fraction and then he shrugged.

'That, too, is common knowledge. But I have heard that it is resented by Tuaim Snámha, who now pays more tribute to Muman and has to accept the overlordship of the Eóganacht dynasty as the price of Osraige's role in that conspiracy.'

'Which does not also please the Uí Máil as well as certain nobles of Osraige. One has to remember that this abbey stands in the middle of Uí Máil territory.'

'What are you saying?' Brother Eochaí asked uncertainly.

Abbot Daircell stared thoughtfully at his stable master.

'I am saying that Princess Gelgéis is seen as having been central to the defeat of Fianamail's plan to extend his territory with the help of Tuaim Snámha of Osraige. She was on her way to visit me and has now disappeared, and her Brehon has been found slain. I received a message by carrier pigeon from her only nine days ago telling me to expect her and her party as she had learnt disturbing news.'

The stable master was thoughtful.

'And you are saying there is a connection between what that news might be and the fact her party has disappeared and one of them, her Brehon, has been killed?'

'Just so. I do not know the details of the news she was bringing but she must have been aware that it was a dangerous journey to make. To ignore the dangers means it was important because her name is reviled by all the Uí Máil, not the least the King of Laigin and his immediate family. Here, in The Cuala, the mountains over which the Uí Máil family hold personal fiefdom, she has vanished. I fear the worst. It also means that it is unlikely that any Brehon linked to these families will attempt to resolve the mystery. Now do you see why I want to entrust a task to someone whose sympathies are neither of this kingdom nor with the ambitions of Osraige?'

'I say again, my sympathies are with the Faith,' the master of the stables said reprovingly. 'But I am not indifferent to the suffering of my people in Osraige. I have heard stories from Osraige that Tuaim Snámha has been recently approached about defying Muman once again and, in doing so, asking for the protection of Laigin. That would be disastrous for Osraige.'

'I knew you would be concerned about the welfare of our people,' exclaimed the abbot, almost in relief. 'I know you have tended our stables well, Eochaí.'

'I have tended the horses in the stables here for three years and you have sent me no complaints,' replied the stable master. There was no complacency in his tone; just a statement of fact. 'That should be recommendation enough.'

'But as a rider? You have been deemed to be excellent?'

'I leave the judgement to others.'

'Then tell me how long it would take, if you had to ride from here to Cashel, in Muman, as a matter of urgency?'

The master of the stables pursed his lips as he considered.

'I would not like to push a horse to extremes, but allowing for any contingency and rest periods, I would say two days.'

'How would you go? Westward across the mountains?'

Brother Eochaí ignored the question. 'Why would I ride to Cashel? If you ask me to take a message, then surely it would be quicker to use the carrier pigeons that you breed and train?'

Like many other important centres, the abbey trained its own pigeons, in which the abbot took a special interest.

Abbot Daircell shook his head. 'This is one message I want to ensure reaches the eyes of Colgú of Cashel and no other. Certain nobles here have devoted time to training their falcons to intercept the pigeons.'

'Then, perhaps, we had better not speak of my route in case someone watches my departure. Not only is the lord of The Cuala known to train peregrine falcons, many others do so, too.'

Abbot Daircell rubbed his chin thoughtfully. 'You are a good man, Brother Eochaí. Then take whatever route you judge is best.'

'What message am I to give when I reach Cashel?'

'Bear my greetings to King Colgú and simply repeat what you have learnt here today: that is his betrothed, Princess Gelgéis of Durlus Éile, was known to have set out for this abbey over a week ago. Of her party, her Brehon was found slaughtered on the route while she and her steward are now missing. Say that I fear for her safety. That is all.'

'Am I to say no more than this?' asked Brother Eochaí, surprised by the terseness of the abbot's message.

The abbot shook his head. There seemed a hidden meaning in his words when he replied: 'I believe that Colgú will know what to do on learning the news.'

CHAPTER THREE

'Law! I am bored by law!'

Eadulf's head jerked up in astonishment as Fidelma suddenly rose to her feet, scattering the papers she had been contemplating and shaking her long red hair from side to side in angry fashion. She glanced belligerently around their private chamber as if expecting someone to leap forward and rebuke her for the statement. Eadulf wisely regained his composure after being startled at the interruption to his own reading. He examined his partner in surprise. They had been sitting quietly studying their respective manuscripts. The fading light of the cold wintery afternoon made necessary the use of candles and oil lamps, and the addition of a crackling log fire to warm them. These conditions did not make reading an ideal occupation. However, some new decisions from the Council of Brehons, which met every three years, had recently arrived and needed to be studied.

'Am I to take that remark seriously?' Eadulf asked in a solemn tone after a pause. He could not entirely disguise the amusement in his eyes and the laughter lines that he knew must be playing at the corners of his mouth.

Fidelma turned on him with an exasperated expression.

'Law, law, law . . . this judgment, that appeal, another new inter-pretation. All to make sure the text has not been outdated by some obscure decision. Appeals from judges who have forgotten that people make the law and not the law make the people. I am fed up with it all . . .'

'That's an interesting statement from one who is the King of Muman's legal adviser,' Eadulf interrupted mildly, letting her anger wash over him. 'But people do change, I am told. What they decide one year, they change the next when more information comes to light. After studying at Brehon Morann's college of law, you have spent years gaining a reputation where you have even been consulted by the High King of the Five Kingdoms. You have gone to many countries because of your knowledge. You have even won fame in many lands between here and Rome. I suppose law can be boring, but you could have had any legal position that you asked for.'

He had barely uttered the words when he realised his mistake.

'On the contrary.' Fidelma's teeth almost clenched. 'You know well that I was rejected when I applied to be Chief Brehon of Muman. Yes, rejected by a council of my fellow Brehons, who did not find me worthy enough in spite of that so-called reputation.' The tone of her voice became a sneer. 'My own brother felt it necessary to assuage my feelings by appointing me his legal adviser.'

'He did so because he needed a good legal counsel to represent him.'

'He did so for charity's sake!' she contradicted.

Eadulf was saddened by her attitude. 'Some would think it is a high honour. In spite of what you say, you must realise that your brother, Colgú, would not have appointed you to that role if he did not think you were capable. And you have proved yourself so.'

Fidelma was not mollified. She pointed to the discarded papers scattered on the door.

'An honour? An honour to have to spend time weeding through all this garbage? Legal claims that any qualified as a *Dos* could sort out.' Eadulf knew that a *Dos* was a fourth-year student at a Bardic school. 'Anyone who has studied the *Bretha Nemed*, the Law of Privilege, could sort out the cases that I am supposed to advise on. I am qualified—'

Eadulf suppressed a groan before interrupting in a heavy tone. 'Qualified to the level of *Anruth*, the second highest degree that either the Bardic or the Ecclesiastical colleges can bestow. You don't have to keep reminding everyone of that.'

Fidelma swung round in annoyance but then checked herself. 'But I did have to remind many that I encountered, especially when I was trying to make my way in this world after I left law school. Now it seems that I must do so again.'

'What has brought this on?' Eadulf asked gently. He paused and indicated the scattered papers. 'I suppose it is an obscure legal matter that is perplexing you?'

'Perplexing me?' She sounded threatening. 'No, it is not obscure; just a paltry argument about rights over a property that could have been dealt with by a junior clerk. No need at all to bring it to the King's legal adviser.'

'Then why was it passed to you?'

Fidelma shrugged, reseated herself and picked up one of the papers.

'Any matter relating to the finding of silver ore in the kingdom has to be reported to the King. I have to consider this and I saw some recent restrictions made by the Brehon Council. Having read them twice, there is still little sense to be made of them.'

Eadulf was interested at the mention of *triun airgit*, silver ore.

'It sounds important,' he ventured, finally setting aside the manuscript that he had been trying to read.

'But not important enough to waste my time over disputes in such matters,' she replied. 'The matter could have been reported directly to my brother, Colgú, and the argument settled by a local Brehon without me having to double-check this reference.'

'But it wasn't. So how long will it take you?'

Fidelma made a cutting gesture with her hand. 'Long enough to waste my time. I could have spent the time playing with little Alchú and giving old Muirgen some time to rest. Since you now take him out for his morning ride, I barely see him at all.'

Eadulf smiled thinly. 'I am quite willing to forgo the morning horse ride,' he said. Eadulf did not consider himself a good horseman and, indeed, preferred any other means of travel than lengthy journeys on horseback. 'It's just that I thought you wanted . . .'

Fidelma's brows creased in frustration. 'I'll tell you what I want and then you won't have to waste time thinking it,' she replied waspishly. 'I don't want to waste time with mundane matters like this.'

'Well, I am sure Muirgen will be happy to allow you to have more time to play with our son.' Eadulf became unusually sarcastic. 'Don't forget that she is getting old now. We've been absent from Cashel enough times over the last years to the point where I am sure that our son does not think of us as his parents at all. He sees more of Muirgen and her husband, Nessan. Let them rest. Give up the law.'

Since Alchú had been a baby, Fidelma had employed Muirgen as nurse to the child while her husband, Nessan, was employed looking after the King's livestock. During the long periods that Fidelma and Eadulf had been away in pursuit of legal missions, Muirgen had been almost a foster parent to the boy. This had been a bone of contention for Eadulf, not because he disliked Muirgen, but because he felt isolated as a parent and, perhaps, somewhat resentful. His son was nephew to the King of Muman, and Eadulf, being an Angle from the kingdom of the East Angles, felt unable to pass on any of his own cultural traditions.

'Give up law? Don't be ridiculous!' Fidelma replied acidly.

'But . . .' Eadulf protested at her change of logic.

'It's better than this litigant's choice.' She held up the paper that she was consulting. 'He spends his life wasting time, digging a well to find silver.'

Eadulf hesitated as he had not recognised the word that she had used.

'Did you say "mining" a well?'

Fidelma failed to understand for a moment and then she actually smiled.

'You mean *claide* – it's basically an act of "digging out" so we can use it as *claide mianna* for mining. *Fear cladhaich* – a miner. Or for digging or excavating water wells.'

'Meaning, in this instance?' Eadulf pressed, for he was always anxious to improve his knowledge of the language.

'You are acquainted with the mountains to the north of here – Sliabh Eibhlinne? They are full of minerals. But some of the farmers on those slopes have argued the water that used to drain from the mountains has changed course because of the mines. A local farmer agreed with his neighbour to dig a well for water. It was on the borders of their properties. This was because it was in the best location to find water. In the course of excavation of the well, the first farmer found pieces of silver ore among the lead and copper that he dug up. So the well is on the first farmer's land. But the second farmer demands shared ownership of the proceeds.'

'The well is on the first man's land? But they both agreed to sinking the well to find water?'

'The agreement was that the water was to be divided between the two farmers. So does the second one have any right to the silver?'

'There was no conflict while the subject of the division was water?'

'None, only when silver was found has a conflict arisen.'

'Then I think that the same division should apply.'

Fidelma smiled thinly. 'You have gained a good understanding of the principles of our law system, Eadulf.'

'I was guided by that bee judgment that you taught me. What do you call it – the *Bechbretha*? That the bee-keeper must give a portion of the honey to his neighbours because his bees gather the nectar from their plants just as much as from his own. Doesn't the same principle apply: that items found on another's land, which affect his neighbour, must be shared? If so, I cannot see why you are frustrated or that there is a problem. It is a simple decision.'

Fidelma's smile broadened but without humour. 'In fact, the bee law affirms that any discovery on land, especially the finding of *glith* or ore of various metals, should be notified to the King, or the local lord or abbot. No division is required to the King unless he or the local lord of the territory is also a neighbour.'

'Then, again, I cannot see why you are so frustrated? The judgment is easy.'

'It is not the principle of division. You know that any judgment must be accompanied by precedent so that it is seen to be fairly based on previous authority. For example, citing the bee law that you mention, we have two different judgments. That, as you say, the bee-keeper has to divide a portion of the honey with his four nearest neighbours or, according to another interpretation, that every four or five years, the bee-keeper must present a swarm to his neighbours so that they also become bee-keepers. The two judgments are based on different interpretations as to whether the bee-keeper is the owner and responsible for the bees or whether the bees cannot be owned, as they are not able to be confined, and so are responsible for themselves.'

Eadulf thought for a moment. 'I did not think there was such philosophy behind the laws.'

Fidelma shrugged. 'Law does not come without thought and precedence, therefore much consideration is shown with even the simplest of judgments. In this case I also have to reacquaint myself with the laws on mining, which I have not seen since I was a student at Brehon Morann's school. What I was complaining about was that I have to ensure that I am up to date with the Council of Brehons' latest rulings.'

She knelt on the floor and began to pick up the scattered papers.

24

As she was settling back again to sort them into order there was a sharp knock at the door. It opened in answer to Eadulf's call to enter. The newcomer was Enda, the young warrior of the Golden Collar, the élite bodyguard to the King of Muman. Enda had been their companion in many adventures. However, Enda's usual expression of amusement was now replaced by one of serious concern. Fidelma was the first to spot this as he entered.

'Is something wrong?' she demanded.

Enda stood hesitantly. 'The King, your brother, requests the presence of you and friend Eadulf.'

Many in the King's household tended to use *Comthach* Eadulf as a term of respect. As the husband of Fidelma, rather than a religious mode of address, they felt it more appropriate. It meant a 'friend' and 'comrade', whereas King Colgú used the term *Cáem* Eadulf, indicating that he was a precious and noble friend.

'Is something wrong with my brother?' queried Fidelma, immediately concerned.

'Not exactly, but the King does not appear in the best of moods. He required you both to come at once.'

'Something must have happened to cause this change of mood,' Eadulf muttered. 'This very morning he seemed as cheerful as ever I have seen him.'

'It is not for me to say,' Enda admitted uneasily, 'but a rider arrived at Cashel a short time ago and spent some time with the King. I was then summoned and told to request your presence.'

'We'll come,' Fidelma said, casting her papers aside once more.

'Do you have any idea where this mysterious rider came from?' pressed Eadulf as they left the chamber.

'Oh, there is no mystery in that, friend Eadulf. He had to give that information to the guards before being allowed into the King's presence. He identified himself as Brother Eochaí and said he carried a personal message from Abbot Daircell of the Abbey of the Blessed Cáemgen.'

'Cáemgen's abbey? That's in the Valley of the Two Lakes,' Fidelma reflected.

'Where is that?' Eadulf asked.

'It is an abbey that lies within The Cuala mountains. I have heard about it but never been there. I know only that it is in a small valley a long way from any major township.'

'The Cuala? That is the mountain range in the northern part of the kingdom of Laigin. I have met people who told me about those mountains.' Eadulf's features assumed an expression of distaste, remembering when he had been taken prisoner and nearly executed when travelling through Laigin. 'Laigin is not the friendliest of places.'

Had it not been for Fidelma, and indeed young Enda and some of his comrades, he would have met his death in Laigin.

Fidelma made no further response as they followed Enda, striding purposefully across the courtyard to the King's apartments. At the doors two warriors of the Golden Collar saluted them respectfully as they passed through and along the oak-panelled corridor towards the King's private chambers. An attendant standing outside the doors saw their approach and rapped three times on the door. He waited until he heard the King's voice, then threw it open and stood aside to allow Fidelma and Eadulf to pass through. Enda remained outside with the attendant.

Colgú rose from his chair before a crackling wood fire in order to greet them. Agitation was etched on his features, which were a male counterpart of Fidelma's own. They could almost be twins, with their red hair, except that Fidelma was older. The King's hair was in disarray, showing that he had been running his hands through it in anxiety, which was a habit that he had had since childhood. Unusually, he came to his sister, both hands held out to take hers. He squeezed them for a moment, then disengaged the left one to hold it out to clasp Eadulf momentarily by the shoulder. He had the same blue-green eyes as Fidelma, which at that moment were wide with worry. Silent with emotion, he turned sharply with a gesture for them to take seats on the vacant couch. He returned to his own chair and stood uncomfortably for a moment before seating himself. Neither Fidelma nor Eadulf spoke for they were perplexed by the emotional anxiety that showed not only on the young King's features but in the state of tension in which he held his entire body.

He seemed as though he was making his mind up to speak. When he did so his voice came like a cry of distress.

'It is Gelgéis: she has disappeared and her Brehon has been found dead.'

'Is that the news the messenger from Laigin brought?' Fidelma was the first to recover from the shock.

'She and a small party had left Durlus Éile to go to the Abbey of Cáemgen. They did not arrive and her Brehon's body was found near the trail. He had been murdered,' her brother replied.

Fidelma's eyes widened. 'Are you saying that Gelgéis went on a journey to this abbey? Surely she would not do that? It is in The Cuala mountains of Laigin. That is a hostile territory for her now. She is hated by people there for being instrumental in helping overthrow Cronán's plot.'

'The abbot is her cousin,' Colgú told her. 'It seems she needed to see him urgently. A trader saw them leave Durlus Éile. He later followed, as he traded regularly with the Abbey. On the path they had taken, he found the body of Brehon Brocc. There was no sign of the others. They did not turn up at the abbey. The abbot, Abbot Daircell, sent a messenger to me.'

Eadulf was puzzled. 'What does this Abbot Daircell expect you to do?'

Colgú spread his hands in a despairing gesture. 'You know that Gelgéis and I were to be married on the feastday of the Blessed Ciarán of Saigir, the patron saint of Osraige? That is just over a week away. If I need to march an army through Osraige and into the mountains to find her, I shall do so.'

'You must not, brother,' Fidelma returned immediately. 'If you do so without the authority of the High King and his Chief Brehon, you will have much to lose. In every military problem this kingdom has engaged in during the last several hundred years it was only in defence of the kingdom and not to invade another. You would run the risk of the condemnation of the Five Kingdoms and the High King himself, just as Fianamail of Laigin has often done. I need not remind you of the reparation of the *bóroma*, the tribute, that has been laid on Laigin for the last six centuries. It will continue until they cease their aggressive conspiracies. Do you want your own kingdom to be similarly condemned by the Brehons of the Five Kingdoms?'

Colgú raised his arms helplessly. 'If King Fianamail has taken Gelgéis captive and killed her Brehon, what else can I do? I must rescue her.'

'There are other ways of doing so rather than sending your warriors into Laigin,' returned Fidelma. 'And the first thing to do is to make sure it is the King of Laigin who has acted in this fashion. You cannot act without proof of who has taken her and where she is being held and for what purpose. From what you tell me, this messenger from Abbot Daircell tells us nothing except that this Brehon with whom she was travelling has been killed. There is no sign of her or her steward. Is that sufficient to go to war? I tell you this as your legal adviser.'

Colgú slumped in this chair. 'Battles I can fight when the enemy is identified, but I cannot deal with this. The woman I love is in danger and I don't know what I can do. I am useless.'

Fidelma regarded her brother with a look of pity. She reached forward and, for a moment, laid her hand on his arm.

'Brother, you are a king and you must not reveal a weakness to anyone outside this room. Only your family – only Eadulf and I – should see you so disturbed. Always appear strong to your people. They expect it of you. If you do not, then you are lost.'

Colgú sniffed and spread a hand to wipe his face before glancing apologetically at Eadulf. 'Forgive me, husband of my sister. I forget that a king has obligations as well as duties. Don't worry, Fidelma, I am in control. Tell me, how can we deal with this matter?'

'Send for this messenger from Abbot Daircell so that I might hear his story at first-hand.'

While her brother crossed the room to give instructions to Enda, who was on guard just outside the chamber door, Fidelma looked thoughtfully at Eadulf.

'Are you willing to embark on a lengthy ride on horseback?' she asked softly.

Eadulf sighed. 'I suppose that you have a mind to set out for Laigin to this remote abbey?'

'That is exactly what is in my mind,' she admitted. 'How else can one get information?'

Colgú heard her last words. 'That is insane, Fidelma. You say that Gelgéis would never cross into Laigin because she is hated there for her role in thwarting Cronán's uprising. Then how much more are you hated there? You were the one who uncovered the plot, and brought about that defeat. If Laigin sought vengeance on Gelgéis, then they would seek treble the vengeance on you.'

Fidelma replied with a nonchalant shrug. 'You forget, brother, Gelgéis may be a princess of Osraige but I am a *dálaigh* of the Five Kingdoms, a Brehon of rank, a member of the law courts with some reputation,' she smiled thinly. 'I am not one to rely on undeserved credit but, as Eadulf was only recently reminding me, I have been consulted in matters by the High King in Tara. You know that the shadow of his vengeance would descend on any who would dishonour my rank and role.'

Eadulf pursed his lips cynically. 'Let us hope those in Laigin would appreciate that they stand under vengeance of the High King if they are involved in this matter,' he said with soft cynicism.

Fidelma did not bother to reply. 'The first task is to discover what has happened to Gelgéis,' she said emphatically. 'Something is afoot because, in spite of what has just been said, she felt it necessary to cross into Laigin, and she does not take risks lightly.'

'Then you have a plan, sister, other than travelling to the Abbey of Cáemgen?'

'The abbey is where my investigation must start.'

There was a knock on the door and Enda ushered Brother Eochaí inside. He was about to withdraw when Fidelma ordered him to stay and close the door behind him.

'How much rest do you need, you and your horse, before starting back to your abbey?' she asked the messenger from Laigin without preamble.

Brother Eochaí did not seem surprised.

'For myself, I could start immediately, but for my horse, it should rest until tomorrow. I pushed it hard on the way here. I know its strength, its pace and abilities as I know my own. It must have rest.'

'Your concern for the animal is to be applauded,' Fidelma remarked. 'As someone who cares for horses, I understand that. You are sure tomorrow gives you time enough?'

'I am master of the stables of the abbey, lady. I know horses. They are my friends. I know their capabilities.'

'I do not doubt it. If you and your horse are fit for the return journey then tomorrow it shall be.'

'So shall it be,' Brother Eochaí agreed. 'So I am to return to Abbot Daircell but what message shall I take?'

'No message,' she replied, to his obvious surprise. Then she added: 'We shall be coming with you.'

'We, lady?'

'Myself, Brother Eadulf and Enda.'

Brother Eochaí stared at her with incredulity. 'You are coming with me to Laigin? But are you not sister to the King of Muman?'

Fidelma was amused at the man's concern. 'And why should that be of consequence?' she asked.

'But you are an Eóganacht?'

'Before that I am a *dálaigh* of the courts of the Five Kingdoms. You should know that a Brehon, even of low rank, is not limited by territorial borders but comes under the authority of the Chief Brehon of the Five Kingdoms and thereby the protection of the High King. I should be able to travel where I please with impunity.' She paused as she saw Enda looking surprised and added: 'That protection goes to all in the party I travel with. I am sure, Enda, my brother will be willing to release you from your service in his bodyguard or on any obligation to allow you to accompany me.'

'If the King allows, then I am at your service, lady,' Enda declared.

'If it helps return Gelgéis to safety,' Colgú replied immediately before she could ask him, 'then I am willing to do so.'

'That is good,' Fidelma said, turning back to Enda. 'Gelgéis has disappeared in The Cuala mountains; her Brehon has been murdered. The task is to find her, Enda. I ask you to come with me as you are one of the few friends I can trust.'

The young warrior did not pause but simply said: 'Explain your plan, lady.'

'My plan is not to go overtly into Laigin proclaiming my rank and purpose.' She turned to Brother Eochaí. 'The journey will not be at the pace by which you have brought the news here. We shall have to travel more sedately and in the manner of a group of religious on a pilgrimage to the Abbey of the Blessed Cáemgen. That will mean we travel in appropriate garb.'

'The best way, if I can suggest it, is the way I came,' Brother Eochaí intervened. 'Leisurely riding will take us several days. We could ride on to Gleann Molúra and then it is but a short ride north to the abbey.' He glanced at Eadulf with a thoughtful expression as though assessing his capabilities as a horseman and not being impressed.

'You are not of the Laigin?' Fidelma suddenly asked.

'I am of the Uí Dróna in Osraige,' Brother Eochaí said simply.

'I was once many days among the Uí Dróna, pleading a case

before the local Brehon, Rathend,' Fidelma said. 'As a matter of fact, I went there to defend my former *anam-chara,* Liadin, against the charge of murdering her husband.' She turned to Eadulf. 'That was long before I met you, when I was a young lawyer staying with my cousin Abbot Laisran of the abbey at Darú.'

Brother Eochaí was looking at her thoughtfully. 'It was in the time of Irnan when she ruled at the Ráth of the Uí Dróna. After, her heir apparent was found guilty of collusion in that murder. Because of that she resigned her chieftainship to Aed Rón.'

'So you knew about the case?' Fidelma asked.

'I heard about it,' admitted Brother Eochaí. 'I had left to serve at the abbey just before that time. Was it not Scoriath, the commander of Irnan's bodyguard, who was murdered and he was the husband of Liadin, whom you mention?'

'You are correct,' acknowledged Fidelma shortly. 'However, I can assure you that it is not my intention to seek shelter or hospitality before we reach the abbey, whether it be in Uí Dróna territory or not. I presume that you did not do so, nor speak of your destination, on your journey here.'

Brother Eochaí agreed that he had not used the main tracks and rested in woods and valleys, avoiding contact with people.

'Then it is settled we journey disguised as religious and only seek help if there is no other alternative,' Fidelma declared. 'Now, Brother Eochaí, repeat the story you have brought to my brother so that we may all hear it first-hand.'

At a nod of approval from Colgú, Brother Eochaí once again recited what had happened at the Abbey of the Blessed Cáemgen. No one spoke until he had finished. Colgú looked anxiously at his sister as if expecting her to come forth with questions and ideas, but she merely shrugged.

'There are no details. Only speculation, which does not help. It seems that there is nothing to be done until we can get to the abbey. It is no use speculating from here, at a distance.'

Brother Eochaí shifted his weight uncomfortably. 'You are not forgetting that the body will be disposed of by this time. It is custom to bury it at midnight the day after death and, from what I was told by our physician, Brother Lachtna, it was already in a state of putrefaction.'

'I am aware of that,' Fidelma agreed. 'However, I am hoping that your physician . . . Brother Lachtna? . . . I am hoping he may be able to tell me a few details. Often bodies can tell us more in their state of dumbness than the most vocal of witnesses.'

'Let us hope your physician has a good eye,' muttered Eadulf softly. His medical training had often helped Fidelma solve mysteries over the years that they had been together.

'Well, the sooner you are off, so much the better.' Colgú's tone made his anxiety clear.

'Don't worry, brother,' Fidelma assured him. 'Daybreak is time enough to start our journey.'

Colgú hesitated for a moment and clenched his jaw in resignation.

'You are right, sister. It is just hard . . .'

Fidelma reached forward and once again laid a comforting hand on her brother's arm.

'I know. Believe me, I care for Gelgéis and look forward to greeting her as my sister. She will be a worthy wife and queen to you, brother. I fully expect her to be standing by your side at the feastday of the Blessed Ciarán when you exchange your vows.'

'But The Cuala mountains are a place of darkness and mysteries,' Colgú said softly. 'I have heard that not even the warriors of Laigin like to travel through them. I have heard stories of the Aos Sí that—'

'Come now, brother,' rebuked Fidelma sharply. 'Let us not talk of such insubstantial things.'

'Yet the King says nothing that is not known,' Brother Eochaí muttered. 'It is said that the Aos Sí do haunt those high peaks, being the last bastion of their power against the New Faith in the Five Kingdoms.'

Fidelma turned with annoyance. 'Oh, come! You are of the religious and you speak of the Aos Sí, supernatural demons who wait to seduce the unwary into their mountain lairs?'

Brother Eochaí was not put out. 'How do you rebut me for saying so because I am a religious? Are you not also a religious and believe in a supreme supernatural being and his angels? If you believe in a good supernatural being why do you not accept the evil supernatural beings that are in eternal battle with them? The devils of hell must be as real as are the angels of heaven. You cannot accept one and deny the other.'

'You believe there are evil beings in the mountains?' Fidelma almost sneered.

'The Blessed Luke writes that the Devil came to the Christ to tempt him to abandon the way of good and turn to the dark side. Did not the Devil take the Christ to the mountain top to tempt him? Up among the peaks the local people of The Cuala say the Devil still dwells. Among the peaks and dark valleys, there is a constant war between the forces of Light and Dark.'

For a moment Fidelma was quiet as she wrestled with good argument to the man's logic. It was Eadulf who interrupted.

'Time for theology later,' he declared. 'What we have found so far is that the demons we have discovered are rarely supernatural but appear in the bodies of men and women inspired by the dark caverns of their minds rather than any place on this earth.'

Fidelma glanced at her partner in surprise, for Eadulf had only been converted to the New Faith as a teenager and raised as an Angle, cousins of the Saxons, in the world of Woden and Frige, of Thunor and Tiw. He had often displayed his belief in the supernatural and evil spirits. She suspected he was just trying to put an end to time wasting on the discussion.

Brother Eochaí shrugged. 'Very well. But it is a foolish man who travels The Cuala mountains at night without acknowledging the powers of darkness. There many tales of the shapeshifters dwelling there.'

Enda, showing signs of impatience, turned to Colgú.

'My lord, if we are to depart at first light then there are things to be done. May I have your permission to be about those tasks?'

Colgú glanced at his sister first and then nodded agreement.

'We will meet at the stable before first light and be ready to make an early start,' she declared. 'Oh, and, Enda, take Brother Eochaí to our stable master and see that he has food and a bed for the night, and anything else he requires.'

Enda raised his hand in a gesture of acknowledgement and motioned to Brother Eochaí to follow him from the chamber.

After they had gone, Colgú shook his head. 'I feel it wrong that you and Eadulf should go on this journey and not me.'

Eadulf smiled. 'And what would be the reaction if the King of Muman, the largest of the Five Kingdoms, set out from Cashel to go into Laigin? Fidelma has told you the consequences if you moved an army. And if you went alone that would be even worse, for you would never reach beyond the border. It is not wrong that Fidelma and I, who are able to travel less conspicuously, make this journey.'

Fidelma gave Eadulf a glance of appreciation.

'What Eadulf says is true, my brother. I know you can't relax but you must try to concentrate on the running of the affairs of this kingdom until we can resolve this matter. You will forgive us withdrawing; as Enda pointed out, we have a few things to prepare.'

Outside the King's chambers, as they were crossing the flagstone courtyard to their own chambers, Eadulf asked: 'Do you know much about this mountainous area we are heading to? I have heard something about this Abbey of the Blessed Cáemgen because it attracts many students. But is it as forbidding as everyone claims?'

Fidelma was reassuring. 'When a country is unknown it is always considered forbidding. The Cuala is not the most inviting of places.

I have never ventured among its many mountains but have seen them from a distance. It is a large territory with many very high peaks. Some are said to be the highest in the Five Kingdoms, like Log na Coille, the mountain of the wood, where the Sláine, the river of health, rises. Generally the area is a place of darkness, a place of grey granite and slate. I would not say it is inviting.'

'Then what possessed this Cáemgen to establish his abbey in such a place?'

'He did not; well, not at first. I had the story from my cousin who became abbot at Darú. Cáemgen was one of the royal families of Laigin one hundred years ago. He wanted to escape from the arguments and intrigues that went with being born into such a dynasty. So he became a hermit living in a cave in that valley of two lakes. It was certainly the remotest place in the kingdom. People heard about his frugal life and, like people sadly do because they often want someone to follow, it was those followers who went to that secluded valley in the mountains and built the abbey that now bears his name.'

Eadulf looked despondent. 'I think we are going to be faced with a hard task.'

Fidelma sighed. 'Not so hard as the one immediately before us.'

Eadulf frowned in puzzlement.

'We have to tell our son, Alchú, that we are leaving him again,' she explained.

'And for an indefinite period,' Eadulf added pessimistically.

'No need to put it so bluntly to the child. I'll send for Muirgen and make sure he'll have the support he needs.'

'I do not doubt that your brother will be mindful to maintain the morning ride in spite of the matter he now frets about. Nor will he neglect to take time to play with him.'

Colgú had always been an excellent support for his young nephew.

'We'll make sure that, if Colgú cannot, one of Enda's comrades, a senior warrior of the Golden Collar does so, such as Dego or Luan.'

Eadulf suddenly halted and glanced around the protective ramparts of the royal fortress. Something made him shiver.

Fidelma saw the movement. 'What is wrong?' she demanded.

'I don't know,' Eadulf replied hesitantly. 'I just had a passing feeling; something like a coldness on the back of my neck.'

'A cold feeling on your neck?' Fidelma was curious.

'I suddenly felt that it would be a long time before we saw Cashel again.'

CHAPTER FOUR

It was as the grey skies were hinting at the arrival of dusk on the third day of their journey that Brother Eochaí led the way through the gate of the Abbey of the Blessed Cáemgen situated in the valley of the two lakes. The journey had been surprisingly easy in spite of all the concerns that had been shared between the travellers beforehand. Though the journey was urgent, Fidelma had kept the pace of the horses to only an occasional canter with frequent stops, so that the sight of a group clad as religious travelling at speed would not cause undue alarm. Even Eadulf, mounted on his placid, sturdy cob, did not complain.

Brother Eochaí, the stable master, led the way slightly in front of Fidelma. Eadulf and Enda followed behind them. They had crossed through Osraige, meeting the occasional cowherd or shepherd and sometimes a hunter, more interested in tracking game than in passing strangers. They had passed Cethrae, the main settlement by the great river Bhearú, seeing only a few farmers tending herds and flocks. As they reached Uí Dróna territory, bordering the kingdom of Laigin, Eadulf became aware of the dark mountains on the distant northern horizon, growing higher and more forbidding as they approached. They had found their way through the foothills under Sliabh Meáin, identified by Brother Eochaí as the middle mountain, although it was far from being the centre of the sinister and unwelcoming range.

He pointed out Log na Coille, rising behind it, as the highest peak of the entire range. Although Brother Eochaí tried to keep them to unfrequented paths, they did pass several fellow travellers, even a few merchants, along the way. They exchanged only the briefest of pleasantries, as was the nature of travellers.

Brother Eochaí led the way through narrow twisting passes among the mountains, naming and pointing out the peaks and sights, not only for their interest but also so they might know their route if they needed to come back this way. What surprised Eadulf was the fact the lower slopes of the mountains and valleys provided an abundance of leafless sessile oaks, which would begin to regain their foliage as spring progressed. He noticed broad-leafed conifer species grew higher on the slopes, but here, lower down, rowan, birch, aspen and hazel stood among the prolific ivy and brambles of the mainly deciduous woodland. But, even leafless, the forests merely enhanced the gloomy threatening atmosphere of the over-powering mountain shadows.

The thought that passed through both Fidelma and Eadulf's minds, they found when they spoke about their feelings later, was that the area left them with a remarkable conflict of reactions: feelings of being awed by the tremendous beauty of the landscape and its timeless quality, and menaced by the strange brooding atmosphere. That intimidating quality seemed to increase the more they moved among the impassive and yet hostile peaks.

They travelled through narrow passes, fording a little river, and journeyed on eastwards between high peaks called Charraig Linnín to the south and Chuileannaí to the north, high places with a strange abundance of holly trees and glimpses of ancient stone monuments raised for unknown purposes back in the time beyond time. It seemed, however, that the way was not frequented by humankind because curious feral goats paused to stare at their passage. Even badgers cast them unconcerned glances before moving on, while hares bounded unafraid across their pathway. Now and then they saw little creatures with bushy tails and flashes of yellow collars running along tree branches in search of unwary small mammals for food – pine martens, which even Eadulf knew indicated the lateness of the day by their activity. The wooded hills seemed alive with sounds of all manner of creatures, which confirmed the idea that such creatures did not go in fear of man the hunter so they took little notice of the small group passing through their midst. Eadulf suspected for every creature they saw, they probably missed a hundred more. Once, as they twisted through the grim mountain pass, they caught a glimpse of a group of red deer on a high slope being watched over by a magnificently antlered stag.

They became aware that they were coming to an end of the pass when the forbidding slopes were not as oppressive and the forest areas began to thin. They were even aware of an increasing amount of bird life, which the evergreen trees had previously hidden from them. Birds of prey dominated the skies at this hour. The travellers saw the long pointed wings and short tails of the blue-grey and reddish merlins streaking by with quick, shallow wing beats, looking for prey. Higher, and in competition, were circling dark but similarly winged peregrine falcons. These were mere specks in the sky until their prey was spotted and they began their dive with wings folded back.

Suddenly, or so it seemed, Brother Eochaí halted his horse and pointed ahead. They found themselves on high ground looking across a long valley split in the centre by a broad, swift-flowing river.

'We have passed through Gleann Molúra. This is just called the Big River, An Abhainn Mhór,' he announced. 'We turn northward now. The river really begins to the north, at the confluence of three smaller rivers in a township named Láithreach, after some ancient ruins there. It's become a small trading settlement rather than a township; a good place for trade as folk can bring their goods along the rivers. From Láithreach we will turn westward and enter the valley of the two lakes where the abbey is situated. It is only a short distance. We will be there before dark, so don't worry.'

They certainly became aware of an increased number of travellers, mainly merchants, but, thankfully, no one wanted to engage in conversation as the daylight was waning. A short time later, when they were passing through a stretch of hilly forest, from their high vantage point they could glimpse some of the abbey's buildings. They moved downhill to where the path was intercepted by a river. It was not wide but the current was obviously strong, the white water billowing along the banks and now and then carrying branches along its path. There seemed no way of guessing how deep it was and Eadulf regarded it with some concern. However, Brother Eochaí saw his anxiety and sought to reassure him.

'There is a ford around that bend,' he said. 'It's very shallow so you can almost walk across. It is the build-up of rocks and stones that creates the ford, which then causes the waters to flow so fast at this point.'

Brother Eochaí turned and led them along the bank where it narrowed and the tall trees entwined overhead. Apart from the noise of the waters it was a strangely quiet area and sounded devoid of birds and animals. It was almost too quiet until there came a shriek of a hooded crow, whose grey body and black wings dived across their path, startling their horses.

Enda was nervous. 'A sign of bad luck,' he muttered.

Fidelma shook her head reprovingly. 'Bad luck is what you create yourself,' she chided.

Brother Eochaí, who was now slightly ahead, had swung suddenly into a small clearing before the river where rocks seemed to be strewn along the banks. The travellers could see the waters rippling over a bed of pebbles. Further on, the river dropped into a dark pool held by rocks, creating a waterfall, which then led to the stronger current of the stream beyond. Here, however, the path of the ford was obvious.

'Greetings, Eochaí, son of Dorcha.' The voice was unexpected. It was high pitched, almost wailing, and cracked with age. Fidelma and her party had been so concentrating on negotiating the ford that they had failed to observe a figure almost hidden on the far bank. Startled, they saw an old woman crouched by some bushes, apparently engaged in washing garments in the river. She was obviously very thin and was clad in dirty and torn rags. Her white skeletal arms and hands protruded where she was clutching the scraps of cloth she was washing. Her face was a mask of white, almost skull-like, with wisps of equally white but dirty hair protruding from an odd-shaped bonnet.

Brother Eochaí obviously knew the woman who had greeted him by name.

'You are late abroad with your washing, Iuchra,' he returned. Fidelma noticed a bantering quality in his tone. 'Should you be out so late in these forests?'

'Worry not for me, Eochaí, son of Dorcha, for the Aos Sí are my friends and I have no need to fear them or their servants.' It was said with an icy cackle and it took a moment for the hearers to realise it was a chuckle.

'I was not thinking of the Aos Sí, old one,' the stable master replied firmly. 'There are plenty of wolves and other predators to be more concerned about.'

'Ah, but even they must submit to the folk of the Otherworld, and am I not regarded as the one who speaks and relays their wishes?'

'It may be so,' Brother Eochaí admitted in amusement, 'but for us lesser mortals, we have to reach the abbey before nightfall as we have no agreement with the Aos Sí or with the wild creatures of the night.'

The old woman fell into a high-pitched cackle again.

'Beyond these trees you are within sight of the abbey. As well you know. So hurry on to your sanctuary of the New Faith. Even princes of the old blood resort to such places these days. Thus they pretend to abandon their ancestry and responsibilities to conceal themselves among those of the new religious. Remember, Eochaí, son of Dorcha, there can be no New Faith without it has permission of the Old Faith. Changing one for the other does not mean changing human nature.'

'Go home, Iuchra,' Brother Eochaí replied in a tired voice. He did not sound perturbed at her words and seemed to treat the old woman as an object of amusement, if not derision. 'Your son may have more need of your woodcraft and protection than we do.'

The old woman did not respond but turned her gaze intently on Fidelma.

'Hear a warning, lady. In the days ahead the searchers will ascend into these mountains; brave but arrogant, thinking their knowledge will sustain them. But these are the strongholds of Aos Sí. Only they hold sway from the high peaks to the dark valleys between. The Aos Sí do not look kindly on trespassers in their domain. They are the ever-living ones, the ever-changing ones, for they are the shapeshifters who control our petty existence. Avoid these dark solitudes, lady. You will find only death and danger among the peaks. Shun them!'

In spite of herself, Fidelma felt uncomfortable as the old woman seemed to be directing her remarks solely at her, as if she knew her. She suppressed a faint shiver and, following Brother Eochaí's example, she rode on by, ignoring the crone.

A short distance later Fidelma managed to draw level with Brother Eochaí. 'Who was that old woman?' she asked.

Brother Eochaí twisted his features dismissively. 'Take no notice of old Iuchra. She is a mad one and must be pitied. Her son is a trapper and hunter in these peaks, but wisely puts a distance between his mother and himself. She claims that she is an *ammait* – a woman of supernatural powers. It is even claimed that she is a shapeshifter.'

'She certainly plays the part well,' Fidelma agreed lightly, trying to bring a touch of humour to her voice. 'She obviously knows the stories of the Badh, the crow goddess of death and battles, who sits washing by the ford and calling forth a prophecy of doom.'

Eadulf joined in with a sniff. 'In that case she has trained that grey crow well. Remember, just before we came upon her, a grey crow swooped down upon us? Unless the claim is that she can change her shape from crow to harridan, the crow was a nice touch of drama.'

Fidelma had actually forgotten the crow and now she blinked at the thought. Then she shook herself, annoyed at the idea.

'I would have thought that her son, whom you mentioned, was best exercised in attending his mother more closely,' she observed to Brother Eochaí. 'It is a son's duty to keep his mother from harm.'

Brother Eochaí shook his head. 'For all her appearance, Iuchra does not do so badly. Local people are always consulting her for prophesies – they claim she is a *fáistinech,* a soothsayer, whose eye is all encompassing. She has a place where she lives in the township and does not often haunt the forests. Her son has no time for her beliefs and that is why there is little closeness between them.' He suddenly glanced up at the sky and was anxious. 'It grows late and we must reach the abbey gates before nightfall.'

'Before the shapeshifters are released into the night,' Eadulf could not help adding with irony in his voice.

'The only shapeshifters that concern me are the scavengers,' replied the stable master. 'As I told the old one, I fear wolves, which in darkness turn into the most malevolent hunters of all creatures, including humans.'

'Any idea what she meant about princes being religious and giving up their rights?' Eadulf asked as they rode on.

It was Fidelma who replied. 'That's obvious enough. Not every son or daughter of a king or prince can inherit a kingdom or a territory. Many have taken advantage of the New Faith to become abbots and bishops and heads of religious houses. I, myself, had to choose that path to obtain security. My brother was not king then and my cousin Máenach, who was king, offered me neither encouragement nor security. That's why I eventually joined the Abbey of Cill Dara, as their legal adviser.'

Brother Eochaí was nodding agreement. 'Even our Abbot Daircell is a relation of the Tuaim Snámha, the King of Osraige. You will find a few of our ruling families in the abbey.'

It was almost dusk when they crossed a wooden bridge and entered the abbey complex. A tall, dour-faced man was in the middle of trimming and lighting the gate lamps. Like every keeper of a *bruden,* a tavern or hostel, the gatekeeper of an abbey was required by law to keep at least one light burning outside the entrance gate so that it could be seen at a distance by travellers.

The picturesque bridge did not mean much to Eadulf as they had crossed many bridges over streams and rivers, and forded as many, too. The main abbey gates of oak were set in a granite wall on the far bank. The buildings of the abbey and the fields worked by its inhabitants were of considerable extent. The western end was bounded by a lake, which Brother Eochaí identified as Loch Péist, the lake of the water monster. The boundary wall seemed to stretch forever, encompassing various streams and rivulets. Brother Eochaí was keen to point out the abbey proper, with its church, included buildings for both the community and its guests, with stables for horses and barns for a large variety of animals. There were also fields for growing vegetables, and fruits were cultivated between two elliptical walls. It was a larger complex than most that Eadulf had seen. There were also many trees within the boundary walls shielding some of the buildings from others. The visitors could just make out most of the complex, but the swift descent of dusk made any further inspection impossible. However, one curious building that caught Fidelma's attention looked like a wooden hut on top of one of the stone buildings that rose several storeys. A number of birds perched and clustered around it, and one or two of them took off and circled it in the growing darkness before coming back to rest.

'Carrier pigeons?' Fidelma asked, and Brother Eochaí gave a nod.

'We learnt the art of sending messages from the Romans when they occupied our neighbours, the Britons,' the stable master explained. 'I am told they learnt it from the Greeks, who learnt from the Persians and so on . . .'

'I am aware of that,' interrupted Eadulf, trying not to sound churlish. In fact, he had realised just how much the pigeons were used in the Five Kingdoms only a few months before, when in the country of the Déisi. 'Why would this abbey have need of carrier pigeons?'

'This is an influential abbey in spite of our isolated location,' replied Brother Eochaí complacently. 'Our abbot often needs to be in touch with the royal centres. Our gatekeeper, Brother Dorchú, is an expert on the training of the birds. He was the man attending the lamps just now as we entered.'

By this time Brother Eochaí had led the way from the outer wall gate, where he briefly halted to ring the bell, before crossing to the inner gate on the far side of the wooden bridge. A tall thin man was already waiting for them and they dismounted, following Brother Eochaí's example. The man came forward, with a quick nod of his head in acknowledgement to Brother Eochaí, before holding out his left hand in greeting.

'I am steward of the abbey – Brother Aithrigid.'

'An unusual name? Doesn't it mean a changeling?' Eadulf could not help observing.

The man looked displeased. 'A changer of things,' he corrected curtly. 'On entering the religious some of us change our names to signify our rebirth in the New Faith. It was a style set by the Blessed Patrick, for he originally bore the name of the pagan god of war,

Succat. When he came to preach the New Faith he adopted the Roman name for a nobleman from "patrician". I wanted to change, so hence I adopted this name "change". So, as steward, I bid you welcome. Your reputations go before you.'

'You know us?' queried Fidelma. Brother Eochaí had performed no introductions.

'This is a small community. A merchant has recently passed by, having seen you travelling in this direction.'

Fidelma was puzzled. 'We have come here disguised as religious so as not to excite interest or draw attention to ourselves. However, it seems that our coming is already known so the disguise of religious robes might be superfluous.'

Brother Aithrigid shrugged before turning to the stable master: 'You may take the horses to the stables and ensure they are fed, watered and made comfortable. Get Brother Cuilínn to assist you. I will attend to all else.'

'How do you know who we are?' Fidelma demanded, when the man had left, leading the horses away. 'We sent no word of our coming. Even when Brother Eochaí arrived in Cashel he carried no request that we should do so. Not even Abbot Daircell could have known we were coming.'

'He is a very clever man, lady, but he is not that prescient. He knew you were on your way here only a short time ago when your party was recognised coming along the Great River. So he bid me prepare for your reception.'

This did not seem satisfactory. 'Someone recognised us? *Who*?'

The steward shrugged. 'I have no idea. All I know is some merchant recognised you and sent a rider to tell our gatekeeper. I suggest that you address your further questions to the abbot.' He seemed to hesitate. 'I have to mention that our community was founded for the peace and contemplation of the brethren only. We are not a *conhospitae*, a mixed house. So, as steward, I request all female visitors stay modestly covered and remain within certain confines of our community as prescribed by the abbot or myself. Now, come, we must not keep the abbot waiting.'

Brother Aithrigid indicated another wooden fence and line of oak trees to his left, which seemed to surround an isolated building.

'This is the abbot's house and herb garden. I shall leave you with him and then make arrangements for your accommodations.'

The silver-haired steward was moving swiftly ahead. Members of the community, with heads bowed, covered by their hoods, hands clasped before them, were moving here and there and did not acknowledge even the passage of the steward. The lights – candles and oil lamps – were now being lit throughout the abbey buildings. The steward led the way quickly into the isolated building to a door through which he entered. This was clearly his own workroom and he crossed it immediately to an oak door on the far side. He paused here and rapped loudly three times, waiting until a voice answered, then he threw it open, announcing loudly: 'Fidelma and her husband have arrived from Cashel, Father Abbot. They are accompanied by Enda, a bodyguard.'

Having ushered them inside, the steward exited, closing the door behind him.

A tall figure rose from his chair. Fidelma observed that Abbot Daircell was a man of middle years; thin, with grey hair that had evidently once been blue-black, enhancing the almost white skin with still-black brows that seemed to meet across the brows. His black eyes, in which the pupils seemed entirely lost so that they appeared solid black orbs, darted constantly from side to side in a nervous manner. The cheekbones protruded a little, making the cheeks seem hollower than they actually were. The lips were thin and red. There seemed little to resemble Princess Gelgéis in the man. Although he came forward, he did not hold out his hand in customary greeting. His face was troubled, though the features were hawk-like. The thought came into her mind that Daircell had a face without pity.

'You are most welcome, Fidelma of Cashel, and you also, Brother Eadulf,' Abbot Daircell intoned. The voice, with its musical quality of a rich baritone, was at odds with his austere features. 'It is good to meet with you even though it is because of the unfortunate disappearance of my cousin.' He glanced enquiringly at Enda. 'And you are . . ?'

'Enda is a warrior of my brother's bodyguard. We thought it best to affect some disguise so as not to draw attention. Now I am told there was no need as someone has recognised us and spread the word.'

Abbot Daircell's face expressed no humour when he said, 'The disguise is not well suited to this young man. I cannot say that the wearing of robes to disguise a man of violence as a man of peace is consistent with the morality of this abbey.'

'Disguise was thought necessary,' answered Fidelma, hearing the disapproval in the abbot's tone. 'You will recall that this kingdom of Laigin and my brother's kingdom have long been an enmity. I thought it better to maintain the fiction we are religious visiting your abbey, although that depends now on how many know we are here.'

Abbot Daircell's expression was sour. 'There is no need to continue with the disguises now that you have been seen and identified. And since you have been recognised it seems that you may be of no help at all.'

CHAPTER FIVE

'Why would our recognition exclude our being of help?' Fidelma demanded.

'I suspected that Colgú would send you when I sent to him. But I was hoping that no one would know of your coming,' explained the abbot. 'Now you have been recognised, I do not doubt the word will spread of your coming. Most people know the role you played in thwarting King Fianamail's attempt to annex Osraige. Your own lives may now be in danger.'

'That was unfortunate,' she admitted. 'Let us hope this merchant who recognised us will not be so free with the information as to spread it widely. If he did, I am here as a *dálaigh*, protected by the laws of the Five Kingdoms, under the authority of the Chief Brehon of the High King. I do not have to hide from any authority.'

Abbot Daircell blinked at her directness. 'I understand, but will the people of Laigin accept it?'

'They should know that they will have to answer if harm befalls me or my companions.'

'Yet it is obvious that harm has befallen my cousin, Princess Gelgéis. Very well, I have heard Gelgéis speak highly of you and your skills. Let us hope you will be able to sort matters and for that, it is good to welcome you here to the Abbey of Cáemgen.'

Fidelma hesitated only a moment and then shrugged. 'We thank

50

you for your welcome and presume that there is no further news of the Princess Gelgéis or her steward?'

The abbot waved them to be seated and resumed his own seat, shaking his head at the same time. There was a knock on the door at that moment and, in answer at the abbot's command, Brother Aithrigid entered with a tray on which was a flagon and bronze drinking vessels with little handles decorated at the top with curious animal heads.

'To welcome you to the abbey,' the steward announced solemnly, while pouring a small portion of golden liquid for each of the three of them. 'We forgot the ritual of hospitality to a visiting noble. This is intoxicating liquor that we distil from our apple trees. It is made with a local ancient method of distillation. The mountain folk hereabouts have an unfortunate name for it. They call it *lind dermait Dé* – the liquor that causes forgetfulness of God.'

'Then we had best take only a symbolic taste,' Eadulf grimaced with wry humour, before putting the bronze vessel to his lips. It was a strong cider made thick and sweet with honey.

The ritual over, Abbot Daircell dismissed his steward, who was obviously annoyed at being excluded but declared he was finalising the guests' accommodation. As the door closed on Brother Aithrigid, Fidelma put down her cup.

'You were about to tell is whether there has been any further news?' she prompted.

The abbot gave an eloquent shrug. 'I wish I could tell you some-thing positive. However, in the days since my stable master has been absent, riding to Cashel and back, there has been no news indeed. Two merchant groups have passed along the trail on which Cétach found the body of Brehon Brocc but nothing else has emerged.'

'I have an immediate question,' Fidelma said. 'When the body of Brocc was discovered, what raised your anxiety about the prin-cess? Was it only the word of the pedlar who had seen her leave Durlus Éile in Brocc's company? You seemed to know she was coming here. How did you know that for certain?'

'She communicated to me by carrier pigeon; I keep a loft for important communications.'

'But you did not think the disappearance of Princess Gelgéis was important enough to use this method to inform my brother? Instead you sent a messenger by horse with a few days' ride ahead of him.'

'I wanted to be sure that the message reached your brother. Pigeons can be at risk from falcons, and many local nobles now train birds for the purpose of intercepting messages.'

Fidelma glanced meaningfully to Eadulf. 'Can you confirm that the message she sent to you by pigeon was securely received? That it was not seen by anyone else?'

'Brother Dorchú, who looks after our pigeons as well as myself, brought it straight to me.'

'Did Gelgéis give a reason why she was coming here when she knew Laigin was not the most welcoming place for her, particularly after her association with my brother?'

Abbot Daircell shrugged. 'She said it was a matter to do with the security of Osraige. That was all. Now she and her steward are vanished as if the Púca had thrown a mist over them and caused them to disappear.'

Fidelma raised an eyebrow slightly with a disapproving expression. 'You sound as if you almost believe that.'

The abbot's features grew sombre. 'I take an interest in such local fables. If you have dwelt in these mountains as long as I have, then you will not discount the pagan beliefs that are still in evidence here. And, don't forget, before the coming of the New Faith, which we do our best to teach everyone, we, too, believed implicitly in such sorcery and magic.'

'It seems most local people still believe it. On our path here we met an old woman called Iuchra, who warned us against the Aos Sí.'

'Iuchra?' The abbot gave a sigh. 'There are even some who believe she is a shapeshifter herself; that is, of the Otherworld and can change her shape . . . passing as a mortal. How did she know who you were?'

'I am not sure,' Fidelma replied thoughtfully. 'There was a moment when I thought she knew exactly who I was.' She briefly described the meeting, and tried to ignore the troubled expression that had crossed Eadulf's features. Eadulf had almost grown to manhood among the pagans of his East Anglian kingdom before he heard the word of the New Faith from Fursa, a wandering Christian missionary, who had converted him. He had not entirely abandoned his youthful belief in the *landwrights*, in the *aelfor*, the elves, who were the malevolent entities who caused sickness, madness and death on the innocent. Once or twice, she knew, in extreme moments, he had shouted out to Woden, the god of the Anglo Saxons, for help. It was hard to dismiss the beliefs one was raised with from infancy. 'Anyway, the New Faith taught us to reject such superstitions,' Fidelma pointed out flatly to the abbot. 'You cannot believe in the malign power of ancient spirits dwelling in the mountains.'

'And why not?' The abbot seemed unperturbed. 'If you believe in God then you must inevitably believe in the Devil, for that is the teaching of the apostles.'

Now Fidelma suppressed a tired sigh. 'I have heard the argument before, from your stable master. But we are here to solve the more earthly matter of your missing cousin, the Princess Gelgéis. The sooner we get on with that task, the better.'

The abbot looked annoyed for a moment at the dismissal of what was obviously a favourite subject. 'There is little more I can tell you.'

'Is the pedlar who discovered the body of Brocc still here?'

'Cétach?' Abbot Daircell shook his head. 'You might find him in Láithreach, where he resides when he's not travelling. The township straddles the three rivers. It's only a short ride east of here.'

'We passed within sight of the township on our way here,' confirmed Fidelma. 'We will have to go there in the morning as night is upon us now. Where might we find him?'

'If he is not in a local tavern, then look for him among the women of easy virtue,' replied the abbot sourly.

53

'Did you keep any of the clothes that the body of the Brehon was found in?'

The abbot snorted. 'There was little of value there,' he said.

'I was not thinking of value,' replied Fidelma. 'As we have no body to examine, which might have told us something, then an examination of what he was wearing when he was killed might give us information.'

'I don't see how.'

Eadulf's mouth was grim. 'It is a task that I have proved adept at. So I would like to look at his clothing.'

Abbot Daircell shrugged as he had done on previous occasion. It seemed a favourite gesture of his to indicate negativity.

'I am afraid that the clothes were washed and the sandals cleansed so that one of the brethren could take them to distribute among the poor lepers. There is a community of them that dwell among the marshes to the east of here.'

For a while Fidelma relapsed into thought. Even the abbot started to fidget, while Eadulf remained stoical, knowing that Fidelma's silence was when she was struggling with a difficult thought. Finally she exhaled deeply and turned to Abbot Daircell.

'To sum up what you are saying: we have come on this long journey and all you can tell us is that a pedlar found a body. You recognised that it was the body of Brocc, Brehon to Princess Gelgéis. You have the word of a pedlar that the Brehon had been part of the princess's retinue, which set out from Durlus Éile in this direction. They have not arrived, even though you had a message by pigeon from Gelgéis saying she wanted to discuss with you a matter relating to the security of Osraige. There is no sign of them. We do not even have the body of the dead Brehon now. We do not have his clothes. All we have . . . I am hoping . . . is this pedlar . . . provided that he has not disappeared. There is nothing tangible to start an investigation, especially if this pedlar can tell us no more than you have told us.'

Abbot Daircell paused for a moment, his expression troubled. Then he said brightly, 'Well, at least you are able to talk with Brother Lachtna.'

'And who is Brother Lachtna?'

'Why, he is our physician. He examined the body when the pedlar brought it in and he was the one who removed the clothing and prepared the body for burial.'

For a moment Fidelma closed her eyes in exasperation. When she opened them, she asked coldly: 'Why did you not mention this before? You say that he made an examination of the body?'

'Well, it should have been obvious that I would have our physician examine the body,' Abbot Daircell replied defensively.

Fidelma realised that the abbot was right and she should have thought of it before. Acceptance of the fact made her aware that it was late and she was tired from the journey. Eadulf would also be tired but he would keep on his feet as long as she did. She glanced at Enda, who had not spoken since they entered the abbot's chamber. He was sitting with his eyes closed and she suspected he was asleep. It was time to put further discussion of the matter aside until the morning.

Abbot Daircell was studying her, as if trying to see what was going through her mind. Finally he arose, forcing a smile to his lips.

'I have ordered baths for you in the guesthouse, and afterwards a small repast brought to your chamber, for we have eaten already. I suggest that you rest and start afresh in the morning, when you can turn your minds to these matters with more clarity.'

'You are right,' Fidelma agreed. 'We will begin in the morning by speaking with your physician and hearing what he has to tell us. Your steward has warned us that you are a male-only house so we must be made aware of the limitations of where we may go.'

'Yes; I will have someone on hand to conduct you at all times.'

A young novice was summoned: a thin, fair-haired boy, who seemed constantly tongue-tied.

Sleep seemed to obliterate any memory of time between leaving Abbot Daircell to waking the following morning. The young boy was awaiting Fidelma and Eadulf and, when they declined to follow him to the refectory, for the bell was issuing its invitation, he conducted them to a small isolated building, which was the *potecaire* or the apothecary of the abbey. The balding physician, Brother Lachtna, was waiting at the door to welcome them, having been alerted that they would be coming to question him. At first glance he was not an imposing man but there was something about his features that indicated a shrewdness that made Fidelma think she should not underestimate him. He inclined his head in greeting to her but his eyes seemed to pause on Eadulf.

'I have heard of you, Saxon,' he opened.

'I am an Angle of the kingdom of the East Angles,' Eadulf corrected him mildly. 'I trust you have not heard ill of me?'

Brother Lachtna's thin lips twitched a little. 'I am told that you were an impatient student and left the medical school of Tuaim Brecain without obtaining proper qualification.'

Eadulf expressed surprise. Of course, it was a fact that he had studied at the famous medical school in Uí Néill territory before being persuaded to go to Rome and being converted to Roman liturgy rather than the practices of the insular churches. The physician decided to assuage Eadulf's apparent curiosity.

'I also studied at the college of the Blessed Brecain. The *druimclí*, the head professor, was then Cenn Faelad, the son of Aililla of Baetán.'

Eadulf's eyes widened. 'I thought Cenn Faelad died a long time ago?'

Brother Lachtna shook his head. 'On the contrary, he still lives.'

'Even in Cashel we have heard of Cenn Faelad,' Fidelma interrupted impatiently. 'I am glad he still lives but he must be elderly now. For wasn't he badly wounded during the battle of Magh Rath, and that was in the year of my birth?'

'The ageing of the body does not mean the mind ages also,' said the physician philosophically. 'Cenn Faelad has been a noble success to those who practise the healing arts and he has inspired many of us. And it should be thus. Let me tell you the story . . .'

'I know the story well,' Fidelma interrupted. 'Cenn Faelad was wounded in the head at Magh Rath and it was expected he would die. He was taken to the medical school of the Blessed Brecain, where surgery was performed on him. He recovered and so decided to renounce his warrior family and become a teacher. He was descended from kings. He devoted himself to study and over these last years he has produced a great many books of learning – we have some of them in the library of Cashel: works on the law, on our history and a grammar of our language. And he has also written poetry. So there is little I need to know of the son of Aililla of Baetán.'

Brother Lachtna regarded Fidelma thoughtfully during her quick recitation; then he smiled.

'It is natural that you should know, being wife to a former pupil of Cenn Faelad,' he said dryly.

'I was a pupil only briefly,' Eadulf corrected quickly.

'Well, he remembers you,' Brother Lachtna said quickly.

'Then I am flattered,' Eadulf acknowledged.

'Then, as a student of Cenn Faelad,' Fidelma interposed, 'we may expect a matching thoroughness of proficiency from you.'

Brother Lachtna examined her to see if there was any sarcasm in her comment but her face was without expression.

'I will only answer the questions that I know the answer to.'

'That is good, for we would not wish it otherwise,' she said as the physician stood aside and beckoned them to enter his domain.

They were immediately assailed by the same pungent smell of herbs, both dry and fresh, and mixtures that they were used to in old Brother Conchobhar's apothecary in Cashel. Herbs hung in bunches from the low ceiling or were stored in jars along wooden shelves, while in the centre of the room was a long wooden table, large enough for a body to be rested on it. There were stains, which Eadulf knew were made by blood over the passage of time and which no amount of scrubbing would remove. There were some benches and two chairs, and Brother Lachtna waved them to be seated.

'I am told that you examined the body of Brocc, Brehon to Princess Gelgéis?'

'I examined a body. It was not I who identified whose body it was,' replied the physician pedantically, 'therefore I cannot declare it was that person.'

'So who did identify it?' Eadulf asked.

'Brother Aithrigid, our steward, as I recall. This was confirmed by Abbot Daircell. They are both from Osraige and said the body was that of the Brehon to Princess Gelgéis.'

'Very well,' Fidelma conceded. 'Now, tell us what you observed.'

'That the corpse was in a state of putrefaction. I was told it had lain on the mountain for about seven days. I could confirm the body was dead for that period because I have had some experience in this matter.'

'How is that?' Eadulf queried.

'As a physician I have followed armies into battle and have walked among bodies that have not been removed from those gory fields for days and sometimes weeks. I have observed the rate of decay of the slain bodies and feel that I am, perhaps, an expert.'

'So this is a fact we can agree upon? The Brehon had been dead seven days. Very well. What else?'

'If he had been killed, then he must have spent days away from molestation by scavengers. That means he was placed where Cétach found him on the open mountainside within only hours of being discovered. No longer.'

'Are you saying that he was hidden for nearly a week after being killed, and purposely placed there?' Fidelma tried not to sound intrigued.

'Exactly. The body had not been disturbed by any animals who forage the mountains.'

'Can you tell us more?'

'There were two wounds to the body. He had been shot in the back at fairly close range by an arrow, but that was not the cause of death. The second wound was where his throat had been cut with a sharp blade. He would have been dead in moments.'

Eadulf was frowning. 'How would such a wound have been inflicted?'

The physician hesitated before seeing the purpose of Eadulf's question.

'The man was held from behind and the killer would have reached round with the blade and made a cut that appeared to be from right to left across the throat.'

'Right to left?' pressed Eadulf. 'And made from behind?'

'That is what I said.'

'That might indicate that the killer was left handed, unless he was ambidextrous.'

The physician grimaced. 'For a right-handed man to make such a cut while holding the man from behind would be extremely difficult. I would say the odds on the man being left handed are favourable. But it cannot be declared as proof positive.'

'So Brocc was first debilitated by an arrow. Were there any signs that he fell from his horse after being shot?' asked Fidelma. 'Did the killer have to lift him from the ground and cut his throat?'

'I can only tell you what I know,' Brother Lachtna replied. 'Whether the man fell and was on the ground, or whether he was standing upright, the fatal wound was in the neck. It is not for me to speculate further.'

'We are told that the clothing has been washed and dispensed with. Is that so?'

'It is. The clothes were washed and sent to the leper colony across the mountains.'

'You saw nothing unusual about them? There is nothing to add to what you have told us already?'

'What could be told from clothes?' the physician asked.

'Many things,' Eadulf replied. 'Tears in the cloth might indicate a fight. Perhaps evidence of other attempts to wound the man are on the clothing but not the body.'

Brother Lachtna shook his head. 'There was nothing else apart from bloodstains and, of course, the tear where the arrow went through the clothing.'

'And the arrow itself?' pressed Eadulf. 'Was it ever found?'

Brother Lachtna raised his brows with surprise. 'Found? It was still in the body when it was found.'

CHAPTER SIX

'We were not told,' Fidelma exclaimed in annoyance. 'I don't suppose the arrow has been kept?'

The physician seemed surprised at the question. He glanced around the apothecary shop as if searching for something before he went to some debris in a corner. 'I threw it somewhere. It was a vicious weapon and so shaped that if it had penetrated living flesh then I would have had to dig it out and that would have doubtless killed the man anyway. The arrowhead was bronze, and hollow where the wooden shaft was inserted. The depth of the wound showed the arrow was fired from a very close range.' He continued to peer through a pile of debris in a corner and then uttered a loud 'Ah!' while bending down and extracting something from a pile of wooden sticks. He turned, holding an arrow with a bronze head towards Eadulf. Eadulf took the arrow and examined it. It was as Brother Lachtna had described it. It had a bronze head, winged, for maximum damage to the flesh, if flesh was its target. The wood appeared to be of seasoned ash and it was fletched with feathers from a bird, but dyed brightly in a curious blue and white pattern.

Eadulf handed it to Fidelma. 'All I know is that a bow and arrows is not the weapon of choice among the warriors of your people. They prefer battle with swords and shields.'

'I don't think we can deduce anything from that,' she said, taking the arrow in her hands and peering at it.

The physician watched them, derision in his expression. 'Certainly this is often a hunting weapon. I know warriors prefer to fight at close quarter with sword and shield and often javelins. However, that does not mean the bow is not used when the princes call their warriors to battle.'

'So this arrow is a type anyone can use?' Eadulf asked, disappointed.

'I have witnessed more than a few battles before I decided to follow the way of peace. I have talked with fletchers about their work, since arrows have often caused me much labour, trying to heal the damage they cause. Where there are such weapons, there are often accidents. The arrow will tell you nothing about who fired it, if that is what you are hoping.'

'Did all Brocc's belongings go to aid the lepers?' Fidelma asked.

'All except his leather belt and shoes, which were of good quality and more valuable. I think Brother Gobbán, our smith, claimed the leather sandals as he was in need of a good pair.'

'Also Brocc's leather belt?' queried Eadulf. 'I don't suppose he had anything attached to it?'

'Oh, yes,' replied Brother Lachtna, again to their surprise. 'There was also a *bossán*, a small leather purse.'

'Where is the purse now?' Fidelma sighed, presuming the answer. 'Was that given to the lepers?'

The physician shook his head. 'I think Brother Dorchú, the gatekeeper, asked for that. He joined us only during the last year, and one of our rules is that all personal possessions attached to one's life before joining the brethren are given away. The less one is reminded of the previous life, the better. The old things are discarded. The gatekeeper said he was in need of a purse, so from the charity of the abbey it was given.'

'So it was accepted that the belonging of the dead man was a gift of charity?' Eadulf asked.

'Just so.'

'I don't suppose there was anything in the purse?' Eadulf enquired hopefully.

The physician laughed sourly. 'If the man was a Brehon then he was a frugal one. Of course, he was probably searched and robbed after he was killed. There was nothing there . . .' He hesitated and then smiled at the memory. 'Oh, except a pebble.'

'A Brehon with only a pebble in his purse?' Eadulf asked.

'It is true enough. I found it. In fact, it was more of a small piece of rock than a pebble. It might even have been a piece of metal. It was very round and its surface rough.'

Fidelma frowned. 'Surely it was an odd thing for a Brehon to be carrying in his purse?'

'There is no accounting for what people carry about with them: sometimes things that have sentimental value to them, which to others would seem just useless,' Brother Lachtna said.

'A pebble with sentimental value?' Eadulf laughed.

'Who knows? Of course, maybe the man picked it up to defend himself by throwing it at his assailant.'

'Then changed his mind and put it in his purse just before he was shot by a bowman in the back at close quarters?' Fidelma queried dryly.

Brother Lachtna shrugged. 'I am no investigator of such things, just a physician.'

'I suppose the pebble was thrown away?'

'Why keep it?' Then the physician paused. 'Come to think of it, I handed it to the abbot before I took charge of the corpse. Now, I believe I have told you all I know of the matter and I have many other matters to attend to—'

'Then there is only one thing more,' Fidelma interrupted as they rose. 'I trust you have no objection if I keep this arrow for a while?'

'Keep it for eternity,' the little physician replied. 'I don't see what help it will be. I should think that plenty of fletchers produce arrows like this in these parts.'

Outside Brother Lachtna's apothecary, Fidelma and Eadulf immediately encountered Enda. The young warrior, now without the guise of the religious robes, was not looking cheerful.

'I was searching for you to see if I could assist you,' he greeted them, his features relaxing in relief.

'You didn't look happy. Didn't the steward provide you with a good bed and food last night?'

'I am treated well enough, lady,' Enda replied, pursing his lips reflectively. 'But, to be honest, the brethren here behave as if it were more like a military camp. I am used to military camps, as you know, but I did not expect to find lewd jokes common among religious brethren.'

Fidelma was not surprised. It was not the first time she had encountered a male community fixated on such matters as women and sex, especially among more youthful members. 'I have to say we are all fallible, in spite of religious calling,' she told Enda.

'It seems that some of them often go to the township, although the abbot forbids it,' went on Enda moodily. 'One of them actually said that the steward turns a blind eye to visits to a certain part of the township. Some of the brethren behave like sniggering boys.'

'Perhaps that is what they are,' Fidelma observed dryly. 'I suppose I am surprised that the steward turns a blind eye. I thought he was more inflexible about the rules. This is a male-only community pledged to celibacy, or so he gave us to believe.'

'They were talking about the fact that when he was young he was supposed to be one of the worst offenders. It nearly landed him in trouble.'

'Well, this is all gossip,' Fidelma declared. 'We should get on with our main task. At least we do not have to disguise who we are. Do you sense any problem now that you are known as a warrior of the Golden Collar?'

Enda shook his head. 'The chamber I share has a good bed and the fare is excellent. Yes, there is good food and drink. I only find some of the conversation irritating, not just the lewdness, either.'

'What do you mean?'

'Everyone here seems to talk constantly about the darkness and evils of this place or, rather, of the mountains and valleys around. Brother Dorchú, the gatekeeper, seems to indulge in the telling of strange tales of ghosts and apparitions that haunt the mines in these parts. It seems that he used to be a guard at some mines near here.'

'*Are* there mines near here?' Eadulf asked, interested.

'Apparently there are several,' confirmed the warrior. 'The gate-keeper was a member of the local noble's warriors. Then he turned to religion and joined the brethren here.'

'That's an interesting contrast to life in an abbey,' said Eadulf.

Enda nodded. 'Apparently there are mines in this valley, further to the west, where silver and even gold have been dug. Brother Dorchú has countless stories of strange monsters that lurk in the caves of these mountains or high up in the peaks. He is not the sort of companion I would want with me on a dark winter's night if I was camping in the mountains.'

Fidelma smiled broadly. 'He doesn't seem to be the only person who likes telling these stories of the supernatural. Even the abbot was trying to tell such tales. They seem very superstitious folk here, but you must not be disturbed by such tales.'

Enda grimaced defensively. 'I am not scared, lady. I am not afraid of anything of this world. You know that.'

'I know it well enough, my friend,' Fidelma assured him.

'Show me enemies of flesh and blood and I will draw my sword against an entire army, but against the creatures of the Aos Sí . . . I cannot defy a force that is incorporeal and fills me with apprehension.'

Fidelma shook her head in mild disapproval. 'Then let me tell you that you are defeated before you begin. The only enemy that you are faced with is of this world and entirely human. Anyway, Enda, I need your assistance this morning. We intend to ride to this nearby township. Our next step is to question the pedlar who found the body of Brocc. If possible, I want him to take us to the spot where he found it.'

'Then I shall get our horses.' The young warrior seemed to brighten and headed off to the stables to fulfil his task.

Fidelma turned to find Eadulf giving her a disapproving look.

'You are a little too harsh upon young Enda and his concerns about these supernatural beings. It's a basic fear in all of us. Enda's a good man, as well you know, when we have been in need of protection.'

'I know,' she confessed. 'But I am irritated to see a good warrior disturbed by the superstitions among these mountain folk, Eadulf. This place is replete with ancient tales and superstitions. Remember we are here for a specific purpose. We don't want to be dissuaded from that purpose or led down different paths from the ones dictated by our own logic.'

'You mean being misled purposely so?' queried Eadulf, as a thought struck him.

'I did not think that people here would really tell such tales to put off our search for Princess Gelgéis purposely . . . nevertheless, they do seem enthusiastic in ensuring these tales are passed on.'

Eadulf was not sure whether there was irony in her voice. He shrugged in dismissal of the subject.

'So we are going to find this pedlar, Cétach?'

'Cétach the pedlar seems to be the closest we have to a first-hand witness,' Fidelma confirmed. 'At least, he discovered the body. We should be able to persuade him to take us to where he found it. Enda might be able to find something else in the surrounding tracks to help us. He is a first-class tracker.'

At that moment they were hailed. The tall figure of the abbey's steward, Brother Aithrigid, came towards them, moving with a gliding motion. His features were still morose but he seemed straining to exude good fellowship.

'I have neglected you,' he greeted them. 'I hope you obtained all that you wanted?'

'As far as we are able,' responded Fidelma, uncertain.

'Excellent.' Brother Aithrigid seemed to ignore the nuance. 'I see you have decided to abandon your religious disguise.'

'Since we were recognised, it serves no purpose.'

'Do not forget that you have only to ask and I shall see to any wants that you may have. Just request and I shall ensure it is fulfilled.'

'That is kind of you. At the moment, there is little we want, for we are about to ride to the township where we have been told the pedlar, the one who found the body, lives.'

A disapproving look passed over the steward's features.

'"Lives" is a loose term. I do not call his existence living. I fear that he is a godless drunkard, and what little he gets from his infrequent trading trips through the mountains, he spends in the taverns there. Whether you will get any sense from him, I would not like to wager on it. Still, it is just a week since his last trip so he might have run out of the means to buy liquor and you might find him sober.'

'Let us hope so, for I was hoping he could show us exactly where he found the body of Brehon Brocc,' Fidelma responded.

The steward looked even more disapproving. 'I would not put much trust in that pedlar. Cétach is well known for his unreliability.'

'The problem is that we will never find the exact spot unless he identifies it,' pointed out Eadulf firmly. 'The testimony of the pedlar is important.'

Brother Aithrigid shrugged. 'You will know your own business. I can only warn you not to trust Cétach.' He hesitated. 'But I do not want you to think this matter has left me unaffected. Princess Gelgéis was a distant cousin of mine, although the abbot is of a closer branch of the family. I also understand something of your professional thinking. I am qualified to prepare judgments in law.'

'You are qualified in law?'

'I am,' affirmed the steward almost complacently. 'But only to the level of *Aire Árd*, and such was my role in the Abbey of Scuithin in Osraige until I came to join the abbey here. That is why I am accepted as steward.'

'We have noted your warning about the pedlar,' Fidelma said, 'but I have to find out if Cétach can tell us more.'

'It is up to you. But, as I say, I do not think Cétach will be of much help. Let me know if you need anything.' The steward turned with a quick nod of farewell and walked back to the abbey buildings as Enda was returning with their horses.

Eadulf stared after Brother Aithrigid for a moment with a frown.

'What are you thinking?' Fidelma asked.

'Just that it is curious that there seem to be so many people from Osraige in this abbey.'

CHAPTER SEVEN

They rode their horses at a walking pace along the track that led towards the little township by the confluence of rivers, which had been identified to them as the place of the old ruins. Láithreach was, in fact, only a short ride from the abbey. They entered the township and found it comprised of fewer than two score of homes, with several buildings clearly used for the storage of goods. Most of these stood by wharfs along the river, where a number of large river-going vessels were moored. Eadulf immediately became aware of the significance of the location, for the meeting of the rivers was perfect for traders to gather. Apart from the smaller river that ran by the Abbey of Cáemgen there was one great river flowing from the north-west and another from the north-east joining into the Great River – as Brother Eochaí called it – that flowed south. Láithreach had grown to a strategic position on this major waterway. The Great River, the three visitors had been told, eventually flowed into the eastern ocean, beyond which was the Britannic Island.

They had to negotiate a bridge that led into the central square. It was the ideal location for taverns, blacksmiths, carpenters and other artisans because traders took advantage of the natural meeting points of both the rivers and the tracks. In fact, there was hardly any sign here of buildings of private residence other than those devoted to trade of one sort or another.

One thing caught Eadulf's curiosity. Each building seemed to have a bunch of yellow flowers hanging over the main door. When he peered closely he realised that they were sprigs of furze; gorse whose yellow blossoms were only just beginning to show their small petals to the world. He pointed them out to Fidelma but she shrugged.

'It must signify some local festival,' she dismissed. 'Maybe it is a symbol of Cáemgen, the founder the abbey.'

'For a person seeking a hermitage to live a life of isolated contemplation, the Blessed Cáemgen could hardly have chosen a location less suited to remain isolated,' Eadulf observed dryly.

'I heard his story from Brother Eochaí last night,' Enda joined in. 'Cáemgen tried to retreat into the mountain caves but it was his disciples who built the abbey. From what I learnt, this Cáemgen was a man of strange ideas.'

Eadulf glanced at him with interest. 'What sort of strange ideas?'

'Oh, Brother Eochaí said he was a prince of royal blood and quite handsome, with many admirers among women. When he joined the religious he became one of those curious fanatics who turn to hate all women because, he claimed, the Faith taught that the woman Eve had brought the curse of God on all mankind by disobeying God's law and tempting Adam, which caused them to be driven from the Garden of Eden.'

Fidelma snorted indignantly but said nothing.

'I suppose each must follow their own belief,' Eadulf sighed. 'I know a lot of religious fanatics hate women on those grounds.'

'This Cáemgen was even more extreme,' Enda warmed to the subject. 'Brother Eochaí said the abbey possesses a life story of their founder in which it says that a young princess fell in love with him. Thinking that he was too modest and self-conscious to declare his love for her, she was bold enough to declare her love for him.'

'Very natural,' Fidelma commented. 'So what happened?'

'They were apparently walking in the woods. When she admitted her love for him, Cáemgen went berserk, tore off all his clothes and flung himself into a nearby bed of nettles, rolling back and forth so that they stung and burnt his entire body. The girl was horrified. But worse was to come. Cáemgen rose and, taking handfuls of the stinging plants, he rubbed them over the girl's face and arms, causing her to cry out from the pain he inflicted on her.'

'And then?' Fidelma demanded. 'Was he punished for the infliction of such pain and suffering on a young girl?'

'Apparently not,' Enda replied. 'When challenged under the law, all he said was "the fire without extinguished the fire within". The excuse being that he had done it for the good of the girl's immortal soul and so that she would not slip into licentiousness with men.'

Fidelma's lips thinned. 'So it was a question of women being made to suffer for man's vanity. I cannot see a Brehon approving such an action that is contrary to the law of the Five Kingdoms. Was the man not charged under the laws? Our laws are quite unambiguous about injuries caused to women, especially any injuries inflicted by men. Such things are dealt with harshly. Was this Cáemgen severely punished?'

'As you have seen, lady, he is now regarded as a saintly person, renowned for his piety and the founder of this abbey,' responded Enda, after a moment's thought. 'Sometimes I find aspects of the New Faith hard to understand.'

'Perhaps we should not judge him too harshly,' Eadulf offered. 'Maybe he had other redeeming qualities?'

'We must judge only on the person presented in the story,' Fidelma replied in annoyance. 'If it happened in reality and this is not just a story, then he would be found guilty of a number of transgressions against women, and punished.'

They fell silent as they entered the square. There seemed much activity to the side that bordered on the wooden quays, where a number of boats were moored from which merchants were offloading and loading, according to their business priorities. There was a constant movement of horses, mules and carts and, rising above all these sounds, people shouting to advertise their wares, announcing such bargains as Fidelma had grown used to seeing in major townships. Here, in the small area among the tall mountains, it seemed incongruous. They halted their horses and examined the scene with interest.

Fidelma turned to Enda with a smile. 'Well, I am sure this place should disperse any spectral beings you might be worried about from the stories you heard last night.'

Enda examined the busy port and seemed more relaxed. 'Certainly it is a sanctuary from the isolated dark valleys and gloomy peaks,' he agreed.

'Now we have to find Cétach,' Eadulf reminded them.

'If Brother Aithrigid's estimate of the pedlar's character is to be relied on, then we should make for the first tavern we can see and enquire for him there,' Fidelma replied.

It seemed an easy task because they were outside a rough wooden building whose appearance and odours announced it as exactly the sort of place they were looking for. It was nothing like the usual taverns to be found in most of the small settlements and towns; places where people could eat, drink and get rooms for the night. This appeared to be a single-roomed *tábhairne* or, as it was often called, a 'tippling house', where people just went to drink. It seemed a fairly popular place as it was crowded within, a few people sitting outside. These drinkers, muscular and strong looking, appeared to be workers who manually carried goods to and from the boats or carts of merchants. The place was not smart enough to be frequented by merchants of status or artisans. There was a wooden rail to hitch their horses and so Fidelma, Eadulf and Enda dismounted and did so.

Eadulf looked round with interest at the adjacent buildings. Each housed various artisans and traders. One such business immediately caught his eye. A short distance from the *tábhairne* was a carpenter's workshop. He could see a tall and muscular middle-aged man with greying hair apparently constructing the wheel spokes for a wagon, chiselling the spokes with mallet and sharp chisel. But it was a younger man that caught his attention. He was seated at a bench outside the carpenter's shop with a quiver of arrows at his feet. Moreover, the young man seemed to be fletching: putting the flight on a lengthy strip of yew. It was the colouring of the flight that had caused Eadulf to look twice.

He turned to Fidelma. 'Could I have that arrow that Brother Lachtna gave you for a moment? Something occurs to me.'

Fidelma regarded him with momentary uncertainty and then reached into her saddle bag and took out the arrow. Eadulf took it and made his way to where the young man was busy, concentrating on his task.

'Good day to you, my friend,' he greeted. 'I see you are a fletcher who knows his art.'

The young man stopped and glanced up, taking in Eadulf's appearance and tonsure. He then returned the greeting.

'I suppose you are from the abbey?'

'I am staying there,' Eadulf confirmed. 'I saw you working and wondered if you could give me your opinion on this.' He held out the arrow.

'You want me to make more arrows like this?' asked the puzzled young man, glancing at it.

'Not exactly. I want to know something about it.'

'Something about it?' The young man sounded confused.

The older man had now ceased his own work on the wheel spokes. He rose and came out to stand by his young companion, frowning in curiosity at Eadulf and the arrow he was holding.

'Good day, Brother. What is it you want from my son?'

Eadulf could hear a slight note of suspicion in his tone and he turned to him with a friendly smile. 'I just wanted the opinion on this arrow from a professional maker of arrows, especially a fletcher.'

The carpenter's frown deepened. 'Why?' he asked sharply. 'Are the religious taking up archery to persuade people to come to chapel?'

Eadulf forced a chuckle, although there had been no humour in the man's voice. 'We would prefer to persuade them in a more gentle fashion, my friend. Perhaps that is a good suggestion as a means to induce the more reluctant members of our flock to attend the mass. I am merely seeking information on this type of arrow.'

There was no alteration to the carpenter's expression.

'Why would you want information on this arrow?'

Eadulf tried to keep his expression friendly. He thought rapidly. 'I am a stranger to your country. I was trying to compare it to the arrows made in my land. That brass head, for example, I have not seen the like before.' In truth, Eadulf did not know whether the Angles or the Saxons used brass arrowheads but he thought the man might not know either.

The carpenter was not entirely satisfied. 'For what purpose?'

'Truly, for no other purpose than my own curiosity,' Eadulf assured him, hoping he sounded sincere. 'The ordinary folk in my land usually sharpen the tip of the wood to a point, heating it in the fire to harden it. Alternatively they use a sharpened flint. I was surprised when I found this arrow discarded in the mountains with a brass head on it. Surely that would be the sign of it belonging to someone of wealth to be able to get his smith to cast it? Also, I was thinking, such arrows may be of worth and the owner would be delighted for its return.'

The carpenter unbent a little. 'Brother Foreigner, you are among The Cuala. These mountains are rich in metals. The smelting of zinc-rich copper to make brass objects has been known here from the time beyond time. Many of our hunting horns are cast from brass and have been so back beyond memory.'

'I see,' Eadulf sighed. 'So such arrowheads would be common? This type of arrow could be used by anyone?'

'They would not be very common,' replied the man cautiously.

'You would need to be able to afford them, and if you were hunting regularly then it would be cheaper to sharpen the wood, as you say, in the old manner.'

Eadulf felt he should try to ward off the man's suspicious attitude.

'This is interesting, for it would be unusual in my country—'

'Which is?' demanded the carpenter, obviously determined not to be deflected. 'I was once told by a wandering merchant that the Greeks and Romans used brass in this fashion.'

'I am from one of the kingdoms of the Angles.'

'Where is that?'

'Among the Saxons.' Eadulf felt he had to accept the term more popularly used in Fidelma's country for the men of his own kingdoms.

'So you are a Saxon?'

Eadulf swallowed his pride and nodded quickly. 'I would like to know more about the arrow because it seems so well crafted compared to those arrows produced by my people. Look at the craftsmanship that must have gone into the metal mould for the tip.'

The carpenter examined the arrow with less suspicion. 'There is little out of the ordinary about it.'

'What about the flights?' Eadulf pressed.

'The flight on the arrow is of feathers from a peregrine falcon and the dye on them proclaims the arrow to be used by Uí Máil, usually by warriors rather than folk hunting for food. Also,' the carpenter actually managed to chuckle, 'the fletcher who made the arrow was left handed.'

Eadulf was excited at the mention of the use of the left hand. 'How can you say that with such certainty?'

'The way the flight – that is, the feathers – is placed and, indeed, when you examine it you will find it is from the primary wing feathers. Some fletchers use tail feathers. But you can feel that the quill has an oval feel to it instead of the round stem like other birds.

The peregrine's wing feathers are made for speed. In spite of the dye you can glimpse the original patterns, and my opinion is that it is the left wing of the bird because of the way they run, and it was placed in position by a fletcher who was probably left handed and preferred it to run so. It might even indicate the bowman himself was left handed, but that is uncertain.'

'You said the colouring of the feather indicated it was of the Uí Máil? Where do they dwell?'

For a moment the carpenter appeared surprised and then he grimaced apologetically. 'I forget that you are of another kingdom, Brother Foreigner. We pay tribute to the Uí Máil.' He waved his hand around him to make the point. 'The lord of The Cuala is a noble of the Uí Máil. He is the uncle to King Fianamail.'

'You mean the local noble is related to Fianamail, the King of Laigin?'

The man stared at Eadulf as if he were a half-wit. 'Have I not said so?'

Eadulf turned away excitedly, still clutching the arrow, and made his way back to Fidelma and Enda, who were impatiently standing by the hitching rail outside the *tábhairne*. He handed the arrow back to her with a self-satisfied smile.

'You have learnt something?' she prompted.

He quickly explained the gist of the conversation. 'At least we definitely know we are looking for a left-handed man,' he finished.

To his disappointment, Fidelma dismissed his information. 'That does not really help us in finding the killer or abductor of the princess.'

'At least we have confirmed that he is left handed,' protested Eadulf.

'Or that *she* is left handed,' she corrected. 'So do you think a left-handed person is unique in this world?'

Eadulf pursed his lips in a sulky expression. 'There are fewer of them than right-handed people.'

'That is true. But how many fewer? Old Brother Conchobhair once told me that if you lined up ten people at random and asked them what hand they used, one of them would be a *cittach*, a left-handed person.'

'Oh, come . . . as many as that?'

'When Brother Aithrigid greeted us, I suppose you noticed what hand he used to do so?'

Eadulf shook his head.

'When we sat with the abbot did you notice which hand he favoured?' she went on.

'No, but—'

'In fact, you should have known anyway because my brother told us the abbot was known by a nickname – Daircell Ciotóg – Daircell the Left-handed. So you see, Eadulf, left-handed people are more numerous than you think. The fact of the left-handedness alone does not help us in our search. However, it does apparently confirm what the physician has told us.'

'Hey!'

There was an angry exclamation behind them. They turned to find a short, dirty-looking man, wearing a leather apron over his sweat-stained clothes, standing on the steps of the *tábhairne*. He stood scowling, hands on hips, showing strong muscular arms.

'Do you think I provide hitching posts free for any passers-by? The posts are for the benefit of my customers.' His tone was hostile.

Fidelma regarded his angry red countenance before returning a disarming smile.

'So you are the *óstóir*, the keeper of this alehouse?'

'I am.'

'In that case,' she replied, 'we will be your customers. You may serve us your best ale. And while you do so you may provide us with some information.'

'Information?' The man seemed disconcerted. 'Information is not always cheaply given. What information could I provide to you?'

At that moment Enda moved slightly and his cloak slipped its position around his neck revealing the golden torc, the emblem of the Nasc Niadh, the Golden Collar of the élite warriors of the King of Muman. The tavern-keeper realised the visitors were of rank and his whole demeanour changed.

'I am sorry, lady, for the brusqueness of my manner. But the hitching rail is provided for my customers. Lady, my *tábhairne* is a humble place with none of the amenities to accommodate those of rank. Let me recommend you to somewhere better suited to your taste.'

'Your *tábhairne* will suit us well enough.' She noticed that the two men who had been seated outside had finished their drinks and left. 'We will sit there and you may bring us your best ale.'

The *óstóir* hesitated. 'You will drink ale, lady? I have a sweet cider that might be more to your liking.'

'That will suit me even better,' she replied gravely, glancing at her companions. Eadulf and Enda opted to try the man's ale and he hurried inside to fulfil the task.

Eadulf glanced around. 'I have to say that I would have taken the man's advice and gone to the tavern on the other side of the square,' he said.

Fidelma shook her head. 'It is not for the man's cider or ale that we are here. The information that we want is more likely to be gathered here than in a more expensive inn. That is, if the descriptions of Cétach's tastes are correct.'

The *óstóir* returned, balancing the mugs on a wooden tray with surprising dexterity. He set the drinks down on a small oak table before them. They took a few sips. Fidelma found her cider was far better than she expected and immediately rebuked herself for thinking it would not be of good quality. Often the best of drinks and food were to be found in the less pretentious places and she congratulated the man on it. He had stood waiting patiently. Now he smiled.

'You said you wanted information, lady. What can I help you with?'

'As you have doubtless guessed, we are staying at the abbey,' she began with a smile. 'We want to track down a trader who deals with the abbey.'

'I know all the traders here,' the man agreed eagerly. 'Who is it you seek?'

'A man named Cétach.'

Surprise crossed the man's features. 'He is hardly a trader. He is just a *corr margaid*.' This was said in a tone of distaste.

Eadulf had not heard the term before so Fidelma explained.

'A low class of trader, a pedlar, usually considered a vulgar, base person.'

'Indeed, lady,' the tavern-keeper confirmed. 'A purveyor of cheap goods or rubbish. He is not worthy of your interest, lady. There are better and more trustworthy traders in the township.'

'Nevertheless, it is this particular pedlar that I seek,' she said firmly.

The tavern-keeper scratched behind his ear. 'Cétach. You should know he is a drunk. He only bothers to do what trade and bartering he does in order to buy liquor. You should know he is not to be trusted, lady. Even when his wife divorced him and took his children from him he gave her nothing, in spite of the Brehon's judgment.'

Fidelma was interested. 'Do you imply that his wife achieved a divorce in the secondary category of the laws and she did not receive full compensation?'

'She was awarded compensation by the local Brehon Rónchú but did she get it? She and her father should have been given back her *coibche*, her dowry, and the benefit of the fines. Cétach never paid them.'

Fidelma expression showed her surprise.

'Indeed,' continued the tavern-keeper. 'He even managed to lay hands on his wife's *tinól*, the wedding presents given to the bride by her friends. She had some friends of wealth among her own people so the presents consisted of household goods and some silver and copper and brass.'

It was the law that the *tinól* was gifts whose value was divided, with two-thirds going to the bride and a third to the bride's father. It was not the property of the husband.

'What was the reason for the divorce?'

'Simple enough,' the man said with a grim shrug. 'He used to beat her and she was often seen with bruises and cuts.'

Fidelma knew that this was listed in the law as one of the seven reasons why a woman could seek separation or divorce and demand her dowry be returned, and with compensation.

'Are you saying that Cétach did not pay his wife that which the law demands that he should?'

'That is what I am saying, lady. I tell you, he is not a good man and one you should do well to avoid, for no business is safe in his hands.'

'But if he ignored the law, the ruling of the Brehon, then he should have been punished.'

'He was. He lost his full rights in the clan and is now considered a *saer fuidhir.* But, having lost his rights, he is allowed to work provided he pay some amount of his fine as a tax until he has paid off his debt. But he has such debt that he will never pay it off. So he remains a cheap pedlar. Not worth bothering about.'

'Nevertheless, I still see need to find Cétach,' she insisted. 'He is an important witness in a matter that needs examination.'

The tavern-keeper looked bewildered. 'A witness? Well, if you insist, lady. What information do you need?'

'Where do we find him?'

He turned and pointed to the rise just beyond his tavern. 'You see the path up that rise that twists through the yews and hazels there? If you follow that path you will find Cétach's cabin hidden among them. If he is sober then he might be away seeking goods to peddle. If he is not sober then he might be sleeping it off. You might be lucky. People tell me that if he is not sober you might hear his mule demanding attention, for he keeps the poor animal tied up there.'

'What does Cétach look like?'

'A wizen half-starved *iraóg.*'

Eadulf knew the derogatory term meant a stoat.

'You can't miss him because his hair recedes from the front and grows in a dirty red mass, the back mingling with an unkempt beard.'

'Very well.' Fidelma finished her cider with a gesture of finality. 'We shall go and look for this unpleasant-sounding person.' She was reaching into her purse when Eadulf interrupted.

'One other question. What's the significance of the sprigs of yellow furze that I see hanging over the doors of all the houses? Does it mark some festival?'

The expression of the tavern-keeper suddenly darkened as he half took a step backwards, but then he paused and shook his head.

'My knowledge is limited on that matter,' he said firmly.

He was about to turn away, but Fidelma handed him some coins with a disapproving glance at Eadulf. The coins seemed to ameliorate the man's displeasure and he raised his hand to touch his brow in salute.

'May you have success and protection to the end of the road, lady.'

They mounted their horses and moved slowly off in the direction the *óstóir* had indicated, towards the rise at the back of the township. Eadulf decided to let his question drop for the time being, even though he had noticed that above the tavern doors was the same yellow sprig of furze.

They had now entered a thick wood covering the rise, well away from the strips of agricultural and pastoral land nearer to the river. The path was a wide one and it was clear from the muddy tracks that it had been used often by a cart and mule. The route twisted a little as it climbed between the tall yews at the bottom of the hill, where there was plenty of water and dampness, before the yews gradually gave way to aspen and broad-leaf conifers. There were a lot of patches of ivy, especially among the brambles.

The travellers had risen high above the township, which was now made invisible to them by the screen of trees, before they came to what was a shelflike plateau around which the trees were encroaching on a couple of wood log buildings. One of these was clearly a barn, looking derelict and disused, but before the open doors stood a tired-looking mule. It was patiently nibbling whatever growth was available in its enforced circle, delineated by a rope attached to an iron ring on a wooden post. It took no notice of them as they approached. There was an empty cart nearby, much weathered, with some of its planking rotting.

The other building was an oak log *bothan*, a cabin, which even at a swift glance looked in fairly immediate need of repair. Sackcloth flapped in the wind at the two windows. The door stood wide open but the place had a long-deserted appearance.

'Do you think this is the place the tavern-keeper meant?' Eadulf said, peering round in disapproval. 'It hardly appears habitable.'

'Well, there is a mule as well as a cart here,' Enda pointed out. 'Therefore there must be an owner and, if the tavern-keeper's estimate of the pedlar was right, we should not be surprised at the condition of his cabin.' Without dismounting, he raised his voice and shouted.

The only answer was a sudden scurrying and a flapping of feathered wings as birds arose from the surroundings, making angry noises of protest. After a moment or two, silence fell again.

'Wait here, lady,' Enda instructed. 'I'll check inside, but it seems the pedlar is either drunk or is not here.'

'Well, he can't have gone far, having left his mule and the cart here.'

Enda swung off his horse and walked towards the cabin door. At a short distance he halted and called again. This time there was a noise from inside and then, in a flash of red, a dog-like creature suddenly leapt from the blackness of the interior. It had made an incredibly tight turn, waving its bushy tail and, with three short sharp barks, vanished even before Enda had managed to get his sword in his hand.

For a moment or two they were all silent.

'A fox,' muttered Fidelma.

Enda had now drawn his sword and was keeping it in his hand as he cautiously entered the cabin. A step beyond the threshold he halted and peered about. They heard him gasp. There were a few moments before the young warrior reappeared.

'I am afraid the man, whom the innkeeper described as Cétach, is not drunk, lady. He is dead.'

CHAPTER EIGHT

The body lay on its face on the smooth earth floor of the cabin just beyond the door. The various odours of the interior, the curious abandoned variety of items that should have been discarded years before, combined in a vile stench. The floor consisted of generations of feet-hardened mud and clay with no sign of wooden floorboards ever having been laid. The few bits of furniture – a table and a chair – appeared as rotten as the exterior of the cabin. Fidelma registered them with distaste as she quickly scanned the room, noticing the white ashes of a still-smouldering fire in a crumbling inglenook. In a far corner was a dark mass of material, which she presumed was a bed. Beyond that there was little else. It took but a moment or so for her to observe this and then look down at the body.

Although the door was wide open there was little light in the cabin. The body was close to the door but in shadow. She did not have to request Eadulf to examine it. He was used to this role, thanks to his medical training. Enda, meantime, had gone to the windows and torn away the dirty sackcloth that hung on nails over them. Even this did not help illuminate the interior, for wreaths of ivy hung over most of the apertures and even crept inside the interior.

Eadulf had bent down, first observing how the body was stretched on the ground, head forward towards the fire with one arm outstretched as if trying to reach forward to it. The head was a mass of unruly hair with curious dark patches. It was only when a ray of light caught it that one could see the hair was dirty red rather than black. The dead man's back was towards the door. The dirty shirt had darkness around the collar, which implied dampness. Eadulf touched it with a fingertip and then held up his enquiring digit to examine it in the light.

'Blood,' he said laconically and unnecessarily.

'Was he hit on the head?' Fidelma asked.

To her surprise, Eadulf shook his head. 'Give me a moment and more light.'

Enda had found a candle, but even though the fire was smouldering it was reduced to white ash without the capability of creating sufficient spark. He quickly ignited the candle using his own *tenlach-teinid*, or tinderbox, which all warriors carried in their girdle pocket so that it was often called *teine-creasa* or girdle fire. It was part of a warrior's training that he should possess the ability to light a fire in the briefest possible time using flint and steel with tinder. Now Enda bent and held the flickering candle close, to aid Eadulf in his examination.

It was only a short time before Eadulf was satisfied enough to turn the body face up. He exhaled softly. 'This must be Cétach. He fits the tavern-keeper's description: the dirty red hair, receding at the front, the beard. He is in the pedlar's cabin. There is no one else about.'

'So what can you tell us about his death?' Fidelma prompted.

There was a red weal across the neck. The dead man had been attacked from behind and a blade had been used across the throat with a clean cut rather than a jagged tear. Eadulf moved back a little and glanced at the entire front of the body. There were no further wounds there. Finally he looked up at Fidelma.

'The man was obviously attacked from behind. He did not even have time to turn to confront his killer.'

'He was caught by surprise?'

'In a way. I think he must have known his killer and did not suspect an attack. He was killed where he stood, with his back towards the assassin. More importantly, this man must have been held from behind while the killer brought his knife round and cut his throat, letting the body slump to the floor face downwards. The knife seems to have been honed to a point of sharpness that is fairly unusual.'

'A sharp knife is carried by hunters and warriors,' pointed out Enda.

Fidelma had noticed Eadulf's hesitancy. 'There is something else?' she pressed.

'The cut was made right to left,' he said, his voice flat. 'The wound is deeper on the right where the knife was first plunged in.'

'You mean it was done by a left-handed person?'

'The pedlar was held from the back and to achieve that cut it must have been done by a left-handed man. It was probably the same assassin as killed Brocc.'

'Unless we believe in an extreme coincidence.'

'At least the killing of both men was done by left-handed men.'

'Or women,' Fidelma corrected absently.

'I doubt a woman would do this, lady,' Enda intervened.

'You sound adamant,' Fidelma commented.

'Well, lady, I would exclude a woman by the very method of the killing. True, a woman can shoot a bow as well as a man. But it takes unusual strength in a woman for her to seize a man from behind and hold him while she cuts his throat. Look at the corpse of this pedlar, lady. He might be thin and dirty but he still had strength from the active manner of his life.'

Eadulf was unsure what he meant and said so.

'Whatever the tavern-keeper thought of his business, Cétach had to lift and cart goods about in his wagon, harness his mule and drive long distances. As we know, he drove whatever goods he bartered between here and Durlus Éile, and the road lay through these mountains. A weak man wouldn't be able to do that. So it would take an unusually powerful woman to launch such an attack on this man so strongly and so quickly that there is no sign of a struggle. The conclusion is that the pedlar succumbed very quickly and only a powerful antagonist could have achieved that.'

Fidelma regarded Enda with an expression of amused approval.

'Well, it seems that we have the making of a Brehon in you, Enda,' she said, but could not quite disguise her testiness at being lectured in her own craft. Eadulf frowned as he detected it and glanced anxiously at Enda. The young warrior did not appear to have noticed.

'I am no Brehon,' Enda said. 'I am happy to serve in your brother's bodyguard. I am a warrior and content enough in that role.'

Fidelma's lips pressed for a moment. Even when she made her remark she had regretted it. She knew her faults, and often Eadulf had pointed out her bad temper and impatience with others.

'It is a good point, Enda,' she went on, trying to retrieve her own self-image. 'However, whatever sex the person was, it does lead us into a fog of questions.'

'Such as?' Eadulf asked. 'If the person who killed the Brehon was the same person who killed Cétach, what could have been the motive?'

'That is the fundamental question,' Fidelma agreed. 'Cétach told the abbot that he had seen Princess Gelgéis and her party leave Durlus Éile for the abbey and days later he followed the same road and found the Brehon's body on the wayside. Recognising it as a member of the princess's party, he puts the body in his wagon and brings it to the abbey. His purpose, to hope for a reward. Now why would that necessitate his murder?'

'Agreed,' Eadulf accepted, 'unless he was not being entirely truthful to Abbot Daircell as to what he saw. He says that he saw nothing: he did not see the killer, he could provide no leads. Nothing that he told the abbot could identify the killer. Why, then, would the killer want to silence the pedlar, and after he had already delivered the body to the abbey? This is now a week later. What else could he have done or said, other than what he did a week ago, to bring death on himself?'

'As you say, perhaps he was not telling everything to the abbot,' suggested Enda. 'Perhaps the killer only just discovered that the pedlar had some knowledge that he had to be silenced for?'

'He could just have left the body on the mountainside and not even mentioned it,' Eadulf pointed out. 'So he had no fear of retribution for taking the body to the abbey.'

'It is all speculation.' Fidelma was growing tired of the matter. 'You know my principal rule. No speculation without information. We simply do not have enough information to make *any* speculation.'

'This has proved a dead end, literally as well as figuratively. Where do we go from here?' Eadulf sighed.

'To start with, it is our duty to report this death to the local Brehon, otherwise we could start facing charges ourselves.'

'Can't you take over such a matter, lady?' Enda asked. 'After all, you are qualified to exert authority across borders.'

'You forget, the fewer people know the real reason why we are here – that Princess Gelgéis is missing – the better. Perhaps we could appeal to the local Brehon to keep our presence here a secret.'

'Should we not be concentrating on the disappearance of Princess Gelgéis rather than the pedlar?'

Fidelma hid her impatience. 'I think the two things are related. Cétach was killed by someone whom he knew. The very act of coming here and killing him in almost the same manner as Brocc means a distinct link.'

'Perhaps he was killed to prevent him speaking to us?' suggested Eadulf.

'What else could he have to tell us? It is over a week since he found and delivered the body to the abbey. There is also another point that causes me some thought – the killer wanted Brocc's body discovered.'

'How do you make that out, lady?' asked Enda, bewildered.

'The physician, Brother Lachtna, said that, though he had been dead for seven days, the Brehon's body was not in a condition consistent with lying out on a mountainside for that time, exposed to feral beasts and the weather. So it was placed there for someone, perhaps Cétach, to find.'

'Well, I believe Cétach was killed for what he had not yet told the abbot,' Eadulf declared firmly.

'If the killer knew that Cétach had not told everything, how did the killer know what had been withheld?' Enda mused. 'He must have had some link with Cétach to find this out.'

Fidelma had grown impatient. 'It is time we pushed on and found the local Brehon to take charge of the body,' she said. 'Someone also needs to look after the mule, as it seems to have little fodder enough as it is. We will take it down to the township.'

They made their way back down to the town's square and found the óstóir who had served them watching their approach with bemusement.

'You were not long with the pedlar,' he observed. Then he nodded to the animal that Enda had been leading. 'Has he abandoned that poor beast?'

Fidelma and her companions did not dismount but she replied: 'We found the pedlar dead in his cabin.'

The tavern-keeper's eyes widened. 'So the drink has finally claimed him? Mind you, I would have thought that he might have lasted longer. He was a man of stamina, despite the liquor.'

Fidelma decided not to correct the man's assumption that the pedlar had perished of alcoholism. 'We need to report the pedlar's death to the township's Brehon. I presume there is one?'

'There are two now. The senior is Brehon Rónchú, but he is away on his *Cúairtugad*, visiting outlying hamlets and isolated farmsteads to hear claims and give judgments.'

'*Cúairtugad*?' Eadulf frowned.

'A legal circuit,' Fidelma explained quickly. 'In rural parts like this, the judge is obliged to make a *cuart,* or circuit, of local towns and villages twice a year so that those who cannot come into the township for various reasons can present their cases and be heard.' She turned back to the tavern-keeper. 'You say there is another lawyer here?'

'He has a female assistant. I forget her name as she has not been long in the township. You will find her down at the river by the jetty.'

Thanking the man, Fidelma led the way from the main square and down to where the wharfs lined a wide section of the river front. There were several people about. Fidelma turned to a boatman who was sitting on a stone, using a needle and thread with great dexterity to mend a tear in a sail.

'Which is the Brehon?' queried Fidelma.

'Brehon Rónchú is not here,' the man replied without looking up.

'I am told there is an assistant Brehon.'

The boatman did not bother to reply but raised an arm and pointed. They turned and saw further along the quayside a group of two men and a woman standing engaged in an apparently fierce conversation.

They all dismounted and Fidelma walked towards the group.

'Are you the assistant to Brehon Rónchú?' she called, as she approached the woman.

The woman turned with a look of enquiry on her face. She was not much older than Fidelma, slightly plump, with freckled features that looked more comfortable when smiling than frowning. Her dark eyes widened with incredulity as they gazed at Fidelma.

At the same time, Fidelma halted with a surprised expression, which was quickly replaced by one of recognition.

'It can't be . . .?' she began. 'Is it Beccnat?'

The plump girl gasped. 'Fidelma of Cashel? What are you doing here?'

'Beccnat!' exclaimed Fidelma, a smile on her features. She moved forward, both arms outstretched in greeting. The woman addressed as Beccnat seemed to stiffen but allowed herself to be engulfed by Fidelma's enthusiastic salutation.

Eadulf and Enda exchanged puzzled glances before they went to join them. Enda stood holding the reins of their mounts silently as they both waited for an explanation.

'How long has it been?' Fidelma had drawn away, noticing the coldness of the other's greeting. 'Surely it is not so long that we have become strangers?'

'I suppose it is some twelve years,' replied the other, still sounding more distant than warm at recognising a familiar face.

'You left Brehon Morann's law school just before I did,' Fidelma pointed out, standing back and casting her eye over the woman. 'You have not aged in my eyes.'

'I was already two years in the college when you arrived,' the woman replied. 'So after six years I obtained the degree of *Clí*, which gave me the authority to be a *baran*, a steward judge and judge in minor cases. As I had no ambition to be more than a simple lawyer, I did not study after that.'

In spite of the coolness of the reception, Fidelma was still smiling broadly.

'Ah, those days at Brehon Morann's college in Teamhair – remember how we shared a dormitory? There was Ainder, Grian, Dubressa, you, Beccnat, together with myself. We were all good friends.'

'We all shared the dormitory,' replied the other. 'I doubt we were all good friends. Anyway, Grian was your closest friend.'

'We were all friends,' insisted Fidelma. 'The five of us in our dormitory were friends.'

'I grant you that Ainder was certainly no friend,' the woman accepted dryly.

'Ainder of the Uí Thuirtri – she was just arrogant,' Fidelma chuckled. 'That was because she was senior in the dormitory and felt she could order us about like—'

'Like a princess,' Beccnat intervened sourly. 'She had to amend her ways when you told her that your father had been King of Muman.'

'I did not tell her,' Fidelma corrected. 'It was old Fuicine, the matron, at the college. Anyway, my father had died soon after my birth.'

'And now your brother, Colgú, is king,' Beccnat pointed out. 'So I did not expect to find you here.'

Fidelma frowned slightly. 'But, tell me, Beccnat, I did not think that you were from this area – is this your hometown?'

The woman shook her head. 'I come from a village not far from Darú on the western border of Laigin. I was invited to come here to assist the local Brehon, Brehon Rónchú, only a few weeks ago.' She regarded Fidelma critically. 'I had heard that you had left the religious and were now adviser to your brother in Cashel. What are you doing here in Laigin, especially when there is so much enmity between the kingdoms?'

'I will explain that matter shortly,' Fidelma replied with a glance at the two men who were spectators.

Beccnat continued frowning. 'I have heard many stories about you; you have achieved quite a reputation. I heard you had married a foreigner.'

Fidelma turned and waved Eadulf forward. 'This is Eadulf of Seaxmund's Ham, from the land of the East Angles.' Then: 'Eadulf, this is Beccnat, who was a friend and fellow student when I studied at Brehon Morann's law school.'

Polite greetings were exchanged, and Enda was also brought forward and introduced. They noticed the woman stared hard at the Nasc Niadh symbol that the warrior wore.

At this point the two boatmen whom Beccnat had been talking to, standing impatiently by, were beginning to show signs of losing patience completely.

'We have to go about our business,' one of them scowled.

Beccnat turned with a quick apology to Fidelma. 'Let me deal with these boatmen first. Then we will talk about what you are doing in Laigin. It is not a place I would expect to find representatives of Cashel.'

'I am sure we have much to talk about,' Fidelma agreed in a serious tone. 'Murder, for an example.'

Beccnat's eyes narrowed. 'Murder?' Her voice was sharp. 'Let me finish dealing with this matter on hand. It is a simple affair.'

'Simple?' one of the men protested angrily. 'Not for us, it isn't.'

Beccnat turned to face him. 'Simple,' she repeated flatly. 'The judgment in your case I give under the *Mur Bretha*, the Sea Laws. On the river, as on the sea, that which is found floating and abandoned, with no one in sight, is the property of he who takes it out of the river.'

'I claim it is mine!' scowled one of the men. 'It was knocked over the side of my boat into the river and not noticed until I had moored here.'

'As you have told me. But how can you prove this?'

The second man was scowling. 'He cannot! When I picked up the box there was no other boat in sight in either direction. It was only after I tied up here that this man came by and claimed the box was his. He said that he had lost it overboard.'

'You told me these facts before,' Beccnat nodded, then turned to the protester. 'Did you report this loss to the master of the wharfs when you arrived here? Do you have a witness who saw the box fall from your boat?'

There was a silence.

'A substantial wooden box fell from your boat without anyone noticing. What is in it?'

The claimant hesitated. 'It was something I was asked to transport.'

Beccnat's expression was icy. 'So what were you asked to transport and by whom?'

The man looked around as if in desperation to find the person he claimed had given him the mission.

'Clothes.'

It was a good guess but incorrect, for the Brehon Beccnat had apparently already taken the opportunity to inspect the contents.

'The content was a single book.' She turned to the second man, who had found the box. 'I will allow you to claim the contents of the box, on condition that you take it to the abbey where, I have no doubt, it was intended to be delivered. You may not have noticed the abbey's name is inscribed in Latin on the wood of the box.'

It was clear from their expressions that neither man had noticed, or probably neither could read nor write.

Beccnat continued: 'You may not sell its contents but you are at liberty to accept any reward for delivery if the Abbey is of a mind to offer one.'

The man was not exactly pleased that he was not given ownership of the box and able only to accept a finder's fee, if offered. Still, it was better than nothing.

Beccnat then turned to the other man. 'You will pay me a fine of one *screpal* for my judgment and then I suggest you get in your boat and get about your own business.'

Scowling, the man handed over the coin and turned for his own boat.

Fidelma watched the ending of the affair with a grim smile.

'An interesting division,' she said, as Beccnat joined her. 'Out of interest, what book was in the box?'

'A small vellum book,' Beccnat replied. 'It looked religious in tone with the title *Altus Prosator*. It seems to mean the "writer of high prose" and was a poem attributed to the Blessed Colmcille.

Now you wanted to talk to me about murder. Let us go to my house. It is just over there, behind the main square.' Beccnat's face was grim.

As Fidelma and companions led their horses to follow her, Beccnat noticed the mule was part of the company. She stopped and frowned.

'I know that animal. That belongs to an old pedlar. What are you doing with it?'

Fidelma looked grim in acknowledgement. 'It belonged to the murdered man, whose name was Cétach.'

Beccnat raised her eyebrows but she made no other comment as they walked the short distance to her house. They tied up their mounts and the mule, and followed her into the cabin. It was warm and a fire crackled in the hearth. They were soon seated and enjoying the strong, sweet liquid she had poured for them, as the traditional token of hospitality.

'And now, what of this murder?' Beccnat prompted. 'You say it is the pedlar named Cétach who has been killed?'

'I do.'

Beccnat sniffed disdainfully. 'He is not one of our better citizens. I have not been long in this township but already his name is known to me as a drunkard, a liar and a wife beater. So why does this matter bring you out of your jurisdiction?'

A puzzled expression momentarily crossed Fidelma's face as she heard the implied criticism in the other's words.

'As you know, I hold a qualification that allows me to be consulted in any territory, and kingdom, and have several times been consulted by High King at Tara,' she pointed out.

Beccnat hesitated and then amended her words: 'I meant it is unusual to see you here in Laigin. Especially because of the tensions between our two kingdoms. Yet I suppose it has something to do with the body that Cétach found?'

'So you know the story?'

'Cétach did not have a silent tongue,' replied Beccnat. 'So how did you come to find him murdered? Do you know who killed him?'

Her tone was not exactly one of boredom but certainly not one of alarm or surprise. Fidelma remarked on the fact.

Beccnat sniffed as if dismissing the subject. 'If there was a man destined to be killed, it was that little weasel. As I said, he was a member of this township that brought little credit to it. I would say that there were many who would cheerfully have volunteered to eliminate the man. What does surprise me was the man was still alive, judging by the amount he drank. He was not a successful pedlar and yet he continued to subsist by selling his discarded goods and rubbish.'

'Well, this time he did not survive,' Fidelma said grimly. 'But you said you had not been long in this township. How did you form this opinion about Cétach?'

'I heard much from Brehon Rónchú. He is the senior Brehon. It was he who judged the matter of the petition for divorce by Cétach's wife. Cétach was found guilty of beating her, especially when he got drunk. Brehon Rónchú tried to get her due compensation but found that the man had even kept the returnable *coibche* or dowry for himself. All Brehon Rónchú could do was reduce the man's rights in the society until he paid.'

Fidelma nodded. 'Or until he was murdered. Every dead person removes their liabilities.'

Beccnat examined her former fellow student thoughtfully.

'In the absence of Brehon Rónchú, the legal jurisdiction is mine,' she pointed out abruptly.

'That is why we sought you out,' Fidelma confirmed quietly.

'Then you must tell me the story from the start. You are your brother's legal adviser in Cashel and yet here you are in Laigin, and in this township. Is it that the body Cétach discovered was a Brehon of Osraige, which territory now has to pay tribute to Cashel?'

Fidelma settled back in her chair and recited the story swiftly, but she was frugal with the details, making no mention of Princess Gelgéis, saying only that they had come to the abbey and learnt that Cétach had found the body of Brehon Brocc. They had gone to see Cétach to learn how he had found the body but on arriving at his cabin they had found him obviously murdered.

'So you see, my friend,' Fidelma concluded, 'it is firstly a matter of proprieties and procedure that, as a stranger in this territory, I should give this matter to the local Brehon but – importantly – I do have to ensure my role is not at all compromised.'

Beccnat was thoughtful. 'Even with your legal standing, I think certain nobility in Laigin would not like to see a Brehon from Cashel involved in any matter that should be in the hands of a local Brehon.'

'I have no intention of interfering in the jurisdiction of another Brehon,' Fidelma assured her patiently. 'That is why I came to you, as I said. I presumed that you would take up this investigation.'

'So far as I am concerned, my interest is the law, its jurisdiction here in Laigin and obedience to King Fianamail. I am very aware of territorial jealousies even as I am aware of territorial tensions. My duty is to take charge of this matter.'

Fidelma nodded in sympathy. 'We took an oath, when we were in Brehon Morann's school, to maintain that principle that law does not stop at a border. And so far as Cétach's murder is connected with my inquiry, I am happy to concede the investigation of his murder to your jurisdiction. But I must also be allowed to conduct my own inquiries because, as you seem to know, the body of the man Cétach found was a Brehon from Osraige.'

'I have no objections but I would have to insist that you share all information with me while pursuing such an investigation.'

Fidelma smiled thinly. 'Of course. You have my word all relevant information will be shared.'

'Very well,' Beccnat said rising. 'I will see to it that the practicalities are observed and arrange for someone to bury the pedlar's body.'

'That is good. You may know who Cétach's friends and enemies were, who would have the best information. Perhaps we could share what you learn from them?'

Beccnat was diffident. 'Not so easy because he had no friends, especially after people learnt how he treated his wife when she divorced him. As for enemies . . .' She shrugged eloquently.

'I presume there are too many enemies to choose from?' queried Eadulf with a sardonic tone.

Beccnat examined him with a serious expression for a moment.

'Cétach was not the man to make friends,' she said coldly. 'No one will mourn his death, that is for sure. But I cannot say that anyone here would volunteer to take his murder on themselves. Of course, you never know what drives a person to an act of murder so I suppose my answer is I know no one who would go so far as killing him. He was a drunkard, true; but he paid for his liquor with his petty trading. Local people just disliked him. He was given to trying to form relationships with women, but no respecting woman would want to go with him.' She paused and thought for a moment and then said, 'He used to go to an *echlach*.'

'An *echlach*?' Eadulf frowned. 'Isn't that a household servant?'

Fidelma was a little self-conscious as she explained. 'It is an older name for what we now call *meirdrech*, a prostitute.' She turned to Beccnat. 'I would not have thought there were many such in a place like this. Is there a *mertecht-loc*, a brothel, here?'

Beccnat seemed sourly amused. 'There is no registered brothel, as such. But you forget that this is a crossroads of trade. The merchants come by river and through the mountains, along the tracks. So just south of the township is an area with some abandoned old boats, which constitutes a sort of brothel area. That is where those searching for the services of a prostitute are likely to find them. Many passing traders have been known to visit there in the twilight hours.'

Fidelma was disapproving. 'Are you saying that such places are not regulated by law? If there is a demand, then there ought to be some sort of protection for both the prostitutes and those who visit them.'

'You are probably right, but the laws are not as all-encompassing as they should be on the subject, and what exist are often in conflict with the laws that are being adopted from the Faith that is brought from Rome. Sometimes it is impossible to use the law of the Brehons when it conflicts with the new religious laws.'

'Was there a particular woman that Cétach visited?' Eadulf asked. 'Sometimes a man will give information to a prostitute that he would not give to anyone else.'

Beccnat considered this for a moment. 'There is a woman who works from one of the boats that is moored on the river there,' she pointed. 'If Cétach didn't visit her, then she would probably know which of her colleagues he did visit. But I am sure she was the one I heard most mentioned.' She paused and added: 'People gossip to her. I do not think many secrets are kept. But gossip is not usable in law.'

'Well, it's a start,' Eadulf conceded. 'What's her name?'

'Her name is Serc.'

Enda chuckled and then immediately apologised. 'An appropriate name as it means "love", and this lady makes men pay for it.'

Fidelma cast a disapproving glance at him before turning back to Beccnat.

'Very well,' she said, rising from her seat, an indication that her companions were to follow. 'We will find this woman Serc. Perhaps she would know if there was anyone who might have particular animosity against Cétach. Just so that other motivations can be eliminated. I am afraid we must leave the man's mule in your hands.'

Beccnat did not smile. 'I will take charge of the beast and the cabin, and see to all the matters with our local physician.'

As they were riding away, Eadulf said softly: 'If this Beccnat was an old friend from college, I would not like to encounter one who had been your enemy.'

Fidelma did not respond.

It did not take them long to find the boat on which Beccnat had told them that Serc plied her trade. There was a small inlet of the river just south of the township in which a few ageing and rotting boats were to be found. They appeared like derelict hulks, long since abandoned to time and the elements. Fidelma insisted on confirming, with a passing boatman, that this was indeed where Serc lived. The man confirmed it was but not before giving her and her companions a curious look. It was clear from his expression that he was wondering why the three should be seeking a prostitute.

The man pointed to one of the several hulks moored in the inlet, of which two had rotting wooden planks connecting them to the muddy shore. By one of them, a patient but frail-looking mule was tied to a post. The adjoining hulk was where the boatman indicated that Serc dwelt. It looked as if it had once been used for carrying cargo. It was broad in the beam with cabins at the bow and at the stern. The centre hold was left uncovered and just for'ard of the centre were the sawn-off remains of what had been a tall central mast for the mainsail.

Eadulf was left on the wharf to mind the horses because Enda insisted it was his role to precede Fidelma, leading the way on board, testing the rotting planking carefully with each step. Only when he was safely aboard did he turn and call Fidelma to follow, warning her to be careful. A noise behind him made him turn. A woman had emerged from the stern cabin and was regarding him with a mixture of suspicion and contempt.

She had probably been attractive once, he thought. Age and experience now weathered her face, and the strands of her unkempt hair were greying. The pale lips drooped, as if there was no traction in the muscles that would have added expression to the mouth. Enda was not sure how he read the feelings of suspicion and contempt because, as he examined her, he thought the eyes were dead – grey orbs as if they had no pupils. She was thin, almost to the point of emaciation. The forearms folded before her breast with very thin; the bones of the wrist and elbows seemed painfully sharp. Her clothes, a threadbare dress and ragged woollen shawl, were almost colourless, although the flecks of colour here and there showed they had once been of good quality. He guessed that she was just beyond middle age.

'Is your name Serc?' Enda asked the obvious question.

The woman watched Fidelma negotiating the plank and then without a change of expression or stance, said tonelessly: 'I don't cater for couples.'

Enda felt his cheeks redden in embarrassment. 'We did not come as your customers,' he snapped. 'If your name is Serc, we came to seek answers to certain questions.'

'By what right?' demanded the woman belligerently.

'My right of authority as a *dálaigh*,' Fidelma replied quietly as she came to stand alongside Enda on the deck of the vessel.

Still the face of the woman seemed to be filled with hostility but the contempt had faded.

'You are not the local Brehon,' she said coldly.

'That is true,' Fidelma conceded. 'I am working in conjunction with Brehon Beccnat.'

'I have no liking for lawyers.' Serc's tone was still hostile. 'They make a living out of the suffering of others. What do you want from me?'

'The answers to questions.'

'Why should I answer your questions?'

'It is your obligation under law to answer to my questions,' Fidelma said sharply.

'And if I do not care to answer them?'

'That's right, dear!' came a cackling voice from the quayside.

'Never answer questions, lest the answers be put in the service of the dark forces.'

The visitors turned, surprised by the intrusion. An elderly woman appeared from the neighbouring hulk. It seemed that the half-starved and elderly mule, standing patiently below, belonged to her. The old woman was dragging a heavy sack, which she attempted to haul on the back of the waiting animal. It was obviously a difficult task for her and instinctively Eadulf left their horses secured and went to help her.

'Let me give you assistance, mother,' he greeted in a friendly manner. 'You will do damage to yourself trying to do things that way.'

The old woman turned her hag-like features towards him with a snarling expression that caused him to flinch and take a step backwards.

'Beware, Saxon.' Her harsh cackle sent a coldness rising against the back of his neck. 'I know you and know where your questions will lead. You will not wish to go there. So, I warn you yet again. Do not venture into the realms of the Aos Sí. Do not ask questions that are not meant to be asked. In the dark mountain passes dwells the wizened old man of lies and from his tongue spread chains to catch the ears of those who listen and answer his honey tongue. Others use chains of metal, but beware the chains that you do not see!'

chapter nine

E adulf was momentarily shocked at the vehemence in the crone's voice. Then he reset his features in a grim smile.

'Well, Iuchra, I didn't recognise you for a moment. I don't see any of your Aos Sí springing forward just now to help you with this heavy load, so I will do so.'

Eadulf reached for the sack and swung it up to fasten it to the bow of the saddle of the mule.

'Get away! I don't want your help!' the old woman cried as, with the ease of one long practised, she used a nearby flat raised stone to elevate herself up and on to the scrawny beast's back. She swung round with such determination that she almost knocked Eadulf over and, uttering imprecations at the world in general, went trotting off down the track towards the main square.

Eadulf returned to his horses and, brushing the dust from his clothes, grinned ruefully up at Fidelma standing looking down at him from the wreck of the boat.

'Are you all right?' she asked. 'Wasn't that the old woman Iuchra?'

'It was the old witch, with curses and all,' Eadulf confirmed. 'I think she was merely unused to being offered help,' he added to make light of it.

Serc gave a sharp guffaw, which was meant to be laughter, but then she continued in the same toneless manner as she employed earlier, 'That one never needed nor accepted help in her life. Iuchra is one of those who will outlast us all and woe betide those who try to help her in this world or even in the next one. She's the local *ammait* . . . always boasting of her supernatural powers.'

'But I thought she dwelt in the caves and forests,' Enda said, forgetting Brother Eochaí had mentioned she had a place in the township.

Serc sniffed. 'Sometime she slips out of character as being the mystic of the woods. When the days are cold enough, she sleeps in that hulk, where it is warm. She does all right.'

'Pity about the state of her mule, though,' Eadulf commented. 'She should have devoted some of the foodstuff in her sack to feeding it.'

Fidelma stared curiously at him. 'What do you mean?'

'When I went to lift the sack on to the mule, I could not help but notice that it contained cooked meats, cheese, bread and fruits. She must do well for herself although she looks every bit as emaciated as her animal.'

Serc shook her head. 'It's not her foodstuff. She cooks and delivers things for other people, even your friend, the new assistant to the Brehon. I've often seen them being cordial with each other.'

The mention of Beccnat brought Fidelma back to the matter in hand.

'Ah, yes, we were talking about matters legal. You were going to answer some questions, I hope. You are aware now of your duty to answer the questions of a *dálaigh*?'

'I am aware of my right not to answer if I cannot answer, or if I do not care to answer.' The reply was returned in the same expressionless tone, which seemed to be her natural expression when dealing with figures of authority.

Fidelma glanced to Enda with a slight shake of her head as she

saw that he was growing irritated and feared he was about to say
something that would make further questions impossible. She turned
back to Serc and quickly forced a smile.

'Let us start with simple things then,' she began. 'Is your name
Serc?'

'I do not deny it,' sniffed the woman.

'Is your occupation that of a *meirdrech*?'

The jaw of the woman thrust out a little further. 'That is the
profession that I follow. Is there now a law forbidding it?'

'None that I know of. However, by those that do exist, your rights
are restricted.'

'I know that, and so does my son, who now lies in a quiet grave
on the hill above here. My son was two years old when he was laid
in the cold earth of the hill and I have seen three winters since that
cold day.'

Fidelma frowned, not understanding. 'I am sorry for your loss,
but . . .?'

'I was raped by a man,' the woman intervened sharply. 'He was
not even a customer of mine. He was a religieux from the abbey.
I was told that the rape of even a prostitute is against the law. But
Brehon Rónchú refused me compensation and refused even to
recognise my son in any legal form.'

'Is the person still a member of the abbey?' Fidelma pressed
firmly. 'Would you remember his name?'

'I was told he was called Brother Tóla, but Brehon Rónchú
assured me there was no such member of the abbey by that name,'
she replied. 'I would have recognised him but was not allowed to
visit the abbey. He was of average height but his features were grey
and almost the complexion of stone. I was not able to confront
him and Brehon Rónchú dismissed my claim. My son was born
without a father and died without being acknowledged and I could
obtain no help for him. That is all I know.'

'I thought a prostitute had no recourse to an honour price,' Eadulf called, as he had been overhearing from below. The honour price was the basic guide to fines from personal injury or death.

'It is true, Eadulf,' Fidelma replied firmly. 'But half of what might have been the honour price, before she turned to prostitution, is allowed in compensation if the *meirdrech* was raped, even by a customer, should she report the matter. If there was a child of the rape and the father admitted that the child was his, he has to pay seven *cumals* so that the child could be adopted with full rights into his father's clan or family. In this case no one admitted the offence and no identification of the father could be made.'

Eadulf knew that Fidelma was well acquainted with such problems. He remembered that she had played a leading part in securing rights for her friend Della, who had once been a prostitute, and who had been raped. Not only had she secured the compensation but had managed to reinstate Della into society and secure rights for her son, Gormán, who had become commander of King Colgú's bodyguard.

'Some compensation should have been claimed,' Fidelma pointed out. 'Why was it not allowed?'

Anger replaced the previously flat tone of Serc's voice. 'Except that did not happen to me. I was told that under the law the entire responsibility of looking after my child rested on me. I did not receive half my honour price – as little as it had been because I was daughter of an assistant boat builder downriver. I received nothing and, after a few years, my baby died of the plague.'

'I know some of the laws on the *Maccshléchta* are harsh.' Fidelma, seeing her companion's puzzled glance, added: 'That's the laws on the inheritance of sons.'

'Those laws killed my son.'

'For which I am sorry. The laws also allow interpretation and change as people's values change. Indeed, the laws change according to the progression of the generations. Or, at least, that is the philosophy that many Brehons follow, and that is why, every three years, there is a great council of the Brehons of the Five Kingdoms to discuss and amend the laws. If you wish, I will ask my colleague Beccnat, the assistant to the Brehon here, if there is a basis to re-examine the law in the light of your case.'

The woman snorted derisively. 'What good will that do when my son lies under the sod on the hill?'

'It won't bring him back, but some justice should be done. I will have a word with her on the circumstances.'

When the woman did not respond, Fidelma gave an inward sigh and added: 'Alas, you cannot bring back the past. However, if there is injustice it will be examined. At the moment, Serc, I still require you to answer my questions.'

The woman looked at her with a sneer. 'You expect me to report on someone or other? Well, let me put this to you, high and mighty lawyer . . . If I am merely a *meirdrech* then there is no need to remind you of the *Berrad Airechta.*'

'Why would you say so?' Fidelma was puzzled. 'What has law court procedure to do with the matter?'

'If you want me to give evidence against someone then the *Berrad Airechta* says that, as a prostitute, I am not allowed to give such evidence. That is the one lesson I learnt about your law. The man who raped me and fathered my son was a religious. My evidence against him was not allowed. Brehon Rónchú explained that clearly. Yes, that is the one lesson of the laws I learnt. So if my evidence is not valid in that case, it will not be valid whatever you want me to say.'

Fidelma shifted her weight uncomfortably. She was thoughtful.

'I do not want you to give evidence, just to answer a few questions. But tell me more of this rape and why your case was considered invalid. You are saying the perpetrator of this attack was a religieux from the abbey here?' she asked. 'You are sure?'

'Are they not as any other men as well as being religious?'

'Very well, Serc. But we must get to the matter we came here to discuss. Do you know Cétach the pedlar?'

Serc shrugged indifferently. 'I thought everyone knew him.'

'Was he a client of yours?'

'When he could afford it, which was not often.'

'So, in your eyes, he was poor?'

'Destitute is what most local people would say.'

'It was well known that he was impoverished?'

'It was no secret. Now and then he would take that flea-bitten mule of his and go off, usually across the mountains, to see what he could pick up to sell. If he made a little money, his first preference was the tavern and, if anything remained, he would come here.'

'So, as far as you know, he had no secret source of money?'

Serc frowned. 'Why are you asking me these questions? If he didn't poach or scrounge, he would have been dead.'

'You seem to be the only person here that admits to having some closer contact with him than others.'

'What are you implying?' demanded the woman, her brow furrowing in anger.

'I am implying nothing. Just that we need to know something about Cétach. His lifestyle and habits.'

'Why?'

'Because he was murdered early today.'

Serc's face registered surprise but not shock or upset.

'So why come to me?'

'Let us say that we have to start somewhere. Do you know any of his family or friends?'

'I don't think he had family or friends in the township. He was a lonely person, mostly by choice. He was married once but beat his wife and she divorced him. She went back to her family somewhere on the coast. And, no, he did not ill treat me as that pious son of a pig did from the abbey.'

'Did he ever discuss anything with you about enemies? Did he mention anyone who would have a grievance against him?'

Serc shook her head. 'The only person who had a grievance was his former wife. I heard he was not even able to return any of the marriage settlement or fines.'

'When was this divorce?'

'I suppose it was about three years ago. He was judged by the same Brehon who dismissed my case,' she confirmed. 'Maybe it is he that you should be talking to.'

'Brehon Rónchú? We are told that he is away.'

'Oh, yes,' Serc replied. 'I heard that he went upriver to the Ford of the Cows.'

Fidelma heaved a sigh. 'I am done here,' she announced.

Serc turned and vanished into the cabin without saying another word.

Fidelma realised that matters were not leading her anywhere but to the obvious conclusion that the murder of Cétach was to do solely with the finding of Brehon Brocc's body. Fidelma and Enda made their way carefully off the boat and rejoined Eadulf below on the quayside, waiting patiently with the horses.

'A strange place for a *mertecht-loc*,' he greeted. 'It sounded from here that there was nothing to learn from the woman.'

'Nothing that would help us . . . at least, nothing that would help us at the moment,' Fidelma added punctiliously.

'Where to now?'

'We will see if Beccnat has found anything further, and then there is little more to do today. However, tomorrow we will try to retrace the path that Cétach was following when he found the body of Brehon Brocc. Perhaps we will learn more.'

She led the way with the others following back along the river to the main part of the township before turning up the path that they had previously taken to visit Cétach's hut.

Outside the rotting construction, Beccnat was standing with a nervous-looking man who was in the process of hauling the body of Cétach on to a small ox-cart, assisted by a companion. As the visitors dismounted, Beccnat introduced the nervous man as Síabair, the local physician.

'Is there anything you can tell us that we might have missed?' Eadulf queried, proud of his medical training but anxious to prove it.

Síabair shrugged. 'The man had his throat cut – is that not enough?'

Having glanced at Eadulf's expression, Fidelma turned to the physician with a patient smile.

'I think my companion was seeking something more informative as he has studied the healing arts at Tuaim Brecain.'

An irritated expression crossed Síabair's face as he realised his knowledge was being examined.

'Then you will already know that Cétach was attacked from behind. He was held in that position while his attacker used a knife, cutting his victim's throat from right to left. Of course, to get into that position, one has to suppose that there was only one attacker.'

'And the assailant being behind the victim, would that not indicate something else?' queried Eadulf mildly.

Síabair's browns came together. 'Like what?' he demanded.

'That the killer was known to the victim. You would hardly turn your back on a stranger unless the person was one you trusted.'

The physician shrugged. 'It might,' he conceded indifferently.

Eadulf decided not to bother to point out that the nature of the wounds indicated a left-handed killer.

'Any observations are welcome if they help resolve matters,' Fidelma said quickly, not wishing to alienate the physician.

'Your colleague Brehon Beccnat here already knows what there is to know,' Síabair replied. 'This man was not well liked in the township and every man would probably have a reason to quarrel with him. So there will be no *nuall-guba*, the lamentation of sorrow, chanted over his grave; no *caoine*, the wailing or weeping aloud; the carrying to the grave will not be accompanied by the *lám-airt*. If I did not have my duties as a physician, I would not even be acknowledging the body with the *toncha* or washing, which is a sacred ritual no matter who the dead person was. He will be buried in what shirt he has and not a linen *recholl* or winding sheet. Do I make myself clear?'

Fidelma was a little surprised by the physician's vehemence.

'You make yourself very clear, Síabair.'

The physician man stared up at her, brows lowered. His nervousness was apparent, as if he had spoken more than he intended. Then he tried to explain.

'You will ask me why I had no liking for Cétach,' he said. 'Very well, I will answer. I was the physician that Brehon Rónchú called in to examine Cétach's wife when she accused him of beating her and sought a divorce. I saw her wounds. From that moment I detested the man. In fact, I hated him and will not express any regret that he now lies dead.'

There was a silence and then Eadulf asked with a thin smile: 'Doesn't that admission put you into the position of being suspect? We know that Cétach was disliked, but was there anyone who disliked him enough to do him harm, to kill him in this matter; a person that he knew? You have now admitted you hated him and do not regret his death.'

'I think Síabair knows well what he is saying,' Fidelma admonished Eadulf.

'I am not ashamed. I was in love with Cétach's wife. Her name was Faife. She rejected me for a life with that worthless piece of excrement. I tried to warn her and, in the end, I was right. He turned out to be nothing but a wastrel who was violent and only wanted to use her money, her dowry, to fund his drinking habits. When she knew the truth, she could only seek a divorce. Divorce was a reason for her to return in shame back to her own family on the coast.'

'In shame?' queried Fidelma.

'That she returned to her own kin without her rightful compensation, even without the marriage payments or gifts, as was her due.

That would have been enough to bring about a blood feud between her family and Cétach.'

Beccnat, who had been standing quietly by, decided to intervene in disapproval. 'Little purpose in that.'

Fidelma grimaced thoughtfully. 'Still, there is precedence, and the blood feud or *dígal* – vengeance, if you like – did have legal standing in the old times. Doesn't the *Críth Gablach* refer to it?'

'But with the coming of the New Faith the blood feud is discouraged and vengeance is seen as futile,' replied Beccnat.

'This is true,' Fidelma agreed. 'And I would support the law that the rule of *dígal,* or vengeance, is pointless and a useless way to pursue justice. The Brehon council long ago rejected vengeance as a path to follow. Compensation to the victim and rehabilitation of the perpetrator are the only ways of a true justice. However, perhaps a member of Faife's family might have felt the need to follow the path of vengeance for the insult to their family over her marriage and divorce?'

'That may be so,' agreed Beccnat. 'But the time to do it is when the blood is hot, not some five or six years afterwards when the blood is cold.'

The physician was shaking his head. 'Don't they say that vengeance is a dish best tasted cold?'

'As a motive that may well apply to you, Síabair,' Eadulf pointed out. He had clearly taken a dislike to the physician. 'Cétach's wife did not come from here, so I have been told. Did you come from her hometown?'

'I did not,' snapped the physician.

'I meant to ask, since you bear an unusual name, where do you come from?' Fidelma asked with a disarming smile.

The physician flushed. 'I am of the Síabrad in the lands of the Uí Bairrache, far to the south of this place. I am of Laigin but not of the Uí Máil. I did not have to tell you my story and bring suspicion on my head,' ended the man indignantly.

'Yet you might have thought that by this confession you are seeking to reassure us that you did not kill the pedlar?'

Síabair's lips thinned in a sneer. 'It will be up to you how you interpret matters but, as you will obviously hear my feelings for Faife from someone in the town, it is easier to hear it from me. Now, if I may go about my duties . . .?'

Fidelma glanced to Beccnat and shrugged, making it clear that she was content. For a moment or two, Fidelma and her companions watched the physician and his assistant lead their ox-cart, with its grisly contents, down the hill until they vanished from sight. Then Fidelma turned to her former school companion.

'It seems that Síabair could not add anything to what Eadulf was already able to interpret from the body. Was there anything else that struck you?'

Beccnat shook her head. 'I have searched the hut and shed and found nothing obvious that could lead to identifying a killer. I begin to believe that Faife's own family is worthy of investigation. The idea of a vengeance killing seems to me a likely motivation. Lots of people disliked Cétach, as you know, but the family seem to have the best cause for hatred that could result in what Síabair has pointed out.'

'Tell me,' Fidelma said thoughtfully, 'did you know about this relationship Síabair describes with Faife?'

Beccnat quickly shook her head. 'I remind you that I was not here when Faife was here and received her divorce.'

'But you heard about it?'

'Brehon Rónchú did not make a point of discussing his cases.'

'Did he ever discuss the case of Serc?'

Beccnat hesitated. 'Not particularly. I heard some tavern gossip, that is all.'

'Gossip?'

'There are still stories and speculation because Serc was supposed to have been raped by someone from the abbey. That produced a child, a boy. He died during some plague. The person she claimed was the father did not exist or, if he did, had a false name.'

'Serc told me that Brehon Rónchú upheld him in this defence?'

'It was on the basis that she could not identify him, so far as I know.'

'I thought he was supposed to be one of the brethren at the abbey.'

'Why are you so interested in that matter?'

'I am not sure,' Fidelma replied. 'Put it down to my curiosity. Serc seems to think it was a misjudgment but did not realise that she could have appealed it, that the *taircsiu* or appeal is a right. It seems that Brehon Rónchú did not explain this or, if one is being generous, Serc might have forgotten after such a time has passed.'

'Most likely it was the latter,' Beccnat replied confidently. 'I know Brehon Rónchú is very particular about his cases. He always volunteers the stipulated five ounces of silver in case of a dispute with his judgments. Litigants are always given the explanation that they can appeal and if the judgment is found to be wrong then the silver is forfeited by the judge.'

'And no appeal was made?'

'When Brehon Rónchú returns, you may take it up with him,' Beccnat pointed out impatiently. 'But he would have no reason to give a false judgment.'

'Would the fact that the person involved was supposed to be a member of the abbey not have been a reason enough to be more diligent?' Eadulf asked.

Beccnat flushed. 'That is an outrageous thing to say! You say a Brehon tried to pervert the course of justice because the accused was a religious?'

'An outrageous thing to do, that is, if the Brehon was protecting a senior cleric,' replied Eadulf easily. 'I only propose it as a possibility.'

The woman turned angrily to him. 'I think you would do well

to put a curb on your tongue, Saxon, for Brehon Rónchú is not a man of quiet disposition to take insults.'

'If that is the case it sounds as though Brehon Rónchú lacks the objectivity that is essential for a Brehon to achieve before he can judge others,' Fidelma pointed out sharply. 'Eadulf was an hereditary *gerefa*, a law giver, among his people. He has a right to make suggestions for consideration without threats being returned. Why was Serc not allowed to enter the abbey to identify her assailant?'

Beccnat hesitated. 'I was merely defending the Brehon. Are we not sworn to uphold the law, whether it is for bad people, good people, rich or poor people?'

'I accept that is the intention,' smiled Fidelma. 'Do you know much about Brehon Rónchú? Where did he get his qualification?'

'His qualification is as a *foirceadlaidhe*.'

'A *foirceadlaidhe* is acquired only at an ecclesiastical or monastic college,' pointed out Eadulf, intervening for the first time. He knew the degrees were differentiated and glanced at Fidelma.

Beccnat shrugged. 'The Brehon went to an abbey college and has the fifth order of wisdom.' Then she frowned and her voice grew sharp. 'I know you of old, Fidelma. I lay wager that you are thinking that because he went to an ecclesiastical college, he might be in favour of making a judgment for a religieux even though the man raped a prostitute. I would advise you not to claim Brehon Rónchú lied, for you would find no friends here. I guarantee it.'

chapter ten

Fidelma decided to let the matter drop. She realised there was something troubling her former college companion and she would have to find out what it was, but at the moment she had no time. 'It seems that there is little more that can be done here. We must be thinking of returning to the abbey,' she said for the woman's benefit.

'Will you be staying there long?' Beccnat asked at once.

'It is hard to say. There is little progress we can make now that Cétach has been murdered. I was hoping that he could show me where he found the body he took to the abbey.'

Beccnat was silent, apparently thinking.

'Did Cétach reveal the actual spot?' she asked after a moment.

'He did not. Only that it was in the valley of Glasán. We shall explore along it to see if we learn anything new. A faint hope, but it is the only thing left.'

'I might be able to help,' Beccnat surprised them by saying.

'How so?' asked Fidelma.

'Because I know someone that hunts in that area. He would be a good person to guide you. At least he would know the likely places.'

Fidelma was interested. 'Where might I find such a person?'

'Here. He is a hunter and trapper named Teimel and has recently returned from the mountains around Glasán. He has a cabin on the edge of the township.'

'Is he a trustworthy man?'

'Trustworthy?' Beccnat smiled in amusement. 'He is said to be a man of his word and once commanded a company of the lord of The Cuala's bodyguard.'

Enda, who had been fairly silent ever since they had returned to Cétach's hovel, suddenly burst into a fit of coughing.

Fidelma turned to him with a look of disapproval.

'I hope you have not swallowed pollen from the dried plants that we have encountered?' she asked with irony.

'Lady,' Enda replied, annoyed that she disregarded what he had considered a subtle warning. 'The lord of The Cuala is uncle to King Fianamail. He is Dicuil Dóna of the Uí Máil; a powerful noble among these mountains and controls most of the north of this kingdom.'

Beccnat's eyes widened. 'Your companion has a good knowledge. Dicuil Dóna is lord of all this territory. Most people here fall under his patronage. Is that a problem in your current investigation?'

Fidelma gave it some thought. 'You say the hunter you know used to be in his bodyguard?'

'But is no longer,' affirmed the woman quickly. 'It could well be good to consider taking a guide with you when venturing along that valley.'

'I agree,' Fidelma replied after a moment.

'I will point out his hut for you,' Beccnat offered immediately. 'I can assure you that he has turned his back on military things, if that is a concern.'

'Why would that be?'

'He has since devoted himself to being a *cuthchaire*, a hunter and a trapper among the mountains here.'

They passed to the township square and towards the bridge that guarded the entrance to the towns. They were moving across the bridge when Beccnat gave a short cry of recognition.

'There is the very man himself,' she exclaimed, turning and waving.

Not far beyond the bridge, on the track towards the abbey, stood a well-constructed wooden cabin. Outside was a man apparently in the process of brushing down a horse, which stood patiently tied to a post outside. The man straightened and turned at Beccnat's cry. He was tall and his rough, untidy hair blew this way and that as the wind caught it. He had an equally large and straggling beard. The eyes were deep set and blue, yet with the trace of ice about them. He was thin and did not appear to be very muscular. Only the weather-beaten skin betrayed the fact that he was a man who pursued an outdoor life. Certainly, he did not give the appearance of one who had been a warrior, let alone a *cenn feadhna*, the commander of a company. He examined Beccnat's companions with curiosity as they approached.

'Ticks,' he said laconically, nodding towards the horse. 'You go through the yew woods here and no matter how carefully you proceed, you will find they leap on to a sweaty horse.'

'It is well that you are here, Teimel,' replied Beccnat. 'This is a colleague of mine, Fidelma. She seeks your assistance.'

Fidelma had felt the urge to stop her introduction but it was too late. She had wanted to give more thought to the idea of getting a guide who had been a bodyguard to a powerful local Uí Máil noble. She noticed a swift look of surprise cross the man's features.

'What assistance do you seek?' the hunter asked.

'She and her companions want to be taken along the river Glasán,' went on Beccnat.

'It is an isolated route.' The hunter was thoughtful, having brought his surprise under control. 'How far along the river do you wish to go?'

'Not far, I think,' replied Fidelma. 'Perhaps not beyond a mountain called, I am told, Céim an Doire, the oak pass.'

'It's quite an isolated route,' Teimel repeated.

'I thought the route was often used and called the Path of the Blessed Cáemgen,' Beccnat pointed out.

Teimel sniffed dismissively. 'Ah, that route. Cáemgen is welcome to it because there are better paths and tracks across the mountains.'

'But none that I want to see,' Fidelma replied irritably.

'Are you staying in the abbey?' The question was sudden and direct.

'They are staying there,' Beccnat confirmed before Fidelma could reply.

'So you want to go along the Glasán?' The hunter eyed them in amusement. To their surprise, he said: 'I suppose it is coincidence that it is along that route that Cétach found a body and took it to the abbey.'

The blue eyes examined them with their trace of icy humour as he noticed the reaction on Fidelma's features.

'How did you know about that?' she asked.

'What Cétach knows he will never keep secret,' the hunter said simply.

'He will now,' Fidelma replied coldly. 'He has been murdered.'

There was a moment's silence before Teimel spoke. 'Murdered? Then his past has caught up with him.'

'Why do you say that?' Fidelma questioned.

'For many reasons. Cétach was not a nice person and that fact was widely known. He was the sort of person who thought all the folk in the world were thieves because he was one. That is why most people would have nothing to do with him. Then there was the abuse of his wife. I doubt that you would find one person in this area who would be prepared to step forward in Cétach's defence if he were attacked.'

'Including you?'

'Especially me,' the hunter confirmed gravely. 'Cétach once tried to steal from me so I thrashed him within an inch of his life. He never tried to steal from me again.'

The words were said as a matter of fact and not with any tone of self-justification.

'Well, that's honest enough,' Fidelma remarked.

'You will always find me honest,' smiled the hunter. 'I might have thrashed Cétach for theft but I did not kill him. I am one who does not praise honesty and then neglect it. I expect people to be equally honest with me. Therefore, this request for a guide along the valley of Glasán is about the body that Cétach found there. Whose body was it? I presume it was of someone of importance, otherwise we would not be having a lawyer from Cashel asking questions in this township.'

'If I say the body was a Brehon, will that suffice for my reason in being interested in the place where this body was discovered?' asked Fidelma.

Teimel smiled broadly. 'It will do unless it needs amending. It must have been a Brehon of importance to bring you, your husband and a warrior of your brother's bodyguard here.' He paused and added with quiet sharpness, 'I would advise you not to lower your hand to your sword hilt, warrior.'

Fidelma realised that Enda had slid his hand to grasp his sword.

'It's all right, Enda. Leave your sword alone.' She turned thoughtfully back at the hunter. 'Unless you have second sight we must have encountered one another before as you seem to know who we are, although Beccnat has not introduced us fully. Where did we meet?'

'We did not meet formally so there is no reason why you should remember me,' replied the hunter, seemingly pleased that he had caused some reaction among the visitors. 'It was when your husband, the Saxon there, was about to be executed. I was at Fearna as escort for Fianamail's uncle, Dicuil Dóna, who is lord of this territory.'

'It was a long time ago,' mused Fidelma, remembering the anguish she had gone through at the time, rescuing Eadulf from execution for a crime he had not committed, having fallen captive to an abbess who had converted to the Penitential rules of Rome. Revenge and execution were not part of the native system, just compensation and rehabilitation.

'A long time ago?' Eadulf said, raising a hand to massage his neck and remembering how the evil Abbess Fainder and Bishop Forbassach had conspired to have him executed. 'Not long enough for me.'

'Very well, Teimel, as you know who we are, tell me, what are your intentions?'

Teimel chuckled. 'Intentions? You have asked me for help. At least that is what our good friend Beccnat says. You want to be shown along the glen of the Glasán where Cétach found a body. You have told me that the body was that of a Brehon and I have to presume he was a person of importance for you to be involved. Well, I see no difficulties in showing you the place. Cétach was quite loquacious about his discovery, so I can take you to the actual spot, if that is what you need.'

Fidelma examined the man carefully. There was something about him that she did not entirely trust. It was not merely what he said but the way he said it. There was also some expression around those cold blue eyes. They did not reflect his humour. She finally reached a decision.

'For that we would be most grateful. You may consider yourself hired as our guide. I should also tell you that the body of the Brehon was—'

'. . . Brehon to Princess Gelgéis,' ended Teimel. 'Don't be surprised,' he went on quickly. 'Cétach found out when he delivered the body to the abbey. Did I not tell you that Cétach could never keep his mouth shut?'

Fidelma's eyes narrowed. 'So how many people know this?'

The hunter shrugged. 'Outside the abbey? As many as the pedlar tried to sell his story to, as I have no doubt he would exchange the information for money.' Teimel looked satisfied. 'I am glad we can now be honest. Cétach told me that he had found the body of the Brehon and knew it to be Brocc. He even said that he had seen him in the company of the Princess Gelgéis leaving Durlus Éile some days before he found the body.'

'Might Cétach have passed on this information to others?' Eadulf asked.

'So that was why you were concerned – this is not some simple murder of a man of no consequence?' Beccnat asked.

'I am afraid that is correct,' Fidelma said. 'Until I have investigated this, I hope it will remain a secret between us.'

Beccnat shrugged. 'So long as it does not interfere with my duties as assistant to the local Brehon.'

'We go back a long way, Beccnat,' Fidelma reminded her. 'We were young students at Brehon Morann's law school in Tara, so you will know I am not in a position of betraying my legal trust. I shall not interfere in the domestic duties you have.'

'I must report matters to Brehon Rónchú when he returns. For the time being I will continue with the investigation of Cétach's murder and keep you informed, but will say nothing to anyone else. What do you intend to do now?' she asked.

'If Teimel is still agreeable, we will follow the valley of the Glasán and see if we can discover anything about the place where Cétach found the body.'

'When do you want to start?' the hunter enquired.

'At first light tomorrow.'

'I can meet you outside the gates of the abbey.'

'That will be fine. We shall be ready.'

Fidelma, Eadulf and Enda left Beccnat and Teimel conversing together and set off for the abbey.

Fidelma was reflective on the journey back. Only once did Eadulf attempt to intervene in her thoughts.

'How did you know the physician was not from this area?' he asked. 'I've been puzzling that.'

'It was his curious name,' Fidelma replied shortly.

'His name?'

'It means a spectre.'

As they followed the path to the abbey, Eadulf kept silent, respecting the privacy of his wife's thoughts. Meeting an old friend of her student days should have brought some joy but it had not. She seemed depressed by it. Enda, too, had nothing to say. So they rode on in the silence, coming to the abbey as twilight was descending. Brother Dorchú, the gatekeeper, was preparing to shut the gates for the approaching evening and paused to acknowledge them as they rode by. At the stable entrance they were met by the stable master, Brother Eochaí, who greeted them with his familiar lopsided grin and took charge of their horses.

Eadulf and Enda went to their respective accommodations to wash before the evening meal while Fidelma went to find Abbot Daircell. The abbot was just leaving his herb garden and greeted her with an anxious look.

'Have you discovered anything?' he asked before she had a chance to greet him.

'I have no news of your cousin, Princess Gelgéis. However, Cétach, the pedlar, has been murdered.'

The abbot stared at her, momentarily shocked, and then crossed himself. 'God between us and all evil. Murdered, you say? Is this death connected to the Brehon's?'

Fidelma lowered herself to the wooden bench. 'I believe it is. He was killed in exactly the same way as Brehon Brocc. That makes a connection. But while we made enquiries in the township we have not been able to discover anything other than he was not a liked person.'

The abbot exhaled slowly. 'We have occasionally bought goods from him at this abbey but more from charity than liking him or his goods. Perhaps it is best not to say anything to the brethren, although I suspect the news will not be long spreading. It seems strange that Cétach was killed over a week after bringing the body of Brocc to this abbey. If that was cause of his being murdered, why not before?'

'Perhaps the killer knew that we had arrived here and were about to make enquiries. If the motive was just that he had found the body then I cannot understand it. I think he knew something else more dangerous, in addition to merely finding the body.'

'But it's a possibility that the killer did not realise that Cétach had brought the body here,' suggested the abbot.

Fidelma shook her head. 'Cétach probably told many people. I understand he had a loose tongue.'

'What do you plan to do now?'

'I have enlisted the aid of a local hunter and trapper, Teimel, to guide us along the valley to where Cétach apparently told him that he had found the body.'

'So Cétach told Teimel where he had found the body?' he demanded in surprise.

'As I said, I am told that Cétach was a person who could not keep secrets.'

'True enough,' muttered the abbot, but he was clearly worried.

'You seem dismayed that Teimel was told. Is something wrong with Teimel?' Fidelma asked.

'Not with Teimel himself, but his mother is a cause of trouble. She will make much of this matter.'

'Why?'

'She is an evil woman. It is best to shun her company.'

'Why is that?'

'She is an *ammait* and forbidden to enter any sanctified land in my keeping. I thought you had encountered her. His mother is Iuchra, a woman of supernatural powers; a woman in league with the Devil. Frequently local folk claim to have seen her among the mountains, appearing in many guises.'

Fidelma grinned in amusement. 'It seems shapeshifters are common in this country.'

'You should not make so light of it, lady. If you had heard the tales that I have heard . . .' the abbot protested.

Once again Fidelma was reminded of the importance that the abbot had placed on the beliefs held by local people in the solitary dark mountains of the area. It was all very well to talk generally but to accuse one specifically of being a shapeshifter was another matter.

'Yes, we have already encountered her,' she confirmed. 'She was warning about the devils that dwelt among the high peaks. Is there any reason for the accusation of her being in league with the Devil? I mean a specific reason in law as our native system does not recognise the concept of consorting with the folk of the Otherworld as a crime? If we make a law against the Old Religion then we would have to include the priests of the New Religion for consorting with their saints and martyrs in their Otherworld.'

The abbot hesitated a moment. 'It is the testimony of several people,' he said simply. 'People go to her to hear prophesies. That cannot be condoned. They testify she is in league with the powers of darkness.'

'Testimony from credible witnesses who saw specific instances?' Fidelma asked coldly.

'If you mean witnesses who actually saw a change with their own eyes, then I would have to say – no. But there are honest folk who heard from someone who—'

Fidelma exhaled angrily. 'You should know that a lawyer and a judge do not accept gossip without consideration of the actual facts. Even the very word for a witness means "one who sees" not "one who hears". The law states that a person can only give evidence about what he has *seen*. What does not take place before a witness's eyes is regarded as "dead".'

The abbot coloured. 'The law of the Roman Church does not agree with that.'

'Thankfully we are not yet ruled entirely by the law of the

Romans, which I know has been adopted by some ecclesiastics and is the basis for these Penitentials. I did not think that they were in usage here.'

The abbot was annoyed. 'This abbey is governed by the laws of this land,' he snapped. 'But many are turning to the new ways.'

'I will not accept hearsay in my judgment from any faction without corroborative evidence.'

The abbot's mouth pressed for a moment and then he shrugged. 'There is no disagreement between us, Fidelma. But one cannot help but listen to the opinions of many good townsfolk.'

'The next time they air their options, they should be asked for their evidence and be prepared to take an oath of its validity, for there are forms of vicarious oath taking, of perjury, or purgatory . . .'

The abbot held up his hand as he realised he might be on dangerous legal ground. 'I know, I know . . . I mentioned only about Iuchra as a means of telling you what is thought about her locally. She is to be avoided and not taken into your confidence. I meant nothing else.'

Fidelma eyed the man cynically. She was about to tell the abbot that his exclusion of Iuchra from the churches under his authority was unlawful, though she did not want to push the man into admitting what he had no means of escaping with some dignity. He would probably cite the new Penitential laws from Rome. However, it was Eadulf, arriving just then, who interrupted.

'As you are an expert on local folklore and customs, I wonder if you could explain a small matter. I have seen many habitations in the town and most of them, if not all, have a small sprig of furze above the main door, with yellow flowers. I wonder what it signifies. Is there some festival that we do not know of?'

The abbot paled slightly. 'You do not know?'

'That is why I ask,' replied Eadulf.

'An old custom of these parts. It's supposed to ward off bad spirits.'

'It does?' queried Fidelma.

'It is particularly meant as a protection against shapeshifters,' the abbot said sharply as if the words were reluctantly dragged from him.

He looked at her moodily, deciding to change the subject. 'So you are going to look at the spot where the Brehon's body was found. It is some time since the event occurred. Do you really think that there is anything that would be left now?'

'We won't know until we look. There was one thing I meant to ask. Your physician told me that the purse on the body was empty except for a pebble. It is curious that a Brehon had nothing in his purse but a pebble. The Brother Lachtna said he gave it to you. I do not imagine that you kept it.'

Abbot Daircell frowned. 'I had forgotten that.' He thought for a moment or two. 'It was just a pebble. I threw it away.' Fidelma was about to express her disappointment when his face lightened. 'No; I was sitting here with it when I sent for Brother Eochaí. When I spoke to him, I put it into my *bossán*.' He thrust his hand into the deep purse and felt about, finally emerging with what certainly looked like a small pebble.

Fidelma took it and examined it thoughtfully.

'It's certainly heavy. Not made of rock, although it looks like it.'

'It's probably a piece of metal,' the abbot dismissed.

'Metal?'

The abbot was not interested. 'So you are going to go wandering in the mountains and hoping to find . . . what?'

'Something. I know there is a slim hope. But we stand some chance because Cétach told Teimel where he found the body. And I'm hoping Teimel is a good tracker. Between him and my comrade Enda, they might be able to see much that we would not be able to.'

'I hope that Gelgéis has only been abducted and not suffered the same fate as her Brehon.' The abbot shuddered at the thought.

Fidelma did not comment. Instead she rose to her feet, still holding the heavy pebble. 'May I keep this for a while?' she asked.

The abbot shrugged indifferently.

She inclined her head in thanks. 'Then we shall depart for the mountains just before first light.'

CHAPTER ELEVEN

T he clang of the abbey bell to signal the time of the evening
meal had begun its summons when Fidelma and Eadulf emerged
from the guest quarters and joined the groups of brethren making
their way to the *praintech* or refectory. They were greeted at the
door by Brother Aithrigid, the steward. To one side, behind him,
was a small stone area, raised from the main floor of the refectory,
which gave entrance to a doorway that was obviously the abbey bell
tower, where one of the brethren was pulling on the rope. The gaunt
steward beckoned them to follow him to the far end of the hall.
There was a raised wooden platform, immediately recognisable as
where senior members of the brethren were seated. The length of
the hall was filled with long tables at which members of the community were sitting. Apparently the rules did not extend to excluding
female guests from dining with the brethren.

The hall itself was filled not only with the aroma of freshly
cooked meats, pies and vegetables, but with the overpowering smell
of scented candles. There were other more unpleasant aromas, too,
from the many bodies crammed into the small dining hall, for
although the rules on washing were strict and the *fothrucud*, or full
body wash, was performed daily before the evening meal, robes
and underclothing were only washed on a weekly basis and thus

odours still clung to their wearers and permeated the air in the heat and intimacy of communal dining.

Fidelma noticed that a chair at the head of the table at which they sat was empty. Brother Aithrigid offered an explanation to the unasked question. 'Abbot Daircell is taking his meal in his chamber this evening for he has much work to do. He begs forgiveness for his absence.'

They were now joined at this table by Brother Lachtna, the physician, and various leading members of the community whose names meant nothing to Fidelma and Eadulf, with the exception of Brother Dorchú, the gatekeeper, and Brother Eochaí, the master of the stables. In fact, as they entered they had realised that everyone was seated in total silence.

The bell had stopped its solemn toll and there suddenly came the quick tinkle of a higher note, this time from a handbell. Brother Aithrigid glanced at a small curtained alcove set high in the wall at the far end of the hall. He nodded, as if in agreement to something. Then he rose from his seat and, at this motion, everyone rose almost soundlessly with bowed heads.

'*Benedic nos, Domine, et haec tua dona, quae de tua largitate sumus sumpturi . . .*'

The *Gratias* was intoned in Latin by the brethren. The bell gave a single high chime. Then, as one, the brethren resumed their seats and attendants – young boys, presumably novices – started to bring round the hot dishes and already carved meats, demonstrating that this was not a community that adhered to vows of poverty. Bread, cheeses and fruits were already on the table. The idea of frugality with meals apparently had not been accepted as part of Abbot Daircell's rules for life in his abbey. The dishes that were served that evening consisted of both goat and pork, with boiled duck eggs and various choices of greens, all washed down with *íarlinn*, ale, which Eadulf found was rather inferior to what he was used to. He doubted whether the abbot contented himself with this and suspected that he would be drinking wine. He had seen some of the glazed amphorae outside the storehouse by the kitchen, and knew that native ships, as well as vessels from Gaul and Britain, did a thriving business around this part of the coast.

Unlike in many abbeys, there seemed no proscription of silence during the meals. Everyone had burst into animated conversations immediately after the *Gratias* had been intoned.

Those seated near Fidelma and Eadulf glanced at them as if waiting for them to make some remark. So when neither Fidelma nor Eadulf volunteered to open a conversation, it was the physician, Brother Lachtna, who turned to Fidelma.

'There is a rumour that the pedlar Cétach has been murdered,' he said. 'Didn't you go to see him this morning?'

Fidelma knew the abbot had asked her not to mention the death of the pedlar. It was a promise that she had kept, as had Eadulf and Enda.

The physician pursed his lips on seeing her non-responsive expression. 'No mystery in us knowing the news. You must know the ancient saying, lady. Rumours travel fast.'

'How did this one travel here?' she asked non-committally.

'They say that a story that is heard by three people is no secret.'

'Given that,' Fidelma observed, 'we have barely returned from the township of Láithreach and yet you say that this rumour is already acknowledged here. How is that?'

The physician smiled, although there was no humour in it. 'The physician from Láithreach, Síabair, arrived just before you. He had to come here to deliver some herbs that I had requested. I did not see him but I understand he left the herbs with the gatekeeper and was eager to impart the gossip.'

Fidelma suppressed a sigh. She had forgotten that in a small community, even though the abbey was considered isolated, most things were interconnected. She was surprised that the abbot had not thought of it either.

'The important matter is not the pedlar's death but the Brehon's death,' Brother Dorchú observed sharply. He had been sitting silent for a time with head lowered as if concentrating on his meal. 'Cétach's death probably has nothing to do with it. We know that the Osraige people would like to blame Laigin for some conspiracy or other. I believe that is why we have certain guests from Cashel among us.' He stared belligerently at Fidelma and Eadulf. 'Osraige seeks Cashel's help to claim a conspiracy against us!'

Brother Aithrigid was angry as he turned to the gatekeeper. 'Be cautious with your words. You should remember that the abbot is a noble of Osraige.'

'I know several who are of Osraige who have settled here,' snapped the gatekeeper. 'This abbey should have insisted on having our own Brehon, Brehon Rónchú, investigate the matter. In spite of the fact that you are of Osraige, you are a close friend of Rónchú. You should have sent for him, not allowed the abbot to send for someone outside the kingdom, especially one who has an obvious bias to Osraige and Muman.'

He had said the words in a heated tone. Before Fidelma could summon a response, the steward turned to the gatekeeper in stern rebuke.

'I would have thought you should be very concerned about the murder of the pedlar. You knew Cétach well, back in the days when you guarded the lead mines near here on behalf of the lord of The Cuala. Cétach was employed hauling the ore from the mines to the township.'

'I had little to do with him. He was just one of those who trans- ported the ore to the town. And that mine I guarded was closed a year or so ago, before I joined as a member of the brethren here. Why should I be concerned about Cétach? He was no friend of mine. All I say is that this is a matter that concerns Osraige and that the abbot and you are from Osraige.'

Brother Aithrigid was increasingly annoyed.

'So are many here. The master of the stables is from Osraige, as are others. It is a serious accusation that you are making, gate-keeper! Do you openly accuse your abbot of sending for Fidelma of Cashel so that she could come here and attempt to conceal something about the death of Brehon Brocc? What mystery or conspiracy do you suspect? That is insulting to the abbot as well as to the office of a *dálaigh*. If your accusations are not specific then I trust you will offer an apology.'

The muttered expressions of disapproval of the gatekeeper were not lost on him and it was obvious that his fellows felt he had gone too far. Brother Dorchú hesitated before turning to Fidelma.

'I meant no personal offence to you or anyone here. I apologise if I phrased things badly. It is simply that I feel that if a crime is committed locally, then it is surely the local Brehon, in whose jurisdiction it occurs, that should be consulted. Am I wrong in this conclusion?'

Fidelma gazed thoughtfully at the man for a moment or two, realising it was no use developing an argument against his insults. He had merely side-stepped it, turning it into an academic question rather than the accusation of bias that he had first meant. She wondered whether she should accept the diversion or go back to the original accusation.

'You are both right and wrong, Brother Dorchú,' she finally told him, not without some coldness in her tone, for insults cannot lightly be dismissed. 'In some crimes, the local judge should take control. But if an advocate or judge of senior rank or professional service is invited to do so, then they can take charge, no matter in which of the Five Kingdoms the infraction of the law is committed.' She paused for effect, a habit she had developed in making pleas in the courts. 'I am qualified to the level of *Anruth*. That degree allows me to be invited to make enquiries in most territories. I would like to think that I am sent here to help because my bias, as you call it, Brother Dorchú, is towards the path of justice. I was not invited to look into this matter by your abbot for any other reason.'

'I am sure that Brother Dorchú, who has now apologised, didn't really mean anything that would imply bias on your part, lady,' Brother Aithrigid said, apparently hoping to end the awkwardness. 'He has admitted that his words were ill chosen.'

Brother Dorchú did not look happy. He confirmed the matter with a grimace that had more of defiance in it than apology. 'As I have implied, it is merely my ignorance of the law that prompted the question. I do not have the legal mind that you have, Brother Aithrigid.'

At that moment one of the brethren came hurrying up and spoke directly to Brother Dorchú. He arose with an apology and some relief on his face.

'It seems there is a problem. A wandering wild boar is creating damage at the fencing. I am called to attend,' he said. 'Will you excuse me if I leave you to attend my duties?'

When he had gone, Eadulf observed with some irony in his voice: 'It seems you have a conscientious gatekeeper. From what I have heard, he is a man of these mountains and seems fond of telling people about the beliefs in demons that dwell in them.'

Brother Lachtna gave a derisive snort. 'I presume, at least,' he replied with dry humour, 'that folks here are not going to say that Cétach's death was also due to the Aos Sí?'

Brother Aithrigid cast him a withering look as he rose from the table. 'We know all about your cynicism, Brother Lachtna. The old beliefs run deep among the people here, as well you know. Remember that Dorchú was raised on Tóin le Gaoith, the mountain at the back of the wind. Many believe what Iuchra tells them.'

The physician sniffed disparagingly. 'Iuchra? The old woman gives a good entertainment with her stories of the Aos Sí and her warnings of retribution on whoever crosses their paths.'

'I would like to debate it, but my duties also call me,' the steward said, leaving them to finish their meal.

'You have not been alone among the high peaks,' Brother Gobbán, the abbey's smith, said. He had hardly spoken before. 'I have, and was born and brought up on the slopes of these dark mountains. I also grew up on the slopes of Tóin le Gaoith. I know the spirits of evil guard them.'

'The mountain at the back of the wind?' mused Fidelma. 'Is that near here?'

'Close by,' confirmed the smith. 'It is one of the highest of the mountains here and we have many stories—'

'Keep the stories for those who want to be entertained by them,' sneered Brother Lachtna. 'Anyway, one would expect more sense from one trained as a warrior.'

'You are talking of Brother Dorchú?' asked Eadulf with interest.

'He was one of the lord of The Cuala's warriors before he joined the brethren,' confirmed the physician. 'He was trained, but I do not think he was held in high regard. He was appointed to guard the lead mines near here and when they fell into disuse he was set to watch over the stored metals from neighbouring mines until they were ready to be shipped. All he had to do was sit outside a bolted door all day and sometimes at night too.'

'So it was boredom that caused him to join you?' Eadulf queried mischievously. 'Not religion?'

'Boredom?' Brother Gobbán laughed hollowly. 'He saw things . . . and I believe him when he says so.'

'It doesn't help that the old hag Iuchra was always about with her tales of doom and gloom,' the physician observed with resignation. 'Abbot Daircell encourages her.'

'Abbot Daircell says he is recording folklore,' cut in Brother Gobbán. 'Such ancient knowledge is sacrosanct and should not be written down.'

'Especially when he is from Osraige?' the physician said in amusement. 'Just as Iuchra is. Superstition is not confined to one place.'

The smith sniffed. 'The Cuala mountains cast their shadows over all our lives, whether we live north, west, south or east of them. So there is no significance as to where their shadows fall.'

Eadulf turned to him with a look of interest. 'Coming from the mountains here, you must know all about these legends?'

'I know many of the legends,' replied the smith.

'The Aos Sí,' Eadulf said. 'I thought they were just the former gods and goddesses who had been vanquished by the New Faith?'

Brother Gobbán assumed the manner of a master addressing pupils. 'The Aos Dána were the old deities. But they say that the Aos Sí, the phantasms of the mountains, have always dwelt in the caverns that lie deep below The Cuala, and only started to stir when the New Faith drove the good gods and goddesses into the hills.'

'And this is believed by many in this region?'

Brother Lachtna chuckled. 'Only by some,' he said, glancing at the smith. 'In fact, if the truth were known, I believe that some of the local nobles propagated the idea to protect their property.'

'In what way can this protect their property?' Eadulf asked, missing the point.

'When you have mines rich in metal ores, they are often difficult places to guard from theft,' replied Brother Lachtna. 'Ask our friend Brother Dorchú when you next see him. But stories of the Aos Sí seeking vengeance on humankind . . . well, that is a different story.'

'So who owns the mines in these mountains?' Fidelma asked.

'Well, each local chieftain governs his own territory but they have to pay tribute to the lord of The Cuala, to Dicuil Dóna of the Uí Máil. All the gold and silver is his to dispose of. I have heard many of the chieftains encourage old Iuchra to spread her stories. The more she can frighten folk with bizarre tales the better they like it.'

'I, too, maintain that she is encouraged by the local chieftains,' Brother Eochaí suggested. He had been quiet some time. 'I suspect even the lord of The Cuala himself pays her.'

'What were the local mines that Brother Dorchú mentioned? Are they still worked?' Fidelma asked.

'This area is rich in metals,' Brother Lachtna replied. 'You will find many mines here – not just iron, lead and copper, but silver and gold. Was it not said that Tigernmas was the first to have the smiths of The Cuala smelt gold, over a thousand years ago? Look at the great granite mountains that surround you. It is around the edges of the granite that you will find such metal ore. The nobles who discovered these metals were quick to exploit them. Whole caves in the mountains were excavated and from the north side of the mountain of Céim an Doire through to this valley many tunnels were made. Metal is precious and has made the nobles here rich.'

Brother Gobbán grimaced sourly. 'These mines do not make this abbey wealthy.'

'And do not forget this is the territory of the Uí Máil, the family of Fianamail mac Máele Tuile, our king,' Brother Lachtna added meaningfully as he also rose. 'The Uí Máil guard their wealth as a mother guards her new-born child.'

'I thought the Uí Máil capital was in Fearna, to the south?' queried Eadulf.

The physician shook his head. 'The real power of the Uí Máil is not with King Fianamail in Fearna but with his uncle. If you cross the mountains a short distance to the west, you will come to an isolated valley called Gleann Uí Máil. That is the chief territory of the Uí Mail. It is there that Dicuil Dóna, the uncle of the King, has his stronghold. His control of The Cuala mountains is such that hardly anything passes among them without his knowledge of it.'

Fidelma glanced thoughtfully at the physician. 'I did not know this.'

Brother Lachtna smiled quickly. 'Dicuil Dóna is a power to be reckoned with. Some say that he would have made a better king than his nephew, Fianamail.'

'So one could presume that he should know about the finding

of the body of Brehon Brocc and any activity of brigands in the mountains that might have led to it?'

Brother Lachtna said, 'Well, you can be assured that the lord of The Cuala has informers throughout the mountains.'

'Some folk speak of him with hushed tones,' admitted the smith, Brother Gobbán, with a dramatic shiver. 'It is said that he knows of things before they happen.'

Brother Lachtna began to smile but Eadulf cut in: 'You were talking of the belief in the Aos Sí. Are you saying that people see some connection with the lord of The Cuala and malignant spirits?'

'There are many folk who have not truly embraced the New Faith and new thinking,' Brother Eochaí answered dryly.

'Is one of them this lord of The Cuala?' pressed Eadulf.

Brother Gobbán was uncomfortable now. 'Dicuil Dóna is a descendant of Laignich Faelann,' he said, as if the name had meaning.

Eadulf glanced at Fidelma for enlightenment but she shrugged; the name meant nothing to her.

'What is the significance of that name?' Eadulf asked the smith.

Brother Gobbán glanced round as if nervous that someone would overhear him. 'According to the old scribes, Laignich Faelann lived a century ago. By the accounts he was the Laigin King who made himself Lord of Osraige for a time. On certain days, when twilight fell, when the evening frost began to settle among the mountains of The Cuala, he was said to assume the form of a wolf and go hunting in the mountains, returning to his body before dawn with the red meat and blood of his kill on him.'

Brother Lachtna began to chuckle. 'Stories from ancient times! Half-wits with delusions of being dogs. Peasants with irrational fears of evil spirits. People have used the idea to instil fear into their enemies since the time beyond time. Any warriors will tell you that the Fianna used to howl like wolves as they ran into battle. It was said to bring fear to the timid. So are all such stories. Fantasy, that is all.'

Brother Gobbán glowered. 'If such things did not exist, then why is it that our legends and the stories told around the fire at night are full of cynanthropy and shapeshifting? What about the story of the daughters of Airitecht?'

Again, Eadulf did not know the story and said so.

Fidelma was tired by the subject but felt she should explain. 'The story is that Airitecht had three daughters. On a certain night, usually on feast of Samhain, they would change into wolves and go into the countryside and feast on sheep. The shepherds and farmers called on a famous hero of the Fianna, the High King's bodyguard, called Cailte, son of Ronán, to save their flocks. They asked him to track down the three she-wolves. It was said that they were fond of music and that it caused them to shapeshift back into their original human forms. So Cailte asked a famous harper, Cos Corach, to join him as a companion on the hunt. They found the she-wolves and Cos Corach started to play. As they changed shape into humans, Cailte threw his spears. He killed all three. The shepherds were never troubled thereafter.'

Brother Lachtna chuckled. 'It's just one of a number of similar stories to fill the winter nights. It's a story to scare children.'

Brother Gobbán rose to his feet with an expression of extreme annoyance. 'You believe what you will, I do not mock you for those beliefs. Just have some respect and do not mock others until you know better.' He began to turn away from the table, then hesitated and then turned back, frowning at Fidelma.

'One thing, lady; you were asking about Dicuil Dóna of the Uí Máil. As you have been told, he is a descendant of Laignich Faelann. Further, it is said that he has inherited the abilities of his shapeshifter ancestor. I would say, if you wanted to know what happened to the Brehon and his companions, then seek answers at the dark fortress of Dicuil Dóna.'

The smith turned abruptly and made his way out of the feasting hall.

Brother Lachtna was chuckling. 'I suppose you hardly imagined finding a senior member of the brethren who has barely moved from the old superstitions.'

'It happens, my friend,' Brother Eochaí said, in the process of rising. Then he paused. 'Stories are quickly spread, lady.'

'I am interested in this lord Dicuil Dóna.' Fidelma turned to the stable master. 'Perhaps Brother Gobbán has a point that the lord of The Cuala might have knowledge of what happened to Princess Gelgéis? Any person who can engender the sort of respect and fear in the smith, whether it is based on beliefs of evil spirits or not, should be worthy of a visit.'

Brother Eochaí gazed at her in some surprise.

'Are you saying that you are prepared to cross the mountains to try to see Dicuil Dóna, lord of The Cuala? I would not advise it.'

'Why not? You don't surely believe that this noble is a werewolf?'

Brother Eochaí flushed indignantly. 'Of course not. But he is a man with a bad reputation. They call his fortress Dún Droch Fhola – the fortress of bad blood – for much blood was shed there as the Uí Máil rose to power. It is a place to shun, and the lord of The Cuala is a man that should be shunned.'

'You intrigue me even more,' Fidelma smiled.

'I have no wish to intrigue you, lady, only to give you warning. Dicuil Dóna is an evil man, wild and profane, caring neither for God nor the Devil. He is a man of dark passions, it is true. No true member of the religious will enter that glen of darkness where his fortress rises.'

'Then it is good that I have left the religious and am not likely to be a saint,' Fidelma, not disguising her sarcasm.

'I have given warning in good faith,' Brother Eochaí said indignantly.

'And it was received in good faith, Brother,' Fidelma replied. She rose, followed by Eadulf. They were conscious of the physician staring after them as they crossed to the doors and left the feasting hall.

Outside, Eadulf turned to her. 'Are you really interested in going to meet this Lord Dicuil? Isn't it dangerous that he is of the Uí Máil and you are of the Eóganacht, families who have long been enemies?'

'I would not have mentioned it if I were not serious,' Fidelma replied dryly.

'What if he is all the things he is claimed to be?'

Fidelma chuckled in surprise. 'You mean a werewolf?'

'You know I don't mean that.' Eadulf was piqued. 'I mean, what if he controls these mountains and the disappearance of Princess Gelgéis is his responsibility? Aren't we putting ourselves in danger?'

'The sooner we find that out, the better. So far we have had no leads at all. If this lord Dicuil Dóna knows anything at all then we have nothing to lose in going to find him.'

'I'd say we have much to lose. For example, our freedom, on the one hand, and perhaps our lives on the other.'

'Don't worry, Eadulf. We will not go rushing up to his fortress gates and ask what he has done with Princess Gelgéis. You know me better than that.'

It was the very fact that Eadulf did know her intemperate moods so well that worried him. She made her way towards the guests' residence. So he contented himself with a dismissive rise and fall of one shoulder to indicate his compliance and then followed.

CHAPTER TWELVE

It was still dark the next morning when Fidelma, Eadulf and Enda walked their horses through the abbey gates. The oil in the gate lantern was running low but still gave enough illumination to guide them across the bridge. They could also see thin rays of light glimmering over the eastern peaks as they crossed the little stream that surrounded the abbey and the lakes. By the time they reached the main track where they were due to meet Teimel, the morning sky had become speckled with clouds of a pinkish hue turning red here and there with a warning of the weather to come. In fact, the weather had, so far, not been typical for the time of year. It had been mild. Usually they would expect to be passing through boisterous winds and unsettled conditions. Fidelma felt that the turbulence would be starting soon, with short bursts of rain interspersed with sunny spells so that, with rising temperatures, early spring flowers would begin to appear.

They had reached the main track and halted, peering round for Teimel. Fidelma felt impatient when there was no sign of him, and she was about to make a remark when the hunter emerged unexpectedly from the dark trees that lined the track. He did not greet them but merely pointed northward.

'We will cross through this forest. There is an easy ford across the river of watercress. It is called such as there is a preponderance of cress around it. Then we will join the main track. It runs on the north side of the river all the way along the valley to the spot where Cétach said he found the body.'

'You are the guide,' acknowledged Fidelma. 'We will follow your lead.'

The sky was brighter now, or as bright as the altocumulus clouds, now stretching across the sky, would allow. They reflected the red dappled sunlight as the sun itself had not yet fully risen above the mountain peaks.

They fell quiet as the hunter led the way along the track that crossed over the shoulder of a tall mountain into the valley of Glasán. Teimel made directly to the river bank, leading to a ford. Once safely across, they turned north-west, following the bank of the fast-flowing river. Teimel occasionally raised his head, almost as if he was sniffing at the air. He seemed sensitive to his surroundings and was not disturbed when a wild boar emerged on the path ahead of them. It turned in their direction, examining them with wicked tiny red eyes and sharp threatening tusks, before tossing its head disdainfully. With a loud grunt, it turned and trotted back into the forest. It was clear that the track was one well used, and Teimel reminded them that it was a straight route through the mountains to the border of Osraige. For this reason Fidelma examined their route carefully.

The forest now seemed to crowd in around the river, which snaked through the valley bottom, in the shadows of the mountain that the hunter called Céim an Doire on the one side, and the slopes of another peak called 'mountain of badgers' on the opposite side of the river. The water, though shallow, flowed roughly, with a lot of white water as the course was over a rocky bed. They were approaching a bend where groups of alders – common in such areas, where their strong fibrous roots helped keep the river bank secure – obscured their forward view.As they were emerging into an open area of grassland, which pushed back on both sides of the river, Teimel halted and signalled that the others do likewise.

'Someone is approaching on horseback along the track,' he told them quietly. 'We'll wait here until they have passed.'

Whoever the approaching rider was, they were certainly not stealthy. The animal was blowing and dragging its hoofs so that twigs underfoot were scattered noisily. Fidelma's party waited patiently for the animal and its rider to approach through the trees. When they came into the clear patch Eadulf was the first to recognise a mule, not a horse, with the old woman astride it.

'It's Iuchra!'

Teimel turned with a frown. 'You know her?'

'We have encountered her twice,' Eadulf explained with a rueful grin. 'She was in Láithreach just before we met you. I tried to help her on to her mule and was not thanked for my pains.'

'She is a proud woman,' Teimel replied. 'What made you go to her assistance?'

Eadulf quickly related the circumstances. Fidelma suddenly realised that Eadulf had not been there when the abbot mentioned that Iuchra was Teimel's mother. She decided, out of curiousness, to see if the hunter would acknowledge the fact.

By this time the old woman had reached them and was staring suspiciously at the group.

'Good day to you, my son,' she called to Teimel.

'I presume you have been delivering food to mountain folk, Mother,' Teimel greeted her with a smile. 'How are they?'

The old woman made an inarticulate grunting sound in the back her throat. Then she wiped her mouth and nose with the back of her shawl and coughed disdainfully.

'They still live, my son.' Her tone was one of amusement. 'Did you think otherwise?'

'That is good to hear, Mother,' returned the hunter. 'Folk like that deserve all the support we of the mountain community can give them. It would be a great shame if ill befell them.'

'I do my best to look after them,' the old woman said with a tired shrug.

'Indeed you do, and you are thanked for it,' agreed Teimel. 'I am sure that your charity will be met with a full reward.' He hesitated and then added: 'But I am glad to hear your charges want for nothing. They are all well, you say?'

'They are well,' the old woman agreed.

'That is good. Safe home, Mother.'

The old woman negotiated her tired-looking beast through the group and continued on down the valley towards the settlement.

Eadulf was puzzled. 'You addressed her as "Mother" and she addressed you as "son". That wasn't just a polite term because of age,' he said to Teimel.

'Iuchra is his mother,' explained Fidelma.

The tall hunter grimaced. 'I do not boast of it. I have disowned her stories of shapeshifters and supernatural beings. I have no wish to be associated with such things, so I greet her formally but wish for no other contact.'

'One is not always responsible for one's relatives,' Enda contributed.

'I know how lawyers' minds work,' Teimel said stiffly. 'So I will tell you this: I was born and raised here in The Cuala. My mother is from the Osraige side of the mountains. She is wise in the ways of healing herbs but she is also a believer in the Old Faith. For all three differences she is whispered about, even by people who use her to frighten their children into obedience.'

'It should be a matter of no concern where people are from but who they are,' replied Fidelma easily. 'Eadulf, my husband, came as a stranger to this land. He studied at Tuaim Brecain and is also wise in the way of healing herbs. He wears the tonsure of the

Blessed Peter of Rome and not that of the Blessed John, which the religious use in these kingdoms. So all that you say about your mother could equally be said about Eadulf. There is no need to defend yourself.'

At this, Teimel unbent a little. 'Well, I can see why you are a lawyer, Fidelma of Cashel. You can certainly counter any arguments with logic.'

'Only when logic and justice dictate. The New Faith came to us only two centuries ago. Once, everyone believed in the Old Faith. That was a faith that was here in the time beyond time. It seemed many decided that the faith of the people in countries to the east was more appealing. It is often foreign to us. But who can truly say which is the right path to follow?'

Eadulf frowned slightly. He was always uncomfortable with Fidelma's liberal attitude to the New Faith. He had been raised, as a hereditary *gerefa*, or magistrate of his people, and followed the old gods and goddesses of the Angles – Tyr, the one-handed hero; Woden; Thunor, god of thunder; Freya, goddess of death, and others. His father had frightened him into obedience as a child by threats of the ravening moon hound, Garn. But he had been converted by missionaries of the New Faith from the Five Kingdoms led by Fursa and his brothers. He had then attended Tuaim Brecain, the famous school of medicine in the kingdom of Connacht. Eadulf had finally decided to make a pilgrimage to Rome, been impressed, and opted to follow the Roman interpretation of the New Faith. So it was, at the Council in Hilda's Abbey, as one of the delegates from the Roman faction of the Faith led by Wilfrid, that he had met Fidelma. She had been advising on law to the advocates of native churches of the Faith. Now and then, he worried about Fidelma's tolerance to the old ways. Perhaps this was because he was a convert himself and often found himself uncomfortable with thoughts of the old gods and goddesses.

'But you are uncomfortable with your mother's talk of the old gods?' Eadulf asked Teimel.

'Uncomfortable?' The hunter was stony faced. 'I am a member of the True Faith. The local people are even more pagan than she is, for all their piousness about the New Faith. They pay to hear her prophecies – the fools!'

'Is that how she is able to buy food to take up the mountain to poorer folk?' Fidelma asked with abrupt curiosity. 'It is an act of generosity.'

There was a moment's hesitation before the hunter replied, 'Local people, relatives in the township, contribute and she takes it up the mountain. Now we must push on.'

They moved on through the encroaching trees, skirting the bank of the river just below on their left. The day was growing warmer although the sunshine above the trees was still pale. There was movement in a clearing by the river. Fidelma was the first to spot a group of red hinds drinking at the water's edge, watched over by a magnificent red-brown stag.

Teimel immediately raised his hand to stop his companions, recognising the great muscular stag was guarding his harem. The beast was giving curious snorts, which the hunter knew were both warning and challenge. The stag raised his head up and slightly back, the nostrils flaring as he tried to identify the danger. With a quick snort, the hinds were warned and turned, dashing into the forest as the stag gave a disdainful look around and bellowed a couple of times before chasing after his harem.

Fidelma and her companions seemed to wait a long time before Teimel indicated it was safe for them to proceed. Fidelma knew that it was never a wise thing to ride near where a stag was watching over the hinds while they were watering and nursing their young.

As the travellers emerged into the small open grassland vacated by the small deer herd they could see the trackway was some short distance from the river bank, where generations of users had cut across the open stretches.

'This is the bend described to me by Cétach,' Teimel said, pointing.

'The body, as far as I can judge from his description, was lying on that far bank.'

Enda had been examining the area and now grimaced wryly.

'I don't think we'll have much luck finding anything of significance here, lady. Look at the way the deer herd has almost ploughed the entire area as they gathered to drink at the river. It has been many days since the body was found. I'd say this point was used as a waterhole for many animals.' He looked at Teimel as if for confirmation.

'You have that right,' Teimel agreed. 'This has always been a good place for animals to water as the lack of trees dispenses with the steeper banks and makes it easier for them to reach the river.'

Fidelma suggested that they spread themselves around the area to see what they could find, but the search proved useless. They found nothing of interest that would help them about the death of Brehon Brocc. Fidelma soon realised that it would be time wasting to continue and so she asked Teimel to lead them back across the shallow river and continue north-westward on the main path, which, a little way on, rose to form a higher path.

'As this is where the body was found,' Teimel pointed out, 'is there any point to searching further on?'

Fidelma had already admitted to herself that it was probably a fruitless task, but she could not help thinking that there was a logic in widening the search. If Princess Gelgéis's party had been ambushed at the point they had searched, then surely there would be something for the sharp eye of Enda to spot. Perhaps simple tracks showing which way a small body of horse riders had been taken away from the scene. She said as much to Eadulf before telling Enda and Teimel to keep a sharp look out for anything they could not make sense of that might be relevant.

She allowed them to continue to search for a short while before voicing the inevitable conclusion: 'It doesn't look as if there's anything to help us in our quest.' Then her eye caught something.

'What is that on the far side, further up the hill, among the trees? It looks like a cave entrance and some huts.'

'It's an old working of the *lucht a cladhi* – one of the mines of these mountains,' Teimel replied. 'They have long since been abandoned. There are plenty of them around here.'

'Mines? What type of mines?' she asked, remembering the 'pebble' of metal that Brother Lachtna had said had been carried by Brocc.

Teimel grinned. 'If you think that is one of the old gold or silver workings, you are going to be disappointed. It produced nothing but *lúaide* – lead.'

'I wasn't after gold or silver,' Fidelma replied. 'Perhaps we should explore the mine as, even when deserted, such places often reveal something.'

Teimel was not enthusiastic. 'There are many such workings.'

'As this one is so near to where you say Cétach found the body, it might well be worth examining,' she replied.

The hunter gave a slight shrug, which she had noticed was a characteristic of his. Then he led the way across the shallow waters to the far bank, where they dismounted, having made sure there were no longer any boars or stags to contend with. The largest mammals in the area now seemed to be a few mountain hares, which was unusual because they normally fed at night. It showed that they had not built up any fears of predators who had the ability to slay them from afar and of which there was only one species: man. It also indicated that these buildings were long abandoned.

It did not need more than a cursory glance to see the mine was little more than an open area where the miners had dug only the surface granite rock of the mountains. A glance revealed no depth to the cave entrance. It was merely a shadowy indent. Nothing was hidden. There was no sign of recent use.

'There might be more caves around that outcrop further along,' Enda pointed out.

'There are many deserted areas like this,' Teimel said. 'You could be looking for years. I would have thought it is best to see if there are signs on the other side of the river.'

Fidelma agreed it would be better to search near where the body had been found. With her consent, they turned and rode back down towards the river.

Not a rustle in the undergrowth, not the faintest whisper of a movement in the air warned them before three arrows struck at precisely the same moment. One penetrated the centre of the path before them, while, of the other two, one embedded itself in the pommel of Eadulf's saddle and the other in almost exactly the same position in Enda's saddle.

An imperious voice called from the cover of the undergrowth of the dark woods, 'Halt! Stay still! One movement towards your weapons and you are all dead!'

Teimel had already summed up the peril of their situation and held his hands palms outwards and away from his sides. Enda glanced at Fidelma, as if he needed her confirmation, but she had also spread her hands, palm outwards, so he followed her example. Eadulf had no choice but to copy them.

The harsh authoritative voice came again. 'Remain on your horses and do not try to do anything stupid. Keep your hands where they can be seen at all times.'

There was a silence and no movement from the undergrowth to betray the position of their assailants, not even the slightest brush of a tuft of grass. The moment of shock was over and Fidelma raised her voice in a commanding tone.

'Know that you have stopped a *dálaigh* in the pursuit of the King's justice.'

'The question arises – which king?' the same voice asked in a sardonic tone.

'All kings are answerable to the law of the people,' returned Fidelma. 'So you may say that I represent the law of the people as administered by the Brehons of the Five Kingdoms and under the jurisdiction of kings from all the provinces to the High King himself.'

'Not every king is welcome in these mountains,' came the reply. 'So we shall see which king you represent.'

'The interests of the law should be welcome in any place,' she retorted, controlling her astonishment that the words implied some knowledge that she was not of the kingdom of Laigin.

There was a snort of dismissal from the voice beyond the bushes.

'It is said that lawyers will talk the hind leg off a mule. I am not interested in philosophy. In a moment my men will come to relieve you of your weapons. You will oblige me by making no moves. Keep your hands as they are now. I trust you have understood that my men are excellent bowmen? Your lives hang by a simple jerk of the fingers on a taut string. In a moment you will hear a hunter's horn. Do not respond. Remain still.'

Fidelma did not bother to answer as the man had mentioned the arrows. She had suddenly focused on the arrow protruding from the pommel of Enda's saddle. It was disturbingly familiar. She glanced quickly to the missile embedded in Eadulf's saddle. It was the same. It was fletched with feathers dyed brightly blue and white.

They sat in silence and a moment later there came three short notes sounded on a hunting horn, which almost startled them in spite of the warning. The notes were long and low, and while their horses flicked their ears and snorted and jerked their heads, they did not move nor precipitated their riders into any action. Almost before the sounds died away, half a dozen riders appeared from the shelter of the trees on the far side of the river and rode directly across to them. The water barely came up to the hocks of the hind legs of their horses, showing there was a ford at this point and perhaps that was why the ambush had been placed there.

Eadulf was watching their approach and assessing the way they held themselves and the weapons they carried. Now that he could see their demeanour he realised that these were disciplined warriors. As the men urged their mounts up the shallow bank, it was obvious they knew their profession. They approached from behind so that they did not obstruct the bodies of their prisoners from the bowmen still concealed in front of them. They moved from the river side to the stationary horses, making for Enda and Teimel first, carrying sacks for them to put their weapons in before making for Fidelma and Eadulf. Fidelma saw they were cautious, even to reaching forward to pluck the arrows from the pommels and put those with the confiscated weapons safely in the sacks. They eased their horses backwards, keeping everyone in sight and showing their skills as riders, and that their horses were well trained. At no time did they give their prisoners opportunity to make an assault.

There came a word of command and, at the same time, a stocky man led three bowmen from the bushes before them. The bowmen each had their longbows strung, the arrows ready and pointing unerringly to the prisoners. The leader came forward to where the first arrow was still rooted in the track before them. He bent and picked it up and stood toying with it in his hands as he examined his prisoners with a faint, almost derisive smile.

He had long black hair, streaked with a little grey from the forehead and temples. His skin was weather-beaten, showing he was used to the outdoor life and his dark eyes had a peculiar intensity as they seemed to possess no pupils. He was clad in a warrior's leather jerkin and trousers, with a finely embroidered linen shirt, a silver chain around his neck, and an ornate scabbard round his waist, showing the bejewelled hilt of the sword that it enclosed. He halted before them and stood, feet splayed apart, his hands quietly turning over the arrow before him.

There came an involuntary expression of recognition as the man glanced at Teimel, which caused Fidelma to look quickly in the direction of their guide. It was clear that Teimel had recognised the man too. A smile slowly spread over the features of the ambusher.

'Well, well, Teimel. I did not know you were of this company.'

The hunter briefly inclined his head towards the man. 'Greetings, Corbmac,' he replied shortly.

'In what capacity are you among these folk?' the leader of the ambushers went on, speaking in a pleasant tone as if passing the time as one might when meeting a friend unexpectedly on the highway.

'I am their guide through the mountains. Well you know my skills.'

There were a few moments' silence and then the man called Corbmac shrugged.

'Your reputation is well known, Teimel. If that is all your role is here then I have no need to delay you. You may take your weapons and return to Láithreach.'

Eadulf cast a puzzled glance at their erstwhile guide. The question raced through his mind: had the man betrayed them into this ambush? But an ambush by whom and for what?

Teimel was leaning forward to the leader and spoke with deliberateness. 'Corbmac, I think you insult me.'

'Insult?' queried the leader with amusement. 'How so?'

'You know me, so you say. You know that I was once a warrior and swore a warrior's oath. Oaths are sacred things. You should know that. So when I say that I have undertaken a task, I do so to the best of my ability and see the undertaking of the task as an oath that I will perform it. My *minn*, my oath, is my honour and I will not violate it for any reason. So I will remain with the people I have given my word to act as guide to.'

Fidelma interrupted by turning to him. 'If these people are offering you freedom, Teimel, you are under no obligation to remain with us.'

'No obligation except my honour, lady,' the hunter declared firmly. 'I will stay.'

At this, the man called Corbmac gave Fidelma a close scrutiny.

'Lady? So you are not just a lawyer? My thanks, Teimel, for confirming the rank of your companion. I have given you the opportunity to depart in peace but if you insist you shall accompany us. One last opportunity . . . do you still wish to remain?'

Teimel grimaced. 'I thought I had spoken clearly enough. I stay with my companions as I am honour bound to do.'

'Well, you must do as your honour bids you, and as you are bound by your honour it now binds you as my prisoner. Very well.' He turned back to Fidelma. 'There are rumours that a *dálaigh* from Cashel is making enquiries among The Cuala; that she is accompanied by a warrior and a Saxon religieux. I learn that this lawyer is addressed with the respect due to one of high birth. Will you confirm your identity yourself?'

'Do you not think that the onus is on you to introduce yourself?' countered Fidelma.

The man scowled. 'I suggest you identify yourself so that our time is not wasted.'

Fidelma realised there was no point in pursuing the etiquette of the encounter.

'I will do so as there is no secrecy on my part,' she said with emphasis. 'I am Fidelma of Cashel. I hold the degree of *Anruth*. I can sit before the High King without his permission. Such is my status. So who are you and what status do you hold to stop my passage?'

The man, who had been named Corbmac by Teimel, now raised his brows slightly and his smile broadened.

'Then our information is right,' he said in satisfaction. 'I have heard of you, Fidelma of Cashel. You are not just a *dálaigh*, but the sister of Colgú, King of Muman, and enemy to the Uí Máil of Laigin. I was sent to find out why there was a lawyer from Cashel. So you are your brother's spy?'

'Not so,' Fidelma replied hotly. 'I and my companions are not spies.'

'Why else are you here, if not to spy?'

'You are talking to a *dálaigh* of the courts, one who has served several High Kings. You are engaged in an action that is not without repercussions,' she warned. 'You know who I am. This is Eadulf of Seaxmund's Ham, whom you may know to be my husband. With us is Enda, my bodyguard . . .'

'And all spies?' sneered the man. 'Now you and your companions will have to accompany me to the fortress of my lord. You can come bound or I will accept your word not to escape.'

'If we are your prisoners, then there is no need for our word to be given to you,' snapped Fidelma.

'Prisoners?' smiled the man. 'Oh, no. We are inviting you to be our guests. Perhaps we are a little forceful with the invitation, that I will grant you, but we do insist that you be guests and partake of our hospitality.'

'And if we refuse?'

'That would hurt me very much for it would mean I would have to increase the force that I am already exerting. It might even be that one of your companions, that dour-faced Saxon there, might be required to come to a close study of the art of combat. Personally, I do not think he would stand much of a chance.'

'You realise that violence against a *dálaigh* and any member of their party is unlawful on many points, irrespective of rank?'

'The main point is that you are here in a territory where you do not belong. That is point enough for me to apprehend you and take you before my lord to question you.'

'Your claim that we are spying is spurious. So now you question me for what purpose?'

'We would have to be shown proof of your claim.' The man was now clearly growing impatient. 'That will be done in the fortress of my lord.'

'And your lord is . . .?'

'My lord is Dicuil Dóna of the Uí Máil, lord of all The Cuala,' was the unpromising response. 'I am Corbmac, commander of his warriors.'

Corbmac turned and gave a sharp order and, from the shelter of the bushes, another warrior appeared leading five horses. Corbmac mounted while his bowmen replaced their arrows in their quivers, loosened their bowstrings and then mounted, too. Once again, Eadulf was impressed by the proficiency with which this was done and was aware that even in that moment, the guards behind had unsheathed their swords to pre-empt any movement if the prisoners attempted to escape.

Eadulf drew his features into a droll expression, glancing at Fidelma.

'Well, you did say that you wanted to have a talk with this noble. It seems our friends have saved you the trouble of looking for him,' he said with irony.

Fidelma wondered if Eadulf had noticed the same design of arrows as the one taken from the body of Brehon Brocc; the brass heads and the fletching. More importantly, she had noticed that Corbmac was left handed.

Corbmac gestured them forward to cross the ford of the river. On the other side they began to ascend through the forest along a path that was at first broad until reaching beyond the tree line, where it became a single track. They had to lean forward in the saddle to maintain balance and Corbmac eventually ordered them to dismount to make the way easier to cross the shoulder of the mountain.

The high hills were quite spectacular and Fidelma spotted little lakes and pools among them. One lake was quite large, even though it stood at such a high elevation. They pushed on slowly up through the breathtaking scenery. Now and then they saw grazing flocks of sheep but no sign of any shepherd. As they began to descend again into more sheltered wooded countryside, it was Eadulf who raised a protest to the grim-faced leader.

'Allow us to stop for refreshment,' he called. 'We have been travelling since first light and I see dusk descending behind us.'

Corbmac glanced back with a callous grin. 'You are weak, Saxon,' he observed viciously. 'My men could ride all night without fatigue.'

'I am no warrior; that is true. But I am no Saxon,' Eadulf snapped.

'I have heard enough Saxon spoken in the eastern seaports. I know their grating accent and words. You even wear the tonsure of the Roman religieux. You are a Saxon.'

'I am an Angle from the kingdom of the East Angles,' Eadulf returned sharply.

'Angles, Saxons, no difference,' dismissed the warrior.

Eadulf scowled, his face reddening as his voice rose in a vehemence that surprised his companions. 'My patience is exhausted with constantly being insulted. I am an Uffingas. We are the descendants of Uffa, son of Wehha, direct descent of Kjárr, fourth son of Woden, and his wife, Frigg. It was Uffa that led our people across the great sea to the land of the Welisc, the foreigners, and drove them westward, creating the kingdom that is called that of the East Angles. We are not Saxons!'

Corbmac stared at him with a look halfway between surprise and amusement. He began to reply but Fidelma spoke softly, seeing the glint in the warrior's eyes.

'Remember, Corbmac, Eadulf is my husband and accepted into the family of the Eóganacht. Among his own people he was an hereditary *gerefa*, which is the equivalent of a *dálaigh*. Do nothing rash against the Eóganacht and their kin, for the law of *dígal* still applies.'

Corbmac's eyes narrowed slightly as he turned this over in his mind. He did not know whether Fidelma was exaggerating or not. *Dígal*, or vengeance, was often used for a blood feud when the kin of a family member killed by an outsider did not receive or accept the fines and honour-price payment. Then he shrugged, smiled and said: 'Very well, Angle, if it pleases you better.' Then he turned away and called to his men. 'The hour does grow late and darkness will eventually be upon us. We will camp here overnight.'

The trees protected them from the winds that swept across the mountain in gusts while also providing dry wood to kindle fires, and a selection of nuts and berries. There were acorns and beech nuts lying about, and the red flash of rowan berries were still on the trees as well as an odour from wild garlic plants. Even the green leaves of the hawthorn were in their edible stage, for they had yet to unfurl and toughen into unpalatable. A stream, rising somewhere higher on the mountain, meandered down through the wood towards the valley below. Just before the wood itself were stretches of grasslands, with chickweed, new growth of *nentóg*, nettles, and *bernán*, dandelions, with their bright yellow flowers, as well as gorse bushes where the horses could be tethered for the night. It was a good choice for an encampment.

It was soon evident, however, that their captors would not allow them any opportunity to use the rest for escape after darkness fell. As large fires were lit ready for an evening meal and darkness, Enda whispered to Fidelma: 'Corbmac has divided his men into watches. I am afraid he is very professional.'

Fidelma shrugged. 'It was not my intention to escape. As Eadulf said earlier, I wanted to see this Dicuil Dóna anyway. So we will accompany our friends to this valley and have a word with this person whom everyone seems to be in fear of.'

It turned out that they were grateful for the fire and the shelter of the trees, for the night turned cold and the gusty wind made it seem even colder. However, they did not want for food as provisions had been supplied by the abbey and it seemed that Corbmac's men had their own food. The only thing that spoilt the serenity of the forest, the fires and food was the constant presence of the guards. When they had finished their meal, Corbmac insisted on one foot of each prisoner being secured to the next companion in a way that they would not be able to move in the night without alerting the guards.

Fidelma decided to make the best of it by reposing herself and entering the *dercad*, or the ancient art of meditation of which she was a regular practitioner, having learnt it at an early age. By this means she could clear or calm extraneous thought and mental irritations and achieve *sitchán*, the state of peace. *Dercad* was once taught and practised by the Druids before the coming of the New Faith, but the practice had been expressly condemned as pagan idolatry by sanctified Patrick, whom some claimed had taught the New Faith to the Five Kingdoms. However, wise teachers – especially among those who had changed their Faith long before the coming of Patrick, such as the Blessed Ailbhe, who converted Muman – had retained the art as worthwhile, linking the old and new. It was certainly useful now and allowed Fidelma to rest and be at one with her surroundings so that she slipped into a deep refreshing sleep.

When she awoke, she was aware of a dawn chorus of many birds. To Fidelma's ears they sounded almost like musicians, each with different vocal instruments, playing their separate themes to contribute to the whole; first the pipes, next the *bodhran*, the goat-skin drum, then the horn, then the harp, and then all coming together to join in one melodious sound. She had heard the short song bursts of the blackbird, the soft melody of the thrush, and the gentle sound of the robin . . . all of whom seemed to have no problems living with one another in this isolated spot.

The discordant sounds that broke into her contemplation were those of the men stirring, preparing a first meal and checking their horses and equipment. It was Corbmac who came and personally untied the constraint on her ankle as he passed along the row of prisoners.

He said nothing in greeting, neither to her nor to any of her companions.

Eadulf looked a little the worst for his experience, tired and irritable. Enda and Teimel, being warriors, had taken things in their stride and were eager for a warming drink and something to eat.

'I'll be all right,' Eadulf said shortly in answer to Fidelma's solicitous question. She did not press him further.

While they were eating they saw one of the warriors having a brief word with Corbmac, then mount his horse and ride off at a fairly hurried pace across the mountain.

After a short time, Corbmac gave the order for everyone to resaddle the horses, douse the fires and prepare to move on.

It was basically an unexciting journey, through gusting winds, across bald hills, now bathed in a faint sunlight. From this elevation, they could see the mountains stretching in all directions. Some of the higher peaks were obscured by misty clouds but these soon dispersed. The sun was nearing its zenith when they began to descend into a narrow marshland valley between two mountains. Directly towards the west they could see by the light variations that the way was opening into a wider flat land of a large valley.

Corbmac halted on a rise and turned to them with a smile that had a grim quality about it. He pointed downwards.

'This is the valley of the Uí Máil. There is the fortress of the lord of The Cuala.'

CHAPTER THIRTEEN

The valley that lay before them was impressively verdant in spite of the fact that it was still many weeks before spring would cast its multicolours over it. There were two rivers running through it, one to the north and one to the south. They later learnt that these rivers had the same name as they rose from a single source on the mountain on the western side. A hill rose within the valley to the south. It was not a large hill compared to the surrounding mountains but it dominated the valley. The group of large buildings that occupied its crown was obviously a fortress. There was no doubt from its appearance that the great granite construction was not merely built to create awe in people approaching it.

Corbmac, observing Fidelma's gaze, nodded as if confirming a silent question.

'That is Dún Droch Fhola, the fortress of Dicuil Dóna.'

'The fortress of bad blood,' Eadulf repeated, pursing his lips in disapproval. 'I presume that relates to the blood of those who dwell there?'

Corbmac glowered at his insult.

'On the contrary, Saxon. It is meant as a reminder of the fate of those who harbour bad blood against the Uí Máil. It is a reminder that their blood will find a resting place there.'

He turned his horse to lead the way down the hill into the valley, towards where the fortress rose.

As Fidelma and her companions followed it seemed the day suddenly grew colder. Eadulf noticed this and was trying to persuade himself that it was the shadows of the surrounding tall mountains sheltering the valley from the sun's warmth that caused the temperature to drop. But even when they rode outside the shadows of the mountains into sunlight there was only an uncomfortable feeling of clamminess. It was a dampness that chilled them to the bone. Even the groups of land workers they met, such as shepherds trying to keep their flocks off the main track, looked dispirited. Eadulf realised that as they came closer to the fortress of the Uí Máil, it seem to rise up higher into the sky, looming larger and more dominant than when they had first seen it from the mountainside. Along the path to the main gates of the fortress were various banners set at equal distance and over the gates from a parapet was hung a great banner of sky-blue satin on which was the image of a blood-red falcon. Sentinels stood watchfully everywhere.

Eadulf leant forward and whispered softly to Fidelma: 'The person who dwells here certainly has no small opinion of himself.'

Fidelma was thinking the same thing but made no reply.

Eadulf had seen many fortresses on his travels. He had been to the complex of the High King in Tara but, even there, such displays of importance were discreetly done. The difference here was the aggressiveness of the building itself, with the sentinels' flamboyant uniforms and weaponry. One was left in no doubt that this was where a powerful noble dwelt; a lord who was used to being obeyed and reminded those who dwelt below the fortress that he had the means to enforce obedience. A person who wanted people to know he held power.

As they crossed the valley floor and approached the cold granite edifice, they were struck with the dark, threatening atmosphere that the place exuded in spite of the fluttering colourful banners. The word 'foreboding' sprang into Eadulf's mind from his own language – '*forbéodan*'. The place was designed to challenge and warn off those who approached the dark shadows of its walls. They could hear the sound of a trumpet blast from within the walls, doubtless warning of their approach. They saw the stout dark oak doors swinging inwards as they headed up the ramp towards them.

A figure appeared on foot and stood in the centre of the entrance watching their advance with hands folded in front of him. Corbmac halted with hand upraised in salute to the figure, who barely acknowledged him but turned his curious gaze immediately to Fidelma.

The man was very young and she realised he was hardly more than a boy. She guessed he must be scarcely more than twenty years. He had black hair, almost the colour of a raven's feathers, a white skin, and eyes that were almost as black as his hair, and wide as if in an expression of perpetual astonishment. In contrast to his features, the thin red lips formed a small grim line with the corners turning down in disapproval, which seemed to be at odds with his almost boyish appearance.

'You have safely come to the fortress of the Uí Máil. May you find your stay pleasant and, when you leave, it is our wish that you will leave some of the happiness and health that you bring.'

Fidelma found the archaic welcoming formula strangely at odds with the youth of the speaker. Nevertheless she thanked the boy although the tone of her thanks was cold.

'I am named Scáth, steward of the house of Dicuil Dóna, lord of The Cuala. Corbmac's messenger has arrived and informed us that he escorts Fidelma of Cashel to the gates of the fortress.' He glanced at Fidelma, obviously expecting confirmation.

'"Escort" is a term full of meaning,' she replied coldly. 'Nevertheless, it does not convey the fact that my companions and I were ambushed and brought here under duress.'

It was as if Scáth's face had been frozen because he did not betray any emotion, not even by a blink of his eyes, as though he had not even heard her protest.

'When my lord heard who you were he instructed me to take you directly to him.'

He turned and issued an order. Several attendants appeared to take charge of their horses as they dismounted.

'I have no wish to be discourteous to your lord,' Fidelma said as she stood face to face with the young man, 'any more than he has knowingly wished to antagonise me. My companions and I will expect an explanation for the way we were brought here. After that, we will see if courtesy can be accepted.'

Now the young man's features expressed shock.

'My lord asked for you to be brought into his presence as soon as you arrived. Let us not keep him waiting. Corbmac will escort your companions to their accommodations.'

Fidelma allowed herself a thin smile. 'I see no reason why I should hurry when my companions and I have been brought to this fortress as prisoners.'

It seemed that Scáth had difficulty with this refusal. Obviously he was unused to anyone acting contrary to instruction.

'But you must come with me,' he finally said, but his youthful voice lacked strength of purpose.

'I will wait here with my husband and my bodyguard,' replied Fidelma, and folded her hands in front of her. Eadulf took a stand beside her, trying to look equally determined, while Enda closed in protectively behind her. Teimel hesitated a moment or two before taking a position beside Enda.

'I am now a member of this party,' he smiled at the young steward. The young man had cast him a look of recognition, which was not lost on Fidelma.

Corbmac stepped forward and drew his sword with a threatening motion.

'You will obey the steward,' he said, his voice grating.

'Or you will do . . . what?' Fidelma replied coldly. 'Would you kill us, as you tried to provoke the death of my husband on the mountain? You may want to reflect on the consequences of the slaughter of the sister of the King of Muman, her husband, their bodyguard and their guide. Whether you do so or not, that is out of my hands. The consequence will be on the head of the lord of this fortress. You may well want to remember that. The consequences of your action will be severe and so you might wish to have your lord consider them before action is taken.'

The young steward was clearly perplexed.

'Consequences? You say your husband was threatened with death? I have heard no word of your husband,' he frowned, as if trying to resolve a puzzle.

Eadulf moved a step forward. 'I am Eadulf of Seaxmund's Ham, in the kingdom of the East Angles,' he announced solemnly. 'I am husband to Fidelma of Cashel.'

Scáth's lips compressed for a moment before he glanced at Corbmac.

'Your messenger gave me no word of any noble in this party other than Fidelma of Cashel.' His tone was irritated.

'It was not important to name everyone in her party,' retorted the warrior in defence. 'He is just a Saxon foreigner.'

'Even though a foreigner, if he is husband to the sister of the King of Muman he cannot be regarded as just one of her party,' Scáth replied with annoyance.

'I did try to inform your man,' Fidelma nodded to the truculent Corbmac, 'that even being a foreigner, as my husband, Eadulf is placed under the protection of the Eóganacht and is of their kin now. An assault on him is an assault on the Eóganacht and that could result in the pronouncement of a *dígal*.'

The young steward was clearly unhappy, easing his weight from one foot to another in an almost nervous movement as he struggled with the prospect. The result of his inward debate was not long in arriving. 'Very well. I will take you and your husband to my lord, Dicuil Dóna. Your warrior companions—'

'Enda is my personal bodyguard and friend, a warrior of the Golden Collar,' pointed out Fidelma, finding a merciless pleasure in putting pressure on the youth. 'Teimel, as you probably remember, is a former member of Dicuil's bodyguard, who is now a hunter in these mountains, and is also under my protection, being employed as my guide. If their safety is guaranteed, then they can retire to enjoy some hospitality. They were ridden hard across these mountains. I presume our horses are being attended to?'

Scáth frowned, searching her face for a moment and meeting stony resolution. He shrugged. 'If that is acceptable, very well. Corbmac will take your men to the *laechtrech,* the hero's hall, provide them with food and drink and ensure the horses have been attended to.'

Corbmac opened his mouth as if to protest and then, seeing the hard glance the young man gave him, re-sheathed his weapon with a petulant gesture and motioned Enda and Teimel to follow him.

'Lady,' Scáth turned to Fidelma, 'now will you and your husband come to meet my lord?'

Fidelma paused tantalisingly and glanced at Eadulf. He saw the humour in her eyes.

'It seems the obvious thing to do,' he said solemnly, sharing her humour.

She turned back to the agitated young steward. 'Then we will follow you.'

The young man visibly relaxed. He turned and began to lead the way across the courtyard of the fortress towards the main buildings. Eventually they were led into a large circular chamber in which a central fire exuded comforting warmth. To one side were several chairs. One chair stood on a dais facing these other chairs. It was empty but it was clear that this was the seat of Dicuil Dóna. People were standing in the room, evidently waiting for the entrance of the lord of The Cuala. Fidelma summed up the artificial setting. Dicuil Dóna obviously liked his visitors to wait before he made an entrance. Fidelma was already disliking the man's pretensions for, knowing who she was, other nobles would have made a point of coming to greet her at the gates and not have sent a steward – a youth, at that – to bring her into the great hall and would not make her wait before making their own entrance.

To express her irritation, she walked across to one of the chairs and deliberately turned it away from the dais, facing towards the central fire before sitting down. There was an audible gasp from the people in the room. She turned and motioned Eadulf forward, pointing to another chair. He copied her.

The young steward, with white face, came forward.

'Lady, lady,' he sounded as if he was in a panic, 'my lord has not yet entered the room. We must all stand until he does and the chairs are set to face him to show respect.'

She reclined back and gazed up at his anxious features.

'As you know, I am Fidelma of Cashel. I also hold the degree of *Anruth*. I am allowed to sit in the presence of the High King himself without waiting to be asked. If you have a Brehon that is anywhere near competent, he will confirm the custom on this matter.'

Scáth thrust a hand through his hair, shaking his head in troubled fashion. 'I do not know these things, lady. I only know what my lord requires and . . .'

'What he requires can only be that which conforms to the law. Is that not so, or do you not recognise the edicts of the Council of Brehons of the Five Kingdoms?'

The steward was trying to form an answer when a side door was thrown open. Fidelma was aware of a tall man entering. The man halted abruptly and stared around, his brows drawing together in an expression between surprise and anger. Those in the room grew quiet and seemed to physically back away before him. In silence the man took in the scene before finally focusing on Scáth. The young steward looked as if he was trying to shelter the strangers from the thunderous gaze of his master.

'What does this delay mean?' thundered the newcomer harshly. 'Did I not hear Corbmac and his men arrive some time ago? You were to bring the woman to me at once, yet you spent time talking with her at the gate and . . .'

His voice died away as he suddenly saw Fidelma and Eadulf seated in their chairs, turned away from the dais on which he intended to take his seat. The man's face reddened. He began to stutter, trying to articulate his anger.

Fidelma, without rising, waved him forward.

'Come closer, Dicuil Dóna of the Uí Máil; come take your seat with us. I do not demand nor do I expect any formalities. You have doubtless been informed of my rank and legal status? My right is to seat myself before being invited to, even by the High King. You will also have heard of my husband, Eadulf. He is from the kingdom of the East Angles, and he has long studied in the Five Kingdoms. He holds honour and rank among the Eóganacht. So we need not waste time in formalities.'

The tall lord of The Cuala seemed to be frozen to the spot. His mouth opened and closed like a fish's, trying to make sensible words but succeeding only in making sounds like the swallowing of air.

Fidelma continued on easily. 'Although your steward has failed to announce you, I take it that you are Dicuil Dóna, son of Rónán Crach of the line of Maine Máil, uncle to King Fianamail? I trust that I have not addressed the wrong person?'

Dicuil Dóna swallowed again and could only get out the response: 'I am Dicuil Dóna.'

Seeing that he had not moved towards her, Fidelma swung round to the steward.

'Scáth, bring that chair closer for the lord of The Cuala to join us, for there is much we need to talk about.'

The young steward hesitated, glanced to Dicuil Dóna, before pushing a chair into place. Another hesitation and then Dicuil Dóna came forward and reluctantly, so it seemed, lowered himself into the chair opposite her. He had a bewildered expression, as if unable to grasp how Fidelma had robbed him of his demonstration of power. In the moments he was trying to compose himself, Fidelma had time to consider the tall lord of the mountains. His hair was dark in colour, jet black, which contrasted with his pale skin. He had a long face with a broad lofty forehead, and profuse bushy eyebrows above dark eyes that seemed to flash with a malignant fire. There was little colouring in his pale face, the skin stretched tight over the bones so that it appeared almost translucent. Only the thin red line of his lips stood out like a splash of blood. With his height and this imposing face, Fidelma thought it was no wonder that people such as the religieux at the abbey were in awe of him.

'I need to know why my party was ambushed and brought here as prisoners by threat of force?'

Dicuil Dóna had sufficiently recovered now to try to take command of the conversation.

'Your role and status as the sister of the King of Muman, as a daughter of a king and a long line of kings, is sufficient to welcome you to my domain, Fidelma,' he began, though the courtesy of his words did not match his tone. 'That fact that you are an advocate of our law courts is another reason why we extend to you . . . and to your husband . . . our fullest hospitality. So I bid you welcome.'

Fidelma smiled tightly as he sought to regain his authority.

'Your words are courteous, Dicuil Dóna,' she smiled. 'Perhaps more courteous than the adherence to protocol of some of your servants.'

A flash of annoyance swiftly moulded Dicuil's features and then was gone as he tried to keep his temper in check.

'I had heard that there was a *dálaigh* in my territory making enquiries about a murder. I sent the commander of my bodyguard to investigate and I did not know that the person concerned was the sister of the King of Muman until I received word that my man was escorting you here. The commander of my guard was to invite you to accompany him to my fortress. I am sorry that there has been some misunderstanding. But you are most welcome as my guest . . . as is your husband.'

Fidelma bowed her head with a grave expression. At least the man was now reduced to making excuses. But she would not allow him off entirely.

'I was wondering, even when your warriors discovered who I was, why they thought it necessary to take us prisoners and threaten us with violence.'

Dicuil Dona clenched his teeth. It seemed that she had driven him to his limit.

'That was a misunderstanding,' he repeated, with slow emphasis. 'You have my apologies. I can offer no more. Perhaps in reciprocation you could inform me what you and your companions are doing in my land. After all, you are the intruders in this Uí Máil territory and are here without invitation or permission.' He paused and added dryly: 'I do not think, in view of recent conflicts, there is need for further explanation from me on why your appearance here should arouse some suspicion at least.'

'That sounds logical,' Fidelma returned amiably, realising that there was a limit to how far she could push the matter. 'But my legal authority should be enough to ensure me safe passage through any of the Five Kingdoms.'

'Perhaps so. But remember this is the kingdom of Laigin and there is currently much enmity between our kingdoms. As lord of this territory, I must ask you what your business is here.'

'It is my work as a *dálaigh*,' Fidelma explained. 'I am told you are the lord of these northern mountains.'

'I am of the Uí Máil and lord of The Cuala,' Dicuil Dóna responded, unable to hide his pride.

'That being so, I am told there is little that you do not know about what goes on in these mountains, that there is nothing happens without your knowledge.'

'An exaggeration,' Dicuil Dóna replied with a dismissive gesture.

'Even allowing for it, I am sure you will have heard word of the finding of a body of a Brehon in the valley of Glasán.'

'Naturally. It was some time ago,' frowned the man. 'He was from Osraige. I am told that his party was attacked by brigands.'

Fidelma took a moment to hide her surprise.

'So you must have some idea what my purpose is, as a *dálaigh* from Cashel, in these mountains. The dead man was Brehon to Princess Gelgéis and she is now missing.'

Dicuil Dóna smiled cynically. 'It is common knowledge that Princess Gelgéis of Durlus Éile is engaged to your brother. Rumour has it that the Princess Gelgéis was travelling with her Brehon. She has vanished, it seems.'

'You know no more?'

'If she was part of that party, I know no more. Perhaps she was not, because who would abduct her? Brigands? If brigands – and I do not deny such wretches exist – why are there no demands for her safe return? Why have we heard nothing during the last two weeks or so? I think this is an excuse.'

'An excuse?' Fidelma was puzzled. 'For what?'

'Perhaps an excuse for your brother to invade this kingdom.'

'It is the sort of irresponsible and futile reason that an Uí Máil might consider,' returned Fidelma angrily. 'It is the sort of stupidity that brought your nephew, Fianamail, in conflict with the High King after his ineffectual support of the Osraige rebels to invade Muman.'

Her words were uttered calmly and coldly. Eadulf was not the only one within hearing who gasped at her direct challenge, framed without any degree of diplomacy.

The lord of The Cuala's face did not alter for the moment. He sat without expression, almost as if he had not understood. Then he smiled slowly.

'You are not afraid to declare your opinions openly, lady.'

'That is the purpose of a *dálaigh*, not to hide from possibilities in the pursuit for truth and justice under the law.'

'Then, tell me, if the lady Gelgéis has gone missing, why is there a silence? Even I have not heard a whisper about her abductors. If brigands, then they would surely have made demands for a ransom.'

'If she was, indeed, abducted by brigands,' Fidelma replied.

The lord of The Cuala smiled grimly. 'My thoughts exactly. But what if conspiracy plays a part? The dark valleys can be a nest of singing birds, each eager to make their songs heard – especially when one has a *colbur*.'

For a moment Fidelma thought he was referring to someone's name but then she realised the man was talking about a pigeon.

She had already observed that a convenient way of getting information through the inaccessible mountains was by means of pigeons to carry messages. But did the man know more . . . such as the messages that had passed between Princess Gelgéis and her cousin the abbot?

'I came here to discover what has happened to Princess Gelgéis. You say it is not possible that she has just been abducted by brigands. As no ransom demand has been made, then you are right to consider the alternatives. My brother certainly has no hand in this matter. The cause of the princess's disappearance is here in these mountains. You are lord of this territory and we should work together to find her.'

Dicuil Dóna exclaimed with reluctant admiration, 'You are direct, lady.'

'It is a fault of mine,' Fidelma admitted without a trace of irony in her voice. 'So now I would ask you to be direct also. As lord of this mountainous area what do you know or what have you heard relating to the death of the Brehon and the disappearance of Gelgéis?'

'What more would I know?' protested Dicuil Dóna. 'You claim your brother has no intention of entering a conspiracy against the Uí Máil of Laigin. I tell you that the Uí Máil has no intention of entering a conspiracy against either Muman or Osraige. If we accept this, where do our paths meet?'

Dicuil Dóna was silent then. It seemed as if he was weighing up some problem and then he reached a decision. He turned to his young steward, Scáth, who had been witness to the exchanges with increasingly puzzled expressions chasing one another across his face.

'Clear the hall. I now wish to talk to Fidelma and her husband in private,' the lord of The Cuala declared loudly. After the steward had ushered everyone out and was closing the doors behind them, the lord of The Cuala said sharply: 'I meant everyone.'

Scáth seemed to hesitate before following the others from the hall. He then closed the doors perhaps a little more loudly than was necessary.

Dicuil Dóna glanced round as if to ensure that the hall was empty before returning his attention to Fidelma and Eadulf. He shifted his chair so that he could sit back in a more comfortable position in front of them. He seemed to have changed into a different person; more friendly and confidential.

'In my position one creates many enemies,' he began hesitantly. 'I want to be honest with you. Fidelma, your family and mine have long been enemies. I make no excuse, nor do I avoid it. What can I say? You know our history as well as I do. The Uí Máil say we are hard done by the Eóganacht. Oh, yes,' he said firmly as he saw a smile hover on Fidelma's lips, 'we have suffered several times from the imposition of the *bórama*, the cattle tribute. According to our bards and storytellers we first had to pay it to High King Tuathal Techtmar the Legitimate, to be allowed even to live in this land in peace. Five centuries have passed and still the tribute is demanded of us.'

'According to the chroniclers, it was only imposed when Laigin broke its treaty obligations,' Fidelma corrected. 'When Cummascach, son of the High King Aed mac Ainmerch visited Laigin, your King Brandubh murdered him, which was a stupid act that led to war.'

'Brandubh died a long time ago,' Dicuil Dóna dismissed uncomfortably.

'Old men still remember him. And his action ensured the tribute would be demanded by subsequent High Kings.'

'Well, it was demanded again last year,' snapped the lord of The Cuala. 'How long can we continue paying?'

Fidelma shrugged. 'I would say that the *bórama* will be demanded until Laigin ceases its threats against the other kingdoms. You will recall that your nephew, Fianamail, supported Cronán of Gleann an Ghuail in his attempt to use Osraige as the grounds to overthrow my brother?'

'My nephew, Fianamail, didn't even cross the border. The conflict was internal and Laigin's army stood by only at the border to defend our interests.'

Fidelma snorted indignantly. 'Our versions of that event do not agree. Had Cronán adhered to his role just as Abbot of Liath Mór, then a lot of bloodshed would have been avoided. But his conspiracy was to allow Osraige as a passage for Fianamail to cross into my brother's kingdom and attempt to overthrow him. That was why the Chief Brehon judged the tribute of the *bórama* should be paid once more.'

'That is not so!' snapped the lord of The Cuala, reverting to his former temper. 'We pay tribute only because we lost. History is a story told only by the victors. It is not reality.'

'I say it is so because I was involved in it. Therefore I know it is so. Even further, it was only because Cronán was defeated by my brother that Tuaim Snámha, the ruler of Osraige, declared his allegiance to Cashel. Tuaim Snámha had delayed his involvement only to see who was the victor. His sleight-of-hand politics is why he remains King of Osraige. Fianamail also awaited the outcome before marching over the border. Had he marched earlier, there might be a different King of Laigin now.'

Dicuil Dóna flushed and was silent. Then he forced a smile and stretched back in his chair.

'We are sensible people, you and I,' he began, adopting a new jocular tone. 'We should not quarrel; especially as the injustices inflicted on Laigin are beyond our resolution at the moment. They have no bearing on today's problem.'

'Neither have I any wish to dwell on matters that are past unless they impinge on the present,' agreed Fidelma firmly. '*Do* they?'

Dicuil Dóna looked uncomfortable. 'I do not know. I merely make a preamble because I recognise our two families have had conflicts in the past and therefore you will agree that there is cause for suspicion between us. What I am saying is that you cannot blame me if I am suspicious of your actions when you come into my territory without a formal announcement.'

'That much is logical,' Fidelma affirmed with a small gesture of one hand to indicate she was waiting with controlled patience. 'I am here to find out what happened to Princess Gelgéis. So we are both suspicious of one another. How do we progress?'

Dicuil Dóna sat back, brow furrowed in thought.

'On my part, I suspect some conspiracy. You know, of course, that these mountains, The Cuala, are rich in minerals and, most particularly, there are very rich gold and silver seams among the granite. Other metals found here have made our smiths famous throughout all the kingdoms for their ability to fashion them into many tools and ornaments.'

Fidelma waited patiently while he paused before continuing.

'I have come to believe that these precious metals are being stolen regularly from our mines. I believe the theft is for a purpose and that is to fund a conspiracy against this kingdom that involves Osraige. This is why we must be vigilant. When I heard word that someone of Muman was wandering the countryside asking questions I sent my men scouring the hills and valleys in search. I suspect there are some who would deprive us of what is rightfully ours. My agents have reported many major disappearances and thefts, most particular are thefts of gold and silver.'

'Stealing metals for what purpose? You think that people are stealing the metals to fund a conspiracy by Muman?' Eadulf asked, trying to see where the man was leading them.

'Certainly it involves Osraige,' replied Dicuil Dóna.

'You claim that it involves the Eóganacht . . .?' began Fidelma. She halted abruptly and shook her head. 'What need do we in Muman have of your metals? There are enough metals in Muman for us. We have the biggest range of mines of the Five Kingdoms.'

'I am no enemy to peace, Fidelma,' the lord of The Cuala said. 'True, there are some who would like to drag this territory back into war. I have to be suspicious of all people outside this territory who come wandering unannounced into these mountains.'

'Such as Princess Gelgéis from Osraige?' Eadulf pointed out sarcastically. 'Did you think she and her party were coming to steal your gold and silver?'

'I certainly did not attack them,' the lord of The Cuala answered fiercely. 'I am not so deaf that I do not hear whispered accusations.'

'We have not said you are responsible for whatever has happened to Princess Gelgéis,' Fidelma replied. 'Nor would we make a claim without reasonable proof. The fact is that a Brehon from Osraige was murdered. The arrow in him with which he was shot before the killer cut his throat was similar to those used by your warriors.'

Dicuil Dóna made a gesture of dismissal. 'And because my warriors use a similar type of arrow do you claim that he was killed by my men? I am lord of The Cuala,' Dicuil Dóna sighed. 'I heard that you have made enquiries of the fletcher in Láithreach and you were told such an arrow was widely used in this area, not necessarily by my warriors only.'

'So you have informants everywhere who can communicate with you over long distances and in a short space of time? But you say that you know nothing of the fate of Princess Gelgéis?'

Dicuil Dóna shrugged. 'I am not infallible and sometimes my informants can fail to get their messages through. But that of which I have been informed indicates that there is a connection with what you seek and what I seek.'

'You are talking about the rock pigeons that are used to send messages and communicate to each other?' Fidelma asked. 'I would have thought they were unreliable in this terrain with peregrines and merlins seeking prey?'

'My household company of warriors breed them to good effect.' The lord of The Cuala smiled. 'But as good as the intelligence is that comes to me, sometimes it is not complete.'

'We do not appear to be proceeding very far,' Fidelma observed with a heavy sigh. 'You were saying that you think the Osraige's Brehon was murdered by some conspirators who are stealing precious metals from your mines? The purpose being to create some sort of war. But with whom? What purpose would Princess Gelgéis play if she was abducted by these conspirators?'

The lord of The Cuala was thoughtful. 'What I am actually saying is that while the Brehon may have been killed by conspirators or brigands – for I do not deny brigands exist here, robbing the mines – if she was taken by brigands they would have demanded a ransom for her. Of course, it has occurred to me that such brigands might be so ignorant that they did not recognise the worth of the princess as a hostage. They might have simply killed her, as they did her Brehon, and we have not yet discovered the body. I do not think so. I think she has become involved in this conspiracy.'

'I presume that those that work these mines are keeping you informed of the activities of mine robbers?' Eadulf asked. 'Why have your men not caught them?'

'Some were. The local Brehon in Láithreach caught two men smuggling gold and silver on a river boat.'

'Brehon Rónchú?' asked Eadulf.

'He found gold and silver ore in boxes that had been loaded for transportation to An Inbhear Mór, the Great Estuary. The boatman, whose name was Murchad, said the crates had been delivered to his vessel by two men who claimed they contained only some schist or quartz for a sculptor at their destination. The arrangement was that the boatman would be met at the harbour and paid handsomely for their delivery. The boatman was suspicious. He contacted Brehon Rónchú after the men had left. Brehon Rónchú opened one of the boxes and took pieces of the contents to the local smith, a trustworthy man, who was qualified as a *cerd*, a silversmith.'

'What happened?'

'The smith confirmed it was precious ore, prohibited from leaving this territory. Brehon Rónchú called on the services of my two warriors who were in Láithreach. The three went on board the boatman's vessel and sailed with him to the Great Estuary to see who appeared to claim the metals.'

'A good strategy.' Fidelma nodded in approval. 'That is exactly what I would have done. And then what happened?'

'The two boxes were unloaded at their destination on the wharf and Brehon Rónchú and my two warriors waited. A wagon drew up with the same two men who had consigned the boxes to the boat. They must have ridden across country and certainly not in a wagon but on fast horses.'

'Extraordinary. If they were going to Inbhear Mór why not take the metals with them?' Eadulf asked without thinking.

'Heaving metal ore about on horseback is an exhausting process,' Fidelma explained patiently.

'And perhaps they thought it was safer to put the ore in a boat,' pointed out Dicuil Dóna. 'Anyway, Brehon Rónchú challenged them. In spite of the attendance of the warriors, they drew their swords.'

Fidelma groaned. 'And both were killed, so no one is the wiser as to whom they were or where they came from?'

'They attacked the warriors with such ferocity that there was only one way to end the conflict. So we don't know their origin or where the ore came from.'

'So it was not a helpful exercise?'

'Because such metals from my mines, or those under tribute to me, are smelted here and contain a mark to indicate its origin, we knew that, as ore, they had not been mined officially from any of the mines in my territory. As a *dálaigh* you know this is prescribed in the texts on such matters. Brehon Rónchú came here bringing the boxes of ore to see my mining steward, Garrchú. The samples showed good quality gold and silver ore. Garrchú found it purer than many of the samples from this area.'

'So this was why it was concluded that it was from a new mine?' asked Eadulf.

'Exactly. The rumours of a secret mine had started long before this incident. However, the event seemed to confirm what was happening. The boatman told Brehon Rónchú that the two men and their wagon had been observed coming along the Glasán valley from these mountains so it was presumed that the mine was somewhere here.'

'A vast territory,' Fidelma sighed. 'It would take days and weeks to search to find a mine. Perhaps the mine is not secret at all, but one being used from which those two men simply stole the metal without being seen?'

The lord of The Cuala shook his head. 'If they took ore already mined it would be noticed. If they spent time mining the ore themselves, it would be noticed. Garrchú, my mining steward, is confident that the source is from an unknown mine. This is why I suggest some conspiracy that puts to use previous metals that have been stolen.'

'Conspiracy to do what? Why attack Princess Gelgéis, and her steward, Spealáin? Why kill her Brehon?'

'I have heard that Princess Gelgéis was on her way to see her cousin to discuss unrest in Osraige.'

Fidelma tried not to register her surprise at the man's knowledge. 'How did you know that?' she demanded. 'Abbot Daircell thought the message had not been intercepted?'

Dicuil Dóna chuckled dryly. 'I do not reveal all my secrets.'

'Perhaps they were taken as prisoners because they recognised their attackers,' Eadulf suddenly pointed out.

'What do you mean?' demanded the lord of The Cuala.

'Maybe the illegal miners were people Princess Gelgéis or her steward recognised.'

'You mean they were from Osraige?' Dicuil Dóna pointed out sharply.

'If so, why would they be transporting the gold and metal ore eastwards through Laigin to a seaport?' Eadulf countered. 'They would have gone west, over the border back into Osraige.'

'I do not think we know enough to make any assertions,' Fidelma said, becoming frustrated with a discussion in which little seemed to be of positive consequence. 'The lord of The Cuala says there is illegal mining of metals going on in his territory. He suspects it is to do with some conspiracy to involve the kingdoms in war. We know that a Brehon was killed and Princess Gelgéis and her steward have disappeared. But there is nothing to link any of these things together. I fail to see evidence of some conspiracy yet.'

'This is true,' Eadulf admitted, adding humorously with one of Fidelma's favourite sayings: 'We have been speculating without any linking facts.'

'There are facts enough,' Dicuil Dóna protested.

'We are trying to bind a few facts together and not making sense. Perhaps that is the wrong way of looking at things,' Fidelma observed thoughtfully.

'What do you suggest then?' demanded the lord of The Cuala.

'I suggest that some more thought is given to the matter,' she replied with a disarming smile. 'For the moment, it would be helpful to have some refreshment and rest. Then we will talk again.'

It was only then that they all realised that since arriving at the fortress of the Uí Máil, no one had been offered traditional hospitality or refreshment.

In spite of his previous arrogance, the lord of The Cuala was clearly remembering his etiquette and his face reddened in mortification. With a muttered apology he rose and went to a table standing by the chair of office he usually occupied, leant forward, took a small bell and rang it sharply. The tones had hardly died away when the door was thrown open and the youthful steward, Scáth, came in, looking flustered and anxious.

'Why are you employed as my steward when you do not remind me of protocols?' stormed Dicuil Dóna. He obviously did not like accepting responsibility for his own lack of thought. 'Did you forget your duties of hospitality?'

The young man stood in flushed bewilderment.

'Come, boy!' snapped Dicuil Dóna. 'Have you arranged for water to be heated for our guests? Has a chamber been prepared for their needs? Why must I have to think of everything?'

The boy seemed to be making an effort to control his temper.

'It will be done, lord.'

'I hope you have made sure that the welfare of our guests' horses is better attended to?'

The young man apologetically turned to Fidelma and Eadulf. 'I assure you, your chamber will be ready shortly. I will order the water in the *debach* to be heated at once. It will not be long. After that you will hear the bell for the evening feast to commence.'

'And our companions?' asked Eadulf, knowing there were often problems with hierarchy. 'I presume they will be joining us at this feast?'

Dicuil Dóna frowned. 'Your companions?'

'Our bodyguard: Enda of the Nasc Niadh,' Fidelma explained in

old cronies. He seems to have a lot of old friends among the warriors.'

'He was one of them himself, remember, so I would not be unduly surprised that he knows several there. Don't forget, Corbmac offered to let him go.'

'In spite of that, he volunteered to stand by us in his role of guide and trapper,' Eadulf reminded her. 'It seems we can trust him.'

'I must have a final word with Dicuil Dóna.' Fidelma rose from the table. 'You best find Enda and Teimel and get them ready so we can set off for this place Dún Árd.'

It was only a short time later that she entered the lord of The Cuala's chamber. He greeted her with a brief smile that seemed without feeling.

'I understand that you encountered my daughter this morning?' he opened before she had a chance to speak.

'I am afraid I did,' Fidelma replied after a pause for she was sure that Aróc must have given him her version of the encounter. However, it appeared that Dicuil Dóna was not entirely blind to his daughter's behaviour.

'I hope you will understand that she is a headstrong girl. However, she is one who bears the blood of the Uí Máil with justifiable pride and—'

'I understood that she is your daughter,' Fidelma interrupted. 'She made a point of impressing that fact upon me. Even so, she must realise that courtesy is a sign of nobility. No one is better than she but, conversely, she is better than no one. I will grant you, Dicuil Dóna, that the Uí Máil are a proud dynasty but dynasties come and go. Pride is only justifiable when examined by the worth of one's own conduct and achievements.'

Dicuil Dóna was looking uncomfortable.

'The girl is of my blood and she has a right to her pride in her ancestry,' he protested.

'One can feel a respect of one's ancestry but there is no justification in having arrogance about it,' she admonished.

'Well, I am sure that she did not realise who you were,' he tried to amend.

'Courtesy is something that you treat everyone with, and not just those whom you select to be courteous to. Without humility in one's self, you do not possess respect for others.'

Dicuil Dóna glowered resentfully but made no response.

Fidelma decided to change the conversation. 'We shall shortly be off to see the manager of your mines. I will let your steward know of our departure.'

'Ah, my steward . . . you know he is my son? He has just left the fortress. He has an errand to be fulfilled in Láithreach.'

'He told me he was your son,' admitted Fidelma. 'Yet you do not refer to him as your *tánaiste*, your heir apparent?'

'He has not earnt that right as yet,' Dicuil Dóna almost snapped in response. Then he caught himself. 'I am lord of all The Cuala. This is a vast land and the mountains are natural fortifications so that I am compelled to make a circuit of my people. I need to send my son as steward in my place. All he has to do is make lists and receive reports, but that does not require the same talent as my heir apparent.'

The duties of a noble and the duties of the territory he governed always relied on interaction, and the concept of the traditional 'circuit', or visits to the territories under his control, was sacred to nobles. The obligations were laid down in the law text *Bretha aithchesa*, or the judgments of the neighbourhood.

'Scáth has already left on his journey? He did not mention he was leaving this morning.' She was surprised.

'He does what he is told when I tell him,' replied the lord of The Cuala, his brows coming together in an expression of annoyance. 'My son is barely trained for any suitable office. He has yet to prove worthy of this office as steward. I have to watch and instruct him carefully.'

'I would have thought he is worthy of the same respect that his sister is given,' Fidelma could not help the remark.

'Respect has to be earned.'

'And Aróc has earned that respect?' Fidelma observed sharply.

Dicuil Dóna's features tightened. 'Are you a parent? Boys must not be indulged.'

'I have a son,' replied Fidelma. 'He is worthy of my respect until he demonstrates otherwise. If I were parent to a daughter, she also would be given respect until she demonstrated otherwise. Respect is due as one fosters and educates your children, helping them in achieving their knowledge and patterns of moral behaviour. But it is not indulgence.'

'Boys have to earn respect, daughters are indulged. How else do you divide the sexes?' sneered the lord of The Cuala.

'Why would one want to divide the sexes?' Fidelma replied patiently. 'You surely know our law system recognises that women have rights, and such rights should apply to the way they are treated as well as their rights to inheritance and property.'

'I have my ways and you have yours,' was the stony reply.

'So long as both ways are in keeping with the law,' replied Fidelma dryly. 'Anyway, I shall get on with the task we have both agreed, and that so long as it does not interfere with the primary task I have come here to fulfil. I presume that we are all free to leave and that Corbmac has been informed?'

'Of course. Why do you ask?'

'Because I observed him leaving the fortress a short time ago. I would not like to encounter him and his warriors as we journey to Dún Árd, only to find we are taken captive again and threatened with our lives because he does not know of our agreement.'

The lord of The Cuala did not share her irony.

'I can promise you that Corbmac has been informed of the situation. Corbmac left to escort my daughter on a journey.'

Fidelma drew herself up. 'Then I shall gather my party and be off. I shall keep you informed of my investigation as it applies to your concerns.'

For Fidelma and her party departure from the fortress of the lord of The Cuala was at least more relaxed than their arrival. Even Teimel seemed happy to leave the fortress behind him. He took the lead away from its forbidding battlements. In fact, it was Fidelma who commented on his cheerful countenance.

'You told me it was called "the fortress of bad blood". Personally I would have called it the fortress of badly mannered people.'

Teimel gave an amused grimace. 'You are not far wrong. I knew Aróc when she was smaller, and even then she was wilful and spoilt. She has grown even more so. As for young Scáth – he seems a spineless soul. That is to his shame.'

'It is true that he is much put upon and not given a chance to stand up to his dominant father,' replied Fidelma. 'But if you had these thoughts why did you serve as a member of the bodyguard of the lord of The Cuala?'

Teimel exhaled with a derisory sound that resembled a snort. 'You have already been given the reason, lady. He is lord of The Cuala. I was young and had an ambition to learn the art of arms. I am no longer young; I have survived two battles. From what I have seen, I probably would not survive a third, for my heart was not in the killing of men simply because the lord of The Cuala said that they were my enemies. So I turned to hunting and trapping for those who wanted to employ my skills and thus far I have supported myself and been in peace.'

They had descended from the fortress into the valley. It was quite broad, with several streams and a river running through it. Several wooden bridges had been constructed so the route was not impeded. A track led from the fortress to a bridge that crossed the main river, which was called An tSláine. It then continued to the foot of a high peak, but skirting it led to north-west. Teimel assured his companions that the track would bring them to Dún Árd. It was fairly

straight, with the valley and waterways to the left and rising woodland to the right. Here they crossed another wooden bridge over a
torrent running down to join a river in the valley.

'Dún Árd is on the far side of that hill,' called Teimel, pointing
ahead of them. In the distance was a hill that could be no more
than three hundred metres high and thus seemed dwarfed by the
surrounding high peaks of the area.

'It is strange,' Eadulf observed, 'that the least thing you would
expect to find in all these verdant hills and valleys would be mines.'

'A lot of workings were soon overgrown by the grasses, bushes
and trees of this area,' Teimel pointed out. 'It is because we have
cool, wet winters, as you have noticed, and in summer the weather
is usually damp but mild.'

'You have an eye for the weather?' Eadulf asked, impressed.

'Anyone who exists by hunting and trapping must know the
weather as they know the land and forests that the creatures inhabit,'
rejoined the hunter.

'You say that there are many mines here that have been hidden
by growth?' Fidelma asked.

Teimel gestured with his arm to encompass the surrounding
mountains. 'Even in the time beyond time there were copper and
lead mines here. Iron ore was found in abundance, and other
metals. But the man you are going to see will tell you all about
that.'

'Lady!'

A sharp call from Enda made them turn towards the young
warrior.

'To the right of us, up on the hill, just beyond the line of those
saileóg.'

Eadulf looked up, confused until he realised that Enda meant
not goats, but a line of goat willow bushes. There were two riders
making their way along a track not far above them.

'Who is it?' he asked. 'I mean, why the concern?'

'Just that our former captor – what was his name? Corbmac – is the second horseman,' replied Enda.

Fidelma was frowning. 'Our friend is right,' she confirmed. 'And the first rider is Aróc.'

'She always seemed friendly with Corbmac,' Teimel observed darkly.

'I wonder where they would be going. Presumably not in the same direction as we are taking?' asked Fidelma.

'Not exactly,' replied the hunter. 'That way would pass by the entrance into a small valley that leads to a mountain called Lúbán, the little bend. That is fairly high, in spite of the name. There is nothing there, as I recall. No towns or settlements of any sort.'

Enda was continuing to watch the two riders as they passed beyond the willow trees and shrubs and then disappeared.

'Well, they seemed too busy looking forward to glance down and spot us,' he commented.

'What would they have done if they had?' Fidelma said dryly. 'I expect that Dicuil Dóna told his daughter where we are going anyway. Is this place Dún Árd far?'

'Not far, but we will stay there for this night, at least. When the darkness descends among the mountains it is not advisable to be travelling abroad.'

Fidelma regarded Teimel in surprise. 'Are you being superstitious, Teimel?' she observed sarcastically.

'I am not,' responded the trapper stoically. 'But I am thinking of wolves, wild cats and the other animals of the night that come out to chase nocturnal prey. I've had many an encounter with a wild boar at dusk and they are dangerous, I can tell you.'

'Creatures that we are aware of and take precautions,' Eadulf responded. 'However, it is the human creature that can be most unpredictable and therefore they are the most dangerous.'

'That is true, friend Eadulf,' echoed Enda. 'I'll take my stand against a wild boar or a wolf any day. But a human who can ambush you or strike you in the back is not the sort of enemy I like to encounter.'

'The steward of his mines keeps a strict watch on brigands and thieves, or so the lord of The Cuala told me. Do you think they would venture so near his fortress?' Fidelma mused.

Her remark was addressed to Teimel, who thought about it and then shook his head.

'I have never heard of brigands chancing their luck so close to the valley of the Uí Máil. I know the geography here abouts. Besides, what travellers would be passing here that would be worth trying to rob? There are dark valleys and remote mountain gorges. It is the more southerly, or more northerly, main routes that lend them-selves to bands of brigands preying on travellers. The lord of The Cuala's warriors are employed to protect travellers and merchants but sometimes incidents happen. Dicuil Dóna is not a person to defy lightly. His vengeance is swift and his reach is long for he can call on his relatives, even to his nephew, Fianamail, the King of Laigin himself, to extend that reach.'

'Yet something is amiss here, for all his vaunted knowledge and power, because he claims he is unable to deal with robberies from his own mines,' Eadulf said dryly.

'To be accurate, and in his defence,' Fidelma intervened, 'it might be gold and silver ore taken from a working that he does not even know of.'

Eadulf shrugged. 'If it comes from a mine that he does not know of then how can he rightly claim that it is his? How does your law stand with that?'

'I am not sure what you mean.'

'Simple,' Eadulf replied. 'I thought a principle of the law was that land like this was held as the common property of all the members of the *tuath* or kin-group, and decisions have to be made on disposal or otherwise by the *derbfine*, the family of the ruler. If this is so, how can Dicuil Dóna talk of his mines being his when it is not even known if they exist?'

Fidelma was patient. 'You have a good knowledge of the principles of the laws of the Five Kingdoms, Eadulf, but there are many nuances. There are aspects of the principle of private property that are extended through the law system. But, of course, the chief or prince cannot make arbitrary decisions as he is always answerable to his *derbfine*, and the same penalties apply if he is not promoting the common welfare of his people. But to answer your question more directly, the texts are specific about the crime of excavating from someone else's mines without their knowledge. Importantly, for your question, it states that excavating from these mines or from any land owned by the chieftain and his *tuath* constitutes a theft. This means that Dicuil Dóna and his *derbfine* are owners of all the land and anything taken from it – anything known or unknown – is theft.'

'But I still don't understand . . .'

Eadulf's usually placid cob suddenly reared, waving his forelegs, screaming in painful shock. Eadulf was propelled backwards off the beast. The event happened very quickly. Fidelma caught sight of an arrow embedded in the flank of the cob, saw it rearing, almost leaning backwards on its hind quarters, then saw Eadulf tumbling backwards. In fact, it was the very act of being thrown that saved his life, for the next arrow flew straight across the position where Eadulf would have been sitting had he remained seated.

CHAPTER SIXTEEN

E adulf landed on his back with a sickening thump and lay still. Checking on his condition was not their first priority. Fidelma and the others acted almost in unison as they cast themselves to the ground from their horses, using the animals as protective shields.

Enda glanced at Teimel and signalled towards a group of trees to their right a short way ahead of them. The hunter frowned as if not understanding. Enda signalled again to the trees before pointing to himself and then to Teimel and making a circling motion with his hand. It was clear he was indicating the presence of the assailant and his intention to encircle him. He again pointed to Teimel and motioned in the other direction. Teimel grimaced to show he now understood the idea was to outflank the attacker by approaching from either side. They had hardly begun to undertake their objective when they heard hurried movements. It was clear that the attacker himself was already moving. Throwing caution to the wind, Enda stood up and began to run forward with the cry of a warrior going into battle. He quickly vanished into the trees. After a pause Teimel followed his example, running off to the side Enda had previously indicated.

Fidelma waited a moment and then turned to crawl over to Eadulf, who was still lying on his back, his eyes closed.

'Eadulf!' she whispered urgently as she knelt beside him.

He made no response. She knew he had not been hit by the arrows so that his condition was the result of his fall. She felt for his heart. The beat was regular although the breath was a little stertorous. Confident now that the assailant would be more concerned with Enda and Teimel, she rose. Eadulf's cob was also in need of attention, for the arrow was still sticking into his flank and blood was trickling from it. She went to her horse to take her *lessan*, a leather water bag, and dropped some of its contents over Eadulf's face.

His eyes fluttered and he groaned.

'Eadulf, can you hear me?'

He blinked and tried to focus on her. 'What happened?' Then, as if realising it was a superfluous question as memory returned, he gave a groan. 'This seems to be getting repetitive. Arrows and ambushes.' He tried to sit up but she held him firmly back.

'You fell off your horse and landed on your back. Be careful. Can you feel any bones broken?'

He lay for a moment as if checking his limbs. 'I think everything is where it should be,' he replied grimly. 'I can be thankful this track is very muddy and soft. Where did the arrow shots come from?'

'Enda and Teimel are chasing the attacker,' she replied grimly. 'Are you sure that you are all right?'

Eadulf, having assured Fidelma he was not seriously injured, eased himself into a sitting position and looked around.

'No one else is hurt, are they?' he asked.

'Your horse is badly hit.'

'I'm not too knowledgeable about horses. Is it very bad?'

'I am not sure. Remain here and I'll take a look.'

He eased himself to his feet and watched Fidelma walk towards the cob. The animal was clearly feeling discomfort and shied a little at her approach but she spoke to it in a quiet, soothing tone, reaching out a hand to stroke it. She peered closely at the point where the arrow had struck, then turned back to Eadulf.

'I don't think it has entered a muscle, but it is in the fatty tissues at the point of the hip. I am not an expert so I will not pull it out before I know.'

A noise caught her ear and she turned, her brow furrowed, head to one side, listening. Enda's voice gave a loud 'halloo' from a short distance away to ensure Fidelma knew that friends were approaching. She acknowledged.

'Is friend Eadulf badly wounded?' Enda demanded as he emerged to join them.

'I was not hit by the arrow,' Eadulf replied. 'I was thrown off the horse and just feeling a sore posterior and a headache.'

A moment later, Teimel returned. 'The attacker has vanished,' he announced. He glanced at Enda in disapproval. 'That was a thought-less act to rush forward shouting. Had we sneaked around the man's position quietly we might have caught him.'

'The attacker was moving. I could hear him. My thought was only of protecting us from further attack,' he replied. 'It appears that we are walking too often into the same type of ambush.'

Teimel replied curtly: 'I will check the area and make sure there are no others waiting in ambush. It is best that you stay on guard here.'

As he disappeared, Enda looked grimly after him as if displeased, then gazed thoughtfully at the cob.

'I think we must start immediately for this place Dún Árd in case the assailants are still about. Eadulf's horse needs treatment as soon as possible.'

'We will go as soon as Teimel returns,' Fidelma said.

They did not have to wait long.

'There are no signs of the attacker at all,' he reported.

'I didn't hear the sound of a horse,' Enda commented.

'Neither did I,' admitted the hunter. 'But I am sure they have gone.'

'I saw some signs of horses where they must have lain in wait for us,' Enda said, 'but I could find no tracks of any horse or of them departing on foot. That was curious. It is as if they have mysteriously vanished.'

Eadulf sighed, rubbing the back of his head. 'Well, I hope we are not back in the realm of shapeshifters again.'

Enda smiled tightly. 'Not so much a person who can shift their shape by supernatural means but a simple skilled woodsman who knows how to adapt to his environment and fade away without a trace. That's even worse than a supernatural shapeshifter.'

Fidelma had been looking around and suddenly she darted into some undergrowth, reappearing a few seconds later clutching an arrow.

'This is the second arrow they loosed,' she said to Eadulf. 'You should be grateful to your poor cob for throwing you backwards and saving your life.'

'Speaking of which, we need to get the animal attended to,' pointed out Enda.

Fidelma examined the arrow carefully.

'Anything of interest?' queried Eadulf.

'Nothing we do not know already. The only thing of interest is that all these arrows seem to be made by the same fletcher, and are designed for a left-handed bowman . . . or woman. The same brass heads, the same feathers and colouring.'

'The poor horse needs attention,' Enda reminded her again.

She stowed the arrow into her *marsupium* and mounted her pony. Teimel, taking the leading rein of Eadulf's cob, announced that he would go in front as he knew the route. Fidelma came next and behind came Enda, who reached down to help Eadulf swing up behind him. They were cautious now to keep their eyes focused for any signs of danger. Fortunately, the track gave way to a more open area.

As they crossed the shoulder of the hill they became aware of smoke rising in the distance and the banging of a hammer, metal against metal. A group of buildings appeared as they came to the rise and looked down at a circular structure that looked like an old hillfort. There were several buildings and many for storage, plus a number of kilns and what appeared forges. A stream rose from the hill behind and ran down through this group of buildings. A glance showed it was obviously more complex than the usual smith's forge.

At what seemed to be an entrance to the complex, a muscular man was standing, wielding a hammer. His leather apron covered a bare weather-bronzed torso. He looked up with a frown of curiosity, his deep-set brown eyes flickering from one to another as they approached, before alighting on the cob with the blood oozing from the arrow still in its flank. He put down his hammer and came to greet them.

He opened with an obvious comment. 'Your horse is injured.'

'Do you have a horse doctor here?' Fidelma asked. 'The arrow needs to be taken out gently in case it is in the muscle or some part where the animal will bleed to death.'

The smith sniffed disdainfully. 'I am doctor to the horses hereabouts. I am the blacksmith in charge of the stables. Who did this to the animal?'

'We were ambushed on our way here,' Fidelma explained.

The smith seemed surprised. 'Near here?' Then he turned to examine the animal without waiting for an answer.

They all dismounted and stood around watching the smith with fascination as, speaking in soft tones to the animal, he started to press here and there around the wooden shaft of the arrow. Then, to everyone's surprise, he bent forward and gave a swift tug, bringing the arrow out in one piece. Rather than reaching for a piece of cloth to stanch the blood that began flowing, he turned to the nearby stream and tore up tufts of a grey-green lichen that grew on the rocks beside the waters. These he immediately pressed against the wound.

'This will suffice until I dress the wound properly. You are lucky,' he added. 'The arrow went in only a short way and it does not appear to have entered the muscle, for the beast would not have made it thus far had it done so. However, it needs to rest awhile. I can offer to stable it for that time as well as keeping a careful eye on its progress. However, as is the rule here, I think you should report the matter of your attack to our chieftain.'

'I presume your chieftain is Garrchú and this is Dún Árd?' Fidelma asked.

'He is and it is so,' smiled the man.

'Then he is the man we have come to see. Where will we find him?'

'This is he coming down to greet you now.' The smith nodded at a figure moving through the kilns towards them.

Garrchú was a lean man with a mass of greying hair, which was so unruly that it was difficult to tell where his hair stopped and his beard began. It disguised his features so that it was not until one looked closer that one realised that they were sharp and bony. He had a lupine quality. The brows came together above a long sharp nose; the eyes were very dark. There was a flash of yellowing teeth but it was hard to see whether the man was smiling or his jaw was set in this expression. Above all, the impression was of white skin that had never seen daylight.

He listened carefully and respectfully as Fidelma introduced her party and examined the wand of office from the lord of The Cuala that she presented him with.

'So how can I help you?' he finally asked.

'Firstly, do you have room to stable all our horses? We would not depart without knowing that the cob is out of danger and on its way to healing.'

'I have stables enough for your mounts. You are welcome to my hospitality.' He motioned to the smith, who immediately took charge of their horses. Without a pause, or so it seemed, Garrchú then turned and issued orders for someone to take their bags and prepare guests rooms for the night and hot water for bathing before the traditional evening meal. Then he gave them all an encompassing smile and waved them to precede him towards the main building.

'This evening you will share my poor fare and I will answer all your questions as my lord Dicuil Dóna has instructed. But first a drink as the symbol of hospitality while we wait for the water to be heated for your baths.'

'We are most grateful,' began Fidelma, but he made a motion with his hand to dismiss her thanks.

'There is no need for thanks, lady,' he replied in mild rebuke. 'Hospitality is a tradition that we strictly adhere to.'

'Then we thank you for that.'

'Do you have any idea of why you should be attacked?' Garrchú was genuinely concerned.

'I can only think it was something to do with the matter that has brought us here from Dicuil Dóna,' Fidelma replied.

'Then perhaps we had better reserve that explanation until after we have washed and rested,' suggested Teimel unexpectedly.

Garrchú had been looking at Teimel with curiosity. 'I seem to know your features.'

'This is true,' returned the hunter. 'I am Teimel, once a member of the lord of The Cuala's bodyguard. I am now merely a hunter in these hills.'

'So?' was all the response Garrchú gave.

It was sometime later when, having washed and rested, they were brought into Garrchú's feasting hall and seated before traditional dishes of roast wild boar and other meats that lacked the variety for most people's palates but seemed traditional in tough mining communities such this. Even the attending womenfolk, like the buxom wife of Garrchú, ate as much meat at the meal as would have satisfied Fidelma for a week. Ale and mead were consumed in large quantities but there was no wine, for imported wine was reserved only for nobles. The company's manners were certainly coarse, as was their language, but it was not offensive, for laughter and good spirits seemed to be essential to Garrchú's table etiquette. Teimel now and then glanced nervously at Fidelma, Eadulf and Enda, which she ascribed to a concern at the cultural differences.

Garrchú was certainly the garrulous host and regaled his guests with some mining stories. He knew much about the metals that could be extracted from the mountains. He talked seriously with Fidelma about how to heat metals and how to judge those colours to which the metals would turn in the fire to indicate the moments they could be mixed. For example, when tin and copper could be mixed into bronze and become liquid enough to pour into the moulds; or how to use liquid copper and zinc with mixtures from lead or iron to create brass. By the time he was talking about smelting steel, Fidelma found herself longing for a bed to go to sleep.

'We did have some questions to ask relating to our mission from the lord of The Cuala,' she finally said, trying to bring the conversation back to the point she was really interested in.

Garrchú shrugged eloquently. 'Ask any question you like and if it is my knowledge I will answer freely. As we deal with a matter from Dicuil Dóna, would you wish my women and attendants to retire so that the exchange may be private?'

Fidelma shook her head. 'It won't be necessary. There is nothing about my business that they cannot learn from elsewhere. Dicuil Dóna told me that two small wooden boxes containing metal ore were escorted here by the Brehon Rónchú recently.'

'So they were. Thieves had tried to smuggle them to the coast. They were pieces of ore, some of which I was asked to have smelted and assessed. They had been found on a boat on the river at Láithreach. This was a few weeks ago.'

'What did you discover?'

'I made my report to Brehon Rónchú and also to my lord's steward, young Scáth, to confirm matters. He took the report to his father. I ventured that the gold ore was of a better quality than I have usually seen from my lord's mines. It was from a mine I did not know.'

'A better quality? Was it that which made you deduce they came from an unknown mine?'

'The gold was not of great quality but it was fine if purified under heat in the crucible.'

'Do you agree with Dicuíl Dóna that it is likely to have been stolen from his mines and, if not from a working mine, then from a secret mine in his territory? You say you deduced it came from an unknown mine.'

Garrchú sat back and rubbed the back of his head thoughtfully. 'I know metals and I know the qualities in the mines here. I will show you tomorrow. I can best demonstrate at the forge nearby.'

'But in the meantime you can say that the ore came from this area – I mean from The Cuala? Can you say that the ore that Brehon Rónchú recovered was dug out of the mines in these mountains?'

'That is a little too specific to say if I am taking an oath on it,' replied the chief of Dicuil Dóna's mines after a moment.

'In what way?' demanded Fidelma.

'I can say that it is the type of ore found in these mountains. But it can also be found in other areas outside of these peaks. However, given that the thieves, according to Brehon Rónchú, had loaded the ore into a river boat at Láithreach, and had travelled there through the valley of Glasán, it would be a good assumption that it was dug in this area.'

'That is a fair enough response,' Fidelma agreed. 'If that were so, would you agree that the ore was stolen from Dicuil Dóna's mines?'

'If the metal were dug from here, then I think it is more likely than less.'

'But you could not say whether it was from a working mine?'

'No one could be so precise, though, as I said, I spotted a greater purity in the gold than I had previously seen.'

'Are there many working mines here? I mean those mines extracting gold and silver ore. I appreciate many other metals are taken from this area.'

'Not many producing any quantity of gold or, indeed, silver ore.

These are the rarest of metals. In search of gold we have even tried to extract it from the rivers, for little grains of gold can be found in the sediment of the river beds. We still use the ancient method of gathering sand from the beds of the streams. Then we use the fleece of a sheep stretched out and propel the sand through the fleece and this traps the tiny but heavy grains of gold in the wool. The fleece is hung up and dried before it is beaten, but beaten so gently that the gold falls off and is recovered. Often a substantial amount is recovered in this way and placed in a crucible and smelted into a block ready to be sent to the artisan.'

Eadulf heaved a bored sigh. 'This does not help us much.'

'In what way do you need help?' Garrchú queried, slightly annoyed his knowledge did not seem to impress Eadulf. 'At least we can be fairly certain that the ore comes from this area.'

'And that is a help?' Eadulf asked, trying to mute his sarcasm.

'It is of help to the extent that we may not be wandering these mountains indefinitely,' Fidelma corrected him disapprovingly. 'We can be fairly sure it comes from these mountains.' She turned back to Garrchú. 'I understand Brehon Rónchú personally accompanied these boxes?'

'He did,' replied Garrchú. 'It was his legal obligation do so. He seized them from those he considered to be thieves. I can show you the metal, as I still have it stored here until he has determined ownership.'

'No need to show it. But when Brehon Rónchú left you, where did he go? We could not find him in Láithreach.'

Garrchú was clearly puzzled. 'I presumed that he had returned to Láithreach as he said he must make further enquiries about the thieves.'

'He was travelling on horseback?'

'It is long and arduous to travel through these peaks and valleys by any other means,' Garrchú said, slightly sarcastically. 'He was riding a horse. Why do you ask?'

'He could not have brought the boxes of ore here on his horse?' she pressed.

Garrchú smiled thinly. 'He was riding a horse. The ore was in a small wagon that he had hired from a local wagon driver from Láithreach. The man who drove the wagon left as soon as he had unloaded the boxes. So the Brehon Rónchú returned alone by horse. You said that you were attacked on your way here,' Garrchú said thoughtfully. 'Do you think it has something to do with this? It may mean that the Brehon did not reach Láithreach. Do you think the thieves and brigands that Dicuil Dóna fears are still nearby here?'

'There is much that is guesswork, and none of us has seen the attackers so we cannot say who they are.'

'You did not recognise any of your attackers and have no clue other than the arrow?' Garrchú shook his head. 'Well, that sort of arrow is common here. This is very worrying,' Garrchú looked concerned. 'You see, if they are brigands and are near here, they will learn whatever gold and silver ore is dug from these hills is brought here. Here it is separated from the other metal ores – tin, zinc, copper, lead and iron. I have the only forges where metals can be refined or smelted.'

'Your forges are particularly concerned with silver and gold ore?' Eadulf asked.

'Those workers I employ here specialise in smelting these metals and these are rare metals so have to be carefully treated. In fact, this very place developed from the site of a silver mine.'

Fidelma was suddenly thoughtful. 'Not far away from here there is a valley leading up to a peak called . . .' She turned to Teimel. 'I forget the name you called it. It was where we saw Corbmac on our way here.'

Teimel frowned. 'I can't remember exactly . . .'

'I think you called it Lúbán,' Eadulf supplied.

'That was it,' the hunter agreed apologetically. 'It slipped my mind.'

'Are there mine workings in that area?' Fidelma asked.

Garrchú thought for a moment and then shook his head decisively. 'I can't recall any that have recently been exploited. But many years ago, I think there were some attempts at mining in that valley. There are no workings there now. Certainly I have never heard of anyone extracting ore from that area recently.' Then he frowned. 'What was Corbmac doing there? Surely not searching for thieves?'

'Who knows?' Fidelma smiled dismissively 'He was riding towards the area.'

'Maybe they were not heading in that direction at all,' Teimel pointed out. 'There are plenty of other paths leading from the one where we saw them.'

'But it is inaccessible so far as tracks and paths are concerned,' Garrchú said. 'You have a river rising on the slopes of that peak, which comes down into the valley of the Uí Máil, otherwise there is little else there now; just some ruins.'

'You seemed surprised when we mentioned that Corbmac was seen riding in that direction,' Fidelma observed.

'It leads into little inaccessible valleys, with no tracks and not even a farmstead or shepherd's hut for vast distances. I find it strange that he would be riding into such isolated territory. He was never a one for isolation, but known for his liking for feasting and dancing and attending taverns.'

Fidelma shook her head quickly at Eadulf as she realised he was about to mention that the warrior was accompanied by young Aróc.

'And you know that area well, I suppose?'

'I have not been along there since I was young. There used to be an old ruined farmstead on a hill in the valley beyond Lúbán. But I would say no one has lived there since the days of Conaire the Great.'

'That's seven centuries ago, according to the bards,' Enda made one of his rare intercessions.

There was a thoughtful look on Fidelma's face but she now decided to turn the subject back to Garrchú.

'Do you produce much gold and silver here? I mean, are there mine workings around Dún Árd?'

'Not as much these days. In ancient times, the main seams were good but now they are generally worked out. It is further into the high peak areas that most seams are worked these days.'

'So the lord of The Cuala still makes a good profit?'

'A lot of what is discovered is sold to merchants from beyond the seas with the authority of the lord of The Cuala. Gaulish merchants arrive at some of our ports because they seem to like the red gold, which comes from association with the copper seams. They pay good prices. Gold is worth fifteen times more than silver. And a good size bar . . . thus . . .' he described the dimensions with his hands, 'that would pay the wages of a single craftsman for nine years.'

'So gold and silver from these mountains is purchased by Gaulish merchants,' Fidelma asked in surprise, 'but it is already smelted into bars by your kiln and forges?'

'Of course. And with the lord of The Cuala's mark on them. As I say, the merchants prefer the red gold. The white gold we keep and often sell to the smiths of local nobles from the south of this kingdom.' He gestured with his head to Enda's golden torc. 'The élite warriors often affect such emblems and hence the need for the ore.'

Enda's cheeks reddened. 'We do not affect to wear such emblems,' he protested. 'It was back in the days of the High King Muineamhon, son of Cas Clothach, a true descendant of Eibhear Fionn, that it was first decreed that torcs of gold or gold chains should be worn round the necks of the élite warriors of Muman. Only our King can bestow them on us. Hence we are called the Nasc Niadh – warriors of the Golden Collar.'

Garrchú was amused by the warrior's defence of his emblem. 'Such traditions are popularly spoken of,' he said dismissively. 'Perhaps they are true, perhaps they are not. Maybe it is just a legend, just as it is said that two centuries ago Eanna Cennsalach,

King of Laigin, defeated his enemies and received tribute of gold
from Muman.'

Fidelma shook her head as she saw Enda's youthful anger rise.

'It is said that the Chief Poet of Ireland, Dubhthach Ó Lughair,
penned a verse saying it was only a small derisory sum because it
stipulates the tribute was accompanied by insults from the nobles
of Muman.'

'But we can agree that the chroniclers admit Eanna Cennsalach,
when he was King of Laigin, was an influential king and he did
defeat and receive tribute from his enemies,' Teimel suddenly interrupted with a scowl.

'But this has little to do with the problems we are faced with,'
Fidelma pointed out in pacification. She had not forgotten Teimel
had been a warrior of Laigin.

'I suspect the problems remain the same,' the steward of the mines
declared sourly. 'I have heard that in the days when the Romans
ruled in Britain, they used to take much gold and silver from the
western parts of that island. There is still a thirst for gold, and that
thirst will never die. It was the first metal that men found, the easiest
to work into ornaments. In spite of iron and copper, and the discovery
of mixing tin and copper to form bronze, which can be sharpened
into tools – tools for farmers as well as weapons for warriors – it
is still gold that men revere above all things.'

'Have you ever had any trouble before this incident?' Fidelma
asked abruptly. 'I mean have you had thefts from the mines in this
territory? Dicuil Dóna seems to think that thefts from his mines
have continued for some time.'

'I have not heard of anything that is significant before the
discovery by Brehon Rónchú. Certainly not to my knowledge, apart
from small pilfering among the miners, which was soon discouraged
by the fines and compensation the thieves were made to pay.
However . . .' He frowned as if remembering something. 'Now that
you ask, I am reminded that when Brehon Rónchú visited he said

that he had heard from some travellers that officials in the seaports were reporting suspicious behaviour from the Gaulish ships that often put into port.'

'Suspicious in what way?'

'I only repeat what was I was told. Brehon Rónchú said that several times during the last months Gaulish ships have been seen putting into an area south of the port we called the place of grey stones. It is very flat land, barely a few metres above the level of the sea, where there are many little waterways big enough to take large boats, but it is a very marshy land and not much covered by trees and growth that would shelter incoming ships from prying eyes.'

'It sounds a dangerous place for seamen,' Eadulf pointed out.

'That it is.' The confirmation came from Teimel. 'I have travelled that way myself in the past. It is a wild and deserted stretch of the shore and certainly no place to try to land or even anchor offshore unless you know it well. I suspect those stories are not exaggerated. Sailors prefer their ports to have deep waters.'

'There is an area where the River Fheartraí empties into the sea. Due south of that is a little seaport called Church of the Toothless One,' explained Garrchú.

'Cill Mantáin? I know that,' Eadulf said with some nostalgia. He looked at Fidelma. 'Don't you remember it was the port from which we sailed that time when we were cast ashore by a storm in the kingdom of Dyfed?'

'I remember,' she replied quietly.

'Well,' continued Garrchú, 'this area of grey rocks and waterways I refer to is north of that safe little harbour.'

'Why is it called the Church of the Toothless One?' Enda could not help asking, for Laigin was an unknown country to him.

'It seems that two hundred years ago some of the first Christians landed there and were attacked by the locals. One of them had his teeth knocked out before he was able to make friends with the people. They named him Manntach, toothless one, and he built his church there,' Teimel replied. 'I heard the story from Brother Aithrigid at the Abbey of Cáemgen. He apparently spent some of his first years in Laigin, along that coast.'

'What was Brehon Rónchú implying about the sighting of the Gaulish ships in that area?' Fidelma asked, turning back to Garrchú.

The steward of the mines made a dismissive gesture. 'I suppose he suspected the smuggling of gold and silver ore, which is why he suspected the two men with the boxes that were loaded on the river boat at Láithreach.'

'It seems his suspicion was correct,' Enda observed.

'But while there is all this fuss,' sighed Garrchú, 'I should point out the worth of the ore in boxes was not enormous. I would say it would have taken ten times the amount of ore, once broken down and smelted, to maintain a noble in a medium fort for life.'

'But if such transportation of the ore had been going on for some time . . .?' queried Fidelma.

'Then it might be a worthwhile exercise,' concluded Garrchú. 'However, as I said, tomorrow, when it is light, I shall show you the forge so you can see the process for yourselves.'

Fidelma became aware that many of the guests at the evening feast had disappeared. There were only a few attendants remaining, for Garrchú's wife and her attendants and friends had also left.

'It is time for us to get some rest. I fear we have a long day tomorrow,' she said, rising. Her companions followed.

Garrchú waved one of the remaining male attendants forward and instructed him to show them to the rooms that had been prepared.

Once in their room, Eadulf flung himself on to the bed and gave a loud yawn.

'Well, I will have no difficulty in finding sleep tonight.'

Fidelma was unusually quiet. In fact, the silence caused Eadulf to peer at her as she sat in the flickering light of the candle.

'Something is on your mind?' he asked with a sinking feeling that he had spoken too soon about sleep.

'There are two things that intrigue me,' she said.

'Only two?' Eadulf tried to joke. 'This whole business intrigues me.'

'Firstly, why was Corbmac heading with Dicuil Dóna's daughter up that valley that leads to nowhere? Well, leading nowhere according to Garrchú. Were they part of a party who, then seeing we might have observed them, left someone behind to ambush us?'

Eadulf stared at her for a moment and then smiled. 'You are not going to tell me that the young girl, Aróc, came back down the mountain to have another shot at you with her bow?'

Fidelma ignored him. 'Then there is the business of the gold and silver ore. Perhaps there is a link somewhere. Garrchú reports Brehon Rónchú as saying Gaulish ships have been seen during the past months anchoring in a place so difficult that Teimel believes no captain would choose to put his ship to anchor there. Then there is the fact that Garrchú does not think the worth of the ore is much unless there is a lot of it.'

Eadulf remained silent.

'You offer no comment?' she prompted.

'Except that we seem to be questioning all Garrchú's statements. To use your very oft-repeated teaching – no speculation without information.' Eadulf yawned. 'I am not sure we have any facts to reach a conclusion but my brain is not working well without sleep.'

Fidelma allowed herself a tired expression. 'You are probably right. I can't help thinking that in trying to sort this information, I am overlooking something.'

Eadulf shrugged. 'I am afraid you are.'

She turned in amazement. 'You know? What am I overlooking?'

'The disappearance of Princess Gelgéis. That is the important reason that we have come to this gloomy mountain country in the first place.'

Fidelma stared at him for some moments. Then she smiled softly. 'You are right, Eadulf. But I do feel that some pattern is emerging, a framework that I can use. Of course, the finding of Princess Gelgéis is the principal concern. I have taken an oath to my brother on finding her. So do not be concerned. But all these things – the murder of Brehon Brocc, the disappearance of Gelgéis and her steward, Spealáin, the murder of Cétach, the mystery of the precious ore business and the attack on us . . . well, they are all connected. That's what I feel.'

'So what should we do?'

'Firstly, I would like a ride up the valley to see this mountain called Lúbán, the little bend. Something puzzles me. It's like an irritant at the back of my neck, especially with the involvement of Dicuil Dóna's daughter and her relationship with Corbmac. Why would they be going in that direction?'

'Teimel said that they could have taken other routes,' Eadulf pointed out.

Fidelma was determined. 'Tomorrow we ride to Lúbán and then we shall head back to Láithreach to have words with Brehon Rónchú. I suspect he knows more, or suspects more, than we do.'

Eadulf sighed. 'You forget, I am lacking a horse.'

'No. I know the poor beast will take a long time healing but I am sure that Garrchú will be able to find you a suitable replacement.'

'What about the possibility of being ambushed again?'

'I think it is highly likely, so we must take precautions,' she replied, not giving him comfort in the matter. 'Now,' she said brightly, 'we should get some sleep before our travels in the morning.'

As Eadulf had suspected, sleep was now banished from his mind. He was aware of the pre-dawn early birdsong, the blackbird, skylarks, thrushes and robins joining in that unique early chorus, before he finally dozed.

CHAPTER SEVENTEEN

During the first meal of the day, the next morning, Fidelma informed Enda and Teimel that her plan was to visit the isolated valley under the shadow of Lúbán. She asked Garrchú whether he or his smithy would continue to care for the wounded cob until they could return, and if he would provide a similar mount in the meantime. Garrchú was willing to fall in with her plans. While he gave instructions to one of his men to see to the arrangements with the horses he reminded Fidelma that he wanted to show her some of his methods of smelting metal ore. She had hoped he had forgotten, but he had already asked one of his men to rekindle the fires and the kiln in readiness.

He led his guests towards the series of outbuildings. The central kiln, and another fire in a brazier over which a crucible was smoking, were already giving off a glowing heat. There were several men there clad in the familiar leathers of smiths and metal workers. Garrchú drew the visitors to a bench to one side of the kiln, at which a single man was working.

Some lumps of metal had been placed on the bench. Or rather they appeared to be what Fidelma and Eadulf presumed were twisted irregular lumps of some metal ore. Next to them were pieces of worked metal, flattened and ready to be made into tools or other items. They were dark grey with now and then a bright flash as the light caught on the edge.

Garrchú picked up one of the twisted lumps and held it out to them.

'This is a sample of the gold ore that Brehon Rónchú brought here. Why can I identify it was belonging to this area? Simple; because most of our gold is found with a strong mixture of copper and this creates a red gold. Natural gold is generally basically mixtures influenced by the deposit of metals that they are found with.' He paused and picked up another piece, holding it out to them. 'This example has a green hue and indicates a silver alloy. That is not usual here but it is found in the mountains of the Mughdhorma, further north.' He put it down and picked up another piece. 'This piece here is a mixture of silver and tin, which we call *óirchédh*. Each area is individual. So you see, the gold is especially easy to identify as coming from a certain area. For those who have studied the various metal ores it is second nature to see the quality – whether there is more of certain metals along with the gold – to identify its origin.'

Fidelma was impressed. She knew there were parts of her brother's kingdom that produced gold and silver but she had no idea that those who dug out the ore were able to be specific about the area of origin.

It was when Garrchú was explaining about some other examples that an idea suddenly occurred. She reached into her *marsupium* and dug around before emerging with the heavy pebble that Brother Lachtna had taken from the purse of the murdered Brehon Brocc. She handed it to the steward of the mines.

'Can you tell me what that is?' she asked.

Garrchú took it and turned it over between thumb and fingers.

'It's not valuable,' was his first comment.

'I just want to know what sort of ore it is,' she explained.

'That's easy. It's lead. Looks like a piece of discarded ore as there is not much use to it. It's not even lead-silver but it could be zinc lead.'

'And lead is common here?'

To her disappointment, the steward of the mines nodded.

'Common enough.'

'So it could have come from anywhere? But nowhere in particular?'

'Probably towards the north of here. There is a zinc and lead working there. There used to be a good demand for lead but not one that made it a valuable metal. As you know, zinc is a good addition to make the alloy brass. The Romans had a good technique for that and, of course, Roman merchants were always looking for lead for making their water and bathing systems.'

Much of what Garrchú told them was repetition of what he had said the previous evening but Fidelma and Eadulf both listened attentively about identification and how the lord of The Cuala jealously guarded the mining rights of his territory.

It was more than mid-morning when they finally managed to extricate themselves from the almost suffocating hospitality of the mining steward. True to his word, he had found a small cob that, apart from its colour, was similar to Eadulf's previous mount. It would be a straightforward exchange, which Eadulf, not being a horseman, did not mind. He had no emotional attachment to horses, unlike Fidelma. So, with provisions and promises of support from Garrchú, if ever it were needed, Teimel led the way out of Dún Árd, the misnamed 'High Fort', and Fidelma's party began to climb up into the hills to follow the route she had planned.

In spite of the promise of a pleasant early spring day a sombre atmosphere seemed to settle on Fidelma as they crossed the hills and descended into the tree-filled valley where they had seen Corbmac with the daughter of the lord of The Cuala. It was as though a dark cloud had descended on her as she acknowledged that she was nowhere near to a solution to the disappearance of Princess Gelgéis. She wondered if she had been side-tracked over the idea of some connection with the metal theft. Was that purposely done by Dicuil Dóna? Next to her, Eadulf rode with shoulders slightly hunched, glancing at her from time to time, as though trying to read her thoughts.

No one spoke as they rode on in the direction of the hill that Teimel had identified as Lúbán, 'the little bend'. Riding ahead, only the hunter seemed undisturbed by the silence. At the rear, young Enda sat well back on his stallion as if relaxed, but a closer look would have shown the tightness of his neck muscles. The lack of movement of his head was deceptive: his eyes continued to dart hither and thither, searching the surrounding terrain for any signs of danger as well as scanning for any tracks to show the passing of Corbmac and Aróc. He had blamed himself for allowing his companions to walk into two ambushes without warning – the ambush led by Corbmac and the second one in which Eadulf's horse had been injured.

He was sensitive of his position as a warrior of the Golden Collar. His honour had been slighted and he resolved that he should offer his resignation as soon as they were safely back within the walls of Cashel. There was no way to ameliorate his loss of honour other than resignation. Fidelma was too considerate a person to have mentioned his unforgiveable failing as a warrior to whom her life had been entrusted. He had failed; failed miserably. Bitterly, he wondered how his fellows among the warriors of the Golden Collar would now regard him.

The silence was interrupted when Fidelma called to Teimel: 'Any sign of anyone passing this way?'

The hunter twisted slightly to face her. 'Nothing I can see, lady. I reckon they took one of the other paths. Mind you, I have not been this way since I was a youth.'

'So you *have* been this way before? Eadulf asked sharply. 'I thought you said—'

'As I said, not since I was a youth,' the hunter replied firmly.

Eadulf caught the warning look that Fidelma gave him and turned with an apology to the hunter. 'Forgive me,' he said, 'but as your tongue is not my own language, sometimes I am inclined to phrase things wrongly. I was just expressing my own fears.' Only Fidelma realised the irony in his voice.

Teimel accepted the apology at surface value. 'I have seen no sign of any trail yet but the ground here is hard, despite the time of year. I suggest we cut across to those woods to the east and follow the easy path back to Láithreach.'

Enda had ridden a little way ahead when their exchange began and now he held up his hand to attract their attention. He swung off his horse and peered around at the ground before remounting with a smile of satisfaction.

'There are signs here, although not just two riders. Several riders and a cart have passed this way.'

'That can't be Corbmac and Aróc then,' the hunter said defensively.

'How do you read those signs, Enda?' Fidelma asked quickly.

'They are old, much older than yesterday. So, I agree, they are nothing to do with Corbmac and the girl. It looks like a group that were certainly heading over the western shoulder of the mountain, unless they made a turn further on.'

'It was said by Garrchú that the place was isolated and deserted,' Eadulf could not help adding with a soft emphasis.

'I want to see this deserted valley,' Fidelma said firmly. She often trusted Eadulf's intuition and she felt he was suspicious. 'So we will proceed towards it whether or not Corbmac and Aróc have gone there.'

Teimel appeared as if he was going to object but thought better of it. He was silent and there was no disagreement.

They proceeded slowly, following the track. Eadulf took the opportunity to move closer to Fidelma. He did not look comfortable on his new mount.

'It will take me a little time to get used to this animal,' he explained loudly to Fidelma. 'I didn't realise that horses had different personalities.'

Fidelma could not help a smile. She knew Eadulf disliked travelling on horseback and had been pleased that he seemed to be growing out of this shortcoming – a shortcoming in her eyes – when he grew used to riding on the placid cob she had given him. He had grown so confident that he was able to take their son, Alchú, for his morning ride without having to ask one of her brother's warriors to accompany them. But there was little advice she could offer him. She found it surprising that some people did not realise animals, especially such an intelligent species as the horse, were possessed of varied personalities, just as human beings were. Well, Eadulf was doing his best with the fact that his new mount was possessed of more spirit and in need of more guidance than the old cob. However, she guessed he had ridden close for another reason.

'Something worries you?' she asked quietly, picking up on his mood.

'I think Teimel saw those tracks before Enda did. I also saw them, which was why I pointed out that he had not been here before.'

She did not reply. She had also detected that Enda had been displaying signs of suspicion about the hunter.

'Enda also saw that Teimel uses his left hand.'

'It proves nothing, as I have told you. I have seen him use both left and right with the same ease. He is what is known as *comdelb* – ambidextrous.'

They emerged above the tree line of the hill, whose summit was to their east. Enda, his eyes keenly on the tracks now, followed them as they crossed over the western shoulder, continuing north. He and Teimel were very alert as they were now on the bald hillside without any growth of trees to disguise their movements. At least there was no concealment for an ambush. Enda paused on the brow, saw the tall hills spreading out around them, and immediately below them a small valley with some streams crossing it. In the middle was a tiny hill with some ruins on top. It looked like an ancient farmstead, exactly as Garrchú had described.

'Is this the deserted valley?' Enda asked.

'This little valley is called An Láithreach,' Teimel said.

Eadulf frowned. 'But that's the same name as the town near the abbey.'

'It is,' agreed Teimel. 'The name means a place with an old ruin. There is an old ruined farmstead that has been there since folk were old enough to remember.'

'For someone who has not been here since a boy, you have a good memory,' Eadulf observed softly.

Teimel made no response.

'What's that large hill on the north side of the valley?' Fidelma queried in a bland voice. 'I presume you can remember that?'

'As a hunter in these mountains one has to retain as much local knowledge as one can. That is An Mullach Rua – The Red Top. There's a river rises on it, which courses down into the valley. As you can see from here, it is a desolate and abandoned place with no sign of any mining activity.'

'We'll go down and take a look anyway,' Fidelma decided.

They descended into the valley and the shadows of the hills seemed to cut out the pale spring sunshine, increasing the odd sombre feelings they had been experiencing since they left Garrchú's fortress. The valley felt cold and it certainly appeared deserted. It was almost devoid of any springtime growth, which Fidelma put down to the fact that its being surrounded by hills excluded sunshine. It was similar to the feeling she had on entering Gleann Uí Máil. It would take more time for warmth to penetrate and make the spaces of verdure between the rocky areas spring to life. There were just a few trees in the valley, mainly yew. As they descended, there was no sign of any other habitation besides the granite stones of what had once been a farmstead.

It was Enda, peering upwards in case of another threat, who drew their attention to the hill Teimel had called The Red Top.

'There's a cave there, not too far up. It looks like some earthworks have been dug along the front of it. That means there is a large shelf of land there.'

They halted and stared up. Enda was right. They turned to Teimel with questioning looks. He seemed defensive. 'That's new since I was a boy visiting here. As I said, this valley was entirely deserted then.'

'We should proceed carefully,' Eadulf cautioned. 'If that is a mine that was worked recently then there might be hostile eyes watching us. Would it not be wise to check out the ruined farmhouse first before we proceed across the valley and investigate?'

'Good thinking, friend Eadulf,' Enda agreed at once. 'Don't let your enemy position themselves at your back.'

Teimel frowned. 'What enemy? No one has used that place since . . .' He stopped, realising that he was making a silly comment.

'If someone has been mining the valley, which Garrchú, as well as you, claimed was deserted, then it is just as likely they would be using the deserted building as well.'

Without another word Eadulf turned his horse and began to lead the way towards the small circular rise and the deserted grey granite of the buildings. Until they grew closer it was hard to see whether it was a farmhouse or just a construction for animals, the whole place was so old and rotting. If there had been a door then it was long reduced to wood pulp and mingled with the earth. The curious thing was that there was a strong smell of decay about the place, despite there being no roof to ensnare the odours. The main walls of the building were blocks of rough granite, no more than the height of a man's chest in most places. Even Fidelma and Eadulf could see there was sign of recent human use about the place.

Enda had taken the precaution of drawing his sword before dismounting and moving cautiously into the small complex. Teimel followed, while Fidelma and Eadulf remained outside to take charge of the horses. It did not take Enda long to assess the ruins hid no dangers.

'There have been people here,' he announced. 'I do not think they were just miners.' He carried in his hand some lengths of severed ropes. 'It looks as if someone has been bound by these.'

Fidelma frowned, taking them from him and holding them up speculatively.

Teimel said quickly, 'Probably shepherds or goat herders used them to keep their animals from wandering.'

Enda shook his head and pointed to the ends of the rope. 'Those ends were cut, and with a sharp knife. That is a waste of good rope. And just by the ropes I found this . . .'

Like a *clesaidhi*, a conjurer, producing a prize item, he handed Fidelma a small pin brooch of the sort women used to fasten their cloaks on their shoulders. It was an oval silver-framed piece of white enamel with a small cross depicted in small red stones. Fidelma drew in a sharp breath. She had seen it before, or something very like it. It was something her brother had once bought as a gift.

She sat staring at it for such a time that Eadulf became concerned.

'I think this might have belonged to Gelgéis,' she finally said in a flat tone. Then she rose. 'We best take another look around these buildings. We might have missed something.'

It was not long before Enda appeared around the corner of the ruins.

'We nearly did miss something,' he said. He beckoned them to join him.

He walked a short distance to the edge of one of the ruined walls and halted, pointing down in front of him. There was a mound of earth there. It was newly dug. There was no mistaking that the shape and size conveyed what it was: a grave has only one sinister shape.

Fidelma had paled a little at the possibility that came to her mind. She stood staring at the earth for a little while before looking at her companions.

'I am afraid we need to ascertain who reposes in this grave,' she said quietly.

Enda did not hesitate but walked quickly back to his horse. As a warrior he carried certain items that were considered essential on the traditional hosting, or summons to battle. These included a small *ernach*, a sharp iron digging tool, and a *slúasat*, a shovel. When the warriors were called to march as a *sluagh,* an army, with the prospect of a battle in hostile country, they usually went prepared to erect camps or fortify positions. From past experience, Enda, whenever sent to accompany Fidelma on a journey, always included them. Now he returned with the tools and tossed one to Teimel, who caught it deftly. Both men divested themselves of their extra equipment and set to work on the grave mound.

'You really think that this might be the body of Gelgéis?' Eadulf was horrified by the thought.

'I pray it is not,' Fidelma replied grimly. 'But the killing of Brehon Brocc leads me to the conclusion that anything is possible.'

'But it must be some distance from here to the spot where her Brehon was found.'

Fidelma made no reply. Her face was sombre as she watched Enda and Teimel working at their distasteful task. Knowing how much Gelgéis meant to her brother, as well as the fact that she, herself, liked and had become friends with the girl, she was trying her best to control the premonition of horror that she felt. All Eadulf could do was stand ready in a supportive, sympathetic role.

With the two warriors working almost in unison it did not seem long before they were well into the grave, which was fairly shallow anyway.

Enda, who was sensitive to Fidelma's concerns, called immediately to her: 'It's a male.'

Fidelma heaved a breath of relief. That was not what she was expecting. 'Are you sure?'

'There is one body in the grave, lady. It is a male,' Teimel echoed Enda.

'Is it her steward, Spealáin?' Eadulf said, glancing at Fidelma. 'Don't forget, Spealáin . . .'

'I have not,' she responded sharply. She had realised that only she and Eadulf would know what Spealáin looked like. Resolutely she moved forward to the grave.

Enda held out his hand as if to stop her. 'Even if it is a week or more since burial, it might not be a pretty sight, lady,' he warned.

'You forget I am a *dálaigh*, Enda, and am used to looking at dead bodies,' she replied.

Enda stood aside to allow her to peer down into the shallow defile. It was true that the man who lay buried there was not a pretty sight. Those who had buried him had not been too careful with the blade of their shovel and some of the skull had been smashed and the flesh torn. Fidelma was about to turn away in disgust but then she realised something that caused her to focus on the hair of the corpse. She stood back and motioned Eadulf to come forward.

'When did you last see Spealáin?' she asked.

Eadulf was puzzled. 'Why, the same time as you; about six or seven weeks ago when Princess Gelgéis came on a visit to Cashel and brought her entourage.'

'And you recall the colour of his hair?'

'Of course.'

She stepped aside. 'Take a look.'

His look was brief. 'That is not Spealáin,' he declared with some relief in his voice.

'Why?'

'Because Spealáin had greying hair and this man has white hair; white the colour of snow. Also, while the top of this man's skull has been crushed, I see the jawline is of a rounded shape. I remember Spealáin as having a very pronounced jutting jaw. It was square. No; this man is not Spealáin.'

'Perhaps he is just a goatherd or some such worker?' suggested Teimel. 'It is easy to die from some accident or other.'

Before she could answer, Enda reached forward and began to

uncover where he estimated the hands would be under the soil. They watched him in surprise.

'I don't think he is any type of shepherd, goatherd or even a worker in these mines. Look at his hands.'

In spite of the burial, the hands were obviously well manicured. They were not the hands of a person who had done any manual work at all.

'Anyway, we can see that this man did not die of some careless accident,' pointed out Fidelma wearily. 'He was killed and buried purposefully. But this does not help in his identification. There is not even a ring to identify him.'

Eadulf was peering closely at the hands, although his expression showed he would prefer not to.

'There is the mark that shows he did wear a ring on the left hand at some time. It must have been pulled off before they buried him. The wearing of such a ring indicates he was a man of some position, although not necessarily a noble who would usually have a chain of rank.'

'Well spotted, Eadulf,' she smiled. 'But knowing that does not help us much. So is there anything else?'

Eadulf shook his head. 'The clothes he is buried in are of good quality. Certainly he was a man of rank. Interesting that those that buried him did not take those garments off first. That tells us that they were not mere thieves or brigands who would have sold them. The clothes fit in with the appearance of the hands. He was a person of some means.'

'Little point in standing here guessing,' Fidelma said. 'Whoever he was, he is not Spealáin and, apart from the brooch, there is no sign of Gelgéis.'

'I don't suppose you would recognise the body?' It was Enda who asked the question of Teimel.

The hunter shook his head. 'It could be anyone,' he replied. 'I don't recognise him. Not in that mutilated condition.'

Fidelma thought about it. 'We can't even be sure of the man being local. What do we have? A brooch that I think I remember seeing Gelgéis wearing, and some cord that is cut and could have been used to tie the hands of someone. We have the body of someone of status but can't identify him. So, we have to be careful of making facts out of our suppositions. That is not the way to resolving this riddle.'

Eadulf looked disappointed.

'It does not alter the fact that something went on here. I don't mean just this murder.'

It was Enda who pointed out the obvious. 'Perhaps the answer lies in or around that cave we can see on what Teimel here calls Mullach Rua.' He pointed to the dark hill opposite.

The gruesome find had almost pushed the idea of the mine workings from their thoughts.

'You are right,' Fidelma replied shortly and decisively, putting the brooch in her *marsupium*. She led the way back to their horses and was the first to be mounted.

'Be cautious, lady,' Enda warned. 'I should lead the way. We do not know what awaits us there and should be careful.'

'If there is anyone up there who means us harm then they will have seen us by now,' she replied. 'Anyway, while we can be vigilant, I don't see a likely ambush spot ahead of us.'

Enda insisted on riding ahead in spite of her protest. He was concerned that the route across the valley lay over a stream and through a copse of trees. These were likely spots if anyone contemplated an ambush. They were the only places of concealment for anyone keeping down below the bank of the stream. This stream led straight up to the hills ahead, but Enda soon discovered that another stream lay ahead before the ground rose up the facing hillside. He hoped Fidelma had not noticed his oversight in checking it. Since he now blamed himself for the previous two ambushes, he was conscious of every action that could rebound on him. But

Fidelma made no comment as the horses waded across. It was not deep and flowed over a rocky, quartz bed. Here were the first signs of some human occupation and that an area had been used to wash rocks, ridding them of clinging mud in the shallow flowing waters of the stream. Nearby, flattened grass and piles of twigs showed where people had camped and made a fire.

The cave entrance was not too far above them and, in spite of Enda's caution, it seemed quiet and desolate. The entrance itself was a ledge from which a wide track descended at an angle towards the east and a high mountain range that led eventually to the valley where the Abbey of Cáemgen was situated and the town of Láithreach beyond.

There was no doubt that there had been a camp on this little plateau, with signs of campfires and more extensive habitation. There were also abandoned broken tools: picks, axes and shovels. Piles of broken granite and other smashed rocks showed working at extracting the metal ore.

The riders halted and dismounted. Enda, as cautious as ever, had drawn his sword and approached the entrance of the cave. Then he stood back and sounded disappointed.

'It is only a shallow working, not really a cave at all.'

Fidelma could see that it was not a natural cave; it was more as if someone, or a group of men, with pickaxes and spades, had attacked the side of the hill and dug deep into it, creating a large manmade cave. Closer inspection showed that from this cave large amounts of ore had been dug and presumably washed and taken away by handcarts to a place where they could be loaded on to a mule cart and taken away down a wider track to the meeting of the river at Láithreach. She presumed the ore would then be placed on river boats sailing down to the sea coast for shipment by the Gaulish sea-going vessels.

She surveyed the cave-like digging, shaking her head in bewilderment. The amount of gold and silver ore from this digging could barely have been worth all the effort. She was surprised to see that Enda had scrambled up above the man-made cave and had disappeared. It was an optical illusion, apparently, as the indentation could not be seen from the angle at which they were looking up.

He suddenly appeared looking down at them.

'A vein!' he shouted down. 'They were following a vein!'

Eadulf looked bewildered. However, Fidelma had understood.

'Are there more workings up there?'

'A low line of diggings cutting across the hillside just behind this ridge, which have been disguised with bushes and shrubs. That's why it could not be seen from across the valley. They must have struck a vein from somewhere along the hillside to the east and have been digging along it.'

'What does that mean?' demanded Eadulf. He wished he had listened more closely to Garrchú's discourse the previous evening.

Fidelma turned with a smile. 'Gold and silver are often found in what they call veins. If you find one you can usually follow it for long stretches, especially between quartz and granite. That's what the steward of the mines told us.'

She glanced up but Teimel had disappeared now, obviously trying to estimate the extent of the workings.

'So we might have found a solution to Dicuil Dóna's mystery. If he says that he didn't know of this digging then it must be that this is the illegal mine workings and the source of the ore. If that is the case then we have fulfilled our promise to resolve the mystery that Brehon Rónchú gave Dicuil Dóna.' She suddenly went quiet.

'A problem?' Eadulf asked.

'Brehon Rónchú. He is noticeable by his absence.'

'But he is supposed to be on his legal circuit,' Eadulf pointed out.

She glanced across the valley to the abandoned farmhouse with its lonely grave. Eadulf caught her meaning but shook his head.

'Teimel would have recognised the body. It would be foolish not to do so when we could so easily show him to be a liar.'

'Perhaps. Yet we cannot prove him to be so immediately, can we?' she said softly. 'I'll keep an open mind. Anyway, we have learnt nothing more than we knew previously.'

'I don't understand.'

'We knew from this story about the gold being seized that it was illegally mined and, by law, it belonged to the lord of The Cuala. We can be safe in the assumption that we have now learnt where the illegal ore was being mined. We have not resolved if or how Gelgéis and her companions were involved.'

'They could have come across the mine working, and those working here took them prisoners to stop them talking.'

'How would they have deviated so far from their road from Osraige to the Abbey of Cáemgen? Don't forget it was on that road that Brehon Brocc was found. It is more logical that they were all taken prisoner when Brocc was killed and brought here where the body was sheltered for a week before being taken back and left where he had been killed a week before. But why? Why was the body taken back to the original track for Cétach to find?'

'I am confused.'

Fidelma was thoughtful for a moment. 'Consider it a little more. They were not taken prisoner to hide the fact of the killing of the Brehon. They were taken prisoner in order to stop whoever did it being identified.'

Eadulf frowned. 'That means they knew the killer or killers.'

'Or might be able to identify them later,' confirmed Fidelma.

'Assuming she and her steward were brought here as prisoners, as you suggest, why? Why not have them killed immediately?'

'I think the killers must have realised that she was an important person.' Another idea was forming in Fidelma's mind but not quite as sharply.

'You mean they realised her worth as a princess of Osraige?' Eadulf sounded doubtful. 'You mean that she and her party were ambushed because of who she was? Or they discovered who she was after the ambush? And what is the connection with this illegal mine working?'

Fidelma sighed. 'You are asking the questions before we have the facts,' she admitted. 'Somewhere everything must fit in.' She glanced about the site of the workings as if she expected an answer to the puzzle to suddenly appear.

Enda and Teimel rejoined them.

'We can find nothing further of significance,' Enda said. 'What now?'

'Aren't we going back to Dicuil Dóna?' Teimel asked. 'Are we going to report to him about this place?'

'Not until I have more information about the relationship between Corbmac and Aróc,' Fidelma responded quickly. 'Did Dicuil Dóna know about them? Is he using us as the catspaw, sending us after them, perhaps to find out about them? Are they stealing from him or is he sending us on some wild-goose chase for his own reasons? Do not forget, my primary concern is to find out what has happened to Princess Gelgéis.'

'What do you intend to do?' Eadulf asked.

'We shall go back to the abbey first. I want to reflect more on this matter. For some reason, I feel there is more information at the abbey or in the township of Láithreach. Do you know the route back to the Glen of the Two Lakes?' she asked Teimel.

'I can do that journey as if I were blindfolded,' the hunter declared. 'It is a hilly route from here to around that flat-topped mountain ahead to the east.' He pointed in the direction. 'We come to a place where there are three lakes before we follow a single track leading downwards alongside the stream that rises there. That takes us around a tall mountain, Ceann an Bhealaigh – the Head of the Way. From there we join up with the glen called the Glen of the Yews, through which the river flows directly into the Glen of the Two Oaks. It is not difficult to navigate; just tiring to travel.'

'Does that lead us near to the place where Cétach found the body of the Brehon?' Fidelma asked. 'When we were taken prisoner by Corbmac, I seem to remember we crossed by that peak called Ceann an Bhealaigh – that was near to where we had to spend the night.'

'You have a good memory, lady,' admitted the hunter. 'If the point where Corbmac ambushed us was where the body of the Brehon was found, then it was north of where we shall pass.'

'It would have been along that way that they would have been brought here?' The question was rhetorical for she was speaking to herself. She sighed. 'The only positive matter I think we are sure about is that there is some connection with this mine.'

'What do we do about the corpse, lady?' asked Enda.

'How do you mean, what to do about it?' Fidelma was confused by the question.

'We should make a record of it for identification.'

'A record, yes; but we don't know who it is,' pointed out Eadulf. 'At least we know it is not Spealáin.' He glanced at the hunter. 'It was mentioned that he showed signs of having worn a ring. That meant he was a noble or an official. We agreed on that. But if he were a local noble, then you would have known him, wouldn't you, Teimel?'

The hunter gave a shrug but succeeded only in looking uncomfortable. 'I didn't recognise him but then, as you recall, his head had been smashed in, presumably by a shovel during burial, if not before.'

'Before?' Fidelma frowned.

'When he was attacked – murdered, as you say.'

'You are right,' Eadulf agreed. 'It is almost impossible to see how the head of the corpse could have been so damaged accidentally while being buried. I would say that this was the result of an attack with the shovel as a weapon rather than damage after death.'

Fidelma was thoughtful. 'He was not local, based on the fact that Teimel does not recognise him. We know that the killer was so filled with hate and bloodlust that they struck out in a bloody fury. Look at the way that the corpse was mutilated.'

'Well, it should not be hard to find out his identity. Surely a man of noble status would travel in company. Where are his companions?'

Fidelma glanced at him almost sadly. 'So where is the companion of Princess Gelgéis?' she asked dryly.

Teimel was apparently watching the shadows of clouds moving across the mountains.

'If we are going to make a move towards the abbey, I must suggest that we start soon, lady,' he warned.

Fidelma uttered a sigh and nodded. 'Any idea how long it will take us?'

'If we are not slow in the journey then we could be there just at dusk and the lights of the gate at the abbey will be a guide. As for myself, I can reach my cabin on the outskirts of Láithreach in darkness just as easily as in daylight.'

Fidelma was about to say that travelling at night time was not a problem to her even if they were not escorted by Enda, as most children were taught how to spot the Seven Sisters and thence the North Star to guide them at night. As for Enda, it was part of his training as a warrior to be versed in finding his way in all types of weather. But she made no reply.

'Let us get started,' Teimel urged.

As they mounted, Enda cast a searching look around the isolated valley to ensure against any surprises. A mine had been worked here, veins of gold and silver ore had been extracted and someone had been killed. It was enough to tell part of the story. It was still speculation as to who the dead person was. It was certainly beyond Enda's capability to guess. He knew only that lack of diligence had caused them to be ambushed twice. And he also knew that he did not trust Teimel.

Soon they were leaving the valley behind them and moved out across the hills with Teimel apparently avoiding the almost primordial tree-filled gullies. He kept to a narrow path further up the hillside. This caused Eadulf considerable nervousness as he had to lean at an

angle to maintain his balance on his horse. He just hoped that this
new horse was as sure footed as his old cob and would not send him
tumbling down the mountain. The trouble was, Teimel made no allow-
ances and led them along at a brisk pace. Even Fidelma had cause
to call out to him and advise that he slow the pace. She had also
given Eadulf some advice when he'd first began to ride seriously.
She'd pointed out that horses were intelligent creatures and, given
free rein, would follow a safe path without having to be guided. So,
remembering this now, he sat back and allowed the animal its head.

It was during that curious short period before the onset of dusk
that Teimel led them by the point where the River of Yews entered
into the large Upper Lake of the valley of Two Lakes. Dusk was
descending rapidly by the time they reached the end of the lake and
followed the river to the Lower Lake and the lights from the abbey
came in sight. It was here that Teimel reminded her that he would
leave her and her companions at the abbey and ride on to his cabin
on the outskirts of Láithreach.

They had not started to part company when Enda called a soft
cautionary warning.

'Stay back a little and you will be interested to observe who is
coming out of the main gate.'

The area of the gate to the abbey was lit by two strong oil lanterns
hung on tall poles, which flooded the immediate area around the
gate and the bridge over the stream. They had just been about to
approach from scant cover behind the trees into the area of light
when Enda halted them.

Two people were emerging out of the main gate. One was the
dorseóracht, the gatekeeper, Brother Dorchú. The other figure
was that of the person they least expected to see at the abbey. It was
Corbmac, commander of the lord of The Cuala's bodyguard.

chapter eighteen

As they watched, even though they could not hear the words, they could see the manner of the exchange between the two men seemed affable, as if they were old friends. They spoke for a short while and the onlookers heard laughter between them at some shared joke. Then with a friendly handshake they turned in separate directions. Brother Dorchú went back to the abbey and Corbmac mounted his horse and disappeared into the encompassing evening darkness.

It was Teimel who eventually made the first move after Corbmac had left. He raised his hand to Fidelma and quietly said: 'If you need me, I shall be found at my cabin.' He urged his horse forward into the darkness at a trot in the same direction that Corbmac had taken. It was the only track to the township.

'Lady,' whispered Enda, after he had disappeared, 'I am afraid I do not trust that man.'

'Corbmac?' Fidelma asked with a frown, her mind elsewhere.

'No, lady. I mean Teimel. Many things puzzle me about his behaviour.'

'Do not be apologetic, Enda,' Fidelma replied in even tone. 'We should all be cautious by the very nature of where we are and what we are engaged in.'

'Teimel seemed to be trying to mislead us . . . pointing out how friendly Corbmac is with Brother Dorchú.'

'Perhaps Teimel's answers could be ascribed to lack of guile. Also Brother Dorchú served the lord of The Cuala as a warrior before he became a religieux and came to this abbey. Why should he not be friendly with Corbmac, his one-time commander? We will bear all these questions in mind. But we will speak later. Now, the day grows late and it is the time for the evening baths. Also I, for one, am hungry.'

They entered through the gate and across the small river over the wooden bridge to the second gate of the abbey. Brother Dorchú, having heard their approach on the wooden planking, had come forward. They could see little of his features in the flickering lamplight.

'*Pax vobiscum*,' he greeted them.

'And peace to you, Brother Dorchú,' she and the others replied gravely as they rode towards the stables. As they dismounted Fidelma turned to Enda.

'We may have a busy day tomorrow so make sure the stable master has the horses well rested and fed. Now Eadulf and I will make sure our baths are being attended to.'

Enda raised a hand in acknowledgment. As he led the horses away several stable lads emerged from the gloom to take charge. As Fidelma and Eadulf moved towards the guest quarters, Brother Aithrigid appeared.

'We did not expect you back so soon,' he greeted. 'Did you have a fruitful trip, lady?'

'Fruitful enough,' she replied indifferently. 'Where might we find Abbot Daircell?'

'He is in the scriptorium, lady. Shall I take you there?'

'We know the way now,' she assured him.

'It will not be long before the time for the evening bell summons the brethren to the refectory,' he reminded them.

'Have no fear, Brother Aithrigid,' she replied solemnly. 'We do not intend to disrupt the routine of the abbey.'

Abbot Daircell seemed surprised to see them as they entered the scriptorium.

'I did not expect you to return so soon from your sojourn in the mountains,' he greeted them, rising, making a gesture for them to be seated before resuming his own chair. 'Was the trip made with profit?'

'There is no journey that is without profit,' Fidelma smiled, 'or, at least, for those willing to learn.'

'And you have learned something? I mean, in the search for my cousin, Princess Gelgéis?'

Fidelma appeared to be gathering her thoughts. 'I wanted to confirm with you that when she sent word of her coming here, when she sent her message by carrier pigeon, she did not say anything specific about the cause of her concerns?'

'Nothing at all except that she was worried about some conspiracy in Osraige.'

'A conspiracy – by whom and for what?'

'Just that she had heard of a conspiracy.'

'She made no reference to thefts from the mines of The Cuala?'

The abbot looked astonished. 'Why would she mention mines?'

'So she only gave you to understand that she needed to speak to you about the safety of Osraige, related to some conspiracy?'

'My impression was that she had no trust in Tuaim Snámha of Osraige?' the abbot replied. 'Of course, it is well known that Osraige paid tribute only reluctantly to Cashel after the defeat of Cronán of Liath Mór and that a conspiracy was suspected between Fianamail and Tuaim Snámha. So I suspect that it might have been something to do with that.'

'But you know no more?'

'I know no more,' the abbot confirmed.

Fidelma suddenly rose and apologised to the abbot. 'I am afraid we must attend the *fothrucud*, the bathing, before the evening meal.'

The abbot waved his hands distractedly, half in acknowledgement and half in dismissal.

'I presume that you have already met Aróc, the daughter of the lord of The Cuala?' he said unexpectedly as they were almost exiting the door. 'I heard that you were guests at his fortress.'

Fidelma turned back with a frown. 'We were. I have encountered her. How do you know we met?'

'She is a guest here in the abbey tonight,' explained the abbot. 'I thought that you should know. Alas, Aróc is a wilful child; perhaps even more wilful than her father.'

When Eadulf followed Fidelma from the abbot's chambers to the guest rooms he was shaking his head.

'It is difficult to fish for information when you don't know the right bait,' he offered.

'None the less,' she smiled almost mischievously, 'I believe that I have found the right stream to fish in.'

Eadulf stared at her for a moment before giving an exaggerated shrug. 'I presume that you will tell me, at some stage, what stream we are fishing in?'

At that moment they entered the bathing rooms and a serving woman came forward to announce that the bath water was heated ready for them but they must make haste for the bell for the last meal of the day would soon be sounding. It put an end to further conversation. The bell announcing the evening meal was sounding even as they were dressing, and so there was no time at all to have any discussion before they were drawn to the refectory.

Fidelma and Eadulf glanced round in curiosity but the figure of Aróc was certainly not visible among the lines of religious taking their places for the meal. The abbot appeared at the head of the principal table as everyone stood ready for the *Gratias*.

'*Benedic nos, Domine, et haec tua dona, quae de tua largitate . . .*'

Led by the abbot, the prayers were chanted in monotone before the meal began. The bell sounded and everyone fell to eating. As before, there was no rule of silence during the meal but there was little opportunity for privacy to discuss the questions in Eadulf's mind. The abbot finally led the concluding grace and then, following his departure from the hall and the leaving of many of the brethren, some of the senior members grew closer to Fidelma and Eadulf and it was plain they were filled with curiosity and made no show of hiding it.

It was the cynical physician, Brother Lachtna, who opened the questions that many of the brethren seemed to have difficulty in suppressing. The physician leant across the table with a broad, almost derisive, grin.

'So you have made a journey into the dark valleys of these mountains. And did you encounter the Aos Sí in your travels?'

This drew a sharp intake of breath from Brother Dorchú so Fidelma decided to return humour for humour.

'Ah, learned doctor, how can we answer you? We are just lawyers, human and fallible folk. If we encountered a shapeshifter we have no qualifications to identify such a creature. Indeed, if someone can shift their shape, how are we to tell what shape is genuine? You might well be a shapeshifter yourself and we would not be able to recognise if this is your real shape or the shape you have become.'

Brother Lachtna gave a roar of laughter and slapped the table, palm downwards.

'Well said, Fidelma of Cashel,' he replied appreciatively. 'And who can say what a person's true shape is? The mind is the greatest shapeshifter of all.'

Brother Dorchú uttered another contemptuous exhalation of breath. 'I have no understanding of your humours, physician. I know what I know and there are strange things that dwell among the mountains. The Aos Sí did not perish with the coming of the New Faith. They are still there.'

'Is that why you left the lord of The Cuala's service to seek refuge here?' the physician sneered. 'Did you come to shelter from the attentions of the Aos Sí?'

For a moment it seemed that Brother Dorchú was tensed ready

to attack the physician. Then he turned abruptly away and stormed off.

'It is not a good path to tread, belittling the beliefs of others,' reproved Fidelma, shaking her head in disapproval at Brother Lachtna.

The physician shrugged indifferently. 'The man should have more sense. He was once a warrior. He was a guard at Dicuil Dóna's mines. So he ought to know well that the only shapeshifters in the mines were those thieves that shifted the shape of the precious metals from the mines to their own pockets.'

'So you found nothing of interest in your journey?' The query came almost sharply from Brother Eochaí. 'I see Brother Eadulf has returned with a new cob; one that bears the mark of Garrchú, the lord of The Cuala's steward of the mines. So there must have been some incident of interest to lose a good horse and have it replaced.'

'It was a gift of hospitality when my own horse was injured,' replied Eadulf.

Fidelma rose slowly to her feet with a weary smile. 'It was a matter of little interest,' she said, glancing meaningfully at Eadulf. 'You will excuse us but it has been a long day and a tiring journey.'

Fidelma was surprised when Eadulf did not make a move to follow her once they were outside the refectory.

'I'll join you in a moment,' he explained, 'but I need a walk to clear my head. I have spent too long on horseback these last few days and I need to feel there is strength still left in my feet.'

Fidelma did not challenge him though she felt he had another reason to stay behind. She hoped that he was not going to reveal anything that she would prefer was kept secret.

In fact, her suspicions were justified. An idea had occurred to Eadulf. After she had left the refectory, he also rose and made his excuses. Once outside he headed in the direction of the gatehouse of the abbey, guided by the flickering lanterns along the path. He had no trouble finding the person he was looking for. The burly, morose figure of Brother Dorchú was actually seated on a wooden bench just outside the main gate by the bridge that led over the stream. He seemed to be staring in contemplation at the dark, rippling waters before him. There was a lantern over the main gate but, as his head turned to watch Eadulf's approach, it cast too many shadows for Eadulf to see the expression on his features. He guessed they would be belligerent.

'Do you mind if I join you for a moment, Brother Dorchú?'

The gatekeeper grunted in annoyance: 'It is late and I like to sit in isolated contemplation before I prepare myself to repose for the night.'

Eadulf was not put off but lowered himself on the wooden bench.

'I, too, like to follow that habit,' he replied cheerfully, 'so I will not disturb you for long.' He paused for a moment, awaiting a protest, but the gatekeeper seemed nonplussed for a reply. Eadulf let a few moments pass.

'You must not take what Brother Lachtna says too seriously,' he observed. When there was no response, Eadulf pressed further. 'I did not embrace the New Faith until I was a young man. But, having done so, I could not abandon the old ways that were embedded in the roots of my people's memories. While we might accept new interpretations there are still basic fundamentals that remain.'

Brother Dorchú had turned towards him, but Eadulf still could not see his face in the semi-light.

'I have no understanding of what you are saying,' the gatekeeper replied irritably.

'What I am saying is that you must not take it personally when people make comments that show that they have not fully understood the New Faith. The Blessed Paul of Tarsus admits that the evil demons rule the age we live in. Does not the Holy Scripture acknowledge that demons exist in the inaccessible and lonely places, in the dark shadows of the caverns, among the secluded and remote

areas such as your high peaks of The Cuala?' He made a gesture
to the surrounding mountains.

There was a pause before the gatekeeper said hesitantly: 'You
are better read than I am, Brother Saxon.' Eadulf decided that on
this occasion he would let the 'Saxon' reference go. There were
times to challenge it and times not to. Anyway, the people of the
Five Kingdoms used 'Saxon' as they did not seem to possess another
name for his people, the Angles.

'I assure you it is so,' Eadulf affirmed. 'The New Faith says
there is good in the world and, knowing there is good, it must
follow there is evil. Otherwise how do we know what is good? So
the New Faith is replete with references to the evil demons that
beset us.'

The gatekeeper sniffed. 'Then why is it that the Brothers make fun
when I speak of the shapeshifters that dwell among the mountains?'

'They probably do so out of their own fears. I find myself
doing the same thing rather than admit the presence of the water
spirits; the dragons and the like.'

Brother Dorchú sighed.

'Up among the high peaks is the lair of the shapeshifters, Brother.
I know it. I came here seeking protection.'

'You have spent much time in the high peaks?'

'I was a child of goatherds and, having acquired strength and
tenacity in my youth, I was spotted by the commander of the bodyguard of the lord of The Cuala. He it was who chose me for training
in the art of arms.'

'But, surely, that was a good life?'

'So I thought, and did so for years. Then I realised that, while
sons of nobles were sent to the hostings called by the King, and
while they were given every opportunity to prove their courage
and honour in battle, I was designated only to guard the mines.
Why was this? I was told . . . I was not the son of a noble. One of
my standing could only guard mines or other places worthy of a

sentinel. I was told not to try to elevate myself to the levels of the champion warriors . . .'

'So you were usually put in charge of protecting the mines here, among the mountains?' Eadulf was sympathetic. 'And was there much theft from the mines that a guard had to be set?'

'The lord of The Cuala jealously guarded his claims over the mines. However, you have seen the vastness of the territory. He left it to Corbmac, his commander, to appoint a guard on those mines thought to be vulnerable to theft.'

'I have met Corbmac,' Eadulf said quickly. 'Are you a friend of his?'

Eadulf was slightly shocked when Brother Dorchú made a spitting sound in the darkness. A moment passed before Eadulf realised that the gatekeeper was but recently a warrior rather than a religieux.

'You dislike him?' Having seen the two together earlier that evening he wondered at the response.

'I am told by the abbot that I must show friendship to him. But Corbmac is arrogant. He looked down on me because I was the son of goatherds. He was the son of a *bo-aire*, a person of some noble blood. He therefore gave me every worthless job he could think of.'

'Why would you be friendly to him just because the abbot told you to?'

'Remember that this abbey thrives only because of the patronage of Dicuil Dóna. That is why the abbot cannot refuse hospitality to his daughter, Aróc.' The words drew forth a bitter chuckle from the gatekeeper. 'Did you know Aróc stays this very night in the abbey guesthouse?' He went on before Eadulf could comment, 'Corbmac came with her as usual as her escort.'

'As usual? Does she come here often?'

'More frequently than in earlier days.'

'I was surprised to see Corbmac escorting her when we left Dún Droch Fhola. But she is now beyond the age of choice so that she can do as she wishes and go with any man she wishes.' Eadulf frowned in the darkness. 'Do you imply that she has a liaison with Corbmac? And even before she was at the age of choice?'

'Even before I left service at the fortress, I knew she was overly friendly to him. But it is nothing to do with me,' Brother Dorchú said. 'You asked me if I dislike Corbmac. I do. Whatever he is, he is still influential and I will not disobey the abbot.'

'I gather it was about a year since you decided to leave the bodyguards?'

'It was.'

'What made you join this abbey?'

'It would be difficult for me to go to some other territory and expect to be welcomed after I had been in service to the lord of The Cuala. So I came here and I asked Abbot Daircell if he would accept me as a novitiate into the religieux.'

'Which he did.' Eadulf did not mean it as a question because the answer was obvious. He used it more as punctuation.

'Which he did,' repeated Brother Dorchú.

'It must be frustrating.'

'Frustrating?' The gatekeeper sounded puzzled.

'That, of all the tasks in the abbey, you seemed to be fulfilling the same task as in your previous following.'

'The same? I don't . . . ah! You mean I was once guardian of the lord of The Cuala's mines and now I am guardian of the gates of the abbey? I don't see it exactly as the same thing. Anyway, as well as my duties, I am being tutored in the rituals of the New Faith.'

'And that is what you want?'

'That is what I want.'

'Let me ask you a final question because the hour grows late.'

'One more question more or less does not matter. In fact, I am pleased to have had this talk to you, Brother Saxon. What is it you want to ask?'

'In the years that you were used as a guard to the lord of The

Cuala's mine workings, and your resentment to Corbmac, to the way
you were treated and your desire to leave, were you never tempted
to take some of the precious metals that you were guarding rather
than protect it?'

There was a silence and then Eadulf frowned at the sound
emanating from the gatekeeper. It took some time before Eadulf
realised the man was laughing.

'Steal the metals? I am strong, but it takes more than the strength
of one man to shift metal – whether it be gold, silver, or other
metals such as tin and copper. Above all, it needs someone who is
learned in the various metal ores, learned about how they are
extracted and smelted into manageable shape. I certainly do not
have such a group of able accomplices nor anyone with the abilities
needed. If I did, why would I be sheltering here?'

'That's a good argument.'

'It is a true argument.'

'So,' Eadulf finally came to the point, 'who here is knowledgeable about the mining world? Who do you think has the knowledge
and contacts to successfully rob the mines of The Cuala?'

The gatekeeper was quiet for a moment or so. 'Perhaps it is not
a matter of knowledge and contacts. It is a matter of knowledge of
the purpose to which the metals can be put.'

Eadulf reflected on this. 'Surely there is only one purpose? One
sells to the person who pays most.'

'But why? Just to make oneself rich? I was a long time guarding
the mines here. Not far from here are some old deserted mine
workings, mainly lead mines. I saw the numbers involved and the
time it takes to run a mining operation. By the time the ore is
extracted, treated and distributed, it is hardly worth anything.'

'So what are you saying?'

'That maybe the mines are being robbed but of material extracted
unofficially to avoid tribute because everyone has to pay tribute.
The lord of The Cuala has to pay tribute to Fianamail, the King of

Laigin, who, in turn, has to pay tribute to the High King Cenn
Fáelad, son of Blathmaic, So perhaps one should be looking for the
thieves closer to Dún Droch Fhola.'

The gatekeeper suddenly rose. 'I have some duties to attend to,
Brother Saxon.' He turned and was silently gone through the gate,
leaving Eadulf sitting a long time in contemplation.

Later, Eadulf repeated the conversation to Fidelma.

'What prompted you to have this exchange with the gatekeeper?'
she asked with reluctant interest.

'I wanted to know more about the man,' he replied. 'The fact that
he was once a guard at the mines before being a religieux. I thought
it would be helpful.'

Fidelma caught a slightly defensive tone in his voice but she said
nothing, much to his relief.

'It does seem curious that he dwells so much on phantoms and
the like, as if he were doing his best to warn people away from the
remote places of The Cuala,' he added.

'Maybe it is just as he says. He is born of goatherders among
these peaks and grown up with the local superstitions,' Fidelma
observed. 'But I will say, it is interesting that he puts forward the
theory that the stealing of the metal ore from the mines is actually
a conspiracy by the very owner of the mines to avoid paying
tribute.'

'Tribute to either the King of Laigin, or for the King of Laigin's
tribute to the High King,' Eadulf hesitated. 'Could that really be a
possibility?'

'At this time we should examine every possibility.'

'There is one thing that worries me,' he frowned.

'Only one thing?' she said with the ghost of a smile.

'We seem to be dwelling more on the theft of the precious metals
from the mines of The Cuala. That is only a secondary matter. We
came here to find out what has happened to the Princess Gelgéis.
We owe that to your brother.'

For a passing moment, an angry frown crossed her features and she stiffened. Then she relaxed again.

'I have not forgotten my obligation to my brother or to Gelgéis, who has become my friend,' she said coldly. 'The only lead I can see at the moment is that there is a connection between her disappearance and the theft from the mines. How else did we find her brooch at the deserted buildings in Lúbán? I was beginning to formulate a theory but had to abandon it when Teimel did not recognise the male body.'

Eadulf was bewildered but said: 'We said earlier that Princess Gelgéis might have been kidnapped rather than being killed because she recognised the thief. What if Brother Dorchú's theory is right and she recognised Dicuil Dóna?'

Fidelma shook her head immediately. 'If the lord of The Cuala was involved he would not be transporting precious metals personally. What I want to do tomorrow is go into Láithreach and see if the local Brehon, Rónchú, has turned up. I need more details about the story of the men killed while they were trying to transport the metals to the seaport.'

'I find it difficult to accept the attempt to evade tribute as a reason to steal gold and silver from the mines.'

'I am not sure that I follow your reasoning.'

'I have not dismissed the idea of the lord of The Cuala's involvement,' Eadulf explained, 'but think of this. If you were doing this to avoid declaring an income for tribute, to avoid paying a tax on it, why would you dig up the gold and silver from your own land in the first place? Logically, you would not bother to excavate it and draw attention to it. Knowing it was there, you could just leave it. Certainly it would be a futile expenditure of time and energy, to dig it up and then send to the coast with it. If you needed it, why not hide it in your own territory in the deep solitary places that are countless?'

Fidelma agreed. 'You know by now, Eadulf, that an investigation is mainly a process of elimination. Let us gather the fragments of information before we assemble them together and then see what is to be discarded.' She suddenly smothered a yawn. 'It grows late and we should have some sleep. We have much to do and I feel that tomorrow will be an even longer day than today.'

CHAPTER NINETEEN

It was a cold but bright and cloudless day when Fidelma found herself crossing towards the stables in search of Enda. She suddenly heard her name called. The voice seemed soft, feminine and familiar. She turned to see the young daughter of Dicuil Dóna, Aróc, approaching swiftly behind her. She said nothing as the daughter of the lord of The Cuala halted slightly breathlessly before her. The look on the girl's face seemed one of friendship, but there was tightness around the mouth and dullness in the eyes that seemed not to support the sincerity of the intended smile.

'I heard that you were here and was hoping I had not missed you,' the girl opened.

Fidelma did not reply and allowed a few moments of silence between them. So Aróc continued. 'You were right, lady,' she said, interpreting the silence. 'I behaved badly when we met at my father's fortress. I was in a bad mood. What else can I say but that I apologise?'

'An apology would be sufficient,' Fidelma replied coldly.

'Then I give it with all honesty,' the girl responded. 'There were various things on my mind at the time and I should have had a better control of my emotions. And, of course, I did not know who you were at the time otherwise I would not have spoken to you as I did.'

Fidelma did not voice the obvious thought that came to her mind: that this implied she would have had no compunction in speaking to anyone of lesser status in the same manner. That would have made the girl's attitude worse. However, she let the thought pass.

'You have apologised and I accept,' she replied coldly.

Either the girl did not appear to detect her coldness or, if she did, it did not trouble her.

'I was surprised to hear that you had arrived last evening,' Aróc went on. 'I thought I saw you heading for Garrchú's forge to the west.'

Fidelma decided to unbend a little as it would be stupid to pass up the opportunity to extract information that might be of help.

'My companion Enda thought he saw you riding with a warrior in the hills when we were on our journey to Dún Árd?' She framed the question as neutrally as she could.

The girl shrugged. 'The warrior was Corbmac. We were on a task for my father.'

'Is that why you are here at the abbey?' Fidelma asked in a mild tone.

'It is,' confirmed the girl. 'My father trusts me to check on certain properties and ensure that tributes are paid.'

'I thought it was your brother, as steward, who was tasked with such matters?' Fidelma tried to sound offhand but this information was contrary to what Scáth had told her.

The girl scowled. 'My brother is weak. He has no heart for collecting tributes when people claim they have nothing with which to pay. It needs a sterner hand to insist on payments from some of these local chieftains who think to take advantage. In such cases my father puts more trust in me and Corbmac.'

'I did not know Corbmac was also staying in the abbey?' Fidelma made the comment into a question.

'Corbmac and his warriors stay at the fortress of a local chieftain on the slopes of An Doire Bán, the white wood mountain.' She indicated a nearby peak to the south-east, which overlooked the abbey. 'I prefer the comforts offered in the guesthouse here.'

'Even so, it must be a long and tiring journey across these mountains collecting tributes. Are you not afraid, especially with stories of brigands and attacks?'

The girl sniffed dismissively. 'You mean the matters you went to see my father about?' There was a flippant tone in her voice. 'Well, Corbmac and his men are more than a match for any brigands, and I, as you know, can shoot with my bow as well as any warrior. I try to be the warrior my father wanted. I grew up with a bow in one hand and a sword in the other.'

Fidelma was not sure whether the girl spoke in humour or there was a serious quality behind the remark.

'Does it not perturb you that, in spite of this, there are some who intend to rob the mines of your father? That robbery might not stop at murder.'

'I know all about the deaths of a Brehon and the local pedlar. There are always those who will try to take what does not belong to them and they will always be punished.' The girl thrust her chin up belligerently as she said this. 'I understand from my father that your job is to find and punish such people. I will leave such worries to you.'

Fidelma was about to make a further comment when one of the stable attendants appeared leading a horse. Aróc moved forward and took the reins, springing on its back with long-accomplished ease.

'Good luck in your task,' she called. 'Perhaps we shall encounter each other again soon.'

Then she was urging her horse into a gallop across the grounds of the abbey and, dangerously, without pausing, across the bridge through the gate. The thunder of hoofs over the wooden bridge left a disturbing echo. For a moment Fidelma stood shaking her head at the recklessness of Aróc's departure. The stable boy was still standing looking after the girl with a disapproving frown. He had not even been acknowledged for his service. Fidelma smiled sadly at him.

'She neglected to thank you,' she observed.

The boy turned with a bitter grimace. 'She is the daughter of the lord of The Cuala and does not believe that she has a need to thank anyone.'

'Does she often stay here?'

'Too often,' agreed the boy morosely. Then he caught himself as if he had spoken unthinkingly. 'I am sorry, lady. I did not mean . . .'

Fidelma reassured him. 'Never apologise for expressing what one truly thinks. What is your name?'

'I was born in winter and so I was named "holly", which bore berries outside the house.'

'So your name is Cuilínn? Have you often had to deal with Aróc before?'

'To be honest, my father and I once worked the lead mines on what we call "the badgers peak", not far down this glen. It was a good mine and supported a few members of our family who worked there. Then came the day when that girl arrived and demanded so much in tribute in the name of her father that we could not even produce a tenth of what was demanded. At her orders, the mine was closed and we were forbidden even to have access to it.'

Fidelma frowned. 'She is not old. This must have happened recently?'

'Six months ago. At least I had a good knowledge of horses and immediately sought work in the stables here.'

'You seem to have much in common with Brother Dorchú,' Fidelma reflected. 'Tell me, this mine, was it the same one that Brother Dorchú was once a guard to?'

The stable boy shook his head immediately. 'It was not, but I know the one you mean. It was on the other mountain, Céim an Doire, further up the valley. That one had been closed some time before. I was once told it was worked out some years ago.'

'Unlike your mine?'

'Our mine was a good mine but it could never produce as much as the lord of The Cuala wanted in tribute. It was on the hillside behind a rocky outcrop. We never wanted for game, as below was a shallow area of the riverbed that all manner of animals had made their watering hole.'

'Aróc refused to let you continue working the mine for a lesser tribute?'

'She evoked the name of her father to demand the tribute.'

'You say it was a lead mine. Were there any other metals that could be extracted from the veins that you were following?'

For a moment the boy stared at her and then started to chuckle. 'You are thinking the seams – the veins, as you call them – might have led to more valuable ones? That suddenly the mine might start producing silver or gold? I am sorry, lady. Not a hope of that. The mine had once been a cave system with three or four interconnecting caves. We knew the caves and the seams well. It was a moderate living until . . . until the lord of The Cuala grew greedy.'

'You say that it was the girl who had the place closed?'

'To be accurate it was the lord of The Cuala's steward. He said she had reported the tribute value to her father and he had been sent by Dicuil Dóna to close the mine if we did not pay it. Now there are always a couple of his warriors protecting it and anyone wandering too near gets threatened.'

'Isn't that odd?'

'Not odd when it is an order of the lord of The Cuala. He can do what he likes. As for Aróc and her brother . . . they are probably as bad as each other.'

'But the mine only produced lead?' pressed Fidelma. 'Why guard it at all now that you have had to abandon it?'

'It is not my position to seek to question the lord of The Cuala.'

At that moment Eadulf appeared, leading their horses. The stable boy inclined his head as the two of them mounted and moved out of the abbey grounds.

'What were you talking to the stable boy about? Eadulf asked, as they clattered across the wooden bridge and joined the track that led towards Láithreach.

'About a little lead mine.' Fidelma paused for a moment. 'I think I would like to look at it sometime as I am told that although it is not worked out, two of Dicuil Dóna's warriors are permanently stationed there to dissuade anyone trying to reopen it.'

Eadulf glanced at her for a moment, puzzled. He was about to ask another question when a figure appeared abruptly out of the thick woods they were passing.

'Greetings to you, offspring of Eber Finn, son of Golamh, first true King of this land. Greetings, daughter of kings and sister of a king.'

They recognised her immediately. This time the old woman was without her mule. Fidelma smiled softly at her.

'And to you, greetings, Iuchra, who knows my genealogy so well. Is it that you are Iuchra, daughter of Abertach, who has the ability to shapeshift into herons or other forms?'

The old woman stared at her for a moment and then let out a cackle of laughter. 'Well, Fidelma of the long tresses, you know your legends and stories of the shapeshifters. I bid you greetings. You are looking for something that is under the earth, below the rocks and soil. Is this not so?'

Fidelma chuckled and shook her head. 'It is not so. I am not here to steal from the mines of The Cuala.'

Iuchra laughed with her. 'Nevertheless, it is so, and you will know it soon. I say this to you – you will take from the mines of The Cuala that which you desire.'

Eadulf frowned in displeasure. 'Have a care, old woman; by accusing Fidelma of Cashel of contemplating robbery from the mines here you are treading dangerous ground.'

'I still say, she will take what she desires from the mines and I do not lie,' repeated the old woman. 'She does this to return what is illegally held to its rightful owner. That is not robbery.'

'I have no understanding of what you mean,' Fidelma retorted impatiently.

'You will understand when you realise the real secret is exposed in the names of the shapeshifters.'

'I still have no understanding,' repeated Fidelma.

'Then you are not possessed of the knowledge that others say you have,' Iuchra replied. 'Think calmly on what I say. You will find what you seek in the caves of The Cuala, of that there is no doubt.'

'What makes you think we search for metal?' Fidelma asked, frowning.

'There comes a time, and come it must, when metal has to be met with mettle. That is the purpose of your coming. There is a mist crossing the high peaks and that foretells of snows coming. You do not have long to resolve the conundrum. I will give you one more clue. Look for what you seek in the place of soft metal and meet it with mettle that is so hard that it can overcome all metals. The secret is in the names.'

The old woman turned with a wheezy screech of laughter and scampered into the thick underground. It seemed the very earth had swallowed her whole.

'Mad, indeed!' grunted Eadulf. 'It's an insult to claim that we are here to rob the mines of The Cuala. She insulted you by saying you are not intelligent enough to solve her stupid riddle . . .'

'Eadulf,' Fidelma replied quietly, 'let it be for the time being. I must think about what she said.'

'Not much to think about, if you ask me . . .'

'Eadulf!' Fidelma warned.

Eadulf shrugged and was silent. Finally, Fidelma nudged her mount forward and he followed.

They rode into the township, passing by Teimel's cabin without stopping. In fact, Fidelma was too deep in thought to notice it and so the two of them crossed the bridge into the main part of the town. They continued on, passing the wharfs and the few boats along the river's quayside, and passed among the buildings that clustered around the town's square. Eadulf guessed Fidelma was heading to see her friend Beccnat, the assistant to Brehon Rónchú. Because of the rivers and many streams that joined at this point, they had to negotiate another bridge to get to Beccnat's cottage.

'Wait!' Eadulf gave a sibilant whisper, halting Fidelma in surprise before they reached it. 'Stop here,' he urged.

Fidelma turned to him with a questioning frown and pulled rein on her mount.

'Isn't that Beccnat's cabin?' said Eadulf, pointing.

'It is. Why?'

Fidelma followed the direction that his hand was indicating. Her eyes narrowed. There was a young man dismounting from his horse before the cottage where Beccnat had entertained them when they first arrived in the town. Beccnat had now emerged to greet the newcomer. She greeted him rather effusively, as a lover greets the loved one. Fidelma was surprised. It was Scáth, the son of the lord of The Cuala. She knew that Beccnat was her own age, having studied with her at Brehon Morann's law school. That meant she was about thirty-five.

As she looked on, a rapid exchange was taking place. Beccnat was shaking her head while Scáth was gesticulating with one hand, making sweeping motions as if waving at the mountains. Fidelma wished she was nearer to see their facial expressions more clearly. Then Scáth, after another close embrace, was back on his horse and digging his heels in to send it into a gallop, scattering groups of people right and left.

'They seem very friendly,' Eadulf remarked thoughtfully. 'What was that about?'

'I think we should find out,' Fidelma replied.

By the time they had negotiated the path across another bridge there was no sign of the young steward of the lord of The Cuala. The hollow tattoo of their horses crossing the bridge must have alerted Beccnat. They had barely dismounted when she re-emerged from her cabin, her face flushed and looking confused.

'Fidelma!' She tried to put surprise in her voice but only succeeded in sounding suspicious. 'But you have been away for only a few days. I thought Teimel was taking you along the valleys in search of—'

'I think you know where we've been,' Fidelma smiled easily as she dismounted.

Beccnat frowned 'I know that you left with Teimel, whom you hired as your tracker to take you—'

Fidelma was in no mood for prevarication. 'I am sure Teimel or Scáth, or either one, has already told you exactly where we have been and what happened.'

This seemed to stop her immediately. Her flushed face, if anything, reddened further and a curious glint came into her eyes.

'You seem to know Scáth very well.' Fidelma continued to smile but without warmth. 'I was wondering why he came here. Perhaps with a message from his father?'

Beccnat's mouth tightened. Suddenly she seemed to emerge from whatever constraints had been holding her back. 'I am not ashamed that I know him.' Her head rose defiantly, chin pushing upwards. 'Are you disapproving of me, Fidelma? You of all people?'

There was something hidden in her angry tone that puzzled Fidelma. She could not quite interpret it.

'Your life is your own, Beccnat. Why should I either disapprove or approve of anything? He has attained the *aimsir togú*, the age of choice, and so have you. We have free choice to do as we will, providing it harms no one. I am just pointing out that Scáth must have—'

The face of Beccnat seemed to have dissolved into some sort of fit of sullen anger.

'Free choice? You never allowed me any choice before when you stole the person I loved.'

Fidelma was frankly puzzled and she glanced nervously towards Eadulf. He looked equally perplexed.

'Stole the person you loved? I fail to understand—' she began again.

'Have you forgotten so soon?' interrupted Beccnat furiously. 'I am talking about Cian! Have you forgotten him so soon?'

'Cian?' A spark of light was dawning in her mind.

'Cian, who was my lover, and you stole him,' snapped the girl.

Fidelma blinked in shock. 'He was your lover?'

Cian had been a young warrior of the Fianna, the High King's bodyguard, who used to frequent Brehon Morann's law school in the year before she graduated. Fidelma swallowed sharply. She had thought that she had dealt with Cian. He had been youthful and handsome. Many had sought his company for he was a famed athlete. In fact, she had seen him racing at the Féis Teamhrach, which was where a friend named Grian had introduced him to Fidelma. The young Fidelma had fallen for the handsome warrior. But Cian had turned out to be just a weak man. He saw women of all ages as conquests to be achieved and, when done, he had abandoned interest and his victims.

'I never forgave you for what you did,' Beccnat cut into her memories with barely suppressed anger. 'He was my lover. You went off with Grian to the Féis Teamhrach. I remember it like yesterday. That was where you met Cian. Where you seduced him. He abandoned me for you. I would have been with him now had it not been for you. I would have kept his love.'

Fidelma stared in shock at this ghost from the past being conjured in hatred against her. She tried to gather her thoughts.

'Beccnat, Cian was an immature youth in pursuit of conquests,' she with icy hate. 'He made my life a turmoil of conflicting emotions. When I refused to go to bed with him he abandoned me for a more pliant companion. Even Grian recognised that his pursuit was merely superficial. Cian was the sort to boast about his conquests. He did not care once the conquest had been made, although it took me time to believe that he had such a base motive. He was dismissed from the High King's bodyguard for his licentious behaviour. I never allowed him into my bed, nor did I go to his.'

Fidelma glanced at Eadulf as if seeking his reassurance. She had told him the story of her unhappy affair, especially after she had encountered Cian years afterwards on the pilgrim ship, the *Barnacle Goose*. It was while she was trying to sort out her relationship with Eadulf, during the time he was imprisoned in Laigin, that she had made the voyage on the pilgrim ship. Cian was then supposed to be a member of the community of the Abbey of Beannchar. Even that was pretence. It had turned out that Cian had not changed at all, but by then she had been able to see him clearly in his true light. For years Cian had been a thorn in her memory as she recalled the anguished emotions, but she had finally dealt with him, or rather the memories he had inflicted, during that pilgrim voyage. At the end of it she found he had no hold on her emotions or memories She ended the voyage as if a dead weight had fallen from her shoulders and she was able to speak easily and freely to Eadulf about it.

Eadulf smiled encouragingly at her to show he understood and stepped forward to stand by her side.

'I am sure we are sorry for some past problem that has caused your mind to dwell in darkness all these years. It has little to do with the matter that brings us to you now,' he said reasonably to Beccnat. 'We were simply wondering why young Scáth had come to Láithreach. He must have told you that we were taken prisoner by his father's warriors and then released on condition we help him with a problem he was trying to resolve.'

The anger had not left the woman's face.

'Scáth came to see me. He now loves me and I love him.' She spoke directly to Fidelma. 'You will not destroy our love as you seduced Cian from me.'

'There is no reason why I would want to destroy anything, Beccnat,' Fidelma assured her, keeping calm. 'As for Cian, he cheated on everyone. When he did not get what he wanted from me, he went to the next conquest.'

'You will not be given the opportunity to hurt me further.' There was a threat in Beccnat's voice.

Fidelma's jaw hardened. 'I hope you are not threatening me. As a *dálaigh*, I have to take notice of it. You must think of the implications. You are qualified enough in law to ponder on the consequence of any actions from such a threat.'

Beccnat's jaw came up pugnaciously.

Fidelma did not give her time to react further. 'As a *dálaigh*, and of higher qualification than you, I have to call on you to answer my questions. I hope you will now answer.'

Beccnat made no reply but stood staring angrily at Fidelma as if ready to defy her.

Fidelma spoke sharply now. 'As you know, my rank as a *dálaigh* and the qualification of *Anruth* is superior to your rank as a *baran,* Beccnat, so I urge you to answer.'

Eadulf had only recently learnt that *baran* was the lowest rank of a steward judge, which served more or less in the capacity of an assistant judge or lawyer.

The woman did not seem concerned as she defiantly faced Fidelma.

'Very well,' Eadulf intervened as a means of breaking the impasse. 'We are not concerned with your personal relationship to Scáth. All we wanted to know was where we might find your superior, Brehon Rónchú.'

Eadulf glanced at Fidelma in an effort to say that he shared her suspicion that Scáth's call on her was not that merely of a lovesick boy: it was not the real reason for his post haste ride to Láithreach.

Beccnat switched her gaze to Eadulf. The anger had not entirely evaporated but now suspicion had begun to join it. Then she asked Fidelma in a tight voice: 'Are you going to allow me to be subjected to questions from a foreigner?'

Eadulf sighed. It was not going to be easy to get the woman to talk.

'Eadulf is a *gerefa*, that is, an hereditary magistrate of his own culture,' snapped back Fidelma. 'In this country, out of respect of his status as my husband, he is allowed to ask questions. Furthermore, he asks under my observation.'

The woman hesitated and then turned to answer Eadulf.

'He is on *Cúairtugad*. You have already been informed of that. I am his assistant. Why do you want to speak with Brehon Rónchú?' she demanded.

'We need to talk to him personally,' Fidelma said.

'Where is he likely to be?' Eadulf asked.

'He could be anywhere.' Beccnat glanced disapprovingly at Fidelma. 'I am not possessed of second sight.'

'We know that a few weeks ago Brehon Rónchú escorted some recovered stolen items to a man called Garrchú at a place called Dún Árd,' pointed out Eadulf. 'Can you confirm that?'

'So I am told,' Beccnat confirmed.

'Did he return here after that?' Fidelma asked.

'He did.' It was what Teimel had already told them.

'So he returned. For how long was he here before he left again?'

'He went almost immediately.'

'And you don't know where? Isn't that unusual, seeing that you are his assistant?'

Beccnat shrugged but made no other reply.

'Did you have any conversations with Brehon Rónchú about the stolen shipment of ore that he found?' pressed Eadulf. 'I presume that you were here when Brehon Rónchú made the discovery of the gold and silver and went downriver to capture the smugglers?'

'I was adjudicating a case elsewhere when the two men's bodies were brought here. It was Brehon Rónchú's case.'

'But he must have told you about it. He must have had some views about the case.'

'What was there to tell? The two men involved in the theft were dead. Brehon Rónchú took the boxes of ore to the steward of the mines at Dún Árd. That was all I know. After that he came back and then went on his circuit.'

'I gather he was on horseback but the ore was in a wagon? Who drove the wagon?'

Beccnat looked suddenly nervous. 'He hired a man and a wagon to transport them.'

An idea suddenly struck Eadulf. 'This is the sort of job Cétach might have undertaken. Was the driver Cétach? Did he transport the boxes?'

Beccnat hesitated. The answer to the question was clearly affirmative. 'I suppose it was Cétach,' she admitted. 'I had forgotten. I had other matters to see to, another investigation, so that I forgot.'

'And this was some time ago? I presume Cétach did not return with Brehon Rónchú?' pressed Eadulf.

'Why presume that?' Beccnat seemed more nervous as she countered the question with her own.

'Because shortly thereafter, Cétach was in Durlus Éile and witnessed the departure of Brehon Brocc and his party. He was a few days in that town before starting back here when he found the body in the valley of . . .'

Beccnat reluctantly acknowledged his logic. But Eadulf was smiling broadly as he faced Fidelma with his conclusion.

'We were told Cétach left Rónchú after he had delivered the ore to Garrchú's place. He went from Dún Árd to Durlus Éile and thence returned through the mountains to the Abbey of Cáemgen, during which journey he found the body of Brehon Brocc. Then he arrived at the abbey.'

'And then he returned here, where he was murdered.' Fidelma was frowning. She stared at Beccnat. 'Do you not think that it was unusual for Brehon Rónchú not to confide in you about the cases he was involved with, as you are his assistant?'

'He never said much about his cases or maybe I was not listening,' shrugged Beccnat.

'I would urge you to try to remember what exactly happened.' Fidelma was exasperated.

The woman shrugged unhelpfully yet again. 'He was a reticent man, even about the cases he was working on. I have told you all he knew.'

'What about the boatman who undertook the transportation?'

'The boatman?' she frowned. 'I told you I had nothing to do with this matter. I was told that when Brehon Rónchú became suspicious and opened the crates, after the two men had left, he decided to accompany the boatmen and take them prisoner when they picked up the boxes at its destination. He was accompanied by two warriors of a small company that the lord of The Cuala maintains here.'

'Did you know these warriors? Are they here now?'

'Dicuil Dóna has the company changed every few weeks. They are no longer serving here. If their names are known it would be Corbmac, the commander of the warriors, to ask.'

'Not even the steward, Scáth?' Eadulf could not help asking.

Beccnat glared at him for a moment and shook her head.

'Well, what of the boatman himself? Where can we find him, as he must surely know more of this matter? What is his name?'

Beccnat sniffed dismissively. 'Murchad.'

'Murchad was the boatman? Then we will question him.'

'It is no use seeking information from him.'

'Why so?' demanded Eadulf with a frown.

'He had an accident with his boat. He fell overboard during a manoeuvre to bring his boat against the wharf, fell between the boat and the wharf and was crushed. He died a short time later.'

Eadulf saw Fidelma's sudden apprehensive expression. 'Too many people involved in this matter seem to be losing their lives,' he said dryly, interpreting her thoughts.

'Then I think we already know where Brehon Rónchú is,' Fidelma agreed in a flat voice.

CHAPTER TWENTY

E adulf had an instinct that Fidelma was thinking about the grave in the deserted valley of Lúbán.

'We must start immediately.'

Beccnat was staring at them defiantly. 'I remind you, Fidelma of Cashel, that I am the appointed Brehon of this area in the absence of Brehon Rónchú. I will take charge of any such matters. Dicuil Dóna shall hear of your impertinence in his territory.'

Fidelma regarded her with an almost sad expression. Then she sighed.

'I am taking over, Beccnat.' She reached into her *marsupium* and brought forth the wand of office given to her by Dicuil Dóna. 'Here is my authority. There are, in fact, two authorities that I have. One you already know, if you have learnt anything about status in law. The second . . . I am sure you recognise it.'

Beccnat stared unbelievingly at the wand of office and then her mouth pressed into a thin line.

'Look for no more help from me then. I have told you what I know.'

'Very well.' Fidelma glanced at Eadulf and they turned back to their horses and mounted without another word. Fidelma was aware of Beccnat standing at the door, glowering after them.

They were silent until they reached the river bridge, at which point Eadulf asked: 'Do you think the person we found in that grave in the deserted valley was the Brehon?'

Fidelma smiled at him thoughtfully. 'I believe so. It being so, then it means that Teimel plays a role in this business – conspiracy or theft. I am not surprised. Like Enda, I found Teimel's manner curious.'

There was a silence and then Eadulf seemed to make up his mind about another matter he had been brooding on.

'It seems Beccnat has been nursing a grudge against you for many years,' he began nervously. 'Do you think that has impaired her truthfulness in *these* matters?'

'I thought that I knew her, albeit that was a long time ago.' Fidelma was genuinely sad as she reflected on the woman's admitted hatred of her. 'We were students together, as you heard, but I did not know what thoughts she has harboured about me after all these years. I regarded her as just one of my friends at college. I had no idea that she had a relationship with Cian, or, at least, thought she did. I have told you the truth about him, Eadulf. I did think I was really in love with Cian when I was young. It did hurt me when he left with another. It took me until I saw him again on that pilgrim ship to know what he really meant to me. It was a bad experience but one of many in life that we hopefully learn from.'

Eadulf leaned forward, placed a hand on her arm and applied a little pressure.

'You were young and that is when we are all prone to make mistakes.'

'I learnt from my mistake,' she agreed. 'Obviously, Beccnat has not done so.'

'You should be careful of her,' Eadulf pointed out. 'To be harbouring some sort of jealousy and revenge all these years is dangerous.'

'I think there is a saying that jealousy is always born with love but does not always die with it,' Fidelma sighed. 'Her jealousy has grown old with her. Let us hope that this relationship with young Scáth is one based on reality and nothing else.'

She changed the subject. 'Beccnat told us that the boatman who found the ore is dead. A pity as he could have provided some information.'

'If his boat was large enough to have carried the Brehon and the warriors downriver, he would probably have had crew. They might answer your questions.'

'Well done, Eadulf,' Fidelma exclaimed. 'Sometimes when I am looking at the forest I neglect the important tree. I think Beccnat said the boatman was named Murchad.'

Fidelma glanced along the wharfs as they passed. Several people were working with the boats that were moored there.

'I'll ask,' she said, guiding her horse along the banks of the river. There was one man who was instructing a couple of young men rigging a sail on one of the moored vessels. He was dark of hair, barrel chested and slightly bowed in the legs, almost typically like a man who earnt his living on the waterways. He watched her with a suspicious frown as she rode up.

'Did you know Murchad, a boatman along here?' she opened after she had greeted him.

'Why?' came the terse unpromising answer.

'I am a *dálaigh* and wish to know,' she replied equally tersely.

The man grimaced as if dismissing the subject. 'He's dead.'

'I understand that. He ran a boat here. Did he have a crew?'

'You can't prosecute the crew for what happened,' replied the man, defensively.

'Why would I prosecute his crew?' she asked, mystified. 'Anyway, do you say that he did have a crew?'

'Do you mean that there might be some compensation due to the crew?' The boatman's attitude changed. He was suddenly alert and eager.

'That depends,' Fidelma replied, interested. 'Why do you think the crew need compensation? Were you one of them?'

The man shook his head. 'I say it because it is thought that the death of Murchad was no accident. If it was no accident then compensation should be payable.'

'If no accident, are you implying it was murder?'

'I did not witness it, but I have heard that the circumstances were suspicious.'

'What are the details?'

'I cannot give you the details as I did not witness them. If you are a *dálaigh* you should know that.'

'I presume the crewmen would know this, if there was compensation to be paid?'

'That is so,' the man replied keenly.

'So who are these crewmen and where might they be found?' Fidelma struggled to hide her impatience.

The man swung round and pointed to some cabins clustered along the far side of the river bank.

'There was only one in the crew. Muirgel, wife to Murchad. She lives in that second cabin. Speak to her.'

'His wife was the crewman?' It was not unusual for a wife and husband to run a river boat together.

'She was a true adept at handling boats. She and Murchad had been together for many years. They both came from our township.'

'So she was a witness to what happened to her husband?'

'As she tells it,' agreed the man. 'And it is in the telling that she is deserving compensation. See that broad-beamed *barca* across the river?' He pointed to one of the river boats. 'That was their boat . . . it belonged to Murchad and Muirgel. They could sail it in safety along the broadest of rivers and around the storm-swept coast in the worst conditions. That is why it was unjust . . . I mean, what happened to Murchad. It has destroyed her life, anyway.'

'In what way?'

'She can't get anyone to crew the boat with her now, let alone find cargoes to take up or downriver.'

'If she thought there was something suspicious about her husband's death, she should have pursued the matter with the local Brehon.'

'Brehon Rónchú? He had left to go to Gleann Uí Máil at that time. I think she reported it to his assistant.'

'Beccnat?'

'It was. Muirgel was not happy with the way her claim was received.'

Fidelma kept her face impassive. 'So this event happened after Brehon Rónchú had left the township?'

'I remember it well because it was when that drunken pedlar, Cétach, arrived back. There was some talk that he had found a body, which he had taken to the abbey.'

'Why was that significant?'

'Because we thought, at first, the body was that of Brehon Rónchú. He had actually hired Cétach and his wagon to take some boxes to the mining steward. We heard they were the boxes of gold or silver that Murchad had been transporting on the river. I would not trust Cétach. But, of course, we later heard it was the body of a stranger that had been found.'

'Why would you think it was the body of Brehon Rónchú? Did he not return here after taking the boxes to the mining steward?'

'Not that I know of.' The boatman shook his head quickly. 'No, he did not return. I know when Cétach returned. That is why I think Murchad's death was as suspicious as was Cétach's death. Everyone is talking about that. That is why you will find sprigs of furze over the doors of all the houses. Evil is at work here.'

The man had confirmed Fidelma's suspicion that Beccnat had not told the entire truth. The question was, why had she lied, or had she been deliberately trying to mislead her out of her declared spite over an ancient love-affair?

The man's eyes suddenly widened as if a new thought occurred. 'Are you a *dálaigh* who has been sent to sort out this matter?'

'You might say that,' Fidelma replied without explaining the truth of the matter. 'You have been of more help than you know. You said that Muirgel dwells in the second cabin on the far side of the river?'

'In that cottage there,' he confirmed, pointing.

At the man's verification, she raised a hand in a gesture of thanks, and returned to Eadulf. She gave a brief summary of the conversation before leading the way across the bridge towards the row of cabins. It was one of several where sprigs of furze, with their yellowing flowers, were tied in bunches above the doors.

'Well, as a symbol to keep the Aos Sí at bay, they don't seem to be working,' Eadulf muttered ruefully.

Muirgel was nothing like her name – sea bright, sea white. Her features were dark, the skin baked brown by the weather and a life spent outdoors. Yet her eyes were bright blue, deep set in her thickset, almost coarse features. However, they seemed to suit the woman and did not detract from some inner kindness that was displayed on her features. She was heavily built but with muscle rather than fat. Her hair was mostly dark but intermingled with grey. Her sea-bright gaze seemed to miss nothing as she paid them a close scrutiny.

'Are you Muirgel?' Fidelma began by asking the obvious. 'Are you the widow of Murchad?'

'Who are you and what do you want of me?'

They had dismounted before the small granite-built cabin and Eadulf had taken charge of their horses while Fidelma approached the door.

'I am a *dálaigh*. I would like to ask you a few questions about how your husband met his death.'

Muirgel scowled momentarily. 'Have you come in answer to my complaint about the Brehon's assistant?'

'I have heard that you made a report about your husband's death to Brehon Rónchú's assistant and were not satisfied with her response.'

'Response? There was none. Time has gone on and Brehon Rónchú has not returned and I am without satisfaction.'

'Perhaps you should tell me what you know about the death of your husband, Murchad.'

'In that case . . .' The woman stood back and motioned her inside her cabin.

Fidelma glanced at Eadulf with an unasked query, but he shook his head, pointed to a nearby building that looked like a tavern and began leading the horses towards it. Fidelma then turned and obeyed the woman's invitation. The room was tiny and hot, heated by a central log fire. It was one room that served as living room and cooking area, while wooden steps led above to a platform that acted as the sleeping area. There was a chair and some stools about the room and, at Muirgel's invitation, Fidelma seated herself, allowing the woman to maintain her right to the single chair.

She leant forwards towards the fire where a *coire*, a small cauldron, sat on the fire steaming, filling the room with a warm fragrance. Muirgel took two clay mugs from a shelf, filled them and offered her one.

'It's dandelion and burdock sweetened with honey,' she explained.

Fidelma thanked her with the ritual of hospitality given and received.

'Tell me the facts of your husband's death,' began Fidelma immediately. 'Tell me the circumstances.'

'He was murdered, plain and simple,' replied the women. 'We had been up the Great River to the Áth na mBó, the Ford of the Cows, to collect some pieces of furniture for the tavern owner here. They had been ordered from a good worker in wood, who makes chairs, beds and cupboards and the like. We were returning down the river to here and coming in to tie up at the wharf just outside.

You will still find our boat moored there. We had done it so many thousands of times that Murchad could do it by himself blindfolded. I emphasise that because the assistant Brehon even questioned my husband's competence as a riverboat captain.'

She paused for a moment. 'I had gone to the bow and was hauling down the for'ard sail while Murchad was at the tiller, allowing the boat to swing inshore. There was still a gap between the stern and the wooden wharf, whereas the bow had already touched the wharf. I was aware of a smaller vessel overtaking us from the rear of our craft.'

'Did you see whose vessel it was?'

'No. I was just aware of a small craft with a sail fully rigged. And then I saw a long pole, longer than an oar, emerge from behind the sail as if someone was holding it. The holder pushed it and suddenly it caught Murchad in the back. He gave a cry, spun a little, and went over the side. He went over just as the stern of our boat swung towards the jerry.' She choked back a sob that arose in her throat. 'He was crushed against the wood of the jetty and the swing of the boat. He did not fall in by accident. I told the stupid lawyer woman that!'

'You told Beccnat, the assistant to the Brehon, these details?'

'I did, for all the notice she took of me,' replied Muirgel bitterly.

'You say that you did not see the person who was obscured behind the sail? You did not see who held the pole that pushed your husband off the boat?'

'I did not see them.'

'But the boat passed you and that would have given you a clear vision of them?'

'My only thought was for Murchad. As soon as he cried out and I heard him go overboard, I lost interest in the sailboat and was trying to get back to the stern to help him get back on board. Of course it was too late. He had already been crushed.'

'And this you told to Beccnat?'

'I have told you that I did.'

'Was anything more heard or seen of this small boat from which Murchad was attacked?'

'I did not see who did the actual attack, but even in passing I recognised the boat. We are not so large a community here that we river folk do not know who owns what boats.'

Fidelma raised her brows in astonishment. 'You mean that you know who owned the boat?'

'Oh, yes,' Muirgel said firmly. 'It belonged to Síabair.'

'Síabair – the physician?' Fidelma asked in surprise. 'Surely, Beccnat questioned him about your identification.'

'I was told that he claimed that his boat had never left its moorings. Neither had he used the vessel at all during this time I said it passed me and Murchad was pushed overboard.'

'What did the Brehon's assistant do?'

'She merely accepted Síabair's word. Why would she do otherwise? She and he are of the same social status while I . . .' Muirgel's voice was bitter and she was unable to finish.

'Did Síabair ever have any cause to do your husband harm?' Fidelma went on, ignoring the claim of social bias.

'None that I was ever aware of,' Muirgel said, recovering. 'But I swear that it was from that boat that my husband was pushed to his death.'

'What if it had been stolen and returned to the mooring before Síabair had noticed that it was missing?' she mused. 'Is that not a possibility?'

Muirgel was silent for a moment before she answered with some reluctance. 'I suppose it is a possibility. The rivers and small waterways are many in these parts. So if a small craft was taken from Síabair's mooring, it did not have to turn round and come back this way again to return to that mooring.'

'Do you know if this was put to Síabair? I mean, was he asked to examine his boat to make sure that it was in the same condition in which he left it? For example, was that long pole that you saw still part of his boat or was it abandoned somewhere?'

'Nothing was investigated,' Muirgel replied, her anger now subdued. 'The assistant of the Brehon just accepted Síabair's word, as I said.'

'But she must have given you an explanation as to why she was making a decision not to investigate?' pressed Fidelma.

'She told me that she would not deviate from her conclusion that Murchad had died as a result of falling overboard by accident. She declared that it was her judgment.'

'Are you sure . . . her judgment? Those are ritual words.'

'Those were her very words.'

'There is something amiss in this. Tell me, did you ask her to investigate the matter for a specific purpose?'

Muirgel was puzzled by the question. 'I told her the facts and wanted to find out who killed my husband. I wanted to see if I could claim his honour price and compensation.'

'So you presented yourself as a litigant?'

'I am not sure what that words means.'

'If you were a litigant seeking judgment then Beccnat was giving judgment. That being so, she should have presented a pledge so that if you were dissatisfied with her judgment you could demand her actions be re-examined by another Brehon. If her judgment was proved wrong, then some means of compensation could be recovered. I presume there was no other senior judge in this area, other than Brehon Rónchú, that you could appeal to? It is your right to appeal against a judgment.'

The woman shrugged. 'There is only Brehon Rónchú, and I admit that I have been waiting for him to return to tell him. But he has not returned. If you are a lawyer, as you say, then surely you could investigate for me?'

'The problem is that if I appeared as a judge in a claim against Beccnat, she might raise a counterclaim of personal animosity against me.' Fidelma was thinking of the sudden verbal attack that Beccnat had launched against her. 'Do not worry. I will find an answer to this. I am certain that what you say is the truth. I have no doubt that Murchad's death was murder.'

'Can you get justice for me?' Muirgel's voice rose in hope.

'Let me ask a few more questions. Do you remember the day when Brehon Rónchú challenged Murchad about the boxes of ore that he was to take downriver?'

'That was the start of our troubles.'

'Do you remember the details of how these men approached Murchad to take this cargo?'

'We always worked the boat together so I was there when these men arrived. Two men came to the township in a wagon. They wished to transport two boxes to the seaport at Clocha Liatha. They had locks on them and when Murchad asked the contents they said they contained some ancient carved rocks of the old religion. Curiously, they said they would not accompany the boxes. They had arranged for them to be met at the destination. Murchad agreed to take the boxes but he was very suspicious.'

'Then the two men left?'

'Not before they paid what was to be one half of the sum in advance and agreed the second half would be paid when the boxes were handed over.'

'So what happened then?'

'Brehon Rónchú was making a random inspection of goods being transported downriver. He said he was suspicious of the movements of metals. He had been told that the lord of The Cuala had asked him to be vigilant about stolen precious metals from his mines. Murchad told him that he was suspicious about the boxes even though he had agreed to take them. We are honest traders. Murchad told the Brehon that he was sure he had seen one of the men in the local tavern some weeks before. Brehon Rónchú knew about locks and soon opened the boxes. We were shocked when we saw the ore.

Brehon Rónchú believed the ore was valuable when smelted. He checked a piece with the local smith and, when he returned to us, he suggested that he and two warriors accompany our boat to the port at the Clocha Liatha and confront whoever came to collect them. We are a busy crossroads and sometimes the town is rowdy and so the lord of The Cuala places some of his warriors here in case things become too rowdy.'

'So you all went downriver? What happened when you reached Clocha Liatha?'

'To our surprise the same two men that placed the boxes on our boat were there to take delivery of them,' she continued. 'They must have ridden on horseback across the country to do so. When Brehon Rónchú challenged them, they immediately drew their swords but the warriors accompanying the Brehon were more than a match for them. They soon perished in their futile attempt to escape.'

Fidelma grimaced in disapproval. 'Was there any real attempt to capture them alive?'

Muirgel was indifferent. 'They were challenged, but once they had drawn their swords there was nothing to be done except kill them . . . short of their own surrender.'

'Was it then that the Brehon Rónchú decided to return here with the boxes?'

'Brehon Rónchú ordered us to return with the cargo. He allowed us to keep the fees paid as compensation, but said he was escorting the metal ore to Garrchú up at Dún Árd. Garrchú is the steward of the mines to the lord of The Cuala. Brehon Rónchú hired a wagon from that old good-for-nothing Cétach and left. That was it.'

'So Cétach drove the wagon with the ore. He came back here and was murdered. Brehon Rónchú has not returned from that trip. Then your husband met his death.'

Muirgel was staring at Fidelma with a growing expression of horror.

'Are you saying . . .?'

Fidelma suddenly rose and smiled down at the woman. 'I must thank you. Trust me, you will hear from me again on this matter and I will ensure that we will examine the role of the Brehon's assistant. But, if you see her, do not speak to her of this conversation or my intentions. In fact, do not speak to anyone about this conversation until I tell you.'

Muirgel thought for a moment and then inclined her head. 'I will do so, lady, so long as I get justice for my man.'

'I assure you, Muirgel, I am sworn to uphold justice and truth above all . . . even if it contravenes the law.'

'But the law is the law,' gasped the woman, perturbed at the instruction. 'We must obey it.'

'Laws are not created to command obedience or to restrain people. When the law does not support freedom, then it absolves people from obedience to its authority. Above all, people must accept their own moral authority. Justice should always come before law.'

chapter twenty-one

When she left Muirgel's cabin, Fidelma went to the tavern Eadulf had previously indicated. Their horses were outside. Inside, she found not only Eadulf but Enda, too. They were seated in a corner, sipping mugs of honey mead.

'Did you get what you wanted?' Eadulf asked as she sat down.

'Not exactly, but that is the nature of solving riddles,' Fidelma replied seriously.

Enda greeted her and explained: 'I was bored just hanging round the abbey so I came to see if you needed assistance. Did you say you have solved a riddle?'

'I am faced with a *drochtcheist* – a puzzle or riddle,' she explained. 'To resolve it you have to proceed by collecting *brodhe*. By that I mean the particles that you have to piece together until they form a whole. So, in this matter, we have just added a few more particles to the key that solves the puzzle. It seems that we have a conflict between law and justice here.'

Eadulf was mystified. 'Surely without law there can be no justice?'

'But law and justice are not always synonymous. Law often creates the bigger injustice. Brehon Morann used to say, "You will always get justice in the Otherworld. In this one you often get only the law."'

The tavern-keeper came across at that moment. Fidelma was not really in the mood for a drink, but for propriety's sake she joined Enda and Eadulf with a mug of *íarlinn*, a small beer. Eadulf noticed deep furrows had formed on her forehead as she seemed to be wrestling with an elusive problem.

'I think we had better get back to the abbey,' she finally said, finishing her drink. 'I feel there is something that I am missing, although it is staring me in the face.'

'Is it that we should go back to that valley of Lúbán?' Eadulf said.

'I am already sure the body was that of Brehon Rónchú but in no way must we admit it before Teimel,' she replied. 'There is something else, however; something even more important to the solution we are seeking.'

As they were leaving, mounting their horses, Enda caught sight of a familiar figure mounted on a thin and exhausted-looking mule down on the wharfs on the far side of the river.

'There's that old woman again,' he indicated with a faint smile. 'Amazing, she seems so frail and her mule is on its last legs, yet both seem to have hidden strengths. I am presuming she still takes food to those relatives in the mountains?'

It was a rhetorical question but Fidelma's reaction was surprising. She swung round to her companions.

'I am an idiot!' she exclaimed vehemently.

Eadulf raised his eyebrows and forced a grin. 'You are possessed of a bizarre humour, I agree,' he acknowledged. 'However, I would not exactly say an idiot—'

'I don't need humour now,' she snapped back. 'I have just come across the resolution to this mystery.'

Eadulf stared at her. 'You know what has happened to Princess Gelgéis?' he asked.

Fidelma hesitated for only a moment. 'I am sure I do,' she replied firmly. 'It was not until this moment that I realised that I have been told where she is. I was confusing my metals.'

Eadulf looked startled, casting a glance around as if to identify the informant. 'Told where she is? By whom?'

'I'll tell you later. First we must return to the abbey.'

With that she turned her horse back towards the abbey without another word, followed by her bewildered companions.

At the stables Fidelma asked for Brother Cuilínn, but to her disappointment she was told that he had been sent on some errand.

It was a short time later that Fidelma rejoined Eadulf and Enda, who were waiting patiently by the bridge.

'Do you want to tell us what is happening, where we are supposed to be going, and why?' Eadulf demanded. 'I can't understand about the confusion of metals. Gold and silver are surely the only metals concerned in the matter of the theft?'

Fidelma replied with the briefest of smiles. 'I have learnt enough not to raise hopes, before I am sure that the promise I made can be kept.'

'Should we not at least know something, lady?' queried Enda, feeling excluded.

'I will tell you when the time is right. We will ride from here north-westward along the Glasán Valley,' she told them in a tone that forbade anything further to be asked.

She led the way west at an easy canter. However, as soon as they were out of sight of the main abbey buildings, Fidelma turned north, over the hill path into the valley of Glasán.

'We've been on this path before,' Eadulf remarked, after they had been riding for some time. 'Can you tell us now where we are making for?'

Fidelma pointed across the valley to the far side of the river.

'We'll stop the other side of the river, across the ford that is there. Once there I shall explain,' she replied. There was now a bright air of excitement in her tone and, for the first time since they had entered the dark mountains of The Cuala, Eadulf suddenly felt a confidence that they were coming near the end of their quest.

When they had reached the point she had indicated they halted. She turned immediately to them.

'I am sorry not to have told you before but there are ears in the abbey that I do not trust. We are going to the deserted lead mine that is situated along this valley. Do you remember it?'

'The old deserted lead mine? But there is nothing there.'

'That is where I think Princess Gelgéis is held.'

'But we saw it. There was nothing there.'

'We did not see all of it. We saw some deserted outbuildings and some indents in the rocks that had been worked. A little way around an outcrop of rocks was the real cave and mine working.'

Eadulf was puzzled, trying to remember anything that had been said that would lead to this conclusion. He asked the obvious question.

'Basically, I was told by Iuchra,' Fidelma replied.

'You trusted that old hag?' Eadulf exclaimed. 'Are you forgetting that she is the one spreading the stories warning people about venturing in the hills and valleys? Why should she tell you anything? She would not want us searching in the mountains and destroying her fairy tales. Why, she even accused you of being here to rob the mines.'

'I admit that her tales of shapeshifters and demons can be dismissed but I have been adding a few things together.'

'Such as?' Eadulf demanded.

'When we encountered her this morning, we thought she was accusing us. Remember? She said that what I was looking for was under the earth, below rocks and soil.'

'She was surely accusing us of looking for precious metals,' Eadulf agreed. 'I warned her about accusing us of trying to rob the mines of The Cuala. And in spite of our denial, she kept on.'

'Indeed she did. She insisted that what I had come seeking I could find in the caves of The Cuala. We were both so fixated on the idea of robbing mines that I discounted it.'

'Are you trying to say that she was telling you where to find Princess Gelgéis? But why?'

'It is still a guess,' admitted Fidelma, 'but I think it is a logical one.'

'Explain.'

'Let us first accept that Iuchra was trying to tell me that Princess Gelgéis was incarcerated in a disused lead mine. There are many among the mountains. One was actually mentioned by Brother Dorchú. You will remember that conversation when he was being ridiculed by the good physician, Brother Lachtna? He said that Brother Dorchú had joined the lord of The Cuala's guard to be a warrior but found he was given simple guard tasks on the mountains.'

'I remember,' affirmed Eadulf.

'Brother Lachtna said that Brother Dorchú once guarded a disused lead mine near here, that he sat outside a bolted door in the mine for hours on end. Behind the bolted door there used to be stored some of the precious metals. It was the boredom of being a guard that caused him to go to the abbey and become one of the Brothers.'

'But that was a year or so ago and therefore it has nothing to do with Princess Gelgéis' disappearance a few weeks ago,' Eadulf pointed out.

'So it was. Anyway, what he said about the disused lead mine stuck in my memory.'

'And we saw a mine. It was above the watering hole for the animals. Nothing was there,' Enda reminded them. 'Remember we stopped and looked around? The place was open and there was no sign anyone could conceal themselves there, let alone be held prisoner.'

'The workings were in front of a rocky outcrop. The real mine was behind it, which we might have found had I not stupidly accepted Teimel's word and returned down to the river just before Corbmac took us prisoner. The young stable boy, Brother Cuilínn, told me he had also recently joined the abbey because that lead mine, which he and his father worked, had been closed down by Aróc. It was because of tributes that could not be paid. So he had joined the abbey stables. He told me that the mine had separate caves that could be closed off. It was along the same valley but a little way from where Teimel showed us the deserted one. More curiously, young Cuilínn mentioned it was guarded even though it was closed. He thought it was because the mine was still workable and Aróc did not want it reopened.'

'You think that is where the princess and her steward are held prisoner?' Enda asked in surprise. 'How would they survive locked in a cave these past weeks? How would they eat and keep warm?'

Fidelma smiled slightly. 'A good question, Enda, and you yourself pointed out the answer.'

A light dawned on Eadulf face. 'The old woman? The old woman with her heavy sack on her mule? I was surprised that the old woman was carrying a sack of food when it looked like she and her mule were more in need of it. We were told she took food to poor relatives up in the mountains quite regularly.'

'She is supposed to be Teimel's mother,' pointed out Eadulf. 'Why keep the princess a prisoner, and in such conditions? What purpose would it serve? If she had simply recognised her attacker, the person who killed the Brehon Brocc, why not simply kill her? Why keep her alive?'

'An intriguing question, to which I think I know the answer, but before I say so I need to find out a little more,' Fidelma agreed. 'It is interesting that Iuchra made a play on words that confused me but now I understand. I thought she meant my fight was metal against metal. What she was actually saying was one must use mettle against metal: human strength and fortitude against those intending to use the riches of the mines for their own purposes.'

'And we resolve our search for Princess Gelgéis by finding her incarcerated in the disused lead mine?' Eadulf asked.

'That is where we are going,' she agreed firmly.

'Then can I put forward a thought?' asked Enda.

'All thoughts are good,' she replied.

'Perhaps not this one,' smiled the warrior. 'If the Princess Gelgéis and her steward are prisoners in the way you say, and the old woman takes food regularly to their prison, then who is actually guarding them?'

Fidelma gazed thoughtfully at him. 'The point being?' she asked slowly.

'While the old lady takes the food and is quite capable of opening a bolted door, even if it has heavy bolts, she would have no protection from an attack by her prisoners,' Enda explained. 'From what I know of Princess Gelgéis, she would seize the first opportunity to try to overpower the old woman. The captors of Gelgéis could not keep her and her steward constantly bound as prisoners for obvious reasons . . .' Seeing Fidelma frown, he said sharply, 'You should know there are certain times when a person must have their hands free.'

Fidelma grimaced ruefully, realising she had been slow on the uptake.

'That means they also have a guard on the cave who will ensure there can be no attempt to escape when the old women brings the food or when the door needs to be opened for . . . for reasons of toilet necessity.'

'Just so,' Eadulf acknowledged. 'But then we have yet to learn how many guards there are.'

'That is not a difficult task to investigate,' Enda pointed out.

'More difficult to understand is why the princess was captured and held a prisoner while her Brehon was actually killed,' Eadulf sighed. 'Frankly, I do not understand it. It begins to look more sinister than a simple means of stopping Princess Gelgéis from identifying the person who killed the Brehon Brocc.'

'Indeed it does, Eadulf. I think I shall be able to explain that. Of more immediate concern is how we shall effect a rescue now.'

'By surveying what we are up against. That is best left to me, lady,' Enda said. 'We should leave our horses a little way before the deserted mine. I shall proceed on foot to the mine and then come back and report to you so that we may know how many people we must overpower. Let us hope there are not many.'

When they reached a short distance from the deserted lead mine they followed this plan.

It was not long before Enda returned from his reconnaisance. 'We are lucky,' he whispered. 'There seem to be only two warriors standing guard at the cave.'

'Warriors?' Eadulf queried, as Enda was usually specific with words.

'The men I saw carried themselves as though they were trained in arms and wore the accoutrements of professionals.'

'Can they be dealt with?' Fidelma asked.

Enda smiled. 'I do not like praising my own powers, lady, but I think I might be able to handle one if someone can distract the other for a few moments . . . just long enough to render him harmless.'

'Then the sooner we get started, the better,' Fidelma said.

Having committed themselves, they followed Enda's plan. Under his instruction they left their horses in a nearby glade in the woods, one not easily seen from the track. Then they followed Enda's stealthy lead to the edge of the wood and found themselves over-looking a stretch of bare hillside with three or four buildings clustered around the dark mouth of a cave. They could see a trackway on the far side of the valley where they had previously passed these workings on their way to the place they were told the body of Gelgéis's Brehon had been found. Enda indicated the buildings before them. By one of them, two horses were grazing in a small corral. One raised its head and snorted, having caught their scent at their approach, but it soon went back to nibbling at the surrounding grass.

Enda suddenly signalled for them to drop to the ground. Off to one side, they saw a cooking fire was lit and a small iron pot with its bubbling content placed on it. A man was crouched over it. Enda raised a finger to his lips before waving Fidelma and Eadulf to stay where they were. Then he crawled away at an oblique angle. It was a short time before he returned again.

He spoke softly. 'Can you manage the one at the cooking fire, friend Eadulf? You could catch him unawares from behind. I will handle the one in the cave as there will be no means to surprise him.'

Eadulf simply gave a curt nod and started to crawl towards the column of smoke projected by the cooking fire.

He had reached the shack that masked the fire and began to move round it without mishap. As he peered round at the far side, he saw the man crouching before the fire, stirring the contents of the pot with a ladle. He quickly looked round. The shack offered a choice of weapons among the discarded wood. He picked a short wooden pole in the manner of a cudgel and crawled back to the vantage point. The man was still sitting on his haunches before the fire, concentrating on the cooking pot. Without more ado, Eadulf crept forward, the pole raised and he brought it down with a sharp crack on the man's unprotected head. With an almost inaudible grunt the man felt sideways and lay still.

Eadulf looked up and saw Enda, a short distance away, emerging between the other wooden huts, sword in hand. Enda glanced across, saw the inert body of Eadulf's victim and raised his hand in acknowledgement. He pointed to himself and then to the cave mouth and began to move stealthily forward. Eadulf found Fidelma behind him. She was carrying a cord, which she passed to him and pointed to the unconscious man. Eadulf quickly bound the man's hands behind his back although his victim remained unconscious.

Suddenly there were cries and the sound of metal on metal, the clash of blows being struck. Enda's voice cried, 'Yield!' but there were no other sounds but grunts and an odd cry and cursing.

Suddenly all was quiet. Eadulf and Fidelma exchanged anxious glances. For several long moments there was silence and then Eadulf began to move forward to the cave entrance. He halted and tensed himself as the shadow of a man began to emerge. Then he relaxed as he realised it was Enda.

The warrior grinned as Fidelma came forward with a questioning look.

'I am afraid I had to hurt the other man a little, lady,' he said. 'Don't worry, I only hurt him enough to render him unable to do anything for the moment. He was, as I said, the only one standing guard in the cave.'

'And are there prisoners there?' Fidelma asked anxiously.

'I have not searched yet. There is an oil lamp there, so we have light.'

Enda led the way back into the cave. The guard lay groaning on the floor, blood coming from his head.

'Tie him up and check his wounds,' Fidelma instructed Eadulf before looking around.

Enda had taken the oil lamp from its hook and now held it high.

The first thing that was obvious was a heavy oak door. It was set in a natural rocky recess that blocked off what was probably a cave beyond. There was a small aperture in the middle of the door at shoulder height. The door was secured from the outside by two iron bolts.

'So Brother Cuilínn's description was accurate,' Fidelma observed with satisfaction. 'There is a means of keeping things, or people, locked in this cave.'

Fidelma went to the iron grille and called urgently, 'Is there anyone inside?'

There was a silence. She called again.

After a few more seconds a male voice answered in a bitter tone, 'We are still your prisoners.'

Fidelma frowned before calling: 'Is that Spealáin?'

'Who else have you locked in here?' came the sarcastic retort.

'I am hoping my friend Gelgéis is also locked in with you. It is Fidelma.'

There was a stifled gasp. A woman's voice cried, 'Is it really you, Fidelma?'

'Gelgéis! It is I, and with friends. We will have you out in a moment.'

With Enda holding the lamp near, she bent to the large metal bolts, which she quickly withdrew and the door was thrown open. Spealáin, the steward, was the first to emerge, seemingly prepared in case it was a trap. He looked round, blinking against the light of the lamp. Then he gave a shout and his features wreathed into a broad grin as he recognised Fidelma.

'It is true!' he called. A moment later Princess Gelgéis emerged and threw herself into the arms of Fidelma, laughing and crying at the same time.

'How . . .? What . . .?'

'Enough questions for the moment,' Fidelma interrupted. 'I am here with Eadulf and Enda. We must get you and Spealáin to a place of safety where we can discuss the situation in a more relaxed fashion. Firstly, are you both all right? Neither of you is injured?'

'No, but it has not been good to be locked in a cave all these weeks,' confessed Gelgéis.

'Is there anything you need to take with you? Personal items?'

Princess Gelgéis grunted in distaste. 'I never want to see anything associated with that cave again.'

'Were you imprisoned the whole time?' Eadulf asked, astonished. 'Were you not let out at all?'

Spealáin answered with a shake of his head. 'Every three days or so, the warriors would let us out to walk around outside but we had our hands tied first. That was about all . . . except now and then an old woman brought us fresh food.'

'At least we each had a natural cubicle formed by the shape of the cave inside, so we had some privacy from one another,' Gelgéis explained.

'Well, we will hear about that later,' Fidelma said. 'We must move quickly.' She insisted they each took a sleeping blanket apiece for she had an idea in the back of her mind. She turned to Eadulf and Enda. 'Bring the two guards and put them in the cave. I am sure it won't be long for them to wait until their companions come to release them.'

Then, having ensured that the door was swung shut and rebolted to contain the erstwhile gaolers, Fidelma ordered Enda to saddle the two horses that belonged to the guards, leading them and the entire party back to where they had left their own mounts. All this was done in silence as Fidelma made clear there were better opportunities to discuss what had happened and explanations later.

By the time they reached the spot where they had left their horses Fidelma had confirmed her plan in her own mind. She took Enda aside and spoke quietly to him.

'Do you think you can find your way back to the fortress of the lord of The Cuala?'

Enda looked surprised but nodded briefly. 'Your brother did not employ me in his bodyguard without knowing some of my capabilities, lady.'

'I want you to ride to that fortress and see Dicuil Dóna. Remember, you should speak to no one else, especially not to his son, daughter or even Corbmac.'

'And what shall I say?'

Fidelma leant closer and whispered urgently. His eyes grew wide with astonishment.

'Is it true, lady?' the warrior demanded.

'As true as I know it to be, Enda,' she confirmed. 'How soon can you get back to the abbey or to Láithreach, as we might be in either place?'

Enda glanced at the sky. 'At the latest, the day after tomorrow, for it seems there is much to be done.'

'You have the message clear?'

'I have, lady.' Without another word he swung on to his horse and was off.

Fidelma found Eadulf frowning. 'Where is Enda off to?' he asked.

'I'll tell you later,' she replied. 'Meanwhile I want to hear Princess Gelgéis' story, so the sooner we put distance between here and ourselves, the better. We must find a safe place for our friends to hole up for the next two days at least.'

'A safe place?' It was Gelgéis who queried the term.

'I need to keep you and Spealáin hidden for two days. In two days, all should be well. If so, I will demand the establishment of an *airecht*, a court, for I will be able to explain all that has happened here.'

Eadulf was the most surprised of them but he knew better than to start questioning her decision. Finally he said: 'Where is there a safe place near here? Certainly not the abbey, and I don't think we could find a safe place in Láithreach. You don't expect Princess Gelgéis to camp in the forests for two nights or more?'

'Láithreach is where I am thinking of,' Fidelma replied seriously, ignoring the consternation on his face. 'I have a place in mind, although the cave was probably more comfortable. But they must stay hidden until I can be ready to bring the facts into the open.'

'What facts other than that my Brehon Brocc has been killed, and I and my steward imprisoned for weeks in a cold, inhospitable cave?' Princess Gelgéis demanded.

'The serious facts are *why* this happened,' returned Fidelma unperturbed. 'I know that you will have that explanation. Brehon Brocc's death is also serious, but what is at the root of this is the conspiracy, and you can tell us about that.'

Princess Gelgéis was troubled. 'You know of it? Our capture was part of the conspiracy. I heard rumours and that was why I was on my way to see my cousin, Abbot Daircell. So is it true?'

'Because of this, as far as you and Spealáin are concerned, you must remain hidden until I am ready.'

Eadulf looked startled. 'You know everything?'

'Everything? No, not everything, but enough to present sufficient facts to force others to supply those that are missing. For the moment, Eadulf, we must return unseen to the vicinity of Láithreach. If Enda has not returned by the day after tomorrow then I shall have to assume help is not coming and try to work out another plan. Now we must put the Princess and Spealáin out of sight for two days. They must be hidden that long.'

'But where are we to hide them at Láithreach?' Eadulf demanded. 'Even those old barges where that prostitute lived won't be safe.'

Fidelma gave one of her mischievous grins. 'We are going to hide ourselves in Cétach's cabin.'

CHAPTER TWENTY-TWO

Fidelma was soon feeling guilty at bringing Gelgéis and Spealáin into the cold and darkness of Cétach's cabin, with its putrid odours. She reasoned it was the last place anyone would look once they found the cave empty and the prisoners escaped. After they had settled as comfortably as was possible, Fidelma took charge.

'Firstly,' she instructed Gelgéis, 'tell us your story of why you were on your way to the Abbey of Cáemgen and how you were taken prisoner.'

'It is a tale simply told,' replied the princess. 'You know that many rulers of my poor land of Osraige have used its position to extract demands from either the Kings of Laigin or of Muman? They use it as a buffer, a counter in a game of *fidchell* between the two kingdoms by using one against the other.'

Eadulf could immediately see the analogy of the board game where king pieces vied with one another to control the board.

Princess Gelgéis continued, 'More recently, you know how Crónán of Liath Mhór, one of my distant cousins and close to King Tuaim Snámha, conceived a conspiracy to create a situation where Laigin could use Osraige to invade Muman on the excuse that they were protecting us?'

Fidelma said nothing as it had been she and Eadulf who had uncovered the conspiracy, which had led to the defeat of Crónán and forced Tuaim Snámha to accept Osraige as vassal to Cashel, paying tribute and reparation.

'It is known that Tuaim Snámha has never been happy with the peace terms that the High King himself forced him to accept,' Eadulf pointed out.

'Exactly so,' agreed Princess Gelgéis. 'Stories reached me from time to time in Durlus Éile that he had not learnt to accept this position. A relative serving in his fortress visited me before I came into Laigin to tell me a worrying story. Tuaim Snámha had received emissaries from Laigin. They had offered him financial support if he would join with them to declare Osraige independent from Muman and stop paying the tribute. The rumour was that he was offered much gold and silver from the mines of The Cuala.'

Eadulf let out a low breath. 'Just to declare independence?'

'Just to declare independence,' Princess Gelgéis confirmed. 'There is much meaning behind that word – "independence". It meant that Osraige would immediately be in conflict with Muman. That would lead to a call for Laigin's military intervention.'

'I would not have thought that Tuaim Snámha would be so short sighted,' Fidelma commented. 'He would know that it would also bring Osraige into conflict with the High King and Chief Brehon once again.'

'I was also surprised, but then I heard that Tuaim Snámha had rejected the proposition from Laigin.'

'Then, if Tuaim Snámha did not accept the proposition . . .?'

'I was informed that Osraige warriors were known to be training in camps. That gold and silver were being brought into Osraige.'

'Implying?' Fidelma prompted.

'That either the report was untrue and Tuaim Snámha had made a deal with Laigin, or someone in our family had. If the latter, that meant there was a plot to replace Tuaim Snámha with someone more compliant with Laigin's proposal.'

'Who?'

'That I did not learn, but it had to be someone in my family, a member of the *derbfine*, otherwise they would not be accepted by the people.'

The *derbfine* was of the bloodline, consisting of at least three generations of the family from a common grandfather, all of whom had to have reached the age of choice. The *derbfine* always met to decide on the most suitable member of the family to be acknowledged as their leader. They elected the head of the family from the High King down to the most minor chieftain, for there was no such concept as primogeniture in the law.

'So, having heard this, what did you do?' Fidelma asked.

'I thought the best thing was to see my cousin, Abbot Daircell. I knew that he had many connections with the Uí Máil, who rule Laigin and, in spite of being of Osraige, he was trusted by them. If anyone would know if such conspiracies were planned, it would be him.'

'You did not even consider that he might be part of such a conspiracy?' queried Eadulf. 'After all, he was one of your family and with a connection to the Uí Máil. That would make him an ideal suspect.'

Princess Gelgéis was surprised for a moment, then shook her head. 'No, his life has been bound up too long with the religious. Anyway, I sent him a message that I would be coming to talk with him about what I had learnt.'

'You sent this message by pigeon?' Fidelma asked.

'I keep pigeons and use them as messengers, as does the abbey. We often exchange messages, keeping them short and in Latin, but written in Ogham characters, which makes it hard for them to be deciphered by unwelcome eyes.'

'And Abbot Daircell replied?'

'Just the words. He said: "Understood. Am expecting you." So my Brehon and my steward and I took the direct path through The Cuala mountains. It's the wider track that runs on the other side of the river, on the opposite side of the valley. We were coming through woodland near the mountain called Céim an Doire when there was a shout. We were ordered to halt and dismount.'

'By whom?'

'We could not see, but there were men hidden in the trees. Three arrows drove into the pathway before us to halt our progress.'

'And so you obeyed the order to halt?'

'Not at first. The ambushers were well hidden. Brehon Brocc threatened the weight of the law against them. Again we were ordered to dismount and this time we did. It would have been foolish to resist. The attackers emerged – half a dozen of them but they all wore coverings over their faces so there was no chance of recognition. From their clothing, I would say they were professional warriors, and certainly they had the discipline of professionals.'

'Were you not able to identify any of them?' Eadulf pressed.

Princess Gelgéis shook her head. 'Not then, nor even later.'

'What happened then?' Fidelma asked.

'The ambushers took what weapons we had and we were all bound and placed on our horses. We were led over the mountains into some isolated valley. I am not sure where – somewhere south-west.'

'Can you describe it?'

'There was a ruined building there; ancient and deserted. The smell was indescribable. Across the valley we could see and hear several men were working. It looked like a mine.'

'How long were you there?'

'Not long. Several days. One day, a new prisoner arrived. He looked like a nobleman. There was an argument and we heard that this man was killed. Then we were told to prepare for a journey back the way we had come. There was some discussion that we should be taken to a safer place, somewhere from which we could not escape. It seemed we were taken back north and brought to the cave where you found us.'

'But what happened to your Brehon?' Eadulf asked.

'It was when we arrived at the cave that Brocc managed to loosen his bonds and tried to escape. He was shot in the back and then one of our guards bent over him and . . .' She paused and shuddered. 'They took the body to one of those huts nearby. I heard someone say they would wait for orders about what to do.'

'They eventually left his body elsewhere, where it was found and taken to the abbey,' Fidelma explained. 'That is what alerted us to the situation.'

Princess Gelgéis looked surprised. 'We have been a long time prisoners,' she went on. 'Prisoners in that deserted mine, the cave where you found us. I don't know what they did with our horses.'

'Was anything said to you as to why you were prisoners?'

'Nothing at that time.'

'No word of explanation? No threat? Nothing?'

Princess Gelgéis was firm. 'I tell you, nothing was said at that time. The guards always wore some sort of masks.'

'What about the person who brought you food?'

'The cackling old crone? They didn't seem to care about her. But I did not see much of her and probably will not recognise her anyway. She was just a shapeless old woman passing food through the door.'

'You say your captors did not speak at the time they captured you. That implies that they spoke to you afterwards?'

'They did. Well, one of them. After some time passed . . . I don't know how long. Days, I think . . . they bound me and took me from the cave. I was taken to one of the huts outside and sat in a chair. A hood was placed over my head. Then someone came in. It was a male voice and he addressed me courteously.'

'So what was said?'

'He spoke directly and with no attempt to dress things up with explanations. I was told that if I had a mind to, I could become ruler of Osraige. I would have to break off my engagement with

Colgú and declare Osraige to be independent from tribute to Cashel. I refused immediately and was taken back to the cave. This happened three or four times over the period. The same question to which I gave the same answer. I replied that Tuaim Snámha was King of Osraige, chosen by the *derbfine*, as the law prescribed, and would remain so until he was legally declared not so.'

'Do you have any idea who the person was that proposed this?' Eadulf asked.

'No, except the last time he said that there was not much time left for me to make a decision. I was also advised to think seriously about whose side I was on. I would serve the people of Osraige either way by leading them or being a martyr.'

'Or being a martyr?' Fidelma was puzzled.

'The man threatened that it would be easy to prove I had been assassinated by an agent of the Eóganacht to stop my marriage to Colgú.'

'There is nothing else that you can tell us about your captors?'

'Just that it was obvious they were in this conspiracy to overthrow Tuaim Snámha and it was proposed that I should replace him as a figurehead under their patronage. I refused.'

Fidelma sighed and shook her head in bewilderment. 'At least it seems that the conspiracy with Laigin does not involve your cousin, Tuaim Snámha. Everyone knows that you are a popular figure in Osraige. If you appeared as a figure calling for the country to cease its tribute to Cashel and become independent, or if it was somehow proved that you had been assassinated by agents of Cashel . . . either way, Osraige would rise up and turmoil would ensue. Laigin could claim that they were interceding to stop Cashel invading Osraige.'

'It is an horrendous idea. I am engaged to Colgú. Who would think me so duplicitous? Would the people of Osraige not suspect that I was being forced into this situation?'

'Some might suspect, many might not,' replied Fidelma. 'It depends who is behind this conspiracy. I am afraid you must cast your thoughts to members of your own family. Unfortunately your popularity has made you necessary to their plot, either as a puppet or as a martyr, to be used by them.' She glanced at the darkening skies. 'We must return to the abbey, lest we cause suspicion. Try to make yourselves comfortable and we will return in the morning.'

There was no other alternative to leaving them there, as she pointed out to Eadulf. There was even a small fenced-off area where the horses of the guards could be left. Gelgéis and Spealáin had to remain in hiding for at least two nights and a day, for the moment their captors had found out that they had escaped the hunt for them would be intense. Also, if Fidelma and Eadulf were absent from the abbey, certain conclusions would be drawn, especially with Enda also absent. It was not going to be comfortable, Fidelma admitted to Princess Gelgéis, but better than being prisoners in the abandoned mine. They had the blankets they had taken from the cave, which would be enough to keep them warm without the necessity of lighting fires and alerting the local people to the fact that the cabin was occupied.

It seemed very quiet as Fidelma and Eadulf approached the abbey, riding across the echoing wooden bridge and into the main abbey grounds. Then, out of the darkness, the figure of Brother Aithrigid emerged.

'The hour grows late, lady,' he greeted. 'Have you ridden far, lady?'

'Only from the township,' she answered truthfully.

Fidelma swung down from her horse as stable lads came out of the gloom to take their horses and lead them away to the stables.

'The bell for the evening meal will be sounding shortly.'

'Then we will have to eat uncleansed,' Fidelma returned, unperturbed.

'At least we can cleanse our hands in that,' Eadulf suggested, pointing to the water trough.

Brother Aithrigid sounded disapproving. 'The abbot is particular that the rituals are kept.'

'The choice between eating and disobeying ritual is an easy choice to make,' Eadulf replied gravely. 'Nourishment of the inner being comes first before the cleansing of the outer being.'

Eadulf had barely plunged his hands into the water trough than the bell started sounding from the refectory. Fidelma quickly cleansed her hands and followed Eadulf into the feasting hall.

As they did so, Fidelma whispered: 'Tomorrow, we must make ourselves conspicuous. I am sure the conspirators will watch us carefully once they know Gelgéis and Spealáin have escaped.'

Eadulf frowned. 'Who do you suspect of being the conspirators?'

'I have suspicions but no evidence. Tomorrow, get Abbot Daircell to show you his pigeon loft and explain how it works. You might learn something. I shall go to Láithreach and attract attention to myself, asking questions around the township. I shall avoid the area where Cétach's hut is. In this manner, we can confuse the conspirators into thinking we had nothing to do with Gelgéis and Spealáin's escape.'

'You still have not told me where Enda has gone,' protested Eadulf. 'He will be missed tonight.'

As they pushed through the doors into the refectory hall, Abbot Daircell was in his place and already rising to intone the *gratias*, which he did without feeling, running through it as if it were a meaningless ritual. It was clear the abbot was very distracted. They took their places at the table and exchanged formal greetings.

'What word is there of your investigation?' Abbot Daircell asked immediately in a low tone.

'There is little positive to say at this time. But I would hope it will not be long before we have some hypothesis to discuss.'

The physician, Brother Lachtna, leant forward and employed one of his cynical grins. 'An hypothesis only? Come, lady, did you not see any of the Aos Sí in your travels? We are told there are plenty about at this time.'

Brother Dorchú, who had joined them at the table, glared in

annoyance at the jocular physician and was about to speak, but it was Eadulf who replied. 'One sees what one expects to see.'

A puzzled look crossed the physician's brow. 'What does that mean?'

'I think what Eadulf is saying is that if you expect to see Otherworld entities, you will surely find them,' Fidelma intervened seriously. 'I think we have come to agree with your steward, Brother Aithrigid, that the wraiths who haunt these desolate places are entirely human.'

Brother Aithrigid stopped eating for a moment with an almost disconcerted expression on his features.

'You found something then?' he demanded sharply.

'Oh, finding things is easy,' Fidelma said complacently. 'It is what you make of them that is important.'

Eadulf was looking around. 'Is the lady Aróc still a guest in the abbey? Is she not eating here tonight?'

Abbot Daircell shook his head. 'I think she and Corbmac have gone to find her brother, Scáth, who apparently is staying nearby.' Then he switched the conversation back again. 'I was hoping that you had found something specific towards resolving the mystery that has been set on us?'

'We have yet to make such a resolution,' Fidelma replied.

Most of the rest of the meal was eaten in an uncomfortable silence. Finally a bell sounded to mark the canonical period.

'It grows late and it has been a long day,' Fidelma said, rising.

It was Brother Aithrigid who looked at them in disapproval.

'I know you have withdrawn from the religious, Fidelma of Cashel, but I see that you and Brother Eadulf do not bother to observe the *Liturgia Horarum*, even when staying in an abbey. Have you abandoned the religious entirely?'

Eadulf decided to answer. 'I don't mind observing the seven daily prayers when there is time to do so, but, with due respect to the Blessed Benedictus of Nursiae, I object to getting up in the middle of the night for the *Matutinus* and thus exhausting myself for the rest of the day.'

After a disapproving glance from Abbot Daircell, the steward did not reply.

When they left the refectory only Brother Lachtna was still smiling at the riposte while the others' faces were wreathed in disapproval.

The next morning, after attending the *Laudare,* or *Prima*, the first service of the day, to make a point, Eadulf ate a sparse breakfast and went in search of the abbot. He found him in the herb garden, which seemed to be Abbot Daircell's favourite spot. The abbot looked up from the bench on which he had been sitting.

'Are you looking for me, Brother Eadulf?'

'I wondered if I could ask of you a favour? I wanted to see your pigeon loft.'

Abbot Daircell was surprised at the request. 'Why would you want that?'

'I have only recently discovered that you often use pigeons to carry messages,' Eadulf explained disarmingly. 'You seem to know much of this subject and I would learn something about the way it is done.'

Abbot Daircell could not help the look of pride and enthusiasm that came into his features. He hastily composed himself.

'I thought it was a common practice in most places,' he replied. 'I am told that the Persians taught the Greeks, and the Greeks taught the Romans, who then spread it to all parts of their empire.'

'I have heard something of the history,' Eadulf admitted, 'but I did not know it was in use here until a short time ago.'

'All the royal centres use it. The method is used in war as well as to convey important messages and therefore it is now adopted as a means of communication between important ecclesiastical centres . . .'

'Such as this one?'

Abbot Daircell pressed his lips in a grim line of self-satisfaction. 'Especially this one. Although we are isolated we are still a centre to which many students come to learn the Faith. We are in touch with several other centres of the Faith. So I have made this a matter of practical interest.'

'That is what surprised me, for I was told the species used to carry these messages were Rock Doves. Surely they live on the coast and therefore would not fly inland?'

'As you will observe, the birds that we breed are able to fly across land.'

'And so you train them yourself?'

'I did initially. Then, when Brother Dorchú joined us, I found that he too had developed the art of training them.'

'I am fascinated. It would be a privilege if you would take me to show your birds and how you can work this magic.'

Abbot Daircell was nothing loath to escort Eadulf immediately.

The pigeon loft was not the romantic place that Eadulf imagined it might be. The smell of the birds confined together with the accumulated excrement from the nesting or roosting birds was overpowering.

Abbot Daircell saw his nose wrinkling and smiled. 'After a while we soak the dried excrement and remove it to use it in my herb garden. It makes an excellent fertiliser.'

Eadulf choked back a feeling of nausea and tried to concentrate on the task he had been given. He glanced round to check there was no one else within hearing.

'What really intrigues me is how secure these birds are in carrying messages?'

Abbot Daircell looked surprised. 'Nothing is ever completely secure but I would maintain that they are secure enough for our abbey's purposes.'

'That's just it. I was thinking about what you told us when we arrived. You had a message from Princess Gelgéis saying that she wanted to speak to you about intrigue in Osraige. She starts out for the abbey and her Brehon is killed and she disappears.'

'So?' The abbot appeared puzzled.

'Could that message have fallen into the wrong hands and alerted those who then went to waylay her?'

'Not unless she sent another message, which I did not get. The bird bringing her message arrived and was brought straight to me. That was how, when the body of Brehon Brocc was brought here, I knew something must have happened to her.'

'You said the message was brought to you. By whom, and who else knew of this message?'

'Brother Dorchú brought the message to me as soon as the bird arrived.'

'Ah, yes. He more or less is in charge of the pigeon loft now. So he knew of the message?'

'The message was in a small container. Even if he opened it and read it quickly, it would have been impossible to understand, for the message was in Latin but written in Ogham characters.'

'But he could have read it?' pressed Eadulf.

'With respect to him, Brother Dorchú's education is somewhat limited. He would not have had the ability to read it.'

'So you are saying that no one could have known from that message that the princess was on her way here?'

'No one.'

'Who else knew about the message?'

'I told Brother Eochaí when I sent him to Cashel to inform Colgú of my fears.'

'No one else?'

'No one.'

Eadulf thought for a moment. 'You say that Princess Gelgéis mentioned some intrigue in Osraige. You are her cousin and also from Durlus Éile. What did you make of that?'

'You know the recent history of Osraige. You were with Fidelma in Durlus Éile when Crónán set up his coup. We also know that Tuaim Snámha and Fianamail, the King of Laigin, were involved in that plot. But they held back from commitment until Crónán was ready. I do not believe that the fanatics who claim to seek an independent Osraige are all gone away. Nor do I think that members of the ruling family of Laigin, the Uí Máil, have ceased their activities to involve Osraige in war.'

'You think that is the ultimate aim?' Eadulf tried to sound surprised but he knew it was a foregone conclusion.

'I have heard that you have witnessed many attempts by the Uí Fidgente in the west to overthrow the Eóganacht. Both the Uí Fidgente and the Déisi would seize any opportunity to overthrow the rule of the Eóganacht.'

'Surely this is all speculation. Are there any hard facts to indicate that Laigin is encouraging Tuaim Snámha to rise up again? He was lucky that he kept his warriors out of the conflict led by your cousin Crónán, but he still has to pay reparation on his cousin's behalf. He must see that as an injustice?'

'If you want my opinion, all that business about gold and silver being stolen from the lord of The Cuala's mines is a cover. Dicuil Dóna is involved and such gold and silver leaving these mines is used to help Tuaim Snámha rebuild his army. I believe that Dicuil Dóna is the man behind this plot. He is not merely lord of The Cuala but uncle to King Fianamail, who is a powerful king himself.'

It was with his mind filled by such speculations that Eadulf finally parted from the loquacious abbot.

CHAPTER TWENTY-THREE

That same morning, Fidelma was passing the cabin of Teimel. It was as if he had been waiting because his tall form emerged from the doorway at that moment, saw her and raised a hand in greeting. When Fidelma reined in her horse, he came forward with a feigned smile.

'I did not see you yesterday, lady. Are you anywhere nearer to finding the missing Princess Gelgéis and her companion?'

'The mystery is not resolved,' Fidelma replied shortly without actually lying.

'So you have discovered nothing?' He paused but she made no comment. 'It may be a mystery that will be unresolved?' It was almost as if he were probing her to find out her suspicions. He glanced about with a slight frown. 'Where are your companions today?'

'They are tired of aimless searching,' Fidelma replied diffidently. 'Eadulf is with the abbot talking about pigeons. Apparently he is fascinated by the art of sending information by this means.'

'But you are usually accompanied by Enda, your bodyguard.'

'I believe he has taken himself off to do some fishing in one of the lakes. He likes to keep himself in practice.'

Teimel looked at her speculatively. 'I heard he was not at the abbey last night?'

'Some fish are best caught at night,' she replied.

'Then it seems you have given up on your search?'

'I suppose you may say that.'

Teimel looked puzzled, as if trying to interpret her responses and attitude. 'I thought the old saying of your profession was that you only give up when you have achieved your goal?'

Fidelma grimaced sourly. 'The older saying is that you give up when there is no more to be done. Anyway, I was going to see Beccnat to find out if there is any further information about smuggled gold and silver. Do you want to come with me?'

Teimel smiled without humour. 'I heard that you had an argument with her,' he said artfully.

'Did you now?' Fidlema's eyes narrowed.

'Yes, I heard it was over young Scáth, the steward of Dicuil Dóna. Several people know about the affair. This is a small township.'

'So the township knows that the boy is her . . .?'

'Her lover?' Teimel chuckled. There was something lewd about his expression. 'It is known, although no one here dares mention it. It is best that the news does not get back to his father, the lord of The Cuala. Anyway, do you still intend to fulfil Dicuil Dóna's commission about his claim of theft from his mines?'

Fidelma shrugged again. 'After today, there is little time to pursue it. I have done all that I can. In two days at the most, I hope my companions and I will be heading back to Cashel.'

'Won't your failure cause problems with your brother? After all, it is well known that Princess Gelgéis was his betrothed.'

'I think you may leave my brother's response to me,' Fidelma replied coldly.

'I meant no offence, but it is a bad thing that has happened.' Teimel tried to sound apologetic. 'I just wondered if there were loose ends in your mind that needed clarification. For example, the body that we found at Lúbán.'

Fidelma knew she had to be on her guard. 'Obviously it was some traveller who found himself in the wrong place at the wrong time. I would imagine there is no way we can be certain who he was.'

'I know you are concerned with our missing Brehon Rónchú?'

'I presume he will turn up after he has finished his circuit,' she replied, trying to sound uninterested. 'By the way, I will ensure your fees for your services are left with Abbot Daircell before I return to Cashel.'

'Well, if you are sure you do not need my services further . . .?'

Fidelma shook her head. 'I am sure we will probably see one another before I depart.' She raised a hand before he could answer and turned across the bridge into the main square of the township. Out of the corner of her eye, she was aware of him gazing as if in thought for some time before he turned back into his cabin.

She spent the rest of the day somewhat bored as she moved aimlessly about the township, trying to avoid the impulse to go to Cétach's cabin to ensure that all was well with Gelgéis and Spealáin. However, she had a feeling that eyes would be on her and she wanted to ensure she gave no clue to their hiding place. She talked to Síabair, the physician, but the subjects were of little consequence and she avoided the sort of questions that she really wanted to ask him. It seemed he had no suspicion or knowledge that she had spoken with Muirgel. There was certainly no sign of Beccnat, and for that she was quietly thankfully. She spent a little time with Serc, the prostitute. However, Serc could give no further details of the religieux who had raped her, which was something that Fidelma had been thinking about as a legal matter to reopen on the woman's behalf.

The day was a long one and, when she met up with Eadulf before the evening meal at the abbey, both felt it had been the most exhausting day they had ever spent. However, Fidelma thought they should have lulled their opponents into a false sense of security.

Eadulf seemed curiously happy.

'I think I have worked it out,' he announced when they were alone.

'How so?'

'We have now learnt there is a conspiracy to replace the ruler of Osraige. Only a member of the family can hope to succeed. Therefore whoever the successor is must be a relative recognised by the *derbfine*. The most likely person is the abbot himself. He has the contacts, especially with Dicuil Dóna. As a prince of the Uí Máil Dicuil Dóna can afford to raise warriors to help establish Daircell as ruler in Osraige.'

Fidelma pursed her lips thoughtfully. 'And the theft of the gold and silver from his mines? Surely he would need that to pay his warriors and equip them?'

'Well, remember a solution we previously dismissed? He is robbing himself so that he does not have to account for it to his nephew, King Fianamail.'

'So this conspiracy is happening without Fianamail's knowledge? Well, I think you are right on that point.'

Eadulf felt pleased. 'So you agree that Abbot Daircell is behind this, seeking to make himself ruler of Osraige?'

Fidelma sighed. 'I am hoping we shall be able to reveal everything tomorrow. But remember, I think it was Cicero who wrote, *"manifestum est recta solutio semper"*. The obvious is not always the right solution.'

Next morning, there was no sign of Enda returning. There was only a faint light tinge to the low, grey clouds when Fidelma and Eadulf took their horses and rode towards Láithreach. Before they reached the settlement, Fidelma took a route through the woods that circumnavigated the township, coming on Cétach's cabin from the rear. They could see the horses they had taken from the guards at the abandoned mine still loose in the small fenced area behind the cabin. Fidelma paused for a moment and looked cautiously around. Then she glanced at Eadulf.

'Well, so far so good,' she said, before turning to lead the way down the hill to the fenced area. As they dismounted, she called: 'Gelgéis! Spealáin! It is Fidelma and Eadulf. Is all well?'

The door of the cabin opened and Spealáin came out, looking relieved as he recognised them.

'We heard you coming . . . the noise of your horses approaching. Anyway, all is well with us.'

Gelgéis emerged behind him, but her face was not as relaxed as her steward's was.

'All is not well with me. I am cold, hungry for hot food and a bed that is not damp and lice inhabited. I do not wish to hear the noises of animals and vermin nearby, keeping me awake through the night. I am even ready to swap this rotting cabin for the warmth of that abandoned mine.'

Fidelma smiled thinly. 'Well, we have brought some better food and some good honey mead. More than that we cannot do at the moment.'

They entered the darkened cabin.

'I hope it will not be long now before we are able to leave,' Fidelma assured her. 'Meantime we have to make the best of it.'

Princess Gelgéis gestured with distaste to their surroundings. 'You are not serious, Fidelma, are you? We have to make the best of it? You and Eadulf are living in luxury by comparison in the abbey's guest rooms and you tell us that we have to make the best of it? How long do you expect that we make the best of it?' There was not bitterness but just irony in the girl's voice.

'If Enda is not back by this evening then we shall all have to find a better place to hide.'

'After last night I would rather have spent the time in a pigsty under the stars,' Spealáin declared quietly. 'We cannot stay here another night.'

'If Enda does not return with help, then we will have no option but to depart very quickly because all our lives might be in danger,' Fidelma said simply.

Princess Gelgéis was clearly perturbed.

'Let me go to my cousin Daircell and demand sanctuary at the abbey. I don't believe he is responsible for any of this.'

Eadulf glanced at Fidelma and said, 'I don't think we would advise that. All I ask is that you and Spealáin remain here patiently.' Then to distract them from their discomfort he asked Gelgéis: 'Have you considered anything more about members of your family?'

'Maybe we are wrong and it is a plot in which Tuaim Snámha himself is manipulating things. He is more likely to be behind any conspiracy to launch an attack against Cashel,' Spealáin said. 'He played a role in the last conspiracy.'

'It was never proved,' asserted Gelgéis. 'The information we had was that he refused to cooperate with the emissaries from Laigin.'

'And the information now says warriors are being trained and paid in readiness. Anyway, lady, your cousin Daircell is not to be so lightly dismissed as a suspect. He has personal contacts among the Uí Máil nobility. He could certainly be at the centre of a new conspiracy,' said Spealáin.

'This is true,' Eadulf agreed enthusiastically. He wondered if Fidelma would let him come outright with his conclusions.

'More importantly,' Spealáin added, supporting him, 'if there was a plot to overthrow Tuaim Snámha, what better lure is there than the abbot bring the princess into his territory, have her captured and forced to be leader of a new regime in Osraige? The people of Osraige love Gelgéis and would gladly follow her.'

Gelgéis was unconvinced. 'I don't believe that Daircell could be responsible.'

'You also believed that Tuaim Snámha would not jeopardise his principality, especially since his cousin Crónán nearly brought it to disaster,' her steward pointed out. 'I am sure he would like to see Osraige influential again. He was cautious last time and did not commit himself, letting his cousin play the major part. That is why he has survived as ruler of Osraige for over ten years. What is to prevent him working a similar conspiracy?'

'Well, these speculations can only be revealed in an *airecht*,'

Fidelma pointed out firmly, trying to seek to end the escalating argument.

'*Airecht* – a legal hearing?' Princess Gelgéis asked cynically. 'How do you plan to hold such a hearing while we are freezing in this disgusting cabin?'

'I won't be able to make the demand until Enda returns. That is why you must be careful and remain here.'

'But you have refused to tell us where Enda has gone,' Eadulf pointed out bitterly.

'You will find out soon enough – one way or the other.'

The time passed uncomfortably and it was mid-afternoon when Fidelma became restless. It was clear she was anxious for Enda's return. Finally she reminded them: 'We must give him until night-fall. If he has not returned by then, we must move to another refuge.'

'I have been anxious ever since we came here,' Princess Gelgéis complained. 'I am perishing of cold. Let's at least light a fire.'

Fidelma sighed, stifling her exasperation. 'I have told you, if a fire is seen here, your enemies will soon come investigating and you will be seeing the inside of that lead mine again fairly soon.'

She saw Princess Gelgéis cast a nervous glance at Spealáin and an odd feeling prompted her to ask: 'You have obeyed me in that, haven't you? You lit no fires last night?'

'There were no fires,' Spealáin immediately assured her.

'But . . .?' There was certainly a 'but' hanging at the end of the statement.

'We found an old oil lamp with some fuel still in it,' Princess Gelgéis said defensively. 'It provided a little warmth as well as light to keep the rodents at bay.'

'No harm,' added her steward. 'No one saw it as no one has come here.'

As if on cue, Eadulf jerked his head up. 'I think I hear horses. Maybe this is Enda?'

A moment later the sound of horses drawing up outside was clear and before they had time to get to their feet, Beccnat burst in at the head of half a dozen warriors. The fact that some of these warriors were armed with crossbows, ready strung, made their decision simple. Even if the warriors were not expert shots it was obvious there was no hope of even a token defence.

'Stay still and you will not be harmed!' Beccnat ordered in a harsh voice. The order was unnecessary.

'You have no authority here, Beccnat. I am still your superior in law,' Fidelma said quietly as she stood up.

'Is that so?' the lawyer sneered. She paused and peered about. 'A light was seen this morning. A silly place to indulge your conspiracy. In the name of the lord of The Cuala, in spite of your claims, I now hold you prisoners for a charge of fomenting war against Laigin.'

'If you claim that you be acting for the lord of The Cuala, you know I can challenge that.' Fidelma made to take the wand of office out of her bag but Beccnat signalled one of her men to seize it before she could do so.

Beccnat smiled malevolently, 'You secretly entered this kingdom to spy and create insurrection against the King of Laigin. You were trying to foment unrest and rebellion. In other words, you are charged with being a spy, sent to stir up disaffection in this kingdom on behalf of the King of Muman.'

'You are not correct,' Fidelma said firmly.

'Am I not?'

'Also, I say once more that you are not acting on the orders of the lord of The Cuala.'

A look of uncertainty entered the girl's eyes at the firmness in Fidelma's tone.

'We will find out who speaks the truth when you answer before him,' she said.

'Under whose orders do you act?' Fidelma demanded. 'Not those of Dicuil Dóna.'

Beccnat thrust out her chin defiantly. 'I have told you, I do.' She turned to one of her warriors. 'Take charge of the spies. Now, there are only two ways of doing what I say. There is the hard way or the easy way.'

'I must correct you, Beccnat,' replied Fidelma gravely. 'There is another way, which is both the legal and moral way.'

Beccnat seemed uncertain at Fidelma's continued self-assurance, but then a smile spread across her face.

'I am afraid I can only interpret that as my way.'

Fidelma was about to respond when the sound of a distant war horn reached their ears. Fidelma heaved a sigh of relief, at which Beccnat frowned, confused. The accompanying warriors looked at one another in hesitation. Unlike Beccnat, they recognised the sound the horn produced.

'I would advise you to put aside your weapons.' Fidelma took gentle command. 'In a moment you will be surrounded by a company of warriors of Dicuil Dóna – lord of The Cuala – and have to answer for what you are doing.' She glanced back at Beccnat and shook her head. 'Of course, if you are acting under his orders – under the orders of the lord of The Cuala – then, of course, you will have nothing to worry about. If you are not then you will be deemed the conspirators.'

Some moments passed in utter silence; so silent that the approach of horses could clearly be heard. They halted outside and the next sound was Enda's voice calling.

'Lady, are you safe? We are here with Corbmac's men. We see some horses outside here. Is all well? You have not been harmed?'

Fidelma barely glanced at Beccnat. 'We are not harmed yet, Enda,' she called back. 'But we could do with help in persuading some misguided warriors to lay down their weapons.'

A second or so later the voice of the commander of the lord of The Cuala's warrior's was heard in support of Enda.

'This is Corbmac! If there are any warriors true to the lord of The Cuala in there, then they must put their weapons aside and come out to surrender. You have been misled. Give up your weapons now and you will be treated fairly.'

Without waiting for a further order from Beccnat, the warriors quickly took the bolts from their crossbows and dropped them to the ground. One of them went to the door, calling that they were surrendering.

Fidelma looked sorrowfully towards Beccnat. 'I suggest that it is now your turn to surrender yourself.'

'We acted under the orders of the prince Scáth, steward to the lord of The Cuala.'

'You will find the lord of The Cuala at the abbey and may give him your account.'

At that moment Enda entered. He had a broad grin on his face as he greeted Fidelma and then turned to Eadulf.

'Good to see you unharmed, friend Eadulf.' Then he glanced to where the Princess Gelgéis was standing with Spealáin, her steward, and inclined his head in courteous bow.

'As soon as you feel able we should ride for the abbey,' he announced. 'I am told that guest quarters will be at your disposal. Dicuil Dóna himself should be there now.' He turned to Fidelma. 'The lord of The Cuala has asked, on our behalf, that the abbey establish an *airecht* first thing tomorrow. Is that in accordance with your wishes, lady?'

'You have done well, Enda.'

The grim figure of Corbmac had now entered to ensure that those who should be taken as prisoners were in the charge of his men. He raised his hand in salute to them all.

'Lady Fidelma! It is good to see you and your companions alive and well. Dicuil Dóna was especially anxious about you all. He should be at the abbey already. My lord suggests that it would be the best place to set up the court to hear an explanation of what has been happening in his territory. Do you have any objections?'

'None at all. In fact, it is by far the best place. Now that your men are in control, I and my companions will ride directly for the abbey.' She smiled round at her companions. 'I think Princess Gelgéis and her steward stand in need of hot baths immediately, to be followed by hot food and warming drinks before a good night's sleep. In fact, after the stress of recent times, I would say that this would not be far removed from my own desire.'

It was but a short time before Fidelma and her companions rode once more across the familiar wooden bridge over the stream and among the abbey buildings to be greeted by the solemn face of Brother Dorchú, the gatekeeper, ringing the inevitable bell to announce their arrival. The only noticeable difference in the men who crowded the abbey grounds was that, instead of the woollen robes of the brethren, the majority of men wore colourful accoutrements of the warriors of the lord of The Cuala.

The arrivals had barely entered the abbey before Dicuil Dóna himself emerged to greet them as they dismounted. He came forward with both hands outstretched. A smile of appreciation beamed on his features.

'Your message caused me to act immediately, Fidelma. You said members of my family were involved in this conspiracy to foster a war between our peoples and, further, in the theft of the gold and silver from the mines. They dare to rob me to foster war? Are you ready to reveal the names to me?'

Fidelma returned his greeting solemnly. 'I have everything I need to present a case to an *airecht*. However, I shall require the presence of your trusted warriors to ensure the attendance of those involved. They might be reluctant to attend at my request only.'

'Hand a list to Corbmac and the attendance of those you want is guaranteed,' Dicuil Dóna assured her. 'I am told you expect to hold the court tomorrow?'

'I shall start my presentation tomorrow at noon,' Fidelma replied. 'This will allow witnesses time to gather and also give the Princess Gelgéis a chance to recover from her long ordeal.'

Dicuil Dóna nodded after a moment's thought. 'I would agree except that I wonder if a further night might give time for those involved in this affair to put distance between this place and anywhere they want to flee to rather than face the consequence of their actions?'

'I do not believe they will do so because they might think that they have created such a web of intrigue that no one could follow the web to its centre . . . to where the real conspirator thinks he is safely hidden.'

'I cannot emphasise that is a threat to the peace of our southern kingdoms and must be handled carefully. The complications are serious. I know it.'

'It is a conspiracy that not only involves members of your family but others of influence as well,' Fidelma pointed out.

Dicuil Dóna bowed his head for a moment. 'Theft is one thing, but you are accusing my family of a conspiracy that might even bring down the wrath of the High King.'

'Conspiracy to depose a king and start a war is a dangerous business,' Fidelma replied firmly. 'So we must act firmly and when there can be no mistakes.'

'Your facts will be presented tomorrow? That could be dangerous.'

'Most dangerous if the facts are as I believe them to be.'

'You are brave then, lady.'

'It is my job to be brave so that I can demonstrate the truth.'

'How do you know that you can trust me if you suspect that my family are involved in such plots?' demanded the lord of The Cuala. 'If it is a matter of conspiracy to depose a king, who else in my family would be in a position of influence to accomplish it except myself . . . or . . .?'

'Or?' prompted Fidelma.

'My nephew, King Fianamail.'

Fidelma smiled slightly. 'I do not think that you want your family destroyed by taking part in this conspiracy. I shall trust you to accept my word that I do not accuse you. Nor do I believe that your nephew, King Fianamail, is involved. That being so, you must help me to reveal the truth and the real culprits.'

For a while the lord of The Cuala stood frowning at her. Then he gave a deep sigh.

'The *airecht* shall be established exactly as you say. My son and my daughter shall be there. The members of my household shall be there. All who you ask for shall be there, and they shall answer you truthfully. I shall give you my utmost support. But let me be honest, lady, if you do not prove your case, it will not go well with you. I shall be in contact with the Chief Brehon and the High King, and demand extreme action against false allegations.'

'You will find that I do not make false allegations,' Fidelma replied easily. 'I think it best until you wait for things to unravel tomorrow before you leap to any conclusions. Therefore, let us get the *airecht* set up and in its position.'

The lord of The Cuala, still frowning, agreed.

'You are an expert. How shall the court be set up?'

'We will keep to the usual form but I should point out that it is not a usual court of law,' replied Fidelma. 'You, as lord of The Cuala, will preside alongside Abbot Daircell, as he is the head of this abbey where the hearing is to take place.'

'But does it not need another Brehon or at least an independent legal authority? That should have been Brehon Rónchú and I am told he is still missing.'

'Sadly, I shall show that he has been murdered in the same conspiracy. His deputy, Beccnat, is compromised, so she cannot be an unbiased judge.'

'She is involved?' The lord of Cuala seemed surprised. 'Then you are the only senior lawyer here. How can the *airecht* sit with only one lawyer as a judge?'

'I am the principal investigating advocate, so cannot be the independent legal authority. Beccnat is compromised in this matter,' Fidelma confirmed thoughtfully.

'Then I am at a loss to see how we can proceed if this presentation is to have legal authority. We would have to send to the Uí Muiredag, or the Uí Faelge or the Uí Faeláin. Itt would take days for their Brehons to reach here and be sufficiently briefed on matters.'

Fidelma shook her head. Then she smiled. 'There is an alternative. Brother Aithrigid is not as qualified as a Brehon but then neither is Beccnat. Brother Aithrigid, before entering the religious, was an *Áire Árd*, and thus skilled in preparing judgments – there is nothing under law that says that he cannot participate in one. In any case, if I prove my points, it would be a matter of referring the case for judgment to the Chief Brehon of the King of Laigin or to the Chief Brehon of the Five Kingdoms.'

The lord of The Cuala examined her curiously. 'If you prove your case . . .' he echoed dryly.

'It is an advocate's task to demonstrate it to others so that they are in agreement, but often agreement cannot be found. That is why we have judges to listen to the arguments and weigh the evidence.'

'Then you recommend the steward of this abbey to sit with me and the abbot in this matter?'

'I do, unless you have a qualified alternative?'

'I do not. My only concern is to find out who has been stealing the precious metals from my mines and for what purpose.'

'That is what I hope to elucidate,' agreed Fidelma. 'And much more.'

'Very well, Fidelma. It shall be so. The court shall sit tomorrow. Do you have a list of all whom you wish to be present?'

'I have. Your commander, Corbmac, must pick a dozen trustworthy men of his band to ensure their presence. Here is the list of names.'

The lord of Cuala took the list and began to scan it.

'There are names here that shock me,' he said almost immediately.

'The search for truth is often shocking. You will hear everything at the court. I merely give the names of people I would like to be available to give testimony. But it does not mean all these people are guilty of anything. They may just be witnesses.'

The lord of The Cuala pressed his lips tightly before speaking.

'Well, this matter is in yours hands, Fidelma. The structure of the court shall be as you deem it. But I fear of what is to transpire tomorrow.'

CHAPTER TWENTY-FOUR

The abbey's refectory had been converted into a courtroom, an
airecht, by the simple means of using the raised platform where
the senior brethren usually sat as the place from which the three
chosen judges would preside. In view of the gravity of the accusations to be considered, it was not constituted as a full court of law
but as only a place for a preliminary hearing. If a case was found
then those accused would be taken for such a hearing either to the
court of the Chief Brehon of the High King or the Chief Brehon
of the King of Laigin.

Abbot Daircell was accorded his right to preside as principal of
the abbey, with Dicuil Dóna, lord of The Cuala, seated on his right
and, on his left, was Brother Aithrigid, the steward of the abbey.
He looked uncomfortable as he assumed his legal role as *Áire Árd*,
although he was perfectly qualified for it. Scowling Beccnat was
asked to attend but only as Brehon Rónchú's assistant and to argue
defensively if so needed. She took her place to the left, below the
judges. To the right sat Fidelma and Eadulf, with Enda taking a
stand behind them. Immediately next to them was Princess Gelgéis
and Spealáin, her steward. Several of Corbmac's guards had taken
positons around the refectory.

The seats placed in the chapel were filled with most people who
had been summoned to the hearing as witnesses. Fidelma quickly

glanced around to make sure those she wanted to attend were there. She saw not everyone was there and she had barely registered this fact when Corbmac came over.

'I have sent my men out to find those who are not here yet, lady,' he explained quickly.

'We will probably have to start without them,' she said to Eadulf, as Corbmac went off to check with some of his men.

She had already spotted Aróc, Scáth and Síabair at the far end by the main doors. They had taken up positions on a broad raised platform step, which led to the door of the abbey's bell tower. There was just enough room for the three of them to stare out above the heads of those gathered. Close by sat others such as Muirgel, the widow of the murdered boatman, with her friends, interested to hear what was going to be said. Even Serc, the prostitute, was among them. Garrchú, Fidelma knew, had ridden here with Dicuil Dóna on the previous day.

The main seating was filled by many members of the abbey. Brother Lachtna was sitting with a perpetual look of cynicism on his features next to Brother Dorchú, Brother Gobbán, Brother Eochaí and even the young boy, Brother Cuilínn. There was a loud humming as the conversation of the people merged and rose into one strange cacophony.

Abbot Daircell was exchanging a word with the lord of The Cuala and, upon receiving a nod from him, turned to Fidelma.

'Are you ready to begin?'

Fidelma rose, making her voice loud and strong. 'I intend making a start but we seem to be lacking two of the witnesses on the list, Teimel and Iuchra.'

'My men are searching for them as we speak,' called Corbmac.

'But you are able to start the proceedings, lady?' the abbot pressed.

'I am.'

The voices of the gathering died away and then the abbot made a gesture with his hand, indicating that she should proceed.

'Firstly, let it be clearly known that my presence here is as a *dálaigh,* qualified to the level of *Anruth*, a member of the *airli,* the council of Brehons . . .'

'Yes, yes, yes,' interrupted the abbot with an impatient wave of his hand. 'Your qualifications are well known here, Fidelma of Cashel.'

'The point that I am making,' went on Fidelma patiently, 'is that I invoke my qualification as a counsel representing the *airli* of the judges serving the law of the Five Kingdoms. I am not here representing the interests of any faction other than truth and justice.'

After a moment's silence, the lord of The Cuala spoke: 'We have acknowledged that. But it must be admitted that you came here as a representative of your brother when his betrothed, Princess Gelgéis, disappeared. That was the purpose that brought you here.'

Fidelma took out his willow wand of office and held it up.

'In seeking truth, I also accepted to represent and report to the lord of The Cuala, at his request, provided his interest did not conflict with my original purpose. They do not.'

Abbot Daircell was nodding moodily. 'I admit that it was I, as cousin of Princess Gelgéis of Osraige, who alerted Muman of her disappearance and was therefore instrumental in Fidelma's coming here.'

'Thank you, Abbot Daircell,' said Fidelma. 'As the princess is betrothed to my brother, the King of Muman, Abbot Daircell sent for help and advice. As a result, I, with my husband, Eadulf, who is a *gerefa* or lawgiver of his people, rode with an escort to see what advice could be offered in tracing her. The simple fact that one of her party, Brehon Brocc, was killed while she and her steward, Spealáin, had disappeared, changed the situation. The murder of Brehon Brocc was a reason for me to widen my legal authority in this matter, raising a matter that has to be forwarded with recommendation to the Council of Brehons.'

Brother Aithrigid leant forward and whispered to his companions. Then the lord of The Cuala spoke. 'It seems there are no legal objections to that interpretation. We recognised you now represent the Council of Brehons.'

'It seemed Princess Gelgéis came into possession of news about a conspiracy and wished to seek her cousin's advice,' Fidelma continued. 'That was the reason for her coming here.'

She paused dramatically and then indicated where Princess Gelgéis and Spealáin were sitting.

'That fact that they are among us is proof that my search was successful. They had been held prisoners and my companions and I effected their release.'

There was a rise and fall of muttering among those attending.

Fidelma nodded, almost in approval. 'The fact that Princess Gelgéis sits there means that we can hear from her own lips her story of how she and her companions were attacked and abducted. When Brehon Brocc tried to escape, he was murdered. The princess and her steward remained imprisoned. More importantly, you will hear the reason for her abduction.'

Fidelma beckoned to Princess Gelgéis, who rose from her seat. Fidelma asked her to identify herself.

'I am Gelgéis of Durlus Éile, Princess of Osraige, whose cousin Tuaim Snámha rules that small unhappy land. I am also cousin to Abbot Daircell of this abbey.'

'Unhappy?' queried the lord of The Cuala in a sharp tone. 'I know your cousin, the ruler of Osraige. What makes him unhappy?'

'Osraige makes its ruler unhappy because it is a territory between two large and wealthy kingdoms – Muman to the west and Laigin to the east. Often Osraige believes that it must appease the kings of both kingdoms to keep its independence and often by this means it is forced to take a stand against one or the other. To take sides one must make choices. My cousin Tuaim Snámha has, in the past, made some wrong choices . . .'

'According to you!' The lord of The Cuala seemed irritated. 'You would prefer he sided with Muman?'

Gelgéis shook her head. 'I prefer he sided only with the good of Osraige. Osraige being involved in a conspiracy with Laigin against Muman caused the intervention of the High King and his Brehon. That much is recent history and resulted in Osraige having to pay tribute both to Muman and to the High King. My Brehon Brocc had discovered that overtures to Tuaim Snámha were being made to bring conflict into our small kingdom once more. If another war broke out it would spell disaster for Osraige. He brought the information to me. It was with this information that I decided to come to talk with my cousin, Abbot Daircell.'

'Except that you never reached him,' Fidelma pointed out dryly.

'This is true.'

It was Beccnat who suddenly saw an opportunity to raise a question and intervened. 'If the Princess Gelgéis was so concerned, why didn't she go and report what she knew to her lover, Colgú of Cashel!' she shouted from a sedentary position. 'Why did she cross into this kingdom, secretly, to see her cousin, the abbot? Or was this also some conspiracy?'

Fidelma was about to challenge her former college friend when Brother Aithrigid intervened in a warning tone. 'My experience in hearings is limited as I usually just advise on legal documents. However, it is my understanding that certain protocols are adhered to. Counsels stand when addressing the court, they put questions without interrupting a witness and they choose words carefully. Princess Gelgéis is formally engaged to the King of Muman. To imply they have an affair outside of this formality is wrong.'

Beccnat had turned red and she was uncertain whether to stand and respond or not. For a moment Fidelma felt sorry for her.

'I am sure the court is obliged for your guidance,' Fidelma smiled before turning back to Princess Gelgéis. 'What was this information?'

'The simple truth was I did not have specific information. Just that some overtures had been made to Tuaim Snámha. I am told gold was offered. I was told warriors were being trained. I wanted to find out if my cousin, Abbot Daircell, knew more.'

'So, you expected the abbot to betray Laigin and side with your . . . your . . . with Muman?' Beccnat sneered at Gelgéis, having risen to her feet.

Fidelma now swung round in disapproval. 'To speak of betrayal of Laigin implies that my learned colleague has information that there must indeed have been a conspiracy by Laigin. What else does she mean by the word "betraying"? This means the King of Laigin, Fianamail, was engaged in some action against Muman, which, if revealed, would betray it. Is that what she is claiming?'

Beccnat stared angrily at Fidelma in confusion. The anger evaporated as she realised the implication of Fidelma's challenge.

'That is not what I meant.'

'My learned colleague is surely far too experienced in law not to choose words carefully.' Fidelma's tone was one of amusement.

There was a silence and then Beccnat shrugged. 'I accept that I chose the wrong words.'

'Then it behoves the learned advocate to think more carefully before she chooses them,' Abbot Daircell declared firmly. 'While the fact that Gelgéis is betrothed to the King of Muman is acknowledged, we accept that Princess Gelgéis' immediate concern in this matter was for the welfare of her own principality of Osraige. She set out on her journey here concerned that its ruler might be seduced into a policy that could bring further disaster on the territory or, indeed, suffer a coup. That is my understanding.'

'I am expressing a legitimate concern,' Beccnat protested.

'As such a concern impugns my being a partial judge in this inquiry, I am willing to vacant this position,' Abbot Daircell declared.

To some people's surprise, Dicuil Dóna immediately disagreed with the suggestion. 'I see no need for such an action. I am sitting with Abbot Daircell and respect his fairness. I think even the learned advocates would point out that this is a hearing whose findings will be passed on to higher judicial authorities. However, it is a matter of importance that the facts should be made public. If the advocates do not object to the abbot continuing to sit, I, as the lord of The Cuala, propose we continue. If there is an objection, I would have to point out that if the abbot is biased then I, too, must be biased, being the senior member of the Uí Máil dynasty in this territory.' There was a silence. 'Is there a challenge to this?'

There was none and Abbot Daircell glanced to Fidelma. 'I think we may now continue to proceed. I believe the question was being asked what Princess Gelgéis had heard to make her and her companions decide to journey to the abbey here in search of my advice.'

'Your memory is accurate,' conceded Fidelma, before turning to Princess Gelgéis.

'It was simply that Brehon Brocc came to me and reported that a certain member of the household of my cousin, Tuaim Snámha, had approached him. This person wondered if Brocc and my household were supportive of my forthcoming marriage to Colgú of Muman. Brocc was intrigued and asked why there might be doubt. The man suggested that Osraige must demand its full independence from the tutelage of Muman and soon, there had to be changes – *mutatis mutandis* were the actual words used – and how would my household and tenants stand then?'

'When what must be changed has been changed,' translated Fidelma. 'What was Brocc's retort?'

'He thought he should find out as much as he could. However, this member of Tuaim Snámha's household was frugal with his words. But a few days later, word came of certain nobles in the south of Osraige being gathered into a *cró bodba* – a war fort – and training, and that the smiths were concentrating on making shields and swords. One merchant says he saw a *marc-shluagh* being trained . . . a cavalry unit. So who would they be trained against? It was at this stage I decided to bring Brocc and Spealáin and go to see my cousin.'

'Of course, each chieftain is entitled to train his household troop. What made you think this was more than that?' queried the lord of The Cuala. 'It could be that Tuaim Snámha had decided to go on some punitive expedition.'

Gelgéis shook her head with a smile. 'Osraige is not a large territory, nor is it possessed of the ability to call a hosting of great battalions, as are Laigin or Muman. The High King had issued no order demanding hostings from any of the kingdoms or territories. So why was Osraige preparing for war? I believe that it could only be because it was being encouraged to do so. There were rumours, too, that Tuaim Snámha had dismissed emissaries claiming to represent Laigin. That is why I decided to seek the advice of my cousin, the abbot here.'

'Perhaps we should now come to the story of what exactly happened on your journey?' encouraged Fidelma.

'We had taken the track from Durlus Éile and made good time. We followed the pilgrim's path as we headed through the mountains. It's a very thick forest through most of the area but I and my companions had been along that route many times and that track, keeping Céim an Doire, the pass of the oak wood, to the south is an easy route.'

Fidelma now led Princess Gelgéis to repeat the story of the ambush, how she and her companions were taken prisoner and then taken to the disused mine, and then the death of Brehon Brocc.

'So,' Brother Aithrigid intervened, 'we hear that you were attacked, taken prisoner and Brehon Brocc killed. Most of this we know. What is more important today is who did this? You have said that you could not identify your captors. So the next important thing is why were you held? Can you even tell us that?'

There was a pause before Princess Gelgéis continued quietly, 'It was made clear to me why I was held prisoner.'

There was a gasp from the gathering.

'And that reason?' demanded Abbot Daircell.

Princess Gelgéis recounted what she had already told Fidelma – how she had been taken blindfolded from the cave to be told that her captors wanted to overthrow Tuaim Snámha and set her up as a figurehead.

'To what purpose?' Fidelma encouraged. 'After Tuaim Snámha was replaced – what was to happen?'

'The conspirator said I would be a figurehead while they would dictate policy.'

'And the policy was?'

'To declare Osraige's independence and refuse to pay tribute to Muman. If Muman threatened reprisals, to call on a powerful warlord of Laigin to intervene to protect us.'

At that Beccnat exploded, 'This is ridiculous! Do you accuse Dicuil Dóna, who sits there as a judge? He is the most powerful warlord of this territory and he is uncle to our king – King Fianamail. A threat against him is a threat against Laigin! Conspiracies and plots?' she sneered. 'More like fantasies!'

'I think the Princess Gelgéis has excellent reasons for her conclusion,' Fidelma intervened quietly. 'Continue.'

'I was taken three times from the cave where we were imprisoned. I was blindfolded each time. A male questioned me. The same one on all occasions. His question was whether I would be willing to declare myself publicly in the conspirators' favour once my cousin, Tuaim Snámha, was overthrown.'

The words certainly had an impact on the gathering.

'What was your response?' the lord of The Cuala demanded.

'A refusal, naturally.'

'Were you told who was involved in this conspiracy? Please continue at your own pace and in your own way,' Abbot Daircell invited, leaning forward and speaking sharply to be heard above the noise.

'The male voice told me that there was a pact between some nobles of Laigin and leading members of Tuaim Snámha's nobles, who were working to unite Osraige with Laigin.'

'As the lord of The Cuala, Dicuil Dóna of the Uí Máil, I now have to intervene in these proceedings because, as the advocate Beccnat has pointed out, the words of Princess Gelgéis implicate me in the conspiracy. She says that if Tuaim Snámha were overthrown, the conspirators expected a powerful warlord of this area of Laigin to raise warriors to help defend the new regime in Osraige. None can argue that there is no other powerful noble in this area than the lord of The Cuala.'

'This is true,' Fidelma admitted. 'Unless you were not the warlord referred to.'

'What other, then?'

'The princess, with respect, cannot identify any of her captors,' pointed out Brother Aithrigid. 'Unless you *are* claiming that you can identify your captor by his voice, Princess?'

'I have said that I can only identify an old woman called Iuchra, who brought us food,' Gelgéis replied before turning to Fidelma. 'I believe she will be presented before the court.'

The lord of The Cuala also turned to Fidelma. 'The old woman will give testimony?'

'That is the intention,' Fidelma agreed, turning to look for her.

Corbmac, who had been engaged in a brief conversation with a warrior at the door, now came straight across to her.

'She is not here, lady. My men went to collect the old woman as you instructed. She has been found dead. We have not been able to find her son, Teimel.'

'How did she die?' Fidelma asked quietly, trying to keep her face impassive.

'Her throat was cut, in just the same way of Brehon Brocc's,' he replied. 'That is, with a savage cut from behind, and from right to left.'

'To stop her talking or because of what she knew about the cave?' whispered Eadulf.

'Lady,' Corbmac added, 'my men went there, as you instructed Enda to tell me. There was no one in the cave where you said you left those men. They were gone, as is Teimel. And Teimel was last seen heading along the River Glasán.'

'Lady, the court is waiting,' Abbot Daircell called impatiently.

'I can't believe that Teimel would kill his own mother,' Eadulf said aghast.

'It has been known,' Fidelma said bitterly. 'Without Iuchra as witness to who employed her to take the food to the captives, and without her son or the two guards we left trussed there, the case is difficult.'

'Does that mean the court will be abandoned?' Brother Aithrigid demanded.

'Do you wish a pause in these proceedings?' Abbot Daircell asked.

For a moment Fidelma was silent. Then she said: 'I will go ahead.'

'But we were waiting for you to present the old woman Iuchra as a means of identifying these so-called conspirators,' Dicuil Dóna frowned. 'Princess Gelgéis has already told us that she and Spealáin could identify only Iuchra.'

Beccnat was smiling triumphantly. 'And as she is dead you cannot identify your captor or the leader of this so-called conspiracy.'

Suddenly Spealáin stood up. 'Your pardon, lady. That is not entirely correct.'

All eyes focused on him.

'I heard the guards talking of the group they belonged to. They mentioned their leaders, who were coming to question Princess Gelgéis. Two names were mentioned. One was called—'

Spealáin's words ended in a cry of agony as something seemed to flash across the hall. It smacked into his shoulder, sending him backwards with a heavy impact to sprawl on the floor. A hunting knife was embedded in his upper arm. Those gathered hardly had time to take this in when further cries and scuffles drew their eyes to the rear of the refectory, to the small raised stone area, which led to the tower that housed the abbey's bell.

Everyone turned their attention to the slight figure of Scáth, the steward of the lord of The Cuala. He seemed to be wrestling with the diminutive figure of his sister, Aróc. She appeared determined not to let go of a second hunting knife she was holding. She was swearing at her brother, who appeared to be trying to remove it. Síabair, the town's physician, had joined him to help Scáth disarm her.

CHAPTER TWENTY-FIVE

'So the conspirator is uncovered!' Brother Aithrigid cried, rising to his feet and pointing to the girl dramatically. The lord of The Cuala seemed to be sitting in stunned horror by his side.

There was a great deal of noise as people cried accusations and orders to one another. Eadulf went to the side of the fallen steward and quickly assessed the wound. The knife had embedded itself in the upper arm but miraculously escaped the bone. A swift tug and it was loose from the flesh. The abbey's physician, Brother Lachtna, came forward to help stanch the flow of blood. Abbot Daircell called for order and the hubbub died away.

Fidelma stood calmly looking up to the struggling group. The figure of a woman pushed through and came towards her. It was Serc, the prostitute. Before she could open her mouth, Fidelma was shaking her head.

'I believe you have spotted your tormentor. The man who raped you and fathered your child. I understand. I want you to do nothing until I have revealed him guilty of other major crimes. Will you do this for me?'

The woman hesitated. 'I will wait, but if it looks as though he will escape, then I shall kill him.' She turned and made her way across to the far side of the room, just below the dais.

Immediately another woman was seeking Fidelma's attention. It was Muirgel, the widow of the boatman, Murchad. 'Lady, I saw who threw the knife.' Fidelma bent forward to catch the whispered name and then nodded. 'I thought as much.' She stood back. Her voice rang out across the chapel.

'Corbmac! Enda! Take care of the weapon and bring Aróc, Scáth and Síabair here at once!' She turned to the abbot. 'As president of this court, you must seek order and silence.'

Abbot Daircell shuddered nervously in his seat. He was clearly shaken. Corbmac was bellowing orders to his men. Finally the abbot took control. It was a matter of moments to bring the son and daughter of the lord of The Cuala forward, together with Síabair. The noise had quietened into angry murmuring. Enda brought the young girl Aróc forward first. The girl's face was white, and anger and anxiety mingled in her expression.

'I did not throw the knife! I did not!' she blurted defiantly to Fidelma.

To everyone's astonishment Fidelma said loudly, 'I know you did not. Release her.'

Enda, who had been restraining the girl, stared at Fidelma in surprise and she had to repeat the order sharply. He reluctantly dropped his hold.

'What does this mean?' Scáth cried, his face twisted in anger. 'We all saw my sister—'

'That's not the way it happened,' Fidelma replied quietly. 'Your sister grabbed the second knife after you missed with your first throw. A quick change of hand hold and it looked as if you were trying to take the knife from her when you realised you did not have time for a second throw and would be seen. It was not the other way about.'

'But I saw her, lady. I went to help my lord Scáth,' protested Síabair.

'You went to help because you knew that Aróc had seen her brother try to silence Spealáin to stop him naming the leaders of this conspiracy, whose names included his own.'